THE DAMAGE
DONE

THE DAMAGE DONE

HILARY DAVIDSON

A TOM DOHERTY ASSOCIATES BOOK
NEW YORK

This is a work of fiction. All of the characters, organizations, and events portrayed in this novel are either products of the author's imagination or are used fictitiously.

THE DAMAGE DONE

A Forge Book
Published by Tom Doherty Associates, LLC
175 Fifth Avenue
New York, NY 10010

www.tor-forge.com

Forge® is a registered trademark of Tom Doherty Associates, LLC.

ISBN 978-0-7653-2697-3

First Edition: October 2010

Printed in the United States of America

0 9 8 7 6 5 4 3 2 1

For my mother, Sheila Davidson, for so many reasons

ACKNOWLEDGMENTS

This book wouldn't be in your hands if it hadn't been for a short story and the people who took notice of it. I will forever be indebted to Todd Robinson and Allison Glasgow, who gave my story "Anniversary" a home in *Thuglit*. Then Sarah Weinman, Martin H. Greenberg, and Ed Gorman selected it for an anthology, and George Pelecanos and Otto Penzler named it as a distinguished story of the year. Next, agent Nat Sobel took notice, contacting me to ask if I'd thought about writing a novel.

Me? Funny you should ask.

Deepest thanks to my agent, Judith Weber, and to my editor, Paul Stevens, who both worked with me to make this book the best it could be. I'm also grateful to the staffs at Sobel Weber and at Forge, who've been so helpful.

Thanks to my wonderful Thursday night writers' workshop: Susan Shapiro, Kate Walter, Royal Young, Rich Prior, Tony Powell, and Alice Feiring. I owe you an apology for keeping you in suspense for so long while forcing you to read eighteen different versions of Chapter 1. Many thanks as well to my other writers' group—Beth Russell Connelly, Ellen Neuborne, Jenna Schnuer, Jessica DuLong, and Leslie Elman—for years of moral support and endless glasses of wine.

I'm also grateful to two sources, both of whom chose to remain anonymous, who opened up to me about their addictions. Thank you for your openness, your honesty, and your trust.

One of the best things that's happened to me on the road to publishing *The Damage Done* has been meeting other criminally minded types along the way, both in person and online. The crime-writing community is a surprisingly warm and welcoming place, and I'm grateful for the support I've had from many people, including Megan Abbott, Patti Abbott, Elaine Ash, Ken Bruen, Joelle Charbonneau, David Cranmer, Barna Donovan, Linda Fairstein, Lyman Feero, Jen Forbus, Jack Getze, Christopher Grant, Jane Stanton Hitchcock, Lesa Holstine, Chris F. Holm, Naomi Johnson, Jennifer Jordan, Jon Jordan, Chris La Tray, Sophie Littlefield, Dan O'Shea, Barbara Quinn, Keith Rawson, Cornelia Read, Kathy Ryan, Kelli Stanley, Dennis Tafoya, Steve Weddle, Corey Wilde, and Dave Zeltserman. I'm also thankful for the support of my fellow members of Sisters in Crime, Mystery Writers of America, International Thriller Writers, Crime Writers of Canada, American Society of Journalists and Authors, and the Society of American Travel Writers.

Others I'd like to thank: Trish Snyder, Darya Arden, Michael Mejias, Shelly Oria, Annie Levy, Maria Portman Kelly, Helen Lovekin, and the members of my first—and only—fan club, the Newfoundland-based Bernadette Walsh, Gillian Marx, and Lorraine McGrath.

Last, but certainly not least, heartfelt thanks to my incredibly supportive family and friends, who put up with me while I was writing this book. A very special thank-you to my mother, Sheila, and my husband, Dan, for reading this book—more than once—and for giving me honest criticism. I could never have done it without you.

THE DAMAGE DONE

1

It was the bright yellow tape that finally convinced me my sister was dead. When the police had called me, I'd cried for her, but afterward a slender thread of suspicion had snaked into my brain and coiled itself around my thoughts. Claudia was deceitful, like every junkie has to be, but she also had a temper and hated to be ignored. I'd kept my distance from her since September; maybe being the butt of the world's worst practical joke was the price I would pay for four months of silence. That suspicion didn't deter me from getting on the first flight I could out of Barcelona, but it kept my heart beating at a relatively steady pace until I'd arrived in New York. Part of me believed that I would come home and find my sister waiting for me with her dark eyes and twisted smile, pleased with herself for tricking me back into her orbit.

Instead, I'd raced up the stairs of the Lower East Side tenement and found her door crisscrossed with yellow crime-scene tape. My hands shook as I peeled it off the right side of the door frame, leaving tendrils dangling like wilted vines. This was further than Claudia had ever gone for a joke. My old keys still turned the two locks. Then I took a deep breath, pushed the door open, and stepped inside.

The smell wasn't anything like death. Instead, something sweetly floral made my nose twitch. The apartment had always been shortchanged on natural light, but there was enough to make out ghostly silhouettes of furniture. I brushed my hand against the wall and the overhead light flickered on. The living room was painted a robin's egg blue, just as I'd left it when I'd hastily moved out a year ago. One wall was lined with my rickety old bookcases; across from them was the small sofa I'd found on the street and reupholstered, back in the days before bedbugs had made New Yorkers leery of sidewalk finds. There was a walnut night table I'd found at a thrift shop, with a new television and DVD player on it. At the far end of the room, under the window, was an Art Deco desk I'd regretted leaving behind. There was an empty space in the center, with a bright pink rectangle in it. It wasn't until I was right in front of it that I realized it was an iPod. I wondered where my sister had come up with the money, and how she'd held back from pawning the gadgets when she was nauseated with the craving for a fix.

"Claudia?" I called out, my voice cracking on the last syllable. My voice was too loud in this empty room.

The floor was bare wood, cracked and splintered and crying out for refinishing. If the police had searched the apartment or taken any fingerprints, there weren't any traces I could see. *It looks like your sister drowned in her bathtub at home,* the police detective had told me on the phone. Her tone was warm, as if she were sure that the cold body was a suicide or an accident. I'd heard that same soothing score from the police when my mother died. They wouldn't bother with fingerprints in a case like that. I wondered if they'd straightened the place out, because Claudia thrived on chaos. Even when she came out of rehab, bursting with good intentions and energetic as a puppy, she left dirty plates and glasses around and deposited her worn clothing on the floor. There was a pile of magazines next to the sofa, *Elle* and *Vogue* and *Travel & Leisure;* Claudia often laughed at me for writing articles for them. Next to the TV was a stack of DVDs; *Sex and the City* was on top. Had she hidden them from me before? There was something darkly humorous about the fact she'd never kept her drug use a secret from me, but that her unspeakable shame was an indulgence in pop culture.

I set my purse on the sofa and turned to the bookcase. On it sat a framed snapshot of six-year-old Claudia and eight-year-old me hugging in front of a Christmas tree. I had an identical picture in my purse, ripped from a frame in my Barcelona apartment, an ocean away. One shelf above held a photo of our parents on their wedding day. Next to that was the painted porcelain rabbit that had been our father's last Christmas gift to Claudia. The pictures of my sister with her goth posse of art-school dropouts were gone. On the top shelf was a red card with a heart wrapped in a bow on the front. I picked it up.

Claudia, what will I do without you over the holidays? Only nine days until I see you again. I'll be counting the minutes. M

I set it back on the shelf, remembering a couple of Claudia's boyfriends who'd expressed their devotion through tattoos. Did the use of a single initial indicate a certain playfulness or a desire to hide his identity? I wondered if M knew about Claudia yet. I didn't want to track him down just to break his heart, but there wasn't much else I could do for my sister now.

Wandering through the short hallway, past the galley kitchen, I stopped in front of the bathroom door. It was closed, and the cold metal of the knob made my hand freeze. I didn't want to see the room where my sister had died. Nothing would get me to open that door. Letting go, I backed slowly into the bedroom. Here was a hint of the familiar shambles, at least. There were no overflowing ashtrays or used cotton balls, but an open suitcase on the bed was stuffed with clothing that was piled too high for the bag ever to close. A black dress flopped drunkenly over a chair, a pair of black pumps in the gutter beneath. The label on the dress caught my eye. Prada. Claudia, shopping at Prada? Not likely. Shoplifting at Prada was a possibility.

The clothes on the bed bore similar labels. Feeling slightly emboldened, I reached for the closet door. Inside, stacked like bricks in a crumbling wall, sat dozens of shoeboxes. Manolo Blahnik. Christian Louboutin. Jimmy Choo. How did anyone, even Claudia, steal that many shoes? I peeked inside a box and found a pair of black patent stilettos. The smooth red leather sole was virgin. Size nine? My sister and I were the same height, five foot six, and we wore a size seven shoe. She had stolen enough clothes from me over the years that I knew we were the same size, though when Claudia's heroin addiction spiraled out of control, as it always did before each stint in rehab, she vanished into the skeletal range. Had my sister been involved in some scam to fence designer shoes? I pulled down a couple of hangers from the densely packed clothing rack. Gucci. Michael Kors. More Prada. Everything would have fit Claudia, assuming she wasn't subsisting just on junk and tar.

I almost missed the brown cardboard box on the floor. The handwriting on it was flowing and feminine, and I wondered who was sending parcels to my little sister. I tore into the box before I realized it was from me. Before Christmas, I'd phoned in an order for an expensive, impossible-to-find perfume called Tabac Blond that my sister loved. The store had couriered over the box and Claudia had abandoned it in the closet, unopened. An odd sense of rejection made a lump in my throat and I shut the closet door.

As I sat on the edge of the bed, it felt as if the year since the apartment had been mine had multiplied into ten. I'd left it behind with almost everything I owned when I'd moved to Spain. Why had I been in such a rush? My own personal life was a shambles, but . . . My eyes fell on a silver bracelet and I made a strangled sound. It looked almost innocent, sitting atop the scarred wood of the old dresser. I stood and grabbed it, then rolled it around in my hands. It was an inch-wide bangle with an interlacing Irish scrollwork pattern on its surface. The inscription read *For Lily, With Love Always, Dad.*

For a moment I thought I'd burst into tears. It wasn't awful enough that Claudia was dead; now I was reminded how much I hated her sometimes. The bracelet was the last Christmas present I ever had from my father. He'd even let me open it on Christmas Eve. *We'll have to wrap it up tight again*, he'd said, *imagine the hell your mother will give me otherwise.* Then he'd died that night and I'd treasured and guarded his gift. I'd worn it to sleep as a teenager, afraid my mother would sell it for brandy or gin. Eighteen months ago, when I'd allowed a very sick Claudia to move in with me, it went missing. My sister had hepatitis then, and her normally pale skin was flushed yellow with jaundice. *You don't think I took it, do you?* she'd said, the picture of frail innocence. Deep down, I'd always known she had. Even when she wasn't shooting heroin she needed cash to buy her more-than-state-allotted doses of methadone, which provided its own high. But I'd never suspected she would steal it just to take it away from me. Dropping onto the bed, I took deep breaths and tried to pull myself together. I hadn't thought I could be sadder or angrier or more miserable than I was when I found out my sister was dead, but I was wrong.

2 I don't know how long I sat there, surrounded by the ghosts of my past, before I heard the knock at the door. For a moment I lost my breath. Was I hallucinating now—or, more likely, hearing noise from an apartment down the hall? It came again, sharp and insistent. Snapping the silver bracelet securely around my wrist, I retraced my steps to the living room. The peephole revealed a blond woman I didn't recognize. When I opened the door, I noticed that she was tall, five foot ten without her heels, in her mid-forties, broad-shouldered but slender. She was simply but expensively dressed in a silk blouse and tailored pants.

"Hello, I'm Sarah Lyons. I live down the hall." She spoke in a low, mellifluous voice and gestured lazily with a manicured hand at the hallway opposite the stairwell. "I noticed that the police tape was coming off the door and I wanted to make sure . . ." Her voice trailed off. *Make sure you're not a thief breaking into this apartment,* she meant.

"I'm Claudia's sister," I said.

"Lily?" she answered, as if we'd met before. "Oh, hello. You live in Madrid, don't you?"

Her cheerful tone grated on me, but I knew that I was an irrational mess of tattered hopes and dashed prayers. "Barcelona. I just moved there from Madrid." My voice strained with the effort of manners.

"You're a journalist, aren't you? Claudia told me some-thing about that being why you moved there."

"I went to Spain a year ago because I was writing a travel guide about it. I ended up deciding to stay for a while." My answer was mechanical. I wasn't going to admit to a complete stranger that I'd been desperate to escape the emotional undertow of my relationship with my sister, among other things. I'd almost convinced myself that I hadn't abandoned Claudia. After all, I'd given her my apartment, and every month I'd mailed the rent check directly to the superintendent. But now she was gone and I was left with the guilty knowledge that I hadn't really taken care of her at all.

"Spain is such a wonderful country," Sarah said, her smile revealing perfect, pearly teeth before her expression darkened. "I'm so sorry about your sister. I was very fond of Claudia. She was such an unusual person. Unique." Sarah's heart-shaped face was sorrowful, but there was nothing affectionate in her tone. I wondered if she was being sarcastic. Calling Claudia "unusual" was like referring to the pope as religious. Some-times I'd felt guilty about inflicting her on my neighbors, but she had to live somewhere. She'd already put in time in a south Bronx squat and in various shelters around Manhattan.

"Thank you."

"It's such a sad situation," Sarah continued. "Claudia was so young. What was she, twenty-eight?"

"She turned twenty-seven in November."

"I should have remembered—she told me that—but she looked older. I suppose she'd just had such a hard life."

Behind my eyes, there was a sign that was flashing, *Get lost*. Sarah didn't see it, or she didn't care, because she went on. "Claudia told me a little of your family history—"

I had a childish impulse to slam the door in her face. For years, I'd dealt with teachers and social workers and counselors who thought that they could divine my future from the facts of my past. I knew nothing about their personal lives, an imbalance that made me feel both vulnerable and angry. Now, I cut Sarah off before she could get into the gory details. "You live down the hall? In which apartment?"

"I live in C."

"Are you a relative of Mrs. Felesky's?"

"Who?" Sarah's eyes widened slightly.

"Mrs. Felesky lived in 5C. This used to be my apartment," I explained, thinking of the petite powerhouse who slipped whiskey into her tea and told ribald stories from the days she'd been a showgirl. "Mrs. Felesky was in this building for thirty years at least. She's a wonderful lady. I guess she's about ninety now, but she was always so independent. Do you know where she went?"

"I have no idea. I just moved in a few weeks ago. Why would you think *I* was her relative?" Her imperious tone suggested she found the question offensive.

"Rent control." Sarah looked blank. "The people who've been here for decades pay next to nothing in rent," I explained. "When they leave, sometimes a relative moves in, without mentioning it to the landlord." It was pretty much what I'd done with Claudia, only I'd made the mistake of inviting her to live with me first. That hadn't worked out very well.

"Oh, I see." Sarah paused, then tugged the thread of conversation back to the morbid. "I saw Claudia on New Year's Eve, just before I went out. She wasn't in very good spirits. She just seemed so . . . sad."

I wasn't ready to hear anything else she had to say about my sister. "Thanks for coming by."

"I'm glad I got to meet you," said Sarah. "I often won-dered what you were like."

I closed the door quickly, spinning the locks. Suddenly I was drained and empty, and I rested my forehead against the door. I knew from experience that people were awkward when dealing with death. After my father died, kids at my ju-nior high would whisper about me in the hallway. *That's the girl! Her father died on Christmas Eve. It's really sad. My mother said . . .* They weren't being cruel, they were just get-ting a charge from their proximity to death, which was close enough to chill but not to harm. It was worse when I was in college and my mother died over the winter holiday break. It was midway through freshman year, and I found that I was suddenly shunned by people who'd invited me to parties only weeks before. One girl pushed a big, flowery card under the door of my dorm room, but she avoided actually talking to me.

The phone rang, reminding me of where I was. The sound had come from the vintage black rotary-dial phone I'd sal-vaged long ago when another elderly neighbor had left the building. You couldn't use an answering machine with it, but you had to respect technology that had been around for half a century and refused to quit. On impulse, I went to the desk and answered it. "Hello?"

Silence on the other end. Then a sound like a wheezing breath.

"Hello?" I repeated. "Who is this?"

"I think I got the wrong number," replied a woman's voice. She sounded very old or very tired. "Sorry 'bout that." She hung up, and I set the receiver back into its cradle.

I'd spent long enough at Claudia's. I retrieved my bag and grabbed my cell phone. My best friend, Jesse, answered on the second ring. He'd wanted to come to my sister's apartment with me. As a consolation prize, I'd promised to phone him when I was done.

"It's me," I said. "Are you ready to get drunk now?"

3

I woke up early Monday morning, jet-lagged and hungover. What really made me feel ill was the fact that I had to go to the morgue that day. Claudia and I were each other's only family; there was no one else to identify her. Still, when I called the police precinct to let the detectives know I'd arrived in New York, I held a faint hope that I wouldn't have to do it. The police had to be busy right after New Year's. It was January third; they'd be up to their eyeballs in thieves and fighters and would-be terrorists. "Car will pick you up ten-thirty," barked the desk sergeant. "Detective Renfrew will meet you." The name twigged my memory. Norah Renfrew was the sympathetic-sounding officer who'd called about my sister's death. I wasn't looking forward to meeting her.

I was staying at Jesse's apartment, and he was up brewing coffee by the time I'd showered and dressed. "Mornin', Tiger Lily," he said in his deep Oklahoma drawl, handing me a cup.

"You didn't have to get up." I felt guilty. "I know you're not a morning person."

"You're not gonna let me live down that time I fell asleep while eatin' breakfast, are you?" He smiled down at me. Jesse was six foot one, handsome like a thirty-year-old Gregory Peck with his dark brown hair and piercing eyes.

Even on such a grim day, he could make me smile. "You went headfirst into a bowl of cornflakes."

"That's our li'l secret." We clicked coffee cups as if they

were champagne flutes. "Damn, but you look fine first thing in the mornin'. Like Ava in *The Barefoot Contessa*."

Jesse and I had met in college, and we'd bonded instantly over our shared love of movies from the thirties, forties, and fifties. I was thirteen when my father died, and his death sent my mother into a tailspin. She had moved Claudia and me to one upstate New York town after another, and I gave up on making real friends and spent so much time watching Rita Hayworth, Lauren Bacall, and the gorgeous Ava Gardner that I was convinced I really knew them. I'd never met anyone who shared my fascination for old-time cinema goddesses until Jesse, who'd grown up in a conservative Southern Baptist family baffled by his love of retro glamour. We'd stayed up till sunrise in a friend's dorm watching *The Sun Also Rises* just after we met. The movie starred Ava Gardner and Tyrone Power. Afterward I'd admitted that Tyrone was my first crush, and Jesse had confessed that he was his, too.

By the time a bald, jowly cop showed up at Jesse's door, I'd convinced myself I could face the day. "You the husband?" the cop asked Jesse, before informing us that he was only escorting immediate family. Jesse protested but I was relieved. It was one thing to camp out in his apartment, another to drag him to the morgue.

"Where's Detective Renfrew?" I asked as we got in the car.

"She had a shooting early this morning." The officer made it sound like it had been scheduled on her desk calendar. "Stanton and . . . Suffolk? Norfolk? Got everyone tied up in knots. Everybody hates it when tourists get shot." In his offhand tone, he could have just as easily been discussing bad weather. My old neighborhood, nostalgia central for the gritty New York of years past. You could clean her up but still the dirt clung under her nails.

"You look familiar," the cop said as he steered us away from Jesse's building in Greenwich Village. "I think I've seen your picture somewhere."

"I doubt it," I answered. "I'm a travel writer. Maybe you've seen my byline before?"

"Nah, I don't read that stuff. Don't leave the city, 'cept to go fishing upstate. Nah, I've seen you somewhere." He was silent as we soared up First Avenue. We finally screeched to a halt in front of a turquoise brick building at East Thirtieth Street. The color bled out into a dull gray on the upper stories, which were pockmarked with air conditioners hanging out of the windows. *Office of the New York City Medical Examiner* read the letters on the face of the building.

"I know who you look like." He snapped his fingers. "Dita von Teese."

"Is she an actress?" As much as I loved old movies, I was out of touch with new ones.

"Nah, she's a stripper. Real class act." He gave me a laconic wave and sped off.

I shook my head and stared at the blue building, working up the nerve to approach the door. The cold wind convinced me to duck inside the morgue's double doors. Up a short flight of stairs I found a lone attendant sitting behind a giant semicircle of a desk. The spacious waiting area was empty except for the brown-upholstered chairs. One wall bore a framed U.S. flag that had been made using the names of the victims at the World Trade Center. Next to it was a rendering of the World Trade Center itself, made from Chiclet-sized photographs of the victims. I wondered what the turnover was for desk attendants in this office and guessed it was high.

Minutes ticked by on my watch. A couple of couriers hurried in and out, but otherwise the room was as silent as the proverbial tomb. I pulled my cell out to see if I'd missed a call, and discovered I'd left it off. The attendant frowned as I turned it on and silently pointed at a sign banning cell phones. There wasn't anyone to disturb, but I didn't feel like arguing. Cold as it was, I chose the frozen sidewalk over the sensation of death warmed over inside the building.

While I was checking for messages, my phone rang. "Lily," the voice on the other end said. "Sweetheart, it's good to hear your voice."

"Martin?" I said, confused. After two years together, I knew my former fiancé's voice, but two calls from him in less than a week was unusual. "Is everything all right?"

"Fine, fine. I was just thinking about you. It's after five in Barcelona, right? I have a hell of a time keeping time zones straight. You'd think I'd have learned by now." Martin had been born in New York, but after attending Swiss and English schools he went on to build a hotel empire with properties on five continents. He spent his life in transit.

"Actually, I'm back in New York right now. I flew in yesterday."

He laughed. "Are you kidding? Why didn't you tell me you were coming in when we spoke the other day?"

I knew that I had to tell him the truth, but I didn't want to say the words. "I didn't know then that I would be."

"Did some last-minute assignment come up? Are you on deadline?" he teased.

"No." I could have added that the week after New Year's was a quiet one, and that I didn't have any stories due till later in the month. Instead I stared at the sidewalk, wishing I were anywhere but the place I was standing.

"Is something wrong, Lily?" The warmth in his voice could have defrosted the street.

"My sister died," I whispered.

"What? Claudia's dead?" He muttered something under his breath, a curse I didn't quite catch. "I'm so sorry, sweetheart. That's—that's terrible. How awful for you." There was a pause. "Are you all right? Do you need anything? Where are you staying? What can I do to help?"

"Nothing, but thank you. I'm staying with Jesse. He's taking care of me."

"That's good of him, of course. But I wish you'd come stay with me." There was a pause while my heart thudded. "I'm sorry, Lily, that sounded more like a come-on than an offer to help. Would you consider a suite at one of my hotels? You'd have people to cook and clean and you could rest. I know you refuse to relax unless forced to."

Martin's overbuilt, overpriced New York properties were gaudy glass skyscrapers, part condo and part hotel. The thought of staying in one of those sterile monoliths left me cold. "I appreciate the offer. Thanks, anyway."

"I hope you'll let me help you, Lily. Don't shut me out. Do you—would you like me to help with the funeral? I want to do anything I can, sweetheart. You know you mean the world to me."

It was a year since I'd left him, but the control he had over my emotions hadn't died. I covered up my awkwardness with a question. "Was there a reason you were calling? Ridley's not in trouble, is he?" In a way, that was a foolish question, because Martin's teenage son was always in trouble.

"Ridley?" Martin laughed again, but it sounded forced. "No more than usual, I guess. Sweetheart, there was one thing . . ." His voice trailed off. "It doesn't really matter now. I'm sorry, I have to head into a meeting. I'll call you later today. There's a dinner I have to attend, but I want to see you.

In the meantime, will you promise to call me if there's anything you need?"

After we hung up, I paced a little faster. Martin had been calling for a reason but he wouldn't say what. I tried to tamp down my curiosity, but it was too prickly. The smart thing would be to avoid talking to him, but I knew I wasn't going to manage that. I'd just have to be firm about not seeing him. As much as contact with my ex unsettled me, it was easier to think about him than my sister, waiting for me just a few yards away. I wondered if they would let me touch her, or if I'd only see her behind glass. Drowning, I knew, distorted and bloated the features. It wasn't something I wanted to see again. The memory of my mother's lifeless face floated in front of my eyes and I pushed it away.

At eleven-thirty a burgundy sedan pulled up in front of the morgue, and a tall, lean woman in her late thirties with copper skin and a close-cropped Afro got out of the car. She spotted me immediately. "Are you Lily Moore?" she called out in a voice so rich it belonged on a record, maybe one with a few scratches between the grooves. She hurried over and shook my hand. "Norah Renfrew. I'm so sorry for your loss." She glanced over my shoulder. "Where's Malloy? Did he just take off and leave you here?" I nodded mutely. "I'm sorry. I should've known better than to trust him to take care of you when there's a pub in the vicinity. Mind if we step inside?" She was wearing a dark pantsuit and no coat.

"You must be freezing." I didn't mean to say it, but I shivered with cold for her. Maybe a year in Spain had softened up my skin.

" 'Button up your overcoat, when the wind is free'—or so my mother used to tell me." She put a hand on my arm.

She didn't sing the old song lyric, but I heard the music beneath it. "I remember that song," I murmured.

"You a fan of Sassy's?" she asked, guiding me to the door and pulling it open.

"I love Sarah Vaughan—though on some days I'm more partial to Ella or Billie." The doorway behind the attendant's desk caught my eye. It looked so bland, but I knew what was lurking behind it. "This would be a day for Billie."

" 'It had me low, it had me down,' " quoted Renfrew. "Yes, Billie's the one you need when there's a crack in your heart." She nodded at the attendant. "Let's sit a minute. Nice that it's quiet in here today. Do you want to ask me any questions first?"

For a moment my mind went blank. I tried to remember what she'd said to me on the phone, but that seemed like years ago. "Did Claudia overdose on heroin?"

"I didn't see any track marks on her but I'll make sure the ME does a tox screen." Renfrew paused. "We wondered about drugs in a case like this, but the friend who found her said Claudia was 'a healthy person who had the occasional glass of champagne.' That's a quote."

"Who was the friend? It doesn't sound like she knew Claudia."

"Woman's name is Kaylee Quan. Funny thing is, she didn't know Claudia had a sister."

Her words hit me with the force of a punch to the stomach. "Excuse me?"

"We got your name from the super in your sister's building," Renfrew said.

"Mr. Pete?"

"That's the one. He said you lived there, alone, for several years, but your sister moved in with you roughly a year and a half ago. Then, a year ago, you moved to Spain and your sister stayed in your apartment. That about right?"

"Yes." Good old Mr. Pete. "Do you think this Kaylee Quan person had anything to do with Claudia's death?" I almost whispered the last word, as if it were indecent to voice it in a building where the dead outnumbered the living.

"No, not at all. Quan got off a flight from Hong Kong and went right over to your sister's place. When she found the—" Renfrew almost said *the body,* but corrected herself. "Found your sister, she had been dead for at least twelve hours."

"Oh." I was still suspicious of any friend of Claudia's. The people she knew were like her, or far worse. "When will you get the report?"

"The ME's office gets backed up this time of year." Renfrew stared at her black suede loafers, then met my eyes. She seemed a little embarrassed. "Look, Miss Moore, you should know that suicides go to the bottom of the heap. In terms of investigations, I mean. It might be a few more days before we get—"

"Suicide?" My hands balled up into tight fists, my nails cutting into my palms. "Claudia wasn't suicidal."

"I'm sorry, I phrased that badly," said Renfrew. "Unless there are signs of foul play, the case isn't going to the top of the pile at the ME's office. That's going to be true of an accidental death, or a suicide. There was no forced entry at your sister's apartment. There were a couple of minor bruises on her, but no ligature marks or signs of an attack. No screams, according to the neighbors." Her voice was gentle. "I didn't mean to imply that the cause of death had been decided. But I have to be honest with you. There are only so many hands to do the work."

I folded my hands in my lap and nodded silently. Even if I didn't want to admit it, I understood what Renfrew was saying. The police only gave a damn if someone committed a crime. It didn't matter that it made a world of difference to me whether my sister died by an accidental overdose or chose to end her own life.

"Are you ready to do this now?" Renfrew gestured at the doorway to the left of the attendant's desk. I followed her inside and down a long corridor. The doors all looked the same, but she opened one and gestured for me to step inside. The room was bright, with shaded bulbs dangling from the ceiling, and microscopes and other lab equipment on counters. There was a window but it was dark.

"Hey there, Norah." Turning my head, I saw an attractive woman in baggy, wrinkled green scrubs. She looked about my age, and her curly red hair was pulled back in a ponytail. "What are you doing here? Aren't you supposed to be on vacation?"

"Hey, Ruthie," said Renfrew. "I hate to admit it, but this *is* a vacation from my kids. They're probably tearing down the house right now."

"I hear you. My kid's still going through his terrible twos, and I keep threatening to bring him in here for a day. Knowing him, he'd probably get a kick out of it."

Renfrew put her hand on my shoulder. "Let me introduce you to Lily Moore."

Ruthie's smile dimmed as she turned to me. "You're here about your sister, aren't you? Everything's set up in the other room. Just let me know when you're ready." She opened another door and I felt a cold blast of air before it shut behind her.

"I'm going to guess this is your first time," said Renfrew.

"The second. When my mother died I had to do this. But that was a few years ago."

"It's never easy, but it's simple. When you're ready, we'll open the curtain and you'll see your sister through the glass."

"I'm ready," I lied. Who had ever been ready for a moment like that?

"Okay, here we go." Renfrew opened the curtain and I held my breath. Ruthie stood next to a body that was draped with a sheet, lying atop a narrow table. She nodded at us and pulled back the shroud, revealing a woman's head and shoulders. Blood pounded in my ears as I stared through the glass. The woman lying there had shoulder-length black hair hanging loose, Ophelia suspended in midair. Her ivory skin was dotted with freckles and her pale rosebud mouth looked unusually small.

"Lily?" Renfrew prompted.

When my mother had drowned, the water bloated her features and cast a blue pallor over her. It was clear death had staked its claim. This woman could have been sleeping.

As I opened my mouth, the air I'd held in rushed out of my chest and I had to gasp for my next breath. "That's not Claudia."

"Take a good, long look at her, now. I know you've got to be jet-lagged and exhausted . . ."

"That woman isn't my sister," I said. "I've never seen her before in my life."

4 "You just admitted you haven't even talked to your sister in four months," the detective snarled at me as he paced. "Maybe she changed her hairstyle and you don't recognize her."

We'd been going in circles since Renfrew had brought me into the Seventh Precinct and introduced me to her partner. Detective Bruxton was a pit bull disguised as a man, all lean muscle and sharp teeth and chilly blue eyes that never veered away from their target.

"That woman in the morgue looks a bit like Claudia," I admitted. "She has dark hair and she's about the same height. But Claudia has six tattoos—six that I know about, anyway. This woman doesn't even have one. Claudia has a dragon on the back of her left shoulder and—"

"Tattoos can be lasered off." Bruxton popped another piece of nicotine gum into his mouth. "Look, if that woman isn't your sister, who is she?"

Detective Renfrew sat across from me, elbows on the table, hands folded together, amber eyes watching me impassively. I wished she would say something, even if it was just to jump in with her own set of accusatory questions. She hadn't said much to me after leaving the morgue. She'd allowed her partner to take charge of the interview, but I felt the weight of her appraising gaze. She was judging every word that came out of my mouth.

"I told you, I don't know. You've asked me that same question ten times in the past hour, and I still don't know." I pulled my coat around me tightly. I'd walked by the police precinct at 19½ Pitt Street hundreds of times when I'd lived on the Lower East Side. It was literally a block south of my old apartment building on Rivington, and I'd often wondered what it was like inside. Now I knew: it was a freezing block of concrete walls and airless rooms and metal furniture that made me long for the cold winter sun outside. Still, I didn't really give a damn. It wasn't my sister in the morgue, after all, and I couldn't hide my relief.

"It's your sister, admit it," Bruxton said.

"No!" I shook my head. "It's not Claudia."

"I don't like people playing games with us," he said. "There are a lot of things we need to be doing right now. This is an open-and-shut case." I'd lived in upstate New York, and I recognized his broad, flat accent. I guessed he'd made it to the NYPD by proving that he was tougher and harder than anyone else.

"I am not making this up," I protested. "I know, I haven't been in touch with my sister in four months. This is the longest we've ever gone without speaking. I've been trying to call her and e-mail her and I haven't heard anything back. But I know what she looks like, and that woman in the morgue is not Claudia."

"Brux," said Renfrew. "Why don't you tell her what you know?"

"Cards on the table," said Bruxton. He put both hands on the table and leaned forward, so that his face hovered close to mine. I guessed he was in his late thirties, but up close I saw the fault lines etched into his face. The lines made him look older, but the scars made him seem dangerous. "When were you planning to tell us about your mother?"

"My mother?" My mouth was dry. "What does she have to do with this?"

"We know," he said ominously.

"Know what?" I wasn't going to make this easy for him. If he wanted to dredge up the past, he could do it alone.

"Your mother killed herself on New Year's Eve eleven years ago."

I stared back at him silently while my stomach clenched. For a moment I felt eighteen again, as if I were hearing the news for the first time, feeling it with the force of a slap. Bruxton's voice was as flat and jaded as that of the officer who had told me about my mother. There was something triumphant in his face that made it clear he knew more than he was saying. He expected me to roll over in shock, or break down in tears. Instead my hands clenched into fists under the metal table and my nails sliced into my palms. "What does that have to do with this dead woman I've never met before?"

Bruxton stood up straight. "You're a hard case, aren't you?"

"What do you think my mother has to do with this?" I said, my temper boiling over. "What, is that your first line of investigation when you find a dead body?"

"No, but in *this* case . . ." Bruxton snarled back.

"How did you find out about my mother?"

There was an awkward glance between the detectives. "Actually, Brux was—" Renfrew started to say, but her partner cut her off.

"A neighbor mentioned it," he said.

"What neighbor?" I demanded.

"From down the hall. Sarah Lyons."

The face of the woman I'd met the day before flashed through my mind. *Claudia told me a little of your family history,* she'd said. I imagined her gleefully spilling every ounce of gossip she'd gathered to the police. She'd pretend to be concerned, but deep down this was amusing for her. I'd disliked her when she'd shown up at Claudia's door; now I loathed her.

"Lily, it's important you understand," Renfrew continued. "We need to know all the facts in an investigation. Even if they don't seem relevant to you."

Her calm voice was like balm on a wound. I took a deep breath. "My mother killed herself, but before she did, she had made many attempts. She would take pills, then call for help. They had to pump her stomach out at the hospital. You can check with Cayuga Medical Center in Ithaca. She was there four times." My shoulders were trembling. "I don't think she wanted to die. It was her way of controlling Claudia and me. If we did something she didn't like, she would threaten to kill herself."

"Had you done something she didn't like?" Renfrew's voice was soft.

I nodded and looked down at my hands. They were wrestling in my lap like palsied snakes. "She didn't want me to go back to college in New York City. I don't think she meant to die. She just wanted me to come back, and not leave again." The bracelet from my father seemed to gleam as I touched it. "I've been worried for a long time that my sister would kill herself with an overdose. She came close once."

"What happened?"

"About a year and a half ago, Claudia had a bad breakup. That's the wrong way to put it. The guy she'd been living with died of an overdose." My voice was terribly calm to my ears. "Claudia came to my apartment a few days later and overdosed. She almost died. That's why I had to take her in. She wanted proof that I cared about her." I looked up at Bruxton. "That woman at the morgue doesn't have track marks on her arms. Don't try to tell me they heal up. My sister has pits and hollows in her left elbow from infected tracks. Those don't go away."

The detectives glanced at each other, communicating in the silent way of a long-married couple. "I think it's time we went back to the sister's apartment," said Renfrew as she stood up. "I'm going to make a quick call. Be right back." She opened the door and stepped out, leaving it yawning behind her.

"You have to admit, it looks strange, this woman dying on the anniversary of your mother's death," Bruxton said.

"It does. But that doesn't mean it's my sister."

"Here's something for you to think about," he said. "If that girl who died in your sister's apartment isn't your sister, what was she doing there? And what does your sister have to do with her death?"

5

Mr. Pete pulled me into a tight hug when he saw me. "Miss Lily! So sad time. But so good see you." The superintendent of my old building was a delicate, sparrow-boned Chinese man two inches shorter—and ten pounds lighter—than me. His face looked older than it had when I'd last seen him, more lined and more tired. He had to be seventy by now.

"It's good to see you, too, Mr. Pete." His habit of referring to everyone by their first name, with a Mr. or Miss attached, was one I'd always found endearing.

"So sorry about sister. So sad." He didn't seem to notice that two police detectives were lurking in the hall behind me, and I wondered if his eyesight was failing.

"Thank you. How have you been?"

"Good, good, can't complain. Miss you in building. Such pretty girl! Like Miss Ava Gardner! You find husband yet?"

"No, not yet."

"You move back here. Marry nice friend from Oh-cla-hoo-maa." Jesse had spent a lot of time at my apartment, and he'd been a favorite of Mr. Pete's. Without Jesse I might never have learned that seeing the movie *Oklahoma!* had made Mr. Pete want to leave Hong Kong for America. Mr. Pete still hadn't made it south of Atlantic City.

"Excuse me," said Renfrew. "Peter Wu, we wanted to ask you to come upstairs with us."

Mr. Pete glanced over my shoulder. "Ah, you police. You

here Saturday. Detective Norah." Then he rattled off her badge number.

Renfrew was impressed. "Don't think I know it that well myself." She shook Mr. Pete's hand.

"Other one not show badge." Mr. Pete peered at Bruxton like a bouncer at one of the clubs in my old neighborhood would a man trying to talk his way in. Bruxton's hard, thin lips twitched slightly, as if crushing a smile.

"We want you to come up and tell us about the girl who lived in Five B," said Renfrew.

"Miss Claudia? Yes, of course," said Mr. Pete. He collected his keys and the four of us trooped up the stairs together. I'd stuck the yellow vines of police tape back in place over the door of 5B before I'd left yesterday, but now all the tendrils were trailing to the ground.

"Evidence of a break and enter?" Bruxton said.

"I came here yesterday, just after my flight got in," I admitted. I'd already told Renfrew this and she hadn't reacted. "It's my apartment. The lease is in my name and I pay the rent."

"Really? You pay the rent?" Bruxton demanded.

"Miss Lily send check every month. From Spain. Never, ever late," said Mr. Pete. "She best tenant ever."

"Why are you paying for your sister to live in your apartment?"

I looked into Bruxton's cold blue eyes and knew I'd never be able to explain it to him. I'd invited Claudia to come live with me after her boyfriend died of his overdose. She'd been staying with him and I was afraid she'd end up on the street, careening from shelter to shelter, as she had in the past. But six months of living with a junkie was sheer agony, and it drove me out of my own home. "Claudia's been homeless before, and she needed a place to live," I said. "I moved to Spain for work, and I mail the rent so she can't use the money for anything else."

Mr. Pete unlocked the door and stepped back, gesturing for me to go first. I turned on the light next to the door. The room looked just as empty and forlorn as it had the day before, and the sweet perfumey smell I'd disliked so much yesterday still floated through the air.

"Okay, walk us through," said Renfrew. "Think about the things that didn't seem right to you in here."

That wasn't as easy as it sounded. As I looked around the room I thought that something had shifted from when I'd last seen it. Hadn't that tacky red card been on the top shelf of the bookcase rather than the next shelf down? I wasn't certain so I didn't mention it. I was already on shaky ground; the oddities that had caught my eye could be explained away as a simple change in preferences or tastes. They wouldn't seem important to anyone who didn't know Claudia. When I spoke, I sounded silly even to myself. "Yesterday, when I saw the magazines and DVDs here, it made me think that Claudia had really changed."

"What was she into?" asked Bruxton.

"*The Sorrows of Young Werther.*" Both detectives looked blank. "Goethe."

"Very beautiful book," Mr. Pete added. "Tragic, but romantic."

"Don't think I've read it," Renfrew admitted.

"That's the kind of thing Claudia likes." There was a line of Ava Gardner's that Claudia liked to paraphrase. *Deep down, you're pretty superficial,* she would say to me. Sometimes she was contemptuous, like when she bought me *Nausea* by Jean-Paul Sartre and months later I admitted I couldn't finish it because it pushed me into a place darker than I was willing to go. Occasionally Claudia said it fondly, like when she caught me watching *The Barefoot Contessa* for the hundredth time. "Look at her bookcases," I said. "It's all Thomas Mann and Dostoyevsky and Knut Hamsun."

"And Edgar Allan Poe." Bruxton pointed to a row of slender, cloth-bound volumes. *Those used to be mine,* I almost blurted out. It was rare for Claudia's interests to intersect with mine, but we both loved Poe, especially his verse. I'd memorized some of his poems, and Claudia used to ask me to recite them for her. It had been a long time since she had done that.

"So she'd go slumming on Park Avenue?" asked Renfrew.

"Exactly," I said, remembering the Irving Berlin song she was referring to. "Claudia has no interest in pop culture or the bourgeois." I held up a *Sex and the City* DVD. "Not her style."

"All right, what else?" prompted Renfrew. But as I went through the rooms it was hard to put into words what was out of place. She would never have bought the three bottles of Perrier-Jouet "La Belle Epoque" rosé champagne that were in the fridge; her beverage of choice was whiskey, preferably Jack Daniel's, neat. But that was nothing next to the lack of mess, smell, and chaos I associated with Claudia. The apartment had become too sterile. By the time I got around to pointing out the shoeboxes in the closet, I felt as if I'd bored the detectives to tears.

"Claudia and I wear the same size shoe, a seven," I said. The brown box that held the Christmas present from me was cast off to the side, where I'd left it. "These are size nines. They might fit that woman at the morgue, but not my sister."

"Maybe your sister was selling shoes on eBay," Bruxton said. He gestured at one wall. "Why are there three empty picture frames hanging here?"

I looked at the antique carved wood and realized that some things I took for granted would seem odd to anyone else. Claudia's talent was for drawing, and she was good enough to have her work included in several shows at small galleries around New York. I'd framed some of her less disturbing, gothic-inspired subjects, but she'd torn them up one afternoon without explanation. She had apologized and promised to replace them, and I left the frames up as a reminder. Before I could explain any of this to the detectives, Mr. Pete spoke.

"Shoes could be for cousin," he said. He was holding a pink-dyed python pump and examining it seriously. "Cousin have big feet for girl. Big girl, overall."

"We don't have a cousin, Mr. Pete," I said.

"Yes, Miss Claudia, cousin." Mr. Pete gestured with his open palms upward, as if this made everything clear.

"But Mr. Pete, Claudia is my sister." I'd been impressed with how sharp his mind had seemed downstairs, but maybe it wandered off to pasture at intervals. "My parents were both only children. They didn't have other relatives in this country. There was just Claudia and me."

"Miss Claudia. She cousin. She good influence on sister. No more loud music. No more strange friends. Good influence."

The detectives stared at me. "I don't know what he's talking about. Mr. Pete, what was the name of this cousin?"

"Claudia. Just like sister!" he answered triumphantly.

I sat down on my sister's bed and rubbed my temples. Mr. Pete sounded crazy, or confused, but maybe he was right. The girl in the morgue looked a little like Claudia, with her dark hair, upturned nose, and rosebud mouth. "Mr. Pete, who told you that this woman was our cousin?"

"She tell me."

"She introduced herself to you?" I asked.

"October, she ask me fix kitchen sink. She say Miss Claudia visit sister Miss Lily in Spain. She cousin, she visit, stay in apartment."

"How long did she stay in the apartment, Mr. Pete?"

He cocked his head to the side. "Two week, she say," he answered. "Cousin engaged."

"She told you she was getting married?" I asked.

"No, but I see ring," Mr. Pete answered, pointing to his own empty ring finger. "Big rock." He smiled. "Distant vision not so good, but close vision still sharp."

"Can you describe this . . . cousin?" I asked, floundering for a better word.

"Height, like you, but big girl. Black hair. Round face like moon. Big, ah . . ." Mr. Pete tapped on his chest. "You know."

Something wasn't adding up. "This other woman in the apartment . . ." My voice faltered. "Why didn't you think of her when the police said someone died in the apartment?"

"Cousin here *October*." Mr. Pete spoke with emphasis. "November, I have surgery. Shoulder, see?" He shrugged his right arm lightly. "December, cousin gone. Sister back."

"You saw Claudia? Did you speak with her?" I asked.

"No talk, but I see at distance." Mr. Pete nodded his head. "Skinny-minnie, black clothes. Claudia, sister. Not big cousin."

Bruxton and Renfrew took over, trying to shake him off his claim.

"Mr. Wu, did you see Claudia Moore on Saturday?"

"No."

"You didn't look at her body?" said Bruxton. "Are you sure about that?"

Mr. Pete's expression was incredulous. "No want look. What for? So sad this happen."

"Can you tell us what you did see on Saturday?" Renfrew asked.

"Of course. Police come to building. Tell me girl come visit, she find friend dead. In bathtub." Mr. Pete paused, shook his head and blew his nose on a crisp white handkerchief he pulled out of his pocket. "I see girl, she crying. She tell police Miss Claudia dead. I tell police, you call sister, Miss Lily, she in Spain. I have phone number."

"Right, that's what you told me," said Bruxton. "Did you know the woman who found the body?"

"December, I see her. Nice girl. Polite. She from Hong Kong. I tell from accent."

As I sat on the bed listening to them, I thought about Claudia's wide circle of acquaintances—she called them friends. She crashed at their apartments when she was between boyfriends. It made sense that one of them might return the favor one day and come to stay with her. There was one friend, a pink-haired girl, who'd slept on my sofa after her boyfriend had beaten her. I'd been impressed because she'd gone to rehab and actually stayed straight. Of course, Claudia dropped her for the same reason I'd liked her. I wondered idly about the suitcase on the bed. Had someone been planning a trip?

"Did you look through many of these boxes, Lily?" asked Renfrew.

"No. Just a couple on top." I stood and joined Renfrew in front of the closet. She opened several boxes and examined the soles of the shoes. "Some of these have been worn, but lightly," she said. Then she knelt and eased out the scuffed boxes from the bottom of the stack. One held a pair of my own heels that I'd left behind. Another contained a blue terry-cloth hand towel that was wrapped around a knobby bundle.

"Careful, Norah, the girl was a junkie," Bruxton said.

"Calm yourself down, Brux," Renfrew answered, lifting the towel by its edges and turning it over, so that it opened up. We all stared at the contents silently. There was a half-used bag of cotton balls, a black disposable lighter, and a tarnished-looking spoon. I'd never seen Claudia inject herself with heroin, but I recognized the paraphernalia. All that was missing was a hypodermic needle and a tie-off. And the heroin itself, of course.

Renfrew stood up, smoothing the front of her pantsuit, speaking to each of us in turn. "Brux, would you mind taking Mr. Pete's statement? Thanks for your help, Mr. Pete." She shook his hand. "Lily, come with me for a second." I followed her into the living room.

"We talked to the neighbors on Saturday," Renfrew said quietly. "Nobody mentioned a visitor staying here with your sister."

"Claudia kept away from all of our neighbors when she lived with me. She never talked to them, or to Mr. Pete." I'd chided Claudia for being rude, but she'd just rolled her eyes. *They only see me as your screwed-up sister,* she'd shot back. *Your pet project.*

"Okay, but that girl over at the morgue wasn't wearing a diamond when we found her yesterday," Renfrew added. "Brings to mind all kinds of questions, like where the hell is that ring?"

"Was Kaylee Quan wearing a ring?" I couldn't help but ask.

"Couple of big rings, as a matter of fact." Renfrew looked pensive.

"What happens now?"

"First, we need to make sure Mr. Pete's got all his synapses firing. We'll talk to the neighbors again. Run the prints off that girl in the morgue through the system."

"Claudia's fingerprints are on file." I felt stupid for not remembering that when I was at the police station.

"That's good, we can use that." Renfrew didn't ask why they happened to be on file, and I was grateful. "We'll file a missing persons report on your sister. We're going to have to talk to her."

"I know." Something in my chest quivered. I'd been so relieved that Claudia wasn't dead. Now that reality was sinking in, I realized that the police would start hunting her down. My sister, the magpie who had a thing for shiny jewelry, bad boyfriends, and hard drugs.

"We'll bring Kaylee Quan in and go over her statement again, and we'll get Mr. Pete to look at the woman in the morgue. Can you think of anyone else we should talk to?"

"I'll make a list for you."

"Can you think of anyone who might've seen your sister recently?"

"The neighbor across the hall told me she saw my sister on New Year's Eve. Only when she talked about my sister, she could have meant this other woman." As I said it, I realized that didn't make sense. Sarah Lyons had known who I was when she'd met me; she'd referenced sad parts of my family history. I turned that over in my mind, but Renfrew's voice broke in.

"I'm going to have to ask you to leave for a while. CSU— the Crime Scene Unit—needs to come in and go over the place with a fine-tooth comb."

"They didn't do that already?" I asked.

"There was no need to do anything but a cursory examination before. No sign of a crime."

When she said *crime,* my legs seemed to give out under me. I dropped into the sofa.

"Are you all right?" Renfrew knelt in front of me so she could look into my face. "You're really pale. I thought you were going to pass out there for a second."

"I forgot to have lunch," I improvised. "Jet lag has me out of whack." The truth was that my mouth was dry with fear of what my sister had gotten herself into this time. I had no idea how I'd get her out of it.

"Holy hell, Lil. Your sister's alive!" Jesse's voice crackled with excitement over my cell phone. "Praise the Lord!"

"Don't tell anyone," I admonished, watching the police cars on the street and waiting for them to roll away. I was sitting in the Portuguese bakery next to my sister's building, nursing an herbal tea and a sweet roll and wondering when my stomach would stop churning.

"Why not? It's good news!"

"Except for the fact that the police are now looking for my sister in connection with the dead woman that they found in her apartment."

"Damn," he said. "I hadn't got 'round to that part yet. You got any idea where she might be at?"

"Jesse! I thought she was dead this morning, remember?"

"I was thinkin' maybe she left a note or some such in the apartment."

"No note," I answered. "By the way, the friend who identified her body is suddenly missing." When Renfrew had tried calling Kaylee Quan, her office, home, and cell phones rang off into voice mail ether. *So when someone discovers a dead body, you let them give you a phone number and then they waltz off into the sunset?* I'd asked. Renfrew had reminded me that witnesses don't get put in a holding cell.

"I might be able to get a clue if I could get into the apartment again, but the police are there now."

"You need to come on home so we can cook up a plan. We can call your sister's friends, track her down that way."

"The junkie network. Yeah, that will work." I stared into the street, willing the cops to beat it.

"You comin' home now?"

"Soon. I'm going to walk a little, clear my head." That wasn't a lie, but I didn't believe that exercise or crisp air would do anything to relieve my anxiety. Somehow the earth had given way under my feet. *All that we see or seem is but a dream within a dream,*" I thought, remembering a line of Poe's. It was as if the year I'd spent in Spain hadn't happened, and I was back where I was a year ago, agonizing over my sister.

When I left the bakery, I headed west on Rivington, noticing that the buildings got nicer and the ratio of trendy bars to bodegas increased dramatically. At Attorney Street I turned and followed it north past Houston. Along the way I dropped into the little hidey-holes Claudia was fond of. It was too early in the day for her to be listening to live music in the back room at the Parkside Lounge, but I could picture her cadging a free meal at a church or hanging out at her favorite tattoo parlor. I went as far north as Trinity Lower East Side Lutheran, an austere, redbrick church on the eastern edge of Tompkins Square Park. Claudia had made extensive use of its soup kitchen and legal-referrals center in the past, but she wasn't there now, nor in the park.

The next logical spot to look for my sister was west along St. Mark's Place. Her spiky-haired goth friends at Androm-eda Tattoo claimed they hadn't seen Claudia in months,

maybe back in the summer, or was it spring? It was a cold
January day, and when the wind hit my face it made my eyes
water. I made it up to Cooper Square, pausing at the door of
Greenwich House before I could pull myself together and
step inside.

"I'm looking for my sister," I told the tired-looking middle-
aged woman behind the counter. "Her name is Claudia Moore.
She's been in your outpatient program in the past."

"We don't give out information about patients." Her eye-
lids drooped so low that she seemed like a sleepy turtle trying
to blank out the scene around her.

"This isn't a privacy issue. I know she's in your methadone
program, or she used to be. She's missing."

"We don't give out information."

"Can you just tell me if you've seen her?" I held up a picture of Claudia. It was taken at the engagement party Martin
and I had hosted two years ago. Claudia was wearing a black
vintage dress she'd borrowed from me with ebony fishnet
stockings and heels. She wasn't smiling at the camera but
she wasn't scowling, either. When she wanted to, she looked
beautiful.

"We don't give out—"

I turned on my heel and walked out the door before she
finished. Frustrated, I paced the block, watching for people
arriving or leaving. By New York City law, methadone patients weren't allowed to loiter near their clinics—that scared
too many neighborhood residents and business owners. If
I wanted to catch anyone I knew, I'd have to wait.

It took close to an hour, but a familiar face finally materi-
alized just before four. With his relatively clean clothes and
his dark hair slicked back, I didn't recognize him at first.
What gave him away was the shock of recognition on his own

face when he saw me. His head swiveled toward the clinic doors, then to the street, as if judging the best exit. I grabbed the arm of his black leather jacket before he could run. "Mal Sabado. What the hell are you doing here?"

"Hey, Claudia's sister," he said casually, as if we were pals. "Didn't think you were in New York anymore." He grinned up at me, revealing several gold teeth. Even though my boots had only a low kitten heel, I towered over him. "Why you always look so mad when I see you?"

"I'm not a fan of drug dealers. Especially ones who keep my sister hooked."

"It's a free country, Claudia's sister. People got the right to do what they want."

I felt queasy, seeing him up close. He had pale skin that was pockmarked from acne, giving him the look of a worm-eaten apple. "Just tell me where she is."

" 'Scuse me?"

"Claudia is missing. Do you know where she is?"

"Haven't seen her in a while now. You check her apartment, maybe?" Something flickered in his eyes. He stared at me curiously.

"She's not there."

"Maybe she moved?"

"She hasn't moved. When was the last time you saw her?"

"Dunno. Few months, I guess. Police busted me, put me out of business."

"Then why are you out of jail?"

Mal gave me his sickly smile again. "Got me a good lawyer. Case went bye-bye, only I got to go into a program." He shrugged. "It's not so bad. Addicts pay as much for methadone as they do for smack."

I felt like hitting him in the head. I couldn't hold him

accountable for Claudia's choices, but the fact that he'd lured her back with free "samples" of heroin when she'd tried to get clean made me loathe him. "Just tell me where you've seen her."

"Maybe I . . . hey, is that her?" His brown eyes widened as he looked over my shoulder. I glanced back and he pulled free of my grip and ran into the clinic. Kicking myself for falling for the world's oldest trick, I went in after him.

"This crazy lady, she's harassing me," he was telling the turtle at reception. "That's her! Call security."

The receptionist turned her tired turtle eyes on me. "You're going to have to leave the building." I took a last look at Mal's gloating face and walked out, biting my lip.

7

"There are so many things wrong with this picture," I said to Jesse. "I can't believe we're sitting here. Did we really think Claudia was going to wander by?"

"I'm an eternal optimist," answered Jesse. "I'm looking over a four-leaf clover right now. Claudia's kickin' up trouble and she's going to want to check out the carnage. Look at all the cop cars up and down her block. She'll love this."

I stared out the window of Jesse's car at Rivington Street. This had been my neighborhood not long ago, but it had had a face-lift since I'd left. Earlier I'd marveled at the new construction over the Lower East Side, but I'd had to admit that the farther east I went along Rivington, the less of it there was. By the time I got to the block between Ridge and Pitt streets, a strip of road away from the housing projects, gentrification had petered out and everything looked familiar and dodgy. But that was in sunlight. At night, and at a little distance, the redbrick building where Claudia lived didn't look so worn out. The disintegrating but still ornate façade had a certain romance to it in the yellow glow of the street lamp.

"I don't know if I want to find her or not. The police want to talk to her about that dead body." I rolled the bracelet from my father around my wrist and wondered when my stomach would untangle its knots. The freckled face of the girl in the morgue floated by my eyes. Had she drowned by accident?

Maybe she'd bumped her head, or had a seizure. Her drown-ing in Claudia's apartment didn't mean my sister was involved.

"Yeah, she's gonna have to explain that one." Jesse sighed, breaking my hopeful train of thought. He drummed lightly on the steering wheel of Ginger, his prized 1968 baby blue Camaro. He was such an Oklahoma boy at heart, keen to get behind the wheel of a car and take off for an adventure, even if that meant surveillance duty on the Lower East Side, or driving along Canal Street while I scanned the crowds for my sister's face, as we had earlier in the evening. I knew that Mal Sabado lived on or near Canal, and I'd guessed that Claudia wouldn't be far from her favorite dealer. But there had been no sight of her.

"Maybe this woman and Claudia exchanged identities," I suggested. "My sister could be living in her apartment right now. Maybe she doesn't even know this woman is dead." I was angry with myself for not digging deeper at Claudia's when I'd had the chance on Sunday afternoon. I'd had the opportunity to go through her mail. Instead, I'd fixated on a long-lost treasure, a discovery that meant nothing now that my sister was officially missing.

"Why would they swap names and apartments?" Jesse shot back. "Only reason you would was if someone was after you. Pretty far-fetched."

What if it was like that Hitchcock movie, *Strangers on a Train*, two people who agree to kill for each other, creating two perfect crimes? Only instead of murder, my sister and this woman were . . . what exactly? It didn't make any sense. My sister had been arrested for drug possession, shoplifting, van-dalism, trespassing, and a litany of other offenses I probably didn't know about. Who would want to swap lives with a convicted criminal? I watched for any sign of a familiar face on the street, but it was desolate. "We're going to seem like crazy people," I said. "The police are going to notice us. It's already after eight. How long are they going to be in there?"

"Calm down, Tiger Lily. You'll get your chance. Folks are just comin' home from work. Cops might be there a spell." I gave Jesse a sidelong look, which he chose to ignore. Sometimes he poured the Will Rogers charm on thick. "Look, we'll grab some supper, then come back. They're not gonna hang around here all night." As usual, my friend was thinking with his stomach. But his suggestion gave me a sudden inspiration.

"You're brilliant. Have you ever eaten at Jannat?"

"Don't think I've had the pleasure," said Jesse. "How come you move all the way to Spain and you're still up on the new spots in New York?"

"It's not new," I admitted. "It's been around a while. An old friend of Claudia's owns it."

"I thought her circle was all artists and writers and rodeo clowns. Restaurant owner seems too straight."

"Not this restaurant owner," I said, playing with the bangle again. "I think it's just one of his money-laundering operations. Do you remember Tariq Lawrence?"

"Big guy, good-lookin', hoity-toity accent, brags about his polo ponies, carries a gun. Um, yeah, I met him a few times when Claudia was holed up with you. Thanks for introducin' me to a real interestin' cross section of society."

I gave Jesse directions and called the restaurant. Claudia had taken me there several times. They were, in fact, the only nights I remembered going out to dinner with her when I didn't foot the bill. Claudia, and whomever she brought with her, dined with the compliments of the house at Jannat. "I was hoping to make a reservation for dinner tonight," I said to the man who answered the phone.

"I am sorry, but we are completely full." His voice was tinged with respectful regret.

"Oh." So much for that idea. "Would Tariq Lawrence be there, by any chance?"

"I am afraid not. May I tell him who it was that asked for him?"

Tariq wasn't enamored of me, and the feeling was mutual. I doubted he'd tell me much of anything about Claudia's whereabouts, but that didn't mean I couldn't drop some bait. "Would you tell him that Claudia Moore called?"

"Miss Moore!" the man said, warmth infusing his voice with the alacrity of a struck match. "I am so sorry. Of course we always have a table ready for you."

I made a reservation and hung up. "Before you tell me what a horrible person I am for doing that, let me just say that Claudia told me to always use her name at the restaurant."

"Did you hear a peep outta me?" asked Jesse, looking smug. "What's the deal with this place? How come your sister gets the VIP treatment?"

"Tariq has been in love with Claudia for years. They dated, then they lived together for a while, but they broke up. They always stayed close afterward, though." I'd always been suspicious of Tariq and his influence on my sister. He was a fixture in Claudia's life, as constant as the sun in the sky and the addictions in her brain.

"Wait a sec. If they're so tight, how come they broke up?"

"I think Claudia got too crazy even for him." I snapped the bracelet open and shut a couple of times in quick succession. What I really meant was that my sister's habits led her to do whatever she had to for a quick fix. She had told me that she and Tariq smoked opium together. *It's so retro, you'd love it,* she told me. *It's even organic!* But chasing the dragon had given way to the urgency of the needle for Claudia, and Tariq had never followed her there. Every relationship my sister had withered because of her obsessive affair with heroin.

In front of the restaurant, a valet drove off with Ginger, as a nervous Jesse stared after them. "Maybe this wasn't such a good idea . . ." he said, as we walked into the foyer, before he froze in place. "Holy Moses."

It had been a year since I'd set foot in Jannat, and it was, if anything, more spectacular than I remembered. The floor was inlaid black-and-white marble in a spiraling mosaic, and carved narrow columns rose up from it, supporting lavender silk hanging above like a canopy. There was a fountain farther back, its black, gray, and lavender tiles looping in a stylized floral pattern.

The maître d', a short, stocky man in a high-collared navy uniform, made a quick bow. "Good evening, Miss Moore." He regarded me curiously. "You are Miss Moore's sister, are you not?"

Good memory. "Yes, I'm Lily."

"It is a distinct pleasure to have you join us again. Will your sister accompany you for dinner?"

"I don't think so."

"That is a shame. It has been so long since we have had the pleasure of her company." He sounded genuinely forlorn.

"I know how much she loves this place," I said. "When was she last in?"

"It was in the summer. Late August, I believe." His brow furrowed. "You must tell her to come back. The warmth of her spirit is greatly missed."

He led us to a small room that was paneled with carved rosewood. There was a low, legless rectangle for a table and oversized silk and velvet cushions scattered around it on the floor. All of the rooms at Jannat were private, so that you could hardly tell who was dining there unless you staked out the exits.

"Your sister prefers to eat as we do in Lahore," said the maître d', and I nodded. Pakistan was one country I hadn't visited, but I'd eaten at the restaurant a few times and understood what he meant. He stepped out of the room and closed the door softly behind him.

"Where the heck are the chairs?" asked Jesse.

"You sit on the floor. On the cushions. Really, it's comfortable." I knelt on a red silk cushion and swung my legs out to the side, kicking off my shoes for comfort. I'd swapped my boots for heels back at Jesse's, but I was still wearing the same black crepe vintage dress I'd pulled over my head that morning. It had seemed appropriate when I'd believed that I would be identifying Claudia's remains that day. Now I just looked like a mournful mermaid.

"Damn," said Jesse, lowering himself cautiously. "I could be in kindergarten again. Do we get storytime with this? Where are the menus, anyway?"

"They don't have a menu. Someone will come in and ask us about what we like and don't like, and how many courses we want. The food is incredible, I promise." I looked around the room, wondering if it was bugged. It was a paranoid thought, the kind of thing that my mother used to ramble about when she was drunk, which was pretty much always. *You can't trust people,* she would whisper, *even if you think they're your friends.* Claudia had complained many times of Tariq meddling in her life, and I wondered if he would stoop to spying on her. Or on me.

"Tariq's doin' pretty well for himself, ain't he?" said Jesse, interrupting my thoughts. "What kind of business is he in, besides restaurants?"

"Import-export, as far as I know." Claudia had made some references that hinted at a smuggling operation. I'd first suspected drugs, specifically the kind pressed out of poppyseed pods, but when I'd prodded my sister, she'd whispered *priceless antiques* in a reverential way that was unusual for her. Still, Jesse was right about Tariq carrying a gun, and I didn't know any antiques dealers who did that.

"Right, I think he told me that once. He talked a lot more about polo. He was very up on polo."

"Polo is still a big deal in Pakistan," I pointed out. "At least in some circles."

"Oh, those wacky colonials. What else d'you know about him?"

I struggled to remember details that I hadn't cared much about when Claudia had originally shared them. "He's from a rich family. British father, Pakistani mother. He's an only child. I think his parents divorced when he was very young. He went to school in Britain, but I can't remember whether it was Oxford or Cambridge."

"How come you're blushin'?"

"Me? It's hot in here. Don't you think so?" It was a little warm, but Jesse was right. Claudia overshared everything about her personal life, and I squirmed at the recollection of an anecdote about Tariq, a private paddock, and a riding crop.

Dinner was delicious but awkward, with me fending off Jesse's more incisive questions while biting into spicy meat dishes. The more I thought about it, the more likely it seemed that Tariq would be the one person who would know what was going on with Claudia. They had a history together that ran almost a decade. Still, when I'd spoken to my sister over the summer, she'd mentioned that she'd barely seen Tariq lately. I'd long ago learned not to make any bets based on what rolled off a junkie's tongue.

"When the police told you your sister had drowned in the tub at home, all I could think about was your mama," Jesse said. "I thought Claudia had deliberately copied the way your mama did it, even down to the date on the calendar. You know, like Sylvia Plath's son did when he killed himself. Do the police know about her?"

"I didn't tell them, but they knew it from a neighbor." When Bruxton had asked me, *When were you planning to tell us about your mother?* in his broad, upstate accent, my first reaction was that he had contacts who'd filled him in about my crazy family. I wondered what else the neighbor knew, but I was afraid to ask. "They were assuming Claudia was a copycat suicide. That would have been the worst thing of all."

"What do you mean?"

I pushed some food around my plate, aware I was tugging at the scab of an emotional wound that had scarred over but never healed properly. "It would be like a signal that . . . My whole family is so crazy that . . ." I tripped over my words, and it wasn't because of the wine. I swallowed hard. "It would be like finding out you inherited a horrible disease. That your dark fate was written into your stars and genes." I shook my head, hoping Jesse wouldn't notice that my eyes were wet. "That certainly sounded self-pitying and stupid." I took a long gulp of merlot.

Jesse grasped my hand, willing me to look at him. "There's nothing stupid about that. For cryin' out loud, if it is, I'm guilty of the same."

I moved closer to him and put my head on his shoulder.

He wrapped an arm around me. We rarely went into this particular minefield, but around the time of my mother's suicide, Jesse's father had killed his mother and then put a bullet in his own brain. He told me later that his mother's cancer was so advanced that it had paralyzed her from the waist down. In the aftermath of our family tragedies, Jesse and I were shocked out of what should have been carefree student existences marked only by dramas involving the men we slept with. We were fast friends who hid from true intimacy with anyone else behind glamorous armor. An invisible barrier separated us from everyone else. The only consolation had been that we'd been on the same side of that barrier.

By the time we left Jannat, I'd made a decision. "I have to talk to Tariq," I told Jesse, while we waited in the foyer for the valet to bring Ginger back.

"You're itchin' to go on over to his place. I can tell."

"How did you know?" I asked. Jesse rolled his eyes at me. "I'm being predictable again, aren't I?"

"Let's just say you've never been a patient gal, Tiger Lily."

"I'm going to take a cab up to Tariq's," I announced. "Right now."

"Hold your horses. What will that get you?"

"The element of surprise. Tariq won't be able to lie about what Claudia's up to." What I didn't add was that I thought there was a chance that Claudia might even be staying with her ex. They were that close. My sister had bragged to me that she had her own room at Tariq's penthouse apartment, where she stayed every now and then. If she swore Tariq to secrecy, he'd be like a vault. I'd learn nothing over the phone.

The valet parked Jesse's baby blue Camaro at the curb and we went outside. "Hop in," Jesse said to me, opening the passenger door.

"I'll be fine. I'm just going to flag a taxi—"

"Nope," said Jesse. "I'm comin' with you."

"I need to talk to him alone, Jesse." I'd been to Tariq's apartment several times; I'd even conspired with him once to send my sister to rehab, for all the good that had done. I knew Tariq wouldn't talk about anything more personal than polo with Jesse around.

"I don't have to come up to his place, but you're not going over alone, Tiger Lily."

I gave in and got into the car. "Thank you."

As Jesse steered Ginger up Third Avenue, he was quieter than usual. He drummed his fingers on the steering wheel, tapping out an inaudible rhythm. "What if this Tariq guy did something to your sister?" Jesse said suddenly.

"Are you kidding? They're like Bonnie and Clyde."

"I'm thinkin' about the gun aspect, Lil."

I thought about that, too. Back in the summer, when Claudia had convinced me that she was off drugs and doing so well, we'd had a strange conversation about Tariq. *How's Tariq taking the new you?* I'd asked her. *He's happy for me,* Claudia had answered. *But we're not really in touch very much right now. It's just . . . easier this way, better to break established patterns. Old friends, old habits.* She'd sounded as if she were regurgitating a self-help book.

What do you mean? I thought he was your best friend. And you told me Tariq never tried heroin.

Oh, I don't mean that. Claudia laughed. *You always think everything is about drugs, Lily.*

Then what?

He's got his own issues, my sister had said. *All of these awful family problems you couldn't imagine.*

I can imagine quite a lot, Claudia.

Yeah, you're right. But Pakistan is different—someone hurts your family, you have to hit them back twice as hard. Someone attacks your cousin, you have to kill him and maybe his brother, too.

Claudia, did Tariq kill someone? I'd gasped.

Get a grip, Honey Bear. You're tightly wound as ever, aren't you? I thought you said living in Spain was relaxing. It was unusually affectionate for Claudia to call me by her childhood nickname for me; Honey Bear was the nickname of Ava Gardner's character in *Mogambo*. I'd let her turn the conversation around, but I hadn't forgotten what she'd said, and now I wondered about it.

"Are you cold, Lil? Want me to turn up the heat?" Jesse asked, turning a knob on the dashboard. I shivered the rest of the way to Tariq's building, a beautiful prewar structure that had always reminded me of a castle. "You sure you don't want me to come on in with you?" Jesse asked. When I shook my head he shrugged. "I'm gonna park her somewhere safe. I'll be waitin' in the lobby. Make sure Tariq knows that." He squeezed my arm and let me go.

One doorman let me inside. Another waited behind a circular counter and telephoned Tariq's apartment after I gave him my name. "There is a Miss Moore here to see you," he said. He was silent a moment. "Yeah, that's what I said. M-O-R-E."

"Two O's," I corrected him.

He repeated this into the receiver. "Go on up, Miss Moore. Top floor."

I thanked him and went to the elevator bank. I was whisked upstairs so quickly that my ears popped. The doors silently slid open on the twenty-first floor, and I stepped into a broad foyer with an inlaid black-and-white marble floor, not unlike the one at Tariq's restaurant. A hulking man in a tailored suit glowered by the door. His head was shaved and his nose looked as if it had been broken, casually and repeatedly, in the past. Overall, he was merely the size of a refrigerator. He was wearing a shoulder holster that didn't do much for the line of the suit, but did a mean job showcasing his gun.

"Good evening, Miss Moore," he said, in a voice as clear and plummy as a BBC broadcaster's. He had a laptop computer open on a console table. I suspected that it was for security purposes, but the screen showed a soccer game in progress, though the audio was on mute.

"Evening," I said.

"Lovely coat," he added, smiling slightly. He held the door for me. I wondered if Tariq had found him at Harrods in London. A heartbeat after the door clicked shut behind me, I heard the roar of thousands of soccer fans. Game on.

Inside the apartment, draperies were pulled shut over towering windows. In the subdued artificial light, a stranger couldn't have told if the opulent furniture was fake or the real deal, but I knew from previous visits—and the occasional tidbit from Claudia—that Tariq's obsession with the English Regency and its trappings knew no bounds. I wondered if I was supposed to stand there, admiring it all, before the man decided to step from the shadows. "Tariq?" I called as I opened my coat and dropped it over the back of a sofa.

No one answered, but the lights went out in the room. I heard footsteps clacking on the parquet floor and I turned around. For a second I thought it was an animal, but then something hit me in the chest.

8

I took a step back as someone tried to slap me. I ducked to the side and my attacker stumbled. For a breathless second I thought of my mother, who had waited up for me once while I was out late with a boyfriend. She had surprised me as I came in the door, hitting me with her fists for making her worry. This attacker was angry but inept. "You bitch," she hissed. With her French accent, it sounded like *beech*. "How *dare* you come here."

"Are you insane?" I spluttered. She grabbed the front of my dress with one hand and there was a furious rip of fabric as I twisted away.

"I'll get even for what you did," she said, and lunged for my throat. I felt her pointed nails sink into my neck, and instinctively I lashed out, hitting her squarely in the nose.

"Ahhhh!" she screamed.

I wanted to rush to the door, but I was disoriented now. As I got away I tripped over a table. Crystal shattered as I fell. Scrambling to my feet, I made it to the wall. Feeling for the door, I found a light switch instead. A woman sat on the floor, legs akimbo. She wore a black dress that clung to her curvy but slender body, and there was a tattoo of a dragon on her pale shoulder. *Claudia*, I almost said aloud when I saw it. But even though I couldn't see her face—it was hidden in her hands—I knew it wasn't my sister.

"My nose, my nose!" she cried. Had I actually broken it?

I stood back, watching her. When I didn't come closer she eventually dropped her hands. *"Beech,"* she hissed from the floor.

"Who are you?" I demanded, more incredulous than angry. "Why did you hit me?"

The woman blinked at me and her mouth fell open in wordless amazement. There was a trickle of blood running from one nostril, so maybe I really had hurt her. She was lovely, even as a disheveled mess gasping for breath. "But, you are not Claudia!" Her voice was astonished and annoyed. "You look like her, but you are not her!"

"Why would you think I was Claudia?"

"The doorman said Miss Moore was here. I thought it was Claudia Moore. Obviously."

"Wrong sister," I snapped. "I'm Lily."

"Lee-lee," she repeated, as if tasting my name. It was clearly bitter in her mouth. "The sister, of course. I have heard about you. I am Tatiana. I would offer you a drink but as you can see, this is a bad time." She patted her nose gingerly. "Padma!" she called. "Padma!"

A moment later, a pretty girl with long black hair, dark brown skin, and delicate features hurried into the room. I was sure she had been listening on the other side of the door, to come in so fast. She was wearing a black salwar kameez, a knee-length, long-sleeved dress with elegant white embroidery on the bodice over a pair of matching pants, and she couldn't have been more than sixteen. She glanced in my direction, bowed, and whispered an almost inaudible, "Hello," before turning her full attention to the French woman. Tatiana put out her arms like a toddler wanting to be held by her mother. The Pakistani girl was shorter and more slender, but she managed to get Tatiana into a wobbly upright position.

Tatiana had broken the heel of one of her black patent Louboutin pumps, and there was blood smeared on her hands. *What a complete mess,* I gloated, though when I looked down I noticed that my black stockings were torn up, too. How had that happened so fast?

"Why would you want to hurt Claudia?" I sank into the sofa, still mystified by what had happened.

"She snaps her fingers and Tariq goes running, as if he is her dog," she said, her voice full of rage. "I tell Claudia if she does not leave him alone, I will kill her." She breathed in sharply. "Ow! That hurt!" she snapped at the maid.

"Sorry, Tati," said the girl. Maybe it wasn't an odd nickname, but it sounded just like *tatty,* as if referring to a pilled sweater or a scuffed shoe. Tatiana limped to a plush chair and sat down.

"When did you last see Claudia?" I asked.

"Too recently," Tatiana hissed.

"Claudia is missing, you know."

"Missing? I wish it were so. She will always turn up, just at the wrong time, like a black penny." Tatiana shook her head with obvious frustration. "Tariq would marry me if not for her. She is black magic." She turned her head toward the girl, who was surveying the room with obvious despair. "You must clean this up. I must call Dr. Khan. Tariq is not to hear of this, understand?"

"Yes, Tati," said the girl. I felt sorry for her, and my estimation of Tariq dropped further. It was bad enough that he was stashing a cheap replica of my sister in his apartment, but worse that he had imported an underage girl from Pakistan as a servant. Slave was probably more like it.

"I told you not to call me that! It is bad enough Tariq does it." Tati narrowed her eyes at me. "Your sister gives me this awful nickname, and now it is all Tariq will call me. That is her power over him."

"Where is Tariq?" I asked.

"In Pakistan," Tatiana said dismissively. She got to her feet and hobbled toward a doorway. I had an impulse to throw something at her, but there was no point. Tati hated my sister, but she was afraid of Claudia and of her hold over Tariq. She had no idea where my sister was.

"Sorry," said the girl. She knelt and picked up some of the larger shards of crystal and porcelain from the table I'd knocked over. "Could I bring you some tea, perhaps?"

"No, thank you." I braced myself to stand.

"You look like Claudia, much more than Tati does," the girl observed. "Are you really Claudia's sister?" I nodded, and the girl looked at me as if she recognized me for the first time. "You're Lily. Oh, my. I am very glad to meet you. My name is Padma. I have heard about you."

"Really? What have you heard?"

She smiled shyly and bowed her head. Nothing good, that was what I'd thought. I stood and collected my coat from the sofa. The knee that had taken the brunt of my fall ached. "Claudia was here at the beginning of September," Padma said.

"Pardon?"

"You wished to know the date that Claudia was last here," she said, her head bowed. "I believe it was September twelve, but I should check the date. It was certainly that weekend."

"Why do you remember that? That's almost four months ago."

"It was just before Tariq left for Pakistan," said Padma. "I remember that."

"You saw Claudia?"

The girl nodded, glancing at the doorway that Tati had exited through. "Claudia hadn't been by all summer. Tariq was often away as well, but he missed her. They are very close."

"Did something happen with Tati that day?"

"Not then. After Tariq left, Claudia came back to drop off a present for his birthday. Tati was here. She never goes to Pakistan, she just waits for Tariq. Tati wasn't very . . . pleased . . . to see your sister."

"What happened?"

The girl shook her head. "Tati told Claudia to get out and never come back. And she threw"—the girl's voice dropped to a whisper—"a bottle like that . . ." She pointed to a table covered with crystal decanters. "At Claudia."

"Was Claudia hurt?"

"No, miss, but she was angry." The girl glanced at the doorway again, obviously afraid of being overheard. "Claudia hit Tati in the face and knocked out two of her teeth." The girl smiled, covered her mouth with one delicate hand, and ducked her head, a mix of mirth and mortification.

It certainly sounded like we were talking about the same Claudia. "Will you tell Tariq I was here? I don't think Tati will be passing on that message. He can reach me at Jesse Robb's. Tariq has the number." With what I told myself was great albeit slow-moving dignity, I left the apartment.

9   At the end of *Show Boat,* Ava Gardner's character was a wreck of her former self, the result of years of abuse and alcohol. The guard who rang for the elevator said nothing, but when the doors closed, the mirror told me that my transformation into a disaster had taken less than a minute. My hair stuck out as if I'd poked a finger into an electrical socket. My neck had a pair of scratches, not deep but vividly red. The front of my dress was ripped and I was flashing one breast through a sheer black bra. I pulled my coat tightly around me without bothering to button it and tied the belt. There was a little dried blood on my hands, and I rubbed frantically to get it off.

Safe again on the ground floor, I saw Jesse by the doorman's desk, flirting with him. As I came over, Jesse glanced up, blanched, and ran to me. "Lil! Are you okay? What happened?" He grabbed my arm, as if I were about to fall over. "Holy hell, I'm gonna shoot that son of a bitch's head off," he muttered through clenched teeth.

"Tariq wasn't even there," I said. Then I laughed.

Jesse watched me as if I'd lost my mind. "Lil? What happened up there?" Over his shoulder, I could see the doorman staring at both of us.

"Tariq's girlfriend thought I was Claudia and she attacked me."

"But why?" Jesse looked perplexed.

"She was worried I was going to steal her man." I laughed and put my hand over my mouth. Tati's frenzy suddenly seemed funny. Claudia would relish that story, whenever I had the chance to tell her about it.

"Did she hurt you, Lil?"

"No, but she ruined my dress. Maybe I should sue."

"D'you need a doc to look at you?" Jesse examined my neck but decided I would live. I saw the front door open and a middle-aged Pakistani man hurried into the lobby, raising his hand in a wave at the doorman. He brushed by us, bumping Jesse with an old-fashioned black doctor's bag and apologizing. He vanished into the elevator and I wondered if he could have been the Dr. Khan that Tati mentioned, summoned to minister to her wounds. Briefly I wondered if I really had damaged her nose. I hoped I had and immediately felt rotten to the core. That was the kind of thing Claudia would say, not me.

"Can we just go home?" I asked Jesse, and he put his arm around me as we left the building.

I told him everything on the drive back, from Tati's copycat tattoo to Claudia's knocking out two of her teeth. My sister was a magnet for trouble, always had been. What surprised me was Jesse's response. "It's some kind of dirty trick your sister's playin'."

"What, with Tati?" I asked, confused.

"No, with you. She gets herself into some kind of jam, then counts on you to bail her out. Again and again and again."

"That's not fair. Claudia hasn't asked me for anything this time. She probably doesn't even know I'm in New York." It was one thing for me to criticize Claudia, but I hated to hear anyone else do it, even Jesse. It was a holdover from childhood, when my sister wouldn't go to sleep at night unless I got rid of the monsters under her bed. She was convinced that I was the only person who could do it. I'd always been flattered by her belief in me and willing to banish monsters wherever she saw them. But now, the job had gotten too big for me.

Jesse dropped me off in front of his building. "Think you can stay outta trouble while I put Ginger to bed?" I promised to do my best while he parked his beloved Camaro in a garage a few blocks away. I was embarrassed for the doorman to see me, but I told myself that my disheveled appearance could be taken for European insouciance. My legs ached like hell, but if I held my big black bag over the worst of the stocking tears, I might pass for normal. That was the moment I realized I'd left my bag in the car. Fighting the urge to run after Ginger's retreating taillights, I headed into Jesse's building, nodding at the doorman's raised eyebrows, slinking toward the lounge area in front of the elevators, and trying to remember if I'd ever seen anyone seated there before. The sofa, director's chairs, and glass coffee table looked like props from a human-sized diorama, and as I slid onto the couch I wondered if I'd broken some unspoken protocol by disturbing it with my presence. I put my head into my hands, took some deep breaths, and rubbed my eyes. The sofa shifted slightly as someone sat down next to me.

"Hello, beautiful," said a familiar voice. I lifted my head and looked at the man beside me. His green eyes were set off by a golden tan and hair as black as patent leather. He was turning forty-six in April, I knew, and the smile lines around his eyes were deepening.

"Martin," I said, my heart dropping to my feet. It would probably tumble out of a hole in my stockings. "What . . . why . . . what are you doing here?"

10

Martin smiled, bringing out the slight dimple in his cheek. "I barely got to speak with you this morning, and my day was scheduled like a marathon," he said. "I was worried about you. I guess I wanted to see for myself that you were all right."

I was ashamed to sit there in front of him, a raw and battered mess who had sunk below any standard of respectability. I wished he would stop staring at me, but the look in his eyes was concern, not condemnation. I was hypnotized by the sight of him. My former fiancé looked handsome in an old-fashioned black tuxedo that Tyrone Power might have worn. "I've been waiting outside the building for the past hour, hoping to see you."

"Now you're stalking me?" I tried to sound lighthearted, even amused.

"Maybe I am."

"So you put on a tux and hid in the bushes outside Jesse's building?"

"The tux is because some very nice but misguided people decided to give me an award. I know, it's hard to believe. I certainly don't deserve it." He smiled at me again.

"One of your charities?"

He nodded. "The Pediatric Cancer Fund. They do a lot of good work. All I do is write checks."

He was self-deprecating about it, but Martin's support of

children's charities had always impressed me. He had one son, Ridley, from his first marriage, and he'd spent a lot of time in hospitals because Ridley had developed a brain tumor when he was three. The boy was almost sixteen now and healthy, but Martin never forgot what hell he'd gone through, having a desperately ill child.

"How is Ridley doing?" I asked.

"Don't get me started. I love him, but he drives me insane." Martin had sole custody of Ridley since his divorce. In front of me, the boy was sweet but almost painfully shy, and he rarely looked me in the eye. Martin claimed that his son had an Einstein-level IQ, and even if that was an exaggeration, I knew the boy had once won a science competition with a project about topology and abstract algebra that I'd been unable to decipher. But one thing I understood about Ridley was that he had no friends. It was something I'd experienced, albeit in a different way: my mother's drunkenness was something I'd had to keep secret. I couldn't get too close to other girls, because if I spent time after school at their houses, sooner or later they expected to be asked over to mine. It was something that left me feeling lonely, and my heart went out to Ridley.

"Did he get expelled again?" My voice was quiet; this was treacherous ground. Ridley had been forced out of four schools that I knew of. He fought with other boys, or he damaged school property. Martin described it as bad luck, and he wouldn't discuss its causes or listen to any criticism of Ridley. I had a similar protectiveness toward Claudia, so I understood, but it didn't make our relationship any easier.

Martin tried to smile. "He's been expelled from every decent school in the city. I've had to hire a bunch of tutors for him now. We'll see how that goes." Martin reached for my hand and squeezed it gently. "Let's talk about you. Are you okay, Lily?"

So much for the European insouciance. "I went to see one of my sister's old friends. Do you remember Tariq Lawrence? A friend of his thought that I was Claudia and attacked me."

"I don't understand," said Martin. "Your sister just died."

"No, Claudia isn't dead after all." It seemed like a week had whirled past since I'd waited for Detective Renfrew at the morgue, but it had been less than twelve hours. "The woman who died in her apartment was calling herself Claudia Moore, but she wasn't my sister."

Martin swore under his breath and stared at me. "Then where is your sister?"

"I have no idea."

We stared at each other silently. Martin hit his temple lightly with the heel of his palm. "Am I dreaming? Well, that's wonderful. What a relief." He leaned forward, taking both of my hands in his. "I'm so glad for you, sweetheart. I was going to ask if there was anything I could do to help, but . . ." His voice trailed off. "Who is this friend of Tariq's who attacked you? What did your sister do to him, exactly?"

"I was too busy beating *her* up to ask," I deadpanned.

"Her? How sexist of me. You don't have to tell me I'm old. My son does it every day." Martin smiled at me, but it was a fleeting expression. "Now, at least, I don't need to worry about speaking ill of the dead."

"Excuse me?"

"I'm sorry, sweetheart. That was in poor taste on my part. But your sister's exposed you to a seedy world."

"Claudia has her issues," I said, annoyed that he would bring them up now.

"She also has a way of dragging other people into them.

Namely, you." Martin went on when I started to protest. "I wasn't sure whether I should mention this to you, Lily. I wanted to tell you something this morning, but I simply couldn't when you said that Claudia was dead."

"What?" I asked, annoyed and excited at the same time.

"I heard from your sister a few days ago." Martin's green eyes stared into mine without blinking.

"You—what?"

"She called me. A couple of days after Christmas. I think she called before it, too, but I was away on holiday. Ridley wanted to go somewhere sunny, so we went to St. Barts."

"Why would my sister call you?" My voice was loud enough to make the doorman look our way.

"This is awkward," said Martin, grimacing. "She made me promise I wouldn't tell you."

"She made you promise . . ."

"She called out of the blue and asked if she could borrow some money. Quite a lot of money, actually. She said she had to go to rehab, that she had to turn her life around once and for all."

I pulled my hand out of his grasp. "She's been to rehab before. Why would she ask *you* for money?"

"I don't know, except she said she was desperate. I figured she had no one else to ask."

"What did you tell her?"

"I asked if you knew she was calling me. She said yes. When I called you before New Year's, I was trying to figure out what was going on. I was surprised when you said you hadn't been in touch with Claudia for months."

"You didn't mention any of this before!"

"I'm sorry, Lily." Martin looked contrite. "I thought there

was some argument the two of you were in, and I didn't want to make things worse."

I was so angry and preoccupied that I hadn't noticed anyone else come into the lobby. "What the hell is *he* doing here?" Jesse bellowed as he strode over. He dropped my black handbag on the sofa between Martin and me. It landed with a heavy thud.

"Hello, Jesse." Martin stood up and put out his hand to shake. "It's been a while."

"Not nearly long enough." Jesse wasn't giving any ground.

"Well, it's good to see you, in any case." Martin smiled, unfazed, and sat down again. "I wanted to see for myself whether you were taking good care of Lily. Sending flowers and chocolates didn't seem like enough."

I looked up at Jesse. Flowers and chocolates? I'd been back at his apartment before we went to do surveillance on Claudia's building, and I hadn't seen anything. Jesse avoided my eyes. "Now you've seen her, so you can get outta my building."

"You know, Jesse, you're always worked up about something whenever we meet." Martin's voice was calm. "You look as if you just realized you'd handed over your life savings in exchange for the Brooklyn Bridge."

"I'd rather be the man who bought the bridge than the one who sold it," Jesse snapped.

"We were just talking about Claudia," I interrupted. "She called Martin just after Christmas."

"For cryin' out loud, why the hell would she do that?"

Martin shrugged. "I'm not sure. Who knows why she does the things she does?" He looked at me. "Who was the woman who died, if it wasn't Claudia?"

"The police don't know that yet," I said impatiently. "Tell

me everything you remember about the conversation with my sister. How did she seem? Was she upset? Angry? Did she mention a friend who was staying with her?"

"Sweetheart, calm down. All she said was that she'd been having a lot of problems and she was trying to get her life under control. She really wanted to get clean this time, she said something like that."

"How original," said Jesse. He was standing in front of us with his arms crossed. At least he wouldn't be throwing any sudden punches that way.

"Was there a reason she was calling now?" I prodded Martin, desperate for any insight. Interpreting my sister's motives through small hints in her words was an inexact art, like reading tea leaves. I'd been trying for most of my life and still wasn't much good at it. "Tell me *exactly* what she said."

"I don't remember it exactly. We'd just come home from St. Barts and Ridley was going on in the background about some stupid book he'd lost. It was hard to concentrate, and she surprised me. I told her I'd think about giving her the money. I wanted to talk to you first, find out what was going on. Then she called again, maybe a couple of days later, asking for the money. I figured I'd help her out, so I said all right. I told her she could come over and I'd write her a check. But she never came by."

"Why didn't you tell me this before? I've been worried sick about her, and she's probably off at a clinic somewhere. Why didn't you tell me she called you?"

"I didn't want to upset you. I know you've never gotten along with your sister. I'm sorry, I thought it would make things worse."

"What was the rehab called?"

For the first time, Martin was lost for words. "I'm sorry," he said finally. "I'm blanking on it. I know I jotted some notes on a bit of paper, but it's in my desk somewhere. You know what an awful mess that is. I'll find it."

"Thanks for droppin' by," Jesse said. "Tomorrow you'll have a sit-down with New York's finest. They'll want every detail, so you better get your story straight." He reached for my hand and led me to the elevators. "Don't worry if you forget to call," Jesse called over his shoulder. "I'll have 'em call you. They'll be happy to come by your office for a meet-up. They're real obligin' that way."

Once the elevator doors closed, I wilted against the mirrored wall. The hollow feeling in my chest made it oddly hard to draw breath. Jesse was muttering to himself. "Thing I can't figure is what the hell he wants. Slithers over here with a cock-and-bull story about your sister. Slippery as quicksand."

"What do you mean?"

"You believe him?" Jesse demanded.

"Why would he lie about Claudia calling him?"

The elevator doors opened and we stepped into the hallway. "Okay, even if that part of his story's true, you gotta wonder why he has to come over and clap eyes on you to tell you. He knows how a phone works. He's fixin' to worm his way back into your life again."

I tried to ignore the last thing he'd said, even though it made my heart skip a beat. "I can't believe Claudia asked him for money. Why wouldn't she ask me? Or Tariq?"

Jesse sighed and unlocked his door. "She knows you don't have that kind of money, Tiger Lily." He pushed the door open. "Maybe she had a big falling-out with Tariq like she did with you. Or maybe the psycho girlfriend scared her off."

Inside the apartment, I dropped onto the sofa and stared at the ceiling. "When were you going to tell me about the flowers and chocolates Martin sent?" I asked, my tone aiming for casual.

"The . . . oh." Jesse's face gave away his guilt. My friend was many things, but he'd never been a man who could hide his emotions. "Look, I thought it was for the best if you didn't see 'em. You know, you were havin' a tough day, and I didn't want him comin' on in and takin' advantage. Steer clear of him, okay?"

Jesse's meddling was nothing new. Part of me was annoyed with him, but a bigger portion was amused by the lengths he'd go to keep me safe. He was my big brother, gay boyfriend, and father confessor. I'd told him too much about my problems with Martin and now he loathed him on sight. Jesse was better at holding a grudge than I was. After a year of dating Martin, I'd accidentally learned that my lover had been married twice before, not the one trip to the altar he'd admitted. The news had upset me, though I couldn't really explain why; Jesse had been furious about it. Worse was the lady architect, as Jesse dubbed her. She had come to the party Martin and I had thrown to celebrate our engagement. Her wide-eyed expression brought to mind Anne Baxter in *All About Eve,* and I got used to seeing it at dinner parties and events. *That's a bulldozer disguised as a powder puff,* Jesse warned me. Later, I learned that she'd traveled with Martin to London and Dubai and Singapore, a fact she let slip one evening while smiling at me over a martini. When I confronted him, Martin insisted that the trips were for work. I never found out what, if anything, had happened between them, and my questions lingered. I cyber-stalked the lady architect now and then, and had found that she had married and moved back to Virginia.

But the uncertainty had fractured my relationship with Martin.

"I wasn't tryin' to deprive you of chocolate, y'know," Jesse added. "Tomorrow I'm gettin' you a box from MarieBelle. Sweets for the sweet."

He knew how to worm his way back into my heart better than Martin did. MarieBelle was our shared obsession, a SoHo shop with treats worth breaking any diet for. I closed my eyes and sighed. "Do you want to open a bottle of wine?"

"Nah. Don't get too comfy there," Jesse warned. "I'm runnin' you a bath."

I took off my ruined dress and slipped into a robe, then washed my hair in the sink of the guest bathroom. By the time I was finished, Jesse had drawn a bath in the Jacuzzi tub of his own bathroom. There was a fragrance of lavender bath salts in the steamy air.

"Take your time." He closed the door before I could thank him. I slid out of my robe and into the warm water. It felt wonderful, until I sank further into the tub and felt my neck burning. Of course, the scratches. *Amateur,* I thought of Tati, sitting up straight and wondering if she'd ever hit anyone before. I could picture my sister pounding her into pieces. She'd done it to me, after all, back in September, when I'd come home to New York for my first visit since moving to Spain. I'd gone to Claudia's apartment after she'd stood me up. She'd opened the door, looking respectable enough in a light summer dress, as if she'd toyed with the idea of going out. But she was also wearing a wool cardigan on a steamy summer evening in an apartment that didn't have air-conditioning. Her fingernails were painted dark red, but half the polish had chipped away. I grabbed one of her bony wrists and pulled up the sleeve a few inches. Her skin was a map of red marks and sores. I'd let go and stepped back, staring at her eyes now, noticing that the black pinpricks were almost lost in her green irises, like insects being devoured by a carnivorous plant.

How could you? I'd yelled at her. *I believed you. I trusted you. You swore you'd gotten yourself together.*

It was trying to get myself together that got me where I am now, she'd snarled at me.

We fought, standing in the doorway, seething at each other, shouting and not caring what the neighbors heard. But what got to her was my parting shot. *I knew you'd never be able to stay away from your drugs for long.*

Claudia stared at me with such a look of hatred that I dropped my gaze and turned away. Her sharp-taloned hands grabbed my neck and hit my head against the door frame. I started to fall and the only thing that held me up were Claudia's hands around my throat. She was surprisingly strong, and all I could do was stare at her while I fought for a gasp of air.

You think I just gave in to temptation, don't you, Lily?

Her eyes bored into mine, those tiny black dots as searingly hot as lasers. I gurgled in response.

You don't know the first thing about it. How hard I worked to just get clean. I've been off dope since April, you know that? Completely, utterly clean. Do you think I just gave that up one day on a whim? Do you?

I tried to make a sound but nothing came out of my mouth. My peripheral vision had gone dark, so that I was staring at Claudia through a tunnel. I was at one end and those mad eyes were at the other.

I've been abandoned and I've lost every fucking thing I care about. But you don't care, do you, Lily? You're just horrified and ashamed. You didn't even ask me what happened. You don't even care why I'm like this.

Claudia let go then, and I fell backward into the hallway. *I hope you drop dead,* she said, then she kicked my feet out of the doorway and slammed the door. I lay there, staring at the ceiling for a minute before I'd gotten up and stumbled down the stairs. I'd run from the building, swearing to myself I'd never go back. Now, lying in Jesse's bathtub, I was sure that my sister had deliberately lured me back into her web. I was trapped as surely as if her hands were still closing around my throat.

11

Coming up into the chilly sunlight from the Castle Hill subway station, I tried not to retch at the reek of urine. No matter how many stories I heard about the revitalization of the South Bronx, I thought of it as New York's own heart of darkness. Farther north and west were the glories of Belmont and Riverdale; south was Castle Hill itself, a neighborhood that was proudly working-class, much like Norwood, the formerly Irish enclave above the Botanical Garden. But the subway stop was in the no-man's-land between Soundview and East Tremont. Both were textbook cases of grinding poverty, but Soundview had the distinction of a murder rate that soared while the rest of the city's plummeted.

I'd been born in the Bronx, but the only reason I'd ever come back was for my family. Claudia and I had been raised in sight of the Woodlawn Cemetery, on the borough's northern border. It had been a tough neighborhood, but a close one, and not a place where junkies went to score dope. My father was buried in Woodlawn, and I brought flowers to his grave from time to time, and always on his birthday. Soundview was another story: it was early Tuesday morning, and cold enough to keep foot traffic to a minimum, but the juxtaposition of sagging buildings with sleek SUVs parked out front hinted at the score. I kept my head down, lifting it to glance at the mural of the angry eagle as I turned at Newbold Street, and I moved fast.

Claudia's old pal Melissa Ardito had already hung up on me that morning. It was reassuring that at least someone in Claudia's circle was acting in character. I'd found her address via an online directory. It turned out to be in a redbrick four-story building that sat equidistant to the Bronx Psychiatric Center and the St. Raymond's Cemetery. There was a punch line in there somewhere, but I wasn't laughing. I didn't think Melissa was hiding Claudia, but I knew she'd keep tabs on her. They had been rivals for years, jousting over art shows at outer-borough galleries. Melissa would know what Claudia was up to, for spite's sake at least.

I had to lean on the buzzer for five minutes before Melissa answered. A man who had followed me off the 6 train went down the street, passing by her building without a glance. My imagination was getting the better of me. "What?" Melissa finally yelled.

"Flow-ahs, special deliver-ay," I called, borrowing Jesse's hokey-Okie accent.

Upstairs, Melissa answered her door after I knocked a couple of times. Her perfect oval of a face was pinched and sallow, and she dangled a cigarette in her mouth, squinting through the smoke. The honey-blond hair that had been her halo was lank and greasy, and she wore a white T-shirt with yellow sweat stains under the arms. She was twenty-seven, the same age as Claudia, but she'd transformed into the warning poster for why you should just say no to drugs.

"This is the second time you woke me up this morning!" she snapped, but she didn't protest when I strolled into her apartment. "What do you want, anyway?"

There was no point in lying to her. "Claudia's missing, and I'm trying to find her," I said, checking out her arms for track marks. Unlike Claudia, who stayed true to opiates, Melissa did a bit of everything. Claudia referred to her derisively as a chipper, someone who just dabbled in hard drugs for fun. Looking at Melissa's haggard face, the fun had vanished long ago.

"I'm not using." She crossed her arms defensively. "I'm in a program."

"Methadone?"

"Yeah, I get my dose at three." She looked at the clock on her wall, obviously longing for the hands to fly forward. There was a wide, dark brown splotch under it, prominent even in a place where every surface was coated in a layer of grime. "Shit's worse than H. You start crawling out of your skin hours before you get it."

"Claudia told me that. But she also scammed extra doses to get high."

"Yeah." Melissa nodded, as if she'd heard about such people, too. "The waiting drives some people crazy."

"The police know you're a friend of my sister's, so they're going to be calling you soon. I wanted to ask when you last saw Claudia."

"What's in it for me?" said Melissa, stubbing out her cigarette.

If you knew an addict, you knew that's how the conversation turned, sooner or later. "Claudia's your friend. You're doing it for her."

Melissa sat on the tattered couch and put her head in her hands, rubbing her temples. "I was hoping you'd be able to help me out." She ran one hand through her greasy hair and I saw an ugly red welt on her forehead that had been hidden by her bangs. "I've got a liver disease and I haven't been working. It's been really hard."

When she said *working,* I wondered if it was code for prostituting herself. Claudia had told me of the depths that Melissa was willing to sink to in order to get a fix, but right now, from the drained and hollow look of her, there couldn't be many takers. Deep down, I suspected that my sister was equally willing to turn a trick or two when truly desperate. "I really don't have much money," I said. "I'm waiting for a couple of clients to pay me." If I'd wanted to whine about the strain of renting two apartments on different continents on a freelance income, I'd come to the wrong place.

"You look like you're doing really well," Melissa said, appraising me carefully. Did she really have a liver disease? Junkies got jaundice all the time, after all. But looking at her, twenty-seven going on forty-seven, made my heart feel tight in my chest. Where was my sister scrounging for her next fix, and how low would she go to get it? I reached into my bag and, without pulling my wallet out, dislodged a couple of twenty-dollar bills.

Melissa's tired eyes lit up at the sight of cash. "Thanks," she said, snatching the bills out of my hand, quickly folding them together and disappearing them into the elastic band of her black panties. "I saw Claudia in August."

"August?" I repeated, with a sinking feeling. Her information was older than mine.

"Uh-huh. She came to a show at the Littlefield Dix Gallery." Melissa reached for an open pack of cigarettes on the end table and lit up. For a split second I thought about asking her for one. "Claudia was looking pretty good, actually. I mean, she's not bad looking when she puts herself together, instead of gooping herself up in that Cleopatra eyeliner crap."

"My sister has gone for the goth look since she was twelve."

"It's never worked for her. But at the gallery she was wearing a designer dress and great shoes. She actually looked pretty."

"How did you know the dress was designer?" I asked, remembering the luxurious clothes in Claudia's closet. Maybe some of them had belonged to my sister after all.

"She mentioned it. I told her she was looking good and she said, like, that's what a three-thousand-dollar dress could do." She sucked down smoke anxiously, as if irritated by the memory.

"Where would she get three thousand dollars?"

"I know! I asked her that and she said it was a gift from a friend. Tariq, I figured. Who else does she know with that kind of cash?" Melissa shrugged. "Fucking show-off."

"How was she otherwise? I mean, what kind of mood was she in?"

"Fine. Sort of . . ." Melissa squinted, trying to pluck the right adjective out of her brain. "Relaxed, I guess. She just seemed relaxed, like everything was good in the world."

"Was she high?"

Melissa dragged on her cigarette and shook her head. "I don't mean stoned-relaxed. She wasn't smoking, wasn't drinking. I asked her what was up and she said she was 'in a different place,' whatever that means." She stared at the floor and squinted up at me. "It was like she was a different person."

"Are you *sure* it was her?" I asked, my heart picking up speed.

"What's that supposed to mean? I've known her since we were eighteen."

"There was a woman who was staying at Claudia's apartment. She kind of looked like Claudia. People thought they were cousins. I'm wondering if it could have been her instead."

"No way," Melissa insisted. "I wasn't that out of it. And even though Claudia was all dressed up, you could see those weird dragon tattoos crawling on her shoulders. Ugh." She shuddered. "I hate those things. It's like something you see on a bad trip."

"Did Claudia say anything about someone moving in with her, or about going away?"

"Not exactly. She said something about how she wasn't spending much time in the city anymore."

"Where was she staying?"

Melissa looked at me blankly. "I didn't ask. She was nagging me about some rehab center. She'd been there, and she was pushing me to go. She was going on about turning her life around, you know, all the crap people spew when they see the light, just before they go back into the tunnel."

"What was the name of the place?"

"Don't remember." Melissa squinted again. "She said she'd gone in April, or maybe May. No, April. Claudia said something weird, like, if I tried it and didn't like it, there was another place she'd tell me about. It was like there was some big secret she was going to let me in on, but only if I went to rehab first. I told her I didn't need rehab and she looked at me like I'm some kind of street junkie." She gestured with her cigarette, annoyed. "She said the place got her into yoga. She was really obsessed with yoga." Melissa's eyes were slightly glazed, as if picking through her fractured memory for broken bits of conversation. "She had her broken tooth capped. Suddenly she had this big smile like Julia Roberts or something. White Chiclets teeth."

I realized that Melissa was right. When I'd seen my sister over Labor Day weekend, she'd been on a screaming high and I was so angry I couldn't see straight. But the front tooth that Claudia had broken in a drug-fueled fall on the pavement was whole. Sometime after I'd left for Spain in January—and before I'd come back for a visit in September—it had been repaired. "Do you remember anything else?"

Melissa studied her cigarette for a moment, then dragged on it and furrowed her brow. "At the time, I thought she was being a pain in the ass, trying to flaunt how well she was doing."

"She wasn't doing well when I saw her in September. She was shooting up again."

Melissa nodded her head. "You can get away for a while, but after a while it's like an old lover calling to you. Then you realize they've still got you, deep down."

12

"The phrase they used was *criminal element*," Detective Bruxton said, grimacing. "They said it applied to both you and your sister."

The detectives had buzzed up unexpectedly at Jesse's building, just after I'd made the trip back from the South Bronx. I'd pretended I had just gotten up, ditching my jeans for a black pencil skirt that was very Ava in *The Sun Also Rises*, and a pale blue angora sweater that did more than just hint at cleavage. When in distress, distract, that was my new motto. Neither Bruxton nor Renfrew had commented on my appearance, which meant that my concealer and foundation were doing their job. That, or the detectives' eyes had glazed over when Jesse trotted out his collection of family Bibles. He kept a leather-bound one the size of an ink-jet printer on an end table. When guests commented on it, as they always did, Jesse played show-and-tell with the other five in his collection, including a Bible his great-grandfather had used as a boy in prep school in Meno, Oklahoma. Both Renfrew and Bruxton had looked relieved when I'd walked in.

"Mr. and Mrs. Decarno in Five A, right?" I guessed aloud. That elderly couple would never abandon their rent-controlled Lower East Side apartment, even if they loathed their neighbors. They had called sweet Mrs. Felesky "loose."

Jesse carried two white china coffee cups out of his kitchen, setting them in front of the detectives. "Wasn't it ole Mrs. Decarno who called you a 'scarlet woman'?" Jesse grinned at me.

"When she was being polite," I said. "Normally, I was the whore of Babylon to her." Renfrew smiled wickedly from the sofa across from me. Next to her Bruxton blushed to the roots of his blond hair. Today, the pit bull was muzzled, almost shy. Fingerprints had proven that the dead woman was not my sister. The harsh skepticism in his eyes had been muted into annoyed bafflement. Still, I noticed that he was watching me closely, even though his reason for suspicion should have passed.

"That pair across the hall from your sister's wouldn't open the door to me, never mind the badge," Renfrew said. She was wearing a pale gray pantsuit today with a simple strand of pearls that gleamed against her coppery skin. "I could swear I heard Johnny Rebel playing on their stereo. Bruxton had to put his white face up to the peephole before they'd open up."

"Be nice if we could run people in for being schmucks," said Bruxton. "Must've been a real treat to have them down the hall from you."

"I travel a lot for work, so I hardly ever saw them," I said. "When I moved into the building, it was filled with older people on fixed incomes who'd been there forever. The woman who used to live in Five C, Mrs. Felesky, was really feisty and a lot of fun. Most of the older people in the building are like that, just not the Decarnos." I sat back on the sofa, annoyed that the Decarnos were clinging to their rent-controlled apartment like barnacles on the hull of a boat.

"Best thing they had to say was that your sister had been quiet the past few months." Bruxton said, glancing around the room.

"Can I get you something, Detective?" asked Jesse.

"No, I'm fine," said Bruxton.

"He's checking for an ashtray," said Renfrew. "Just ignore him."

"I said I'm fine," Bruxton muttered, his face reddening again. Less than twenty-four hours ago, he'd been interrogating me. Now, he was squirming and I was enjoying the show. He pulled a foil packet out of his wool coat and popped a couple of pieces of nicotine gum in his mouth.

"Quitting's so hard," Jesse said sympathetically. "I have a friend who stopped and started a dozen times before she managed to do it." I gave him a look that said, *You're talking about me, aren't you?*

"He's not actually trying to quit," said Renfrew. "The gum just keeps his head from exploding before he gets his next smoke."

"Can we talk about the case?" said Bruxton. "We're putting together a timeline. You told us you saw your sister over Labor Day weekend at the beginning of September. The woman down the hall—Wendy Malahoff, do you know her?" I nodded and Bruxton continued. "She remembered your sister screaming and breaking things just before Labor Day. She said it sounded like your sister was throwing things and kicking the walls. Malahoff spoke to your sister briefly."

"What did she say?"

"Claudia told her to go fuck herself and slammed the door in her face," said Bruxton. "She said it was definitely Claudia Moore."

"That sounds like my sister," I agreed.

"There's two solid weeks of this. Yelling, cursing, et cetera. Mrs. Decarno said a man came by on September tenth— she's sure about the date, since she was heading out to her hematologist's—and he tried to reason with Claudia. Your sister screamed that he'd abandoned her, then yelled 'I hate you,' and slammed the door in his face."

"Did Mrs. Decarno describe the man?"

Bruxton glanced at his notebook. "She said *tall* and *distinguished*. When pressed, she added *old enough to be that minx's father*. He was white, had an English accent, and he wore a dark suit. That was it."

I could picture Mrs. Decarno watching Claudia through the peephole in her door, as she had done to me when I lived there. She was an evil-minded old woman who spiked every sentence with insults and insinuations. Still, it was hard not to smile at her dubbing Claudia a minx.

"After that, there was no noise from your sister's apartment," said Renfrew. "It might have been empty for two, maybe even three weeks."

"People are fuzzy on dates," said Bruxton. "Wendy Malahoff in Five D went off to Malaysia on a business trip, and she seems to be away most of the time. Mrs. Felesky in Five C hurt her leg in mid-September and moved to Ohio to be with her kids. Of course, your sister didn't tell people she was going away."

"Then, sometime in the fall, this other girl appeared," Renfrew continued. "She was quiet. No one really noticed her, except your superintendent."

"Mr. Pete is amazing," said Jesse. "He has a photographic memory. He can recite every line from every movie he's ever seen."

"He's sharp as a tack," said Renfrew. "He noticed that this girl wore a whopper of an engagement ring. We found a Tiffany box with the diamond in the back of her lingerie drawer. Only, guess what, it's the wrong ring."

"What?"

"The one at the apartment is a two-carat princess cut in a Tiffany setting. We showed it to Mr. Pete, and he said it was nothing compared to the one she was wearing. Smaller ring, wrong style, not an antique."

"The two-carat diamond wasn't big enough for her?" I asked, incredulous. Martin had wanted to buy me a golf-ball-sized diamond when we got engaged, but that didn't appeal to me. He'd finally found a two-carat ring we agreed was beautiful. I'd loved it, but it was so big I felt conspicuous wearing it out. I'd never gotten used to the weight of it on my hand. As sad as I was to give it back to Martin before I left for Spain, it was a relief not to be responsible for it anymore.

"Go figure," said Renfrew. "Assuming Mr. Pete is right, this antique diamond ring is gone. History. It's not in the apartment."

"And somebody stole her laptop computer," Bruxton added.

Now I was completely confused. "What laptop?"

"CSU says there was one on the desk in the living room. The power cable is still there, and there's a credit-card charge to Claudia Moore for the computer. She bought it in the middle of November."

"Are you kidding? My sister doesn't have a credit card."

Renfrew reached into her briefcase and pulled something small out. "Take a look," she said, leaning forward and handing it to me. There were four clear plastic bags, each with a different credit card inside, made out to Claudia Moore. I turned each one over. The signature was a rough approximation of my sister's.

"These aren't Claudia's." I handed them back to Renfrew.

"The oldest credit card was issued end of October. Your sister's prints aren't on them, but the dead woman's are. It looks like that woman had, let's say, *borrowed* her identity. We also found this in her wallet." Renfrew handed me another small plastic pouch. Claudia's driver's license was inside. It was the real thing, not a fake. I stared at it wordlessly before handing it back. Nothing made sense anymore.

"Makes you wonder, doesn't it?" said Bruxton. "The ring would be an easy thing for the person who found the body to grab up, no matter how big the rock. But why not take the cash and credit cards? And if they took the laptop, how did they smuggle it out with no one noticing?" The detectives exchanged a look. I wanted to ask about the mysterious Kaylee Quan, but Renfrew started to speak before I formed a question.

"That's about it for information from the neighbors," she said. "This girl kept quiet. Nobody heard anything from the apartment, but the downstairs neighbor heard footsteps sometimes so she knew someone was up there. She assumed Claudia had come home, and was glad she was being so quiet."

"It's New York. Nobody knows their neighbors, even in a small building," said Bruxton. "No one's close with your sister, and the dead woman only talked to the neighbor down the hall." He leaned forward. "If you think about it, it makes sense. Sarah Lyons moved into the building in November, after this other woman got there. Lyons never met the real Claudia, so the fake Claudia wasn't worried about getting caught out with her."

"Here's what doesn't make sense. I met Sarah Lyons on Sunday afternoon, and she knew exactly who I was. She knew I lived in Spain. Did the impostor fill her in on that?"

Renfrew and Bruxton looked at each other again. They seemed to communicate through quick glances and ESP. "We think it's a sure thing that the dead woman knew your sister," said Renfrew. "She probably wanted to reduce the chances she'd slip up, so she stuck to one story, unless she was dealing with someone who knows your sister."

"Or maybe Sarah Lyons is psychic, or just a total kook," said Bruxton. "You can ask her yourself if you want to come down to the station with us."

"She's at the station?" I was astonished.

"She wasn't home last night when we canvassed the building, but Bruxton left a message on her phone and she called this morning," Renfrew explained.

"This morning? Yeah, if you mean seven A.M.," said Bruxton.

"He's not a morning person," Renfrew explained. She nudged him. "Someday I'm going to murder the bugler . . ."

I got her reference—a lyric from an Irving Berlin song called "Oh! I Hate to Get Up in the Morning"—but Bruxton ignored it. "Sarah Lyons kept saying 'You must be mistaken. This has to be a mistake.' Then she told me I was crazy and hung up on me."

Renfrew shook her head. "You have that effect on women, Brux. In any case, she called back and she's coming in at noon. We thought it would be helpful to have you there."

So there was a reason they had come by, more than curiosity about what they'd see if they caught me unawares. "Definitely," I said. "Count me in."

"Is that actually on the up-and-up?" Jesse interrupted, surprising me. "I mean, if you're questioning a suspect, can you just bring someone else along for the ride?"

"Sarah Lyons is a witness, not a suspect at this point," Renfrew clarified. "As long as she gives her permission—and she was enthusiastic when I suggested that Lily sit in on this—it's on the level."

"Have you found out anything yet about who the dead woman was? What about her fingerprints?" I asked.

"Ran them through the system, came up empty," said Bruxton. "We're trying to match the one photo we have of her to driver's license photos, but you have to run that state by state. No hits yet. It would be easier if we had a photo of her alive."

"Do you have any idea where my sister is? An old friend of mine came over last night and said that Claudia had called just after Christmas, wanting money to go to rehab. I think she must be at some rehab center now." It was a relief to be able to point the detectives in this new direction, feeling sure that Claudia would have a solid alibi for the time that another woman was expiring in her apartment.

"This friend of yours, she have a name?" asked Bruxton.

"It's a he," I said. "Martin Sklar."

"Rings a bell," said Renfrew, writing the name on her note-pad and handing it to me to check the spelling. I added his phone number and home address underneath, embarrassed that I still remembered so much. To be fair, he lived in the Dakota, a landmark building that every New Yorker knew.

"He owns a bunch of boutique hotels and condos," Jesse piped in. "You know that new hotel on Lispenard, the Oracle? That's his."

"The Oracle Hotel?" Bruxton's jaw was taut as it worked the gum. "I just read something about that place, maybe a month ago. Wasn't there some problem with it?" If by *problem*, he meant that Martin had stuffed another unnecessarily chichi hotel into an overcrowded neighborhood, then sure.

"It opened a month ago, Brux. There were articles about it everywhere. Not that I *read* them," Renfrew confessed. "You know how much reading I get away with when my kids are around."

Bruxton looked at me. "Okay. You know Martin Sklar, how?"

"I just told you. He's an old friend."

"Well, we'll definitely have a word with him," said Bruxton. "He was sure it was your sister he spoke with?"

"Yes," I said. "Martin said the woman was Claudia."

"We've pulled the phone LUDs for the apartment's land line," said Renfrew, taking a sheaf of papers out of her briefcase and handing them to me. "We've got everything from September onward. We couldn't find any record of a cell phone."

"Claudia doesn't have one. She hates gadgets," I said. I didn't add that my sister mocked me for writing on a laptop. *Do you think Poe would have composed "Annabel Lee" on a computer?* she'd taunt. I'd remind her that I wasn't writing poetry, and her rejoinder was that I should be.

"Take a look at the records from the land line," Renfrew added, pushing a ballpoint pen across the table. "Any numbers you recognize?"

I glanced over the top pages, then flipped ahead to the end of December, scanning the outgoing numbers from Christmas Eve on. There were none that I recognized. No calls to Martin. I looked again, wondering if I'd missed them. They weren't there. My face felt hot as I realized that Martin had lied to me. I bit my lip and looked at the incoming calls. There was Martin's number. The list swam before my eyes, and jealousy prickled me as I noticed it came up repeatedly. He had called Claudia's apartment three times in the middle of the day on New Year's Eve, then again at nine-fifteen in the morning on New Year's Day. There was a call from Martin on her birthday in November, and another in mid-September. The calls were so brief it didn't seem as if he'd spoken to anyone, but seeing it in black-and-white made my stomach churn. Once, just after Claudia moved in with me, Claudia had gotten out of the shower and let her towel slip off in front of Martin. That was something I'd never be able to forgive her for.

"These calls are from Martin Sklar." I drew a star next to it and wrote his name in the margin. My hand shook only a little. "The international calls are from me, from my cell phone." I marked those, too. "I don't recognize the other numbers. Do you know what they are?"

"The Manhattan ones are mostly a gym off Union Square called Sinotique, and a couple of restaurants that deliver. She used the name Claudia Moore with them, by the way." Renfrew took the list out of my hands. "There are a bunch of calls from Chicago, made with prepaid calling cards on different pay phones. Those only started in the middle of November."

Were the calls for Claudia or her impostor? As far as I knew, my sister didn't have any friends in Chicago. Had one of her old crowd moved there recently? "What about Kaylee Quan? Did you find her yet?"

"She's in the wind," said Bruxton. "We called her husband last night. He's still in Hong Kong. He didn't sound worried about her. Hard to say if he knows where she is, or just doesn't care."

13

"He was an absolutely terrifying man. He looked like a criminal, perhaps even a terrorist." Sarah Lyons looked impeccable, almost regal, as she spoke, reminding me again of a forty-something Grace Kelly. She was beautiful and poised and haughty.

"Can you describe him?" Detective Renfrew asked her. We were sitting together in the detectives' break room at the precinct on Pitt Street. It was arguably cozier than the interrogation cell I'd been in the day before, but its dingy yellow walls and tiny window to the outside permitted no light or air circulation. When I'd come into the precinct the detectives had put me "on ice," as Renfrew had phrased it, in the break room. They'd sent me to the interrogation room after Sarah had come in, but they hadn't followed me in for a few minutes. Then the detectives had swooped over and moved us to what they called "more comfortable" surroundings, back in the break room. If they were this confused about details, I had little hope their investigation would amount to anything. We were seated at a folding metal table that looked only slightly more substantial than a card table. Bruxton was next to me, taking notes and keeping quiet for once.

"Well, he was tall, perhaps six foot three, and broad-shouldered. He wore a suit. He might have been Arab, or Pakistani. He had a very deep voice and a British accent." Sarah's description was impressive. Claudia had told me that

Tariq Lawrence's half-Pakistani, half-English heritage had led him to be mistaken for every nationality from Argentine to Turkish, but people rarely guessed the truth. "He was quite the frightening presence," Sarah added. "I thought about calling the police the last time he showed up."

"Why was that, Ms. Lyons?"

"The man was enraged. He pounded on Claudia's—that girl's—door, then he kicked it and started shouting. I asked that girl about it later but she said she didn't know who he was. I didn't believe her, but I let it drop. I wish I hadn't." Sarah stared at her manicured hands. "That was on December twenty-eighth, just three days before she died."

I thought Sarah was being melodramatic, but I couldn't deny that Tariq could be intimidating. She'd probably never encountered anyone like him. Why would she? I sat in a metal chair, admiring her simple white linen blouse with gold cuff links and tailored black trousers, accessorized with an Hermès Birkin bag, an alligator belt, and a simple strand of pearls. She was impeccably elegant and I felt deflated, the dime-store glamour of my red lipstick and secondhand clothes tawdry by comparison. It was odd that someone so elegant had chosen to live on the Lower East Side, but I supposed that only demonstrated how gentrified the neighborhood had become.

"Ms. Lyons, you saw this neighbor with Kaylee Quan and this aggressive, possibly Arab, man," said Renfrew. "Anyone else?"

"She had a visitor in the middle of November, two weeks after I moved into the building," said Sarah. "A middle-aged woman, tall, brown-haired, mousy. She looked desperate. I remember thinking that she was old enough to be Claudia's mother, but she didn't look anything like her. There was something off about the whole thing."

"What does *off* mean, exactly?"

"I heard Claudia say that the woman shouldn't have come there. Something about how no one should see them together. The other woman said she'd had to come back because she'd run out of money. It was strange."

"How did you hear this, exactly?" Bruxton tossed in.

"I was in the hallway. Noise carries quite easily in the building," Sarah answered with a withering glare. "I was on my way out, and that was all I heard. Claudia was away for a few days after that. When she came back, she never mentioned the woman or what she was doing there, and I didn't ask. Claudia went away for the weekend quite often, but she never mentioned where, only that she was seeing friends."

We pondered that quietly, until Bruxton spoke up. "You have any idea who any of these people were, Lily?"

"I have no idea who the woman was. Claudia didn't introduce many of her friends to me."

"You ever know this neighbor of yours to use drugs?" asked Renfrew.

"Good heavens, no." Sarah looked horrified. Of course she would. Letting Sarah, with her pristine demeanor and formal bearing, in on my family problems made me feel grubby and low. "She was a very healthy person. She told me she only bought organic produce. She did yoga."

My ears perked up, remembering what Melissa Ardito had said about my sister. It was the first healthy thing I'd ever heard of Claudia taking an interest in. "Did this woman go to a class in the neighborhood?" I asked.

"No, she said the ones nearby were filthy," Sarah answered. "She found a studio she liked in Union Square. I'm afraid I don't remember the name."

I remembered the phone records. Renfrew had said there

were calls to a gym around Union Square. That must have been the yoga studio. Had my sister ever been there, or just this woman who used her name?

"That's all right," said Renfrew. "You know, judging from all of the designer goods in the apartment, it sounds like this girl had some expensive tastes."

"Yes, I think she did," Sarah agreed. "She always seemed to come home with a shopping bag."

"So far you've told us that your neighbor didn't have a boyfriend, didn't go out a lot, drank a little but didn't do drugs, and she did yoga," said Renfrew. "What were her other habits like?"

"She just seemed like a nice girl. I remember noticing that she had so many books in her apartment, yet she wasn't much of a reader. I thought it was just an example of the Anthony Burgess axiom, that the purchase of a book is a substitute for the reading of it."

I knew the Burgess line and was impressed that Sarah did, too. I hadn't liked her when she'd interrupted me at Claudia's apartment, but given the frame of mind I was in that day, I'd been in no position to form an opinion. Sarah seemed like someone who could walk into any room and strike up a conversation and sound civilized. What would she make of the real Claudia? I had a pretty good idea what my sister would think of her.

"On Sunday you told us you saw Claudia on New Year's Eve," said Renfrew.

"Yes, I spoke with her that afternoon, just before I went out to run some errands. She had a cold and I asked if I could get her anything. She said no. She said she was just looking forward to having a quiet night at home."

"There was something you said, Ms. Lyons. You told us that the girl had died just like her mother had."

Sarah dabbed her eyes and nodded. "She had told me about her mother before the holidays. She said her father had died on Christmas Eve, and her mother had died on New Year's Eve, and she hated the holidays." Sarah looked at me. "I'm sorry, Lily. It must be hard to hear that someone who wasn't your sister said those things."

I was getting angrier by the minute. Someone pretending to be my sister had traded on our family tragedies to gain sympathy from a stranger. I had a fleeting thought that maybe the girl who died had it coming. "Clearly she talked about me, too." I spoke slowly because my mouth was dry. "You knew I've been living in Spain."

Sarah nodded. "I remember being in her apartment, perhaps a month ago, and I asked about a photograph on her bookcase. It was the one of two young children in front of the Christmas tree. She told me that you were her sister, but that you'd never been close."

I felt tears in my eyes. *We're not talking about my sister,* I told myself. *Those words didn't come out of Claudia's mouth.* But still, Claudia had to have told the dead woman these things. What was their relationship? If they had met in some rehab program, they might have shared a lot of confidences. I'd tried to go to a couple of support meetings for families of drug abusers, and I'd been embarrassed by the details other people revealed. It hit me suddenly that the dead girl might not have known my sister that intimately, that the details she regurgitated could have been culled from a group meeting.

"Lily, is it true that you really have no idea where your sister is?" Sarah asked me.

"None at all," I admitted.

"Ms. Lyons, would you mind taking a look at some mug shots, seeing if there's anyone you recognize?" asked Renfrew. Sarah nodded. "Speaking of shots, let's be clear about this," Renfrew added, setting a snapshot on the table and pushing it toward Sarah. "Is this the woman you knew as Claudia Moore?"

It was a close-up of the woman I'd seen at the morgue. Her hair fanned out like a dark halo around her pale, freckled face. The shot must have been taken from above while she lay on the mortuary table. Her eyes were closed but she didn't seem peaceful. She just looked dead.

Sarah looked at the photograph for a moment without touching it. "Yes."

"Have you ever seen this woman?" Bruxton asked, sliding a second photograph across the table. From the side, I caught a glimpse of Claudia, head cocked slightly and arms crossed, glaring into the camera. It reminded me of those photographs people got on safari, snapping the furious wildebeest before it charged.

Sarah stared at the photograph, picking it up gingerly as if it were a relic. She stared at it silently, taking in every feature, then picked up the photograph of the impostor.

"That's the real Claudia Moore," said Renfrew. "Do you recall ever seeing her?"

Sarah stared at the photograph, as intently as an Egyptologist might regard the Rosetta stone. She blinked a couple of times. "Well . . . this will sound odd, but . . . yes. It was her. I'm certain of it."

"When did you see her?" asked Renfrew.

"On New Year's Eve," said Sarah. "She was walking up the stairs of the building when I was going out. We passed each other on the landing."

14

I got up, dropping my coat on the floor. "Excuse me," I said, grabbing it and bolting. As I stumbled through the squad room, jaded detectives gave me a wide berth. My face was flushed and I kept my head down. Where was the bathroom? I ended up in front of a small window, taking deep breaths and trying not to throw up. A hand touched my shoulder.

"You look like I did the last time I tried to quit smoking," said Bruxton.

I tried to give him even a shadow of a smile, but couldn't manage it.

"You want to sit down? I can get you something to drink."

I was panting and terrified I'd pass out. If Claudia had been in the apartment building on New Year's Eve, it wasn't much of a leap to suspect she was involved in the death of the woman who'd been found in the bathtub. My sister would be the prime suspect.

"Silent treatment. I'm used to that, you know." Bruxton rubbed my shoulder gingerly, maybe expecting me to swat him away. He let go and leaned against the wall, watching me.

"I can't believe that Claudia . . ." I didn't finish the sentence. "I can't believe Sarah said that. She doesn't know what she's talking about. My sister wouldn't . . ." *Kill anyone*, I wanted to say. Claudia wouldn't kill anyone.

"Take a breath," said Bruxton. "These are new shoes. Don't get sick on them."

I stared at his feet. His shoes were scuffed black leather, of an indeterminate style that shouted *discount outlet*. "They don't look new."

"This is what new shoes look like when you're making support payments."

His distraction was working. I breathed easier. "Support payments?"

"I have a son. He lives in New Jersey with his mother."

"You're divorced?"

"Hell, yeah," said Bruxton. "You probably know this already, but don't marry someone who'll sleep with your best friend."

"Your *what*?" I was suddenly riveted. "Are you serious?"

"Want to go outside?" he asked, changing the subject just as it was getting interesting. "They won't let me smoke in the building."

We headed downstairs, me clinging to the wooden railing and Bruxton holding my arm. He lit up the second we were out the door, then bought us coffee from a cart down the street. "Thanks," I said. I thought about asking him for a cigarette but restrained myself. "Why are you being so nice all of a sudden?"

"This is your idea of nice? I'll make a note." His tone was almost playful. Had I misread what had happened in the break room? I'd expected accusations about Claudia, at least from Bruxton. Or was he hoping to trip me up? I tried to play along.

"It's like a piranha being nice," I explained. "You have to wonder why. What was going on up there? Before you and Renfrew came in, you were listening to Sarah and me from behind that two-way mirror, weren't you? Then you made us change rooms before the interview. What was that about?"

THE DAMAGE DONE   107

He took a long drag. "Observant of you. Norah and I were testing a theory."

"What theory?"

"Sarah Lyons responds differently to my partner and me," said Bruxton. "You see this a lot in police work, people will feel comfortable talking with one detective and not another. Sometimes it's a gender thing, or race or age. There's all kinds of unconscious biases people have, and it affects what they give you when you interview them."

"What bias does Sarah have?"

"She doesn't like me. Go ahead and laugh." He'd made me smile and I couldn't hide it. "When she came in, I put her in the interview room and got her a glass of water. She wouldn't even take off her coat, never mind sit in a chair or take a drink in there. When Norah came in, it was her job to calm the feathers I'd ruffled."

"I hate to be the one to tell you this, but you're kind of . . . brusque. Maybe she'd like you better if you weren't so brusque."

"That go for you, too?" he shot back. Then, as if thinking better of the question, he flushed so red that even his ears were burning. There was something a little bit endearing about a pit bull who blushed. "So, what do you think of Sarah Lyons?" he asked.

"She knows a lot about me and I know nothing about her. Why are you interested in her?"

"We think she may have had a significant relationship with the dead woman," said Bruxton. "Possibly a sexual one. Of course, this is based in part on some stuff the Decarnos said, so it could all be crap."

"What did they say?"

"Apparently Sarah was always knocking on the woman's door, inviting her places and giving her little presents."

"Interesting." I tried to remember what Sarah had said about Claudia when she'd met me on Monday. *I'm so sorry about your sister. I was very fond of Claudia. She was such an unusual person. Unique.* It wasn't exactly a passionate declaration. "Is Sarah a suspect?"

"Everyone's a suspect." Bruxton took a long drag. "Think about it. This dame lives down the hall, has easy access to the victim, gets into her apartment and kills her. Damn, that's a case you could sell to a jury, just think up something, maybe a love affair gone bad, for motive. Instead, we got Sarah going to a party on the Upper East Side that night, a fund-raiser for people with Parkinson's disease. Video in the foyer shows her going out at seven-thirty, and a dozen people verified she was at the party." He exhaled loudly. "Not that that proves much. We checked her out. No criminal record. Never been married. Know what she does for a living? She's a life management specialist."

"What's that?"

"She gets suckers to give her money for 'life coaching' over the phone or online. Can you believe that?" He crushed his cigarette and lit another. "She's lived all over the Eastern seaboard—Boston, Philly, Portland—but she spent the past five years in California, taking care of her mother, who had Parkinson's, by the way. Sarah told my partner she just up and moved to New York in November to get away from sad memories. Your superintendent told us that when she moved in, she had the choice of a place on the third floor or the fifth. For some reason, she chose the fifth. In a walkup? Makes you think she's kind of a weirdo."

"In case you're wondering why she doesn't like you, listening to you talk is scary," I said, feeling defensive. What did it say about me that I'd up and moved from New York to Madrid, then uprooted myself again for Barcelona? "It's like you wish you could pin it on her. You're making me glad I was in Spain when this woman died."

"Cops learn to be suspicious," Bruxton said. "People never give you the straight story. The thing that gets her off the hook, at least partway, is that somebody went to a lot of trouble to get into your sister's building without being seen that evening. The power went out briefly just before eight P.M. Not a big deal, except that when the power came back on, somebody had broken the security camera."

"Wait, someone deliberately—"

"Let's put it this way. The power was out for almost two minutes. Long enough to get inside and bust the camera. But there's no forced entry with the outside door, so whoever did it probably had a key. An expert could've jimmied the lock, but not with enough time to take out the camera afterward." He took one last drag and threw the cigarette into the gutter. "We should go back. Norah's got to be wrapping up the interview now."

Upstairs Sarah was in the squad room, sitting at a desk with a framed photograph of two cherubic young boys. Renfrew was next to her, flipping through a giant book of what I assumed were mug shots. "Back already?" said the detective, smiling at me. "We're going to be busy with the books for a little while."

I smiled back, getting it instantly. The detective two-step wasn't just for Sarah's benefit. It was for mine, as well. They'd decided that Bruxton had better odds of getting information out of me. I was his pet project.

"Lily, I was worried we wouldn't get to say good-bye."

Sarah stood and came up to me. "Please believe me when I say I want to help find your sister." She snapped open her elegant Hermès handbag. She handed me a heavy ivory card, with *Sarah Lyons* embossed in black calligraphic script, with a telephone number beneath it. "If I can help in any way, please call."

"I guess we'll leave you two to the books," said Bruxton. "Lily, do you want to grab some lunch?"

"I wish I could, but I've got a deadline today and I need to get back to my friend's apartment to work."

"I can drive you back," said Bruxton.

Persistent bastard. "Great," I said, attempting enthusiasm.

Sarah ignored Bruxton but she leaned forward and gave me a quick hug. "Call if you need anything. I'd be happy to help," she whispered. Renfrew gave me a wave and ruffled the pages of the mug shot book, summoning Sarah back to her seat.

Can I ask you something?" Bruxton asked, once we set off in his battered navy Ford Taurus. Now that I knew his angle, I wanted to hear Bruxton's questions. "Why'd you move to Spain?"

"My parents were from Ireland, and I have dual citizenship. I could work anywhere in the European Union."

"Okay, but why Spain?"

I wasn't about to confide the combination of frazzled nerves and broken heart that had pushed me to leave New York. After Claudia moved in with me, I realized I'd made a terrible mistake. Living with my sister was tough, but living with my sister when she was on drugs was impossible. I spent most of my time instead at Martin's apartment. Then, in the wake of the lady architect debacle, I'd decided that I couldn't trust Martin. After taking temporary refuge at Jesse's place, I'd seized the chance to work on a project in Spain and never looked back.

"I went there originally because I was writing a guide-book, but I ended up staying," I told Bruxton. "It's so beauti-ful there, and the food is amazing, and there's incredible art and architecture. The people are so nice."

"Come on. You're from New York. You didn't move there because people are *nice*."

"I was inspired by Ava Gardner. Do you know who she was?"

"Actress. She was in *The Killers*," said Bruxton, "and *The Sun Also Rises*."

I was impressed. "I wouldn't have taken you for a fan of old movies."

"I'm not. But I like Hemingway. Those two pictures were pretty good, unlike some of the crap they made out of his stories. Like *To Have and Have Not*—I mean, throwing Hoagy Carmichael and a bunch of songs into a Hemingway story? Screw that." Bruxton dragged on his cigarette and I wondered if the style was inspired by Bogart before it be-came a habit. "So what was the Ava Gardner thing?"

"She got sick of Hollywood, and she'd filmed a couple of movies in Spain and loved it there, so she decided to up and move. It was a pretty gutsy thing to do. She really lived it up there, partying with bullfighters . . ."

"You know any bullfighters?"

"No." I laughed. "I write books."

"Books, plural?"

"Three. The Spain guidebook, then city guides to Madrid and Barcelona."

"In one year?" Bruxton stared at me. "You wrote all that?"

"Don't sound so impressed." I was a little bit flattered by

his astonishment. "They're only guidebooks. After the Spain book, I took the research I did and recycled it for the city guides."

"Still . . . that's really something."

If only he knew. Half the guidebook writers I'd encountered did all of their research from the comfort of their own living rooms, thanks to the Internet. Before I could disillusion Bruxton about the travel-guide racket, my cell phone rang. As I pulled it out of my bag, I recognized Martin's number. I was tempted not to answer in front of Bruxton, but curiosity got the better of me. "Yes?"

"Lily, sweetheart," said Martin. "Did I catch you at a bad time?"

"No, it's fine."

"I was wondering if there was any news about your sister?"

"No," I lied. This wasn't the time to share what Sarah had said. My voice was terse, but I was hemmed in with Bruxton there, pretending not to listen. "Sorry, I'm in a police car right now."

"Really? So you can't say much," said Martin playfully. "Don't tell me you got yourself arrested. I know how bad you can be."

"You'd find that amusing, I suppose."

"You in handcuffs, Lily? Better than amusing."

I hoped Bruxton didn't notice me blushing. "I hope you're calling for a reason."

"I found my notes," Martin said. "But calling them 'notes' gives them a status they don't deserve. Basically, it's a card I scrawled on. I'll give it to you when we have dinner tonight."

"Excuse me?"

"I made a reservation for us at One if by Land, Two if by Sea." Martin's voice was smooth as polished glass. "You always loved that restaurant, and you can certainly use some cheering up, with everything going on."

"No," I said flatly. There was a stunned silence from Martin, and I felt cruel. I hadn't meant to be rude, but the image of Martin and me reverting to old habits at old haunts shook me. One if by Land was arguably the most romantic restaurant in the city, a luxurious spot nestled into Aaron Burr's eighteenth-century carriage house, all flowers and fireplaces and candlelight. "I'll meet you for a drink downtown."

"If that's what you'd prefer," said Martin quietly. "I thought you loved One if by Land."

He was the one who adored that restaurant, but I wasn't going to remind him of that now. "I'll meet you at that flamenco bar I used to like so much. Do you remember it?" I glanced at Bruxton, whose eyes were on the road, but I wasn't fooled. There was simply no way I'd give up any detail I didn't have to within earshot of the man.

"Flamenco bar?" There was a pause. "Wait, that place on Crosby you dragged me to a couple of times?"

"See you there at six." We said good-bye, and I snapped the phone closed.

"Sounds like you're going on a date," said Bruxton. "Who's the lucky guy?"

"It's just an old friend." Once the words escaped my lips, I realized how stupid they sounded. I'd called Martin an "old friend" that morning, in front of Bruxton. Now I sounded like I was hiding something. "I meant to ask you before, is there anything new on the girl who died?"

"She was a strawberry blond," said Bruxton. In his upstate accent, *blond* came out *bland*. "She'd dyed her hair black. We're wondering if it's the same woman your superintendent saw back in October."

"But Mr. Pete said that woman was on the, um, full-figured side."

"True, but we found plenty of diet pills and laxatives in the apartment. And we know this woman was bulimic."

"They finally did the autopsy?"

"No, the ME is hoping to get to it this afternoon. But he could tell about the bulimia by the acid damage on the dead woman's teeth. She'd had to have a lot of expensive dental work because of it."

"Ugh." I had a longstanding terror of dentists that I didn't feel like sharing with Bruxton. "That's disgusting."

"Hopefully he'll have more for us soon." He fixed his eyes on the road. "What do you think is going on with your sister? You know her better than anyone. What's your instinct?"

"Claudia and I haven't been close since we were kids."

"Why not?"

"She never forgave me for going away to college and leaving her with our mother." It wasn't something I would normally have admitted, but Bruxton already knew about my family and my mother's death.

"What happened after your mother died? I mean, where did your sister live?"

"She wanted to live with me, but she couldn't stay in the dorm, and I didn't have the money to get an apartment for us." Could he hear the guilt in my voice? "The child services people thought she should finish high school in Ithaca, since she only had a year and a half to go."

"They put her in foster care?" Bruxton asked.

"No, the first home was actually the family of one of her friends. They were really nice people, and it seemed like a perfect arrangement."

"What went wrong?"

"Claudia fought with them over their rules and everything else. She ended up punching her friend's mother in the face. They put her in a foster home, one where the couple was used to dealing with problem teens. Claudia hated it, and she ran away."

"Happens a lot. Where'd they find her?"

"She was arrested three months later for shoplifting, and she had drugs on her, so they got her for that, too. They put her in a juvenile detention center."

"And things went downhill from there." There was no question mark. I guessed it was a familiar story for anyone at the NYPD. "Where was she arrested?"

"Manhattan."

"You were both in New York, and she didn't try to get in touch?"

"Not even once." It had been an agonizing time for me, wondering where my sister was. In a way, it had been a relief that she'd been arrested, after I'd stared at the ceiling through many nights, wondering if she were dead.

"So you weren't kidding about going long stretches without speaking." Bruxton stared at the traffic. "Would you tell us if you heard from her?"

"Of course. Why wouldn't I?" In the back of my mind, I was ticking off the reasons never to trust people in authority. I'd had to lie and playact throughout high school, always in fear of letting anyone too close to the truth about my family. One girl I'd stupidly confided in when I was fifteen ratted out my drunken mother to the principal. Later, when I'd confronted her, she'd sworn she'd felt sorry for me and just wanted to help. The principal, in turn, had invited me to his office, locked the door, and made it clear what it would take for him not to call in child protection services. Normally I hated it when my erratic mother pulled up stakes and moved Claudia and me to a new town, but that was one place I couldn't get away from fast enough.

"Maybe you'd hold things back because you're afraid she'll get dragged into this mess. Maybe because you feel guilty."

He was more perceptive than I'd realized, and I instantly regretted telling him anything. "You're welcome to think what you want. Why don't you tap my phone?"

"It would be great if we got to do that, but we can't. Stupid laws."

We were all of four blocks from Jesse's building, but traffic was so snarled up that it was barely moving. "You know what? I can walk from here." I got out of the car before Bruxton could object. "Thanks for the drive, Detective," I added, slamming the door behind me.

15

The woman in knee-high boots, skinny jeans, black turtleneck sweater, and pink hair didn't look like any church lady I'd seen. "Rachel?" I stared at her and recognized a glimmer of the girl I'd met before. She'd been a friend of Claudia's then, a punk goddess with prominent piercings and enough attitude to power a rocket ship. She'd also had a rotten boyfriend who'd pounded the hell out of her and forced her to turn tricks to feed his drug habit.

"It's so good to see you, Lily." Rachel pulled me into a muscular hug. "You look so beautiful. But then, you always do."

Just after Claudia had moved in with me, I'd woken up one morning to find a pink-haired pixie drooling on my couch. When I'd shaken her awake, she'd pulled a box cutter on me. And yet she'd turned out to be the only friend of Claudia's I liked. "You look fantastic." I smiled at her. "You've still got the pink hair. I love it!"

"People can't believe I work for a church." Rachel looked around at the wooden pews and the stained-glass windows. "This place is part of me, though. It changed my life."

That was, after all, why I liked her. Rachel was the only friend of Claudia's who had kicked her drug habit. Of course, Claudia had cut off the friendship for the same reason. Fortunately, Rachel had a distinctive name—Heidegger—and Google had given up her whereabouts quickly. I was glad to be able to track her down at the Jan Hus Presbyterian Church on East Seventy-fourth Street. Her voice had been warm on the phone, as if she were genuinely glad to hear from me. "What do you do here?" I asked. "When I Googled you, the Web site said you worked for the Neighborhood House."

"I work on outreach to the homeless, but have a lot of programs here at the church—music lessons for kids, meals for the elderly, the Remarkable Theater Brigade, even kendo classes."

"Wait, swordfighting?"

"We're a twenty-first-century church. We don't spend all our time praying, you know."

"There's a rumor that Presbyterians have no fun. Calvinists aren't exactly known for their sense of humor."

"You Catholics are the worst gossips," said Rachel. "We've got a Session—a board of Elders—just like any Presbyterian church, but we're a straight-positive, gay-positive, social-justice kind of place. And we honor other faiths. Our namesake, Jan Hus, was a Catholic priest."

"I recognized the name. I know there's a statue of him in the old town square in Prague, and that he was burned at the stake by the Inquisition, but I don't remember why."

"Jan Hus asked himself *What would Jesus do?*" said Rachel. "The answer was to preach against the clergy getting rich by charging poor people for baptisms and funerals, and to demand that the Bible be translated into Czech so people could read it for themselves, among other things. He preached that Christ rejected orthodoxy, that he didn't want a grand church swathed in money."

"One of those social-justice types. I can see what the Inquisition would have against him."

Rachel smiled. "We have services on Sundays at eleven. Come by while you're in town. We get a lot of lapsed Catholics. You'll fit right in."

"Thanks. Could I ask you about Claudia? I know you're busy, but I'm worried about her."

"I couldn't believe it when you said she was missing. But maybe I shouldn't be surprised." Rachel looked around the church again. "Do you want some coffee or tea?"

I shook my head and we wandered up an aisle and sat down in a pew with a carved back. There were a few people at the back of the church, and a couple of people praying in the front pew, but otherwise we had the place to ourselves.

"I wish I could tell you something that would help," Rachel said. "Claudia got in touch with me back in June. She told me she'd kicked smack's ass for good and she was really upbeat about her life. Things were good. She was drawing again. We met up a couple of times on the Fourth of July weekend. We had coffee, and then she came by the church. Thought this place was great." Rachel glanced toward the altar, smiling. "We used to spend a lot of time in churches. They were often the only places you could get a meal, and even when they wouldn't let you sleep there they'd find you a bed somewhere else."

"I know. Claudia's shown me her favorite ones." I smiled ruefully. Claudia had also sneaked money out of my wallet and donated it to those churches. At least that was a well-intentioned theft. I touched the silver bracelet on my wrist. "Was she in touch with her old friends?"

"I don't think so. We talked about some of them—the ones who'd gone to prison, the ones who died—but I'd heard a lot more than she had. I'm on the other side of the fence now, but I've got my ear to the ground, you know?" I nodded and she continued. "She was in touch with Tariq, of course, but he was always her friend, not part of our scene, you know what I mean? But she said she hadn't seen much of him because she was away a lot. I asked her where and she said 'Lyme-tick country.' That was as specific as she got. The last time I saw her was at the end of August. She still seemed to be doing well, but she was freaking out about something."

"Do you know what it was?"

"Not exactly, but it had to do with the guy she was with."

"What guy?" I asked. "She had a boyfriend?"

"She hadn't mentioned him before that. But yeah, she had a boyfriend. Apparently it started in the spring. He was Svengali and she was Trilby. She'd sing whatever tune he told her to. He told her to stand on her head, she'd stand on her head. She said she was really in love with him, but listening to her talk about this guy was scary. Trust me, I'm an expert on the subject of scary guys." Rachel took a deep breath and tapped her chest with one hand, just above her heart. I remembered her scars, rough-edged craters from the time her ex had flung a pan of hot oil at her. "Claudia wouldn't even tell me his name."

"Why was she so secretive about him?"

"Search me. Claudia said she was forbidden to talk about him. She told me it would ruin his life if anyone found out."

"Forbidden?"

"That's the way she put it, and it scared me," said Rachel. "I asked if she'd told you about this guy and she said you were the last person in the world she'd tell."

"Did she say why?"

"Just that you wouldn't understand, and you'd be furious. Claudia was obsessed with how brilliant he was," Rachel said. "She must have mentioned that twenty times at dinner. He had money, I'm sure about that. Claudia said he would only accept the best of everything, and that that was the only way to live. He'd taken her to One if by Land, Two if by Sea and she said it was like discovering food for the first time. Everything was new with him."

"One if by Land?" My mouth was dry.

"It's a fancy restaurant in the West Village. The name is from a Longfellow poem, 'Paul Revere's Ride,'" Rachel explained. "When Claudia called me to figure out a date for dinner, she told me she had big news. Then a week later, when I saw her, she was upset. She said her boyfriend, the genius, had pretty much thrown her over for his old girlfriend. Apparently Claudia had been staying at his place a lot of the time, but he forced her to go back to her own apartment because his girlfriend was coming back for a visit."

"Wait, this was at the end of August?"

"Yeah. The girlfriend was coming in for a few days over Labor Day weekend."

All of the oxygen left the room suddenly, and I was left in a vacuum with a thudding heart. Labor Day weekend was when I had last visited New York. I'd stayed at Jesse's, but I'd seen Martin for dinner and had ended up spending the night with him. Now, thinking of the calls Martin had made to my sister in the fall—and never told me about—I was starting to put the puzzle pieces together. I thought my sister couldn't shock me anymore, but she'd done it again. Claudia had always wanted whatever I had, but I couldn't believe that she would go after Martin. But what other explanation was there? She could have carved me up with a kitchen knife and it wouldn't have been so painful.

"Lily, are you all right?" asked Rachel. "You look like you've just seen a ghost."

"I'm fine. Just . . . tired. I haven't really been sleeping."

"This has got to be so hard on you." Rachel's voice was warm and sympathetic. "I wish I could help. I feel like I really blew it the last time I saw Claudia."

Behind me, someone coughed and I looked around. There

was a man sitting in the pew just behind us, and even though his head was bowed, I thought for a heartbeat that I recognized him. He looked like the guy I'd seen in the Bronx, the one who'd made the hairs on the back of my neck stand up as I'd left the subway station. But I dismissed the thought almost immediately: the man was wearing a plain black coat and wool cap, a look that was common as subzero temperatures in New York in January.

Rachel's voice broke into my thoughts. "I should have been supportive, but I reacted badly. I told her this guy was a cult leader, and she needed to be deprogrammed. I think she really needed to talk to someone, but she couldn't stand hearing any criticism of him. She got up and left in the middle of dinner."

"Did you talk to her afterward?"

"She avoided my phone calls, and of course I couldn't even leave a message. I sent her an e-mail to apologize, and it bounced back. No surprise there. She hates e-mail because she can never remember her passwords." Rachel rubbed her hands over her eyes. "Then I got a message from her."

"When?"

"Middle of September. I was out of town for a youth retreat. It was short—she said something like 'I just wanted to tell you that I decided to get help.' Then she said she was going away for a while and she would call me when she got back."

"Do you still have the message?"

Rachel shook her head. "I saved it, but my voice mail automatically deletes stuff after thirty days. I'm sorry."

"You didn't hear from her again?"

"No. I sent her a birthday card in November and then a Christmas card in December. That's it."

"So you didn't know anything about another woman living in her apartment?"

"No, but it doesn't totally surprise me," Rachel said. I'd given her a quick rundown on the phone about the woman whose body had been found. "Claudia tries to help people. Maybe she was helping this woman."

"It's hard for me to picture Claudia on the giving end of the relationship," I said, swallowing hard.

"I know, but that was just her relationship with you," said Rachel. "She was always taking from you, I saw that myself. It's like she thinks you have so much that you won't miss it. But she was good to people who didn't have much of anything. Like when she took me in after my boyfriend tried to kill me."

I remembered being surprised by Claudia's kindness at the time, but later I'd felt like Claudia was really taking advantage of my kindness, forcing me to shelter and feed her friend. "I heard that Claudia went to rehab in the spring," I said. "Do you know the name of the place?"

"It's funny you ask. I wanted to know where she'd gone, and she wouldn't tell me. After our dinner from hell, I started wondering if the guy she was seeing was connected to the rehab center. And I don't mean another patient. I think he was a therapist she saw there."

I thought about this. If Rachel was right, why was Claudia worried about my fury? The idea of a doctor taking advantage of my sister made me livid, but that was nothing next to picturing my sister with my former fiancé. "I don't know. Claudia was completely antitherapy. She thought people who went to therapists were suckers."

"Love can do strange things to your brain," Rachel pointed out. "Like a drug."

16

Martin arrived at the flamenco bar almost half an hour late. He'd called me from his car, apologizing and swearing to be there soon. When he finally arrived, he was oddly disheveled in a crumpled suit, and his eyes were frantic as he scanned the room. He spotted me and pushed his way through the crowd, then wrapped his arms around me tightly. He kissed me on the forehead, then lightly on the mouth. "I was afraid you wouldn't wait," he said. "I'm so sorry. I hate being late, especially for you."

I'd had time to think about how I would deal with him while I dressed at Jesse's, then later as I sipped cava at the scarred wooden counter at the bar on Crosby Street. The place was just as I remembered—a long, skinny, dark-paneled room with red velvet curtains that blocked the eyes of the world outside. Rumor had it that the place had been raided a couple of times for fire-code overcrowding violations. Almost every seat snaked along the bar; there were just a couple of plush red velvet seats at tables for the lucky few who had staked an early claim. Later in the evening, the tables would be removed and the space would resonate with guitar music, clapping hands, and the nailed heels of the dancers. I'd visited plenty of flamenco bars in Spain, and my interest in the dance had only grown.

"It's all right," I told Martin. This wasn't how I'd planned to begin. I'd been simmering at the bar, turning over in my mind the best way to get the truth out of him. Since I'd spoken with Rachel, I hadn't been able to shake the image of my sister and my ex together.

He let go of me and took half a step back. "You look absolutely beautiful, Lily. Like Ava in her prime in *The Barefoot Contessa*."

"Thank you."

"That dress is incredibly sexy. Vintage?"

"Yes, it is." I was wearing a rioja-red silk number from the 1950s, low-cut with a narrow waist and full skirt. I'd traded my boots for black patent slingbacks and added a patterned shawl I'd bought in India. Before I could say anything else, Martin turned to the barman.

"Double scotch, neat."

"No scotch," said the barman. "White wine, red, sangria, cava."

"Lily, you've brought me to a place that doesn't serve alcohol?" Martin's expression was incredulous. "I'd forgotten there was a reason I didn't like it." He turned back to the bar. "I'll have whatever my girl is having." The barman procured a champagne flute from under the bar and poured a glass of cava, sparkling white wine from Spain.

Martin drank it in one gulp. "Another, please," he said. The barman gave him a what-the-hell look and poured him a second glass.

"Are you going to tell me what's happened?" I asked.

Martin ran one hand through his hair. "Can't I just say I want to forget about my afternoon?" I gave him a look. "Fine. I've been at a police station the past two hours."

"Is that supposed to be funny?"

Martin took a gulp of cava. "No, Lily. The police were questioning Ridley."

He looked me in the eye and I felt my heart softening. "What happened? Is he all right?"

"He's fine. It's a long story but the short version seems to be that Ridley wanted to get even with one of the bullies who'd tormented him at his last school. So he—allegedly—filled a box with wires and delivered it to the punk's building."

"A box of wires?" I crossed my legs and leaned forward slightly. "I don't understand."

"It looked like a bomb, according to the bully's mother. You should have seen her, Lily. One of those Botoxed bitches in tight designer jeans. Mutton posing as lamb." Martin took another drink. "Of course, her husband makes a lot of money, so the police have to investigate the matter. They brought Ridley in and questioned him before I got there. Which is illegal, by the way. But Ridley, being his usual childish self, admits everything when they do. Apparently he can keep these crazy things he does secret for a time, but then he cracks and has to reveal all. They had a signed confession when I got there." He downed the rest of his drink and gestured for another.

I watched Martin carefully. I knew he wasn't lying; he was telling me what he believed to be the truth. In his mind, Ridley had been silly and childish, but not malicious. The other boy was a vicious monster, probably devil's spawn. Ridley had never been cruel to me when Martin and I had been together, and I couldn't view him as evil, but I knew that there was something wrong with him that his father refused to see. "I'm so sorry." I touched Martin's arm and he grabbed my hand and held it. "What's going to happen to Ridley now?"

"The police can do damn all about it. He's a minor, and the confession won't be allowed in court. That's what they get for listening to that lying little bastard who was bullying him. He's a year older than Ridley, but he told the police that Ridley was older, and bullying him." Martin was quiet while the barman poured another round for both of us. I quietly extracted my hand from his grip.

"But didn't they check his ID?" I asked, before taking a sip from the fresh glass.

"They did," Martin acknowledged wearily. "Ridley had a fake ID that says he's twenty-one. The police were too lazy to bother checking whether it was real." He caught my look. "Ridley had the ID so he could get into clubs. It's not a big deal. I'm sure I had one at his age."

That was how it always went. Martin would find a way to justify whatever his son did. Everyone else was picking on his boy. "Is Ridley still getting counseling?" I asked.

"He had counseling for months. He was just going through a phase then. He's fine now."

We regarded each other warily. I knew that there was only so far I could push Martin on this, but I needed to try anyway. "Martin, your son told Claudia he wanted to try heroin. He told her he would pay her a lot of money to buy it for him."

"Ridley says stupid things he thinks will impress people," Martin countered. "He knew your sister was an addict, and at his age that must have seemed cool to him. He had a silly little crush on her." Martin and I had met each other's relatives when we were first dating, but we hadn't tried to bring them into the same room until we got engaged and decided to throw a big party to celebrate. I found out much later, after Claudia had dropped a series of increasingly less subtle hints, that Ridley had been keenly interested in drugs, even calling Claudia afterward to ask if she could help him get heroin. *I just about keeled over when he asked,* she'd told me. *He's what, thirteen? fourteen? At fourteen maybe you're discovering mushrooms. That kid needs help.* If Claudia thought the boy was in trouble, there was no doubt he was. I'd relayed Claudia's words to Martin and he'd had a "talk" with Ridley, which had resulted in the boy getting counseling. That was well over a year ago.

I shook my head. "Martin, you can't—"

"Lily, please." His eyes were pleading. The skin around them was puffy. Last night he'd been devil-may-care handsome; tonight he was older and tired. I bit my tongue and took another drink. "I shouldn't be bothering you with all of this, anyway. I should be helping you. Any word yet about your sister?"

"Nothing. Everything they learn seems to go back to the woman who was living in her apartment."

"Have they figured out who she was and why she was there?"

I knew he was desperate to steer the subject away from his own problems, and I had reasons for talking about mine. "They don't know who she was, but it's pretty clear she was impersonating my sister. She managed to get credit cards in Claudia's name and went on a spending spree."

Martin seemed lost in thought as I spoke. "So, this woman was exploiting your sister. Another addict?"

"The police don't seem to think so. Not heroin, anyway." I paused, waiting for him to respond. "You were supposed to give me the name of the rehab center Claudia talked to you about."

"I'm ashamed of myself. With what happened with Ridley, I'd let it slip my mind." He reached into his breast pocket and pulled out a business card, which he handed to me. "When I found the names, I looked them up. They seem like respectable places. Some very wealthy people have gone to them."

Them? I looked at the crisp white card. *Sunset Malibu?*

Promises? it read, in Martin's bold print. I turned the card over. Martin's name was embossed in a squared-off font, with the name of his company, Pantheon Worldwide, underneath in smaller type. The ego hadn't deflated any since my departure. I turned the card over again. "Malibu, California?"

"Right," said Martin.

"Claudia, going to California? That's hard to picture." My sister had said, more than once, that the country would be better off if that particular state sank into the Pacific. *We need to get rid of Los Angeles,* she had said once. *Hollywood and the TV industry make people stupid sheep.* "These are two different treatment centers. Which one was she going to?"

"The first one, I think. She said it was like Promises. I didn't know what that meant, so I looked them both up. But she never came by to pick up the check, so maybe she changed her mind. I called both of these places today, and Claudia's not at either one."

I'd been waiting for him to say her name, to call her something other than "your sister," which had always sounded slightly dismissive on his tongue. Now that he'd said it, I watched his face for a flicker of emotion. There was nothing.

"You called her on New Year's Day, in the morning." I fought to keep accusation out of my voice.

"That sounds right. How did you know?"

"The police have the phone records. They show that you called my sister several times."

"I did. I phoned to tell her she could pick up the check. Of course, I couldn't leave a message since you insisted on keeping that old wreck of a phone." He smiled and took another drink.

"And you called her in the fall. September and November, I think."

"Absolutely not," Martin said firmly. "Is that what the records show?" I nodded. He pondered that for a moment. "Your home and cell numbers are programmed into every phone I own. Maybe I pressed a button by mistake."

The calls had been very short, I remembered. There couldn't have been much of a conversation, if any. But I wasn't willing to let it be so easily explained away. "Tell me about your conversation with Claudia again."

"She called me up out of the blue. She didn't sound well. She said that it must be a surprise for me to hear from her. I said it was, and I asked if you were all right." Martin gave me a long look. "When she called, all I could think was that something had happened to you."

He touched my hand again and I fidgeted with my glass. "What then?"

"She said you were fine. I think she said you were doing your own thing in Spain, something like that. Then she told me she'd been going through a rough patch."

"In what way?"

"She wasn't specific. I assumed she was talking about her addictions. I knew she was fighting so many demons when you and I were together, so in a way I wasn't surprised by that. I finally asked her why she was calling me. She said she needed to go to this rehab center, but it was too expensive for you to pay for. She gave me the impression she had talked to you."

"She hadn't," I said.

"Well, that was pretty much the conversation. I said I would have to think about it. She said she would call me back, and she did, a couple of days later. I had talked to you by then and I told her I would lend her the money."

"You must have known you'd never see it again."

"That was a risk I was willing to take. I did want to help

her, and of course I have the resources to do it, if she's finally ready to help herself." He touched my shoulder, then let his fingers slide lightly down my arm. When we were a couple he was constantly, insistently affectionate. At first I'd found it romantic, but I'd later realized that it was more like a craving that never subsided. It wasn't exclusively sexual; once, when I was sick with breakbone fever after a trip to Southeast Asia, he'd taken days off work just to sit with me, holding my hand and stroking my hair. "The money doesn't matter. I thought that by helping your sister, I was, in some small way, doing something for you."

How kind of you, I wanted to say, but there was a lump in my throat and I couldn't get anything out. I stared at my glass.

"That didn't come out right. I sound like I'm bragging." Martin's hand was still on my arm, warm through the thin silk of the dress. "When your sister first called me, I was terrified something had happened to you, Lily. Even after she said everything was all right, I had to talk to you. I had to know that you were all right."

He was trying to seduce me, I knew that, yet part of me melted with his words. "That's sweet of you, Martin. But you don't have to worry about me."

"It made me realize that I don't know what I would do if anything happened to you. I miss you so much, Lily. You have no idea." He picked up my hand and turned my palm over and kissed the inside of my wrist. "You know I love you, don't you?"

I fidgeted in my seat. "Martin, this isn't a good time. I can hardly figure out which end is up these days. I can't—"

"I know. I don't mean to pressure you. I just wish I could fix things. Not only between us, but your past. You've suffered so much. It's made you this incredible person. You're so strong, you can deal with anything, but you're also unbelievably kind and warm and caring underneath that. I've never met anyone like you."

I felt awkward and tried to play it down. "They're not going to let you have any more to drink if they hear you going on like that."

"Don't joke, Lily. I do that all the time and I know how hollow I sound." His eyes were unwavering. "If you come back to me I'll do everything I can to make things right. It's not fair, what you've had to go through. Your father dying when you were a kid. Your mother killing herself, trying to make you feel guilty about her for the rest of your life. That's more than anyone should have to bear. Then your sister—"

"Excuse me. I'll be just a minute." I slid off my barstool as gracefully as I could and wobbled my way to the back of the bar. I had to put some distance between us, before I lost control. Martin knew my family history so intimately I felt like I was already lying naked in front of him. He'd never once been physically forceful with me but I'd sometimes felt overwhelmed by him. Jesse wasn't mistaken when he'd called Martin quicksand.

I went into the bathroom on the left, locked the door, and pulled out my cell phone. Jesse wasn't home, so I dialed my voice mail. There were two hang-ups followed by a message. "Lily, it's Melissa. I found the name of the place Claudia wanted me to go to. It's called 'Idylhaven' and here's the phone number." She rattled off a series of digits, with an area code I didn't recognize. "Would you let me know when you find Claudia? I'd like to know she's okay."

Whether it was the twenty-dollar bills or her own conscience flaring to life, Melissa had come through after all. I listened to her message a couple of times. I'd never heard of

Idylhaven, and I didn't recall Claudia mentioning it. She had been to rehab centers before, and I'd given the names to the police along with those of her friends. This would be a new one to check out.

When I came out of the bathroom I washed my hands as if everything were fine. In the mirror I saw how flushed my face was, even in the dim light. Why would Martin lie to me about his calls to Claudia, or about California rehab centers? Had some attraction been percolating between them over the years, and when I cut myself out of the picture they'd gravitated to each other? The card in my sister's apartment was signed with a mysterious *M*. The handwriting wasn't familiar, but Martin usually had florists handwrite his cards for him.

I reapplied my lipstick and made my way down the crowded bar. As I took my seat I noted that my flute of cava was magically full again. I sat down and pounced before he could say anything. "I was just thinking about how you never gave me my keys back."

"Your keys?" The bar light was dim, but under his St. Barts tan, I thought Martin paled a little.

"The keys to my apartment on Rivington. You didn't give them back when we broke up. When I moved to Spain I guess I forgot about them. But it just hit me, you still have them."

"I certainly haven't given them away." Martin smiled. "They're probably in my desk, but you know what a mess that is."

"You could have dropped by Claudia's apartment any time you liked, you know. She didn't change the locks."

"Why would I visit her?"

"My sister always liked you."

Martin grimaced. "I don't think *liked* is the word I'd use."

"What would you call it?"

"Envy. Jealousy. Selfishness. Greed." His tone was as harsh as his words.

"Where do you think she is?"

Martin rubbed his temple with one hand. "I wish I knew, Lily, I really do. I think we should bring a private investigator into this. The police aren't making any headway."

I pretended that he hadn't just said *we*. "A private eye? Where would I find one?"

"I know one. He's reliable and resourceful. You can count on him."

"Really?" This was getting interesting. I leaned forward. "How do you know?"

Martin's eyes flicked to the crowd waiting for our seats. "People can't be trusted," he said quietly.

"What are you talking about?"

I put my hand on his arm. It worked like truth serum. "When people know you have money, they will stoop to anything to extort it from you. They will even try to drag your family, your children, into it." The words tumbled out of his mouth and he looked surprised by what he'd come out with.

"Has someone blackmailed you?"

He gazed at me and then leaned forward so that his lips almost touched my ear. "A few have tried. They don't get away with it."

"Did someone try to involve Ridley?"

Martin pulled back abruptly and downed the rest of his drink. "This place is more crowded and noisy than I'd like. Why don't we go somewhere else to talk?" There were people lined up against the wall behind us, glasses held high, as if toasting, *To hell with the fire code.*

I was disappointed that he'd shut down when I mentioned

his son, and I tried not to show it. "What did you have in mind?"

"We could go back to my place." He caught my expression. "Or one of my properties?" By *property,* he meant hotel. He may as well have been saying, *Would you like to try out one of the mattresses with me?* "There's one close by, with a stunning bar and a wonderful Japanese restaurant. You would love it."

"I'm sure I would." It was tempting to go with him. I knew he wasn't telling me the whole truth, but I wasn't sure whether he was holding something back, or if he was outright lying. If Sarah Lyons had identified my sister correctly, Claudia came back to her building on New Year's Eve and she might still have been in the apartment when Martin called the next morning. Could there be something going on between them?

Martin took my contemplation for consent. He set a large bill on the countertop, thanked the barman, and stood up. He helped me with my coat, and took my arm as we ducked around the red velvet curtain. He opened the door for me, putting an arm around my waist at the same time.

"It's so good to have you back in New York," said Martin as we stepped into the frosty air. "This city is all wrong without you." He stroked my cheek with one hand and pulled me close to kiss me on the mouth. I hadn't wanted to admit it, but I'd craved his touch, too, and heat sizzled through my body. For a moment I forgot about my sister and everything else.

"New York does seem like her kind of town," said a deep voice that rattled me. I turned away from Martin and saw a man standing head and shoulders above the rest of the cigarette-puffing crowd outside the bar.

"Bruxton? What are you doing here?"

"Enjoying the night air. Oh, yeah, there are some developments in the case I wanted to talk to you about." The corner of Bruxton's mouth seemed to twitch, but he was dangling a cigarette like Bogart and it was hard to read his expression in the pale glow of the streetlight. He put out his hand to Martin. "Bruxton."

Martin stared at him and slowly put out his hand. "Martin Sklar."

"Good to meet you," said Bruxton. "Old friend of Lily's, aren't you?" He said *old friend* in a tone of voice that I would have reserved for *serial killer*.

"Detective Bruxton is investigating my sister's disappearance as well as the death of the woman in Claudia's apartment," I explained.

"You're working overtime, Detective," said Martin dryly. "How rare in a public servant." His son's misadventure with the police that afternoon couldn't have been far from his mind. There was something particularly cold in the way he said *servant*.

"Who knows what those captains of industry might get up to if we didn't?" said Bruxton. "Might hurt themselves burning down a building."

"What did you find out?" I asked Bruxton. "Do you know anything about my sister, or who that woman who died was?"

"We're all ears, Detective," said Martin.

"Let's all go down to the precinct to talk," Bruxton answered. "Since you're an old friend of Lily's, it would be good to get your perspective on her sister's disappearance."

"I wouldn't be able to add anything to your case," Martin said.

"You never know what could be helpful. The tiniest detail can be a dead giveaway," said Bruxton. "Just how intimately acquainted are you with Claudia Moore, anyway?" For the briefest of heartbeats, I wanted to throw my arms around him for asking what I hadn't been able to.

"I would have to consult with my lawyer before answering any questions," said Martin.

"Right." Bruxton nodded. "That's what you told my partner when she called you earlier today."

"I'm aware of how the police can twist the truth to build their case." Martin turned to me and smiled gently. "Good night, my Lily," he said, curling a strand of my hair around his finger. "I'll get you to come home sooner or later," he said, his voice low yet loud enough for Bruxton to hear.

"Good night, Martin."

He turned and started toward the curb, then stopped dead in his tracks. "Where's my car?" Crosby Street wasn't long or broad, so there was nowhere for an idling Town Car to hide.

"Oh, was that your driver who was sitting there with his engine running?" asked Bruxton. "I guess you didn't know the city has a three-minute idling law."

"In the dead of winter?" Martin seethed. He wasn't wearing a coat; why would he when his only exposure to the elements was between curb and building?

"Unless it's forty below." Bruxton shrugged. "It's not."

"Where is my driver?"

"He went that way." Bruxton jerked his head. "He could be on Lafayette. But if you don't find him, the subway's on Spring Street."

17

"You're evil," I said, walking with Bruxton to his car. Martin had stormed off in a wordless rage and disappeared around the corner of Broome Street. I'd never seen him so angry. "How did you figure out I was here?"

"I'm a detective." Under the force of my skeptical glare, Bruxton added, "You mentioned flamenco when you were making plans to meet that guy. There are two places with flamenco music and dancers near your old building. I tried the other one first. Then I came up here, spotted you at the bar, and waited."

"So you're a stalker. Nice to know that about a guy with a gun." I buckled my seat belt.

"We've all got our flaws. Speaking of which, mind if I smoke?"

"Go ahead." I stared at the open pack. Whether it was the near-miss with Martin, or a more general frustration with my sister, I was suddenly overcome with craving. "Do you mind if I have one?" Bruxton's eyebrows shot up, but he handed the pack over and lit me up with the same match he used for his own. Bruxton smoked Camels, which were stronger than the cigarettes Claudia and I used to steal from our mother's purse. In college and after I'd stuck with the thin ultralights that were targeted at women. After my second drag on the Camel I felt light-headed.

"You want to grab something to eat?" he said as we pulled away from the curb.

"Aren't you taking me to the precinct?"

"Only if your *old friend* was coming along. I'd love to get him into an interrogation room."

"Let's go to Jesse's," I said. "He's been working on a shoot all day. He'll go crazy if I don't catch him up on everything."

"Sure. So tell me about the old friend."

"Why?"

"We started digging after he blew us off today. Did he mention he burned down a church?" asked Bruxton. I stared at him, waiting for the punch line. "I'm not kidding. You know the Church of St. Aristarchus?"

"I think I've heard of it."

"On Lispenard, a block south of Canal and east of Church Street. Used to be an Orthodox church, but it hasn't had a parish in decades. Martin Sklar wanted to build a hotel on the site, but a community group got landmark status for the church. Guess what happened?" We stopped at a red light and he watched me. "One night last March the place went up in flames. Then your old friend got to build his hotel."

"I was living in Madrid last March. I never heard anything about it." That wasn't exactly true; the mention of a church fire tugged at my memory. I'd heard about this, but not from Martin.

"I drove by it tonight," Bruxton added. "It's a tacky piece of shit."

I bit my lip. "If there's evidence Martin did it, why not arrest him?"

"He has an alibi, of course. Out of the country. So he didn't actually set the fire himself, and the investigators weren't able to get anyone to admit he'd ordered it. But there was plenty of evidence the blast was deliberate, and the person who benefited from it was Martin Sklar. Proving guilt is tough, especially when you're up against the top fund-raiser for half of City Council. And no one died, so that made the case less pressing. Slippery guy, your old friend."

I couldn't imagine Martin doing anything like that. It was one thing for me to suspect that he scored low on the fidelity scale, another to see him as a criminal. "Martin does a lot of charity work, especially for children's organizations." I delicately tapped ash into the car's overflowing ashtray. "He's not someone who would do what you're suggesting."

"Loyalty is an overrated virtue." Bruxton tossed his cigarette out the window and lit another. I'd smoked maybe a third of mine. "You want to hear about that girl who died in your sister's apartment?"

"What do you think?"

Bruxton's mouth twitched slightly. "Brace yourself. She didn't drown in the tub."

"What?"

"There's no water in her lungs. She was already dead when her head went under."

"Then how did she die?"

"Heart failure," said Bruxton. "The ME said her heart gave out first. He could tell what order her organs shut down in, and the heart was first."

"So a healthy twenty-seven-year-old woman had a heart attack?"

"She wasn't twenty-seven." We were almost at Jesse's building now. Bruxton parked in an illegal space and turned the car off. "The ME thinks she was in her mid-thirties. There's evidence she was anorexic as well as bulimic."

"So her heart just gave out like that?" I glanced at my cigarette surreptitiously.

"It can happen, especially given her health issues. She was hooked on diet pills and laxatives, and she was apparently obsessed with exercise. Believe it or not, too much exercise hurts your heart." Bruxton lit a fresh cigarette. "ME said a jolt to the heart could have killed her. There's no bruising on her chest, though. He told me about a corpse he autopsied a while back, guy had been punched square in the chest and dropped dead. Boring bar fight turned into manslaughter. Guy died so fast there wasn't even a bruise where he'd been hit." He took a long drag.

I was picturing Claudia while he was speaking. My sister had a problem with impulse control and a violent streak. When she was frustrated or furious she lashed out at people. What if she'd gotten into an argument with this woman, hit her, and the woman had dropped dead?

"But there's more," Bruxton said, breaking into my thoughts. "There was Rohypnol in her system."

"The date-rape drug?"

"That's the one. ME's office is still running tests. They said it was a trace amount, like she had a couple sips of a drink laced with it."

As we walked into Jesse's building, I was trying to make sense of it. The woman's death wasn't really like my mother's suicide, but it looked like it on the surface. Had my sister accidentally hurt the other woman, killing her and leaving Claudia with a dead body on her hands? Was it possible that my sister had staged the scene to make it look like an accident or a suicide? That would have taken more cynical calculation than I'd ever known my impulsive sibling to have. Of course, if she had come up with such a plan, I'd come to town and ruined everything. What I wasn't admitting to Bruxton was that I knew Claudia had used Rohypnol from time to time. It was a way to enhance the high from heroin and soften the landing afterward. Still, if I knew that about the drug, so did Bruxton.

"I hope Jesse's home. He hates to miss anything," I said as the elevator doors opened on the floor. But even while I was unlocking the door, I knew my friend wasn't there. The apartment was quiet and dark. I dropped my coat over the back of the sofa and Bruxton shrugged his off and carefully set it beside mine. "Can I get you something to drink? Jesse's got a cache of sauvignon blanc from Chile, but there's also a great malbec from Argentina if you'd rather have red."

"Thanks, but I don't drink."

"Ever?"

"I'm an alcoholic," Bruxton said. "I'm not into the twelve-step crap, but I know what I need to steer clear of."

"Sorry, I didn't mean to pry." I'd known plenty of alcoholics, but none who admitted to it with such matter-of-fact directness. "Would you like a soda? Juice? Or water?" I blurted out, stewardesslike. He asked for water, and I went into the kitchen and poured two glasses from the pitcher in the fridge. When I came back to the living room, Bruxton's taut jawbone was already working furiously on the nicotine gum.

"What else have you found out?" I asked.

"We went over the security tape from the apartment building, what little we have before the power went out. There are so many people going in and out on New Year's Eve, most of them wearing hats or hoods or big coats. Sarah Lyons ID'd a couple different women who might've been the woman she saw on the stairs, but they're wrapped up like mummies. Unfortunately, it was a hell of a cold night." He paused for a minute. "Norah and I talked to your sister's doctors, managed to get a hold of some of her friends. We already had the phone LUDs, bank records, credit. We were able to put together something of your sister's life in the past year. It looks like she pulled away from her life last spring. A lot of her friends haven't seen her in a while."

"Where did she go?"

"We know Claudia Moore, the real one, went to a rehab center in western Massachusetts. Place called Idylhaven," said Bruxton. Score one for Melissa, I thought. "Then she checked herself out of rehab but didn't go home. She just vanishes. For weeks, there's nothing. She didn't spend any money. Didn't call anyone. She was totally off the grid."

There was a question in the air and I tried to answer it. "Claudia and I only talked on the phone once every month or so, and we'd send cards sometimes. She hates e-mail, and she's not on Facebook. I don't know where she went. She never told me anything about it, except that she'd gotten herself clean. She didn't give me details." What I didn't add was that Claudia had been furious at me when I'd called last February to tell her I'd decided to rent an apartment in Madrid for a while. *You're abandoning me?* she'd asked in disbelief. I thought she'd stop speaking to me, but she'd called me repeatedly in March. Then she'd disappeared in April without a word. I knew at the time that her sudden silence was really a form of revenge.

"Okay," said Bruxton. "She's back on the grid in June. Barely. At the end of the month she asked the super to fix her bathroom ceiling. Water damage. Mr. Pete swears it was her. Some of her old friends see her now and then over the summer, usually at art galleries. She made a few calls about taking art classes, getting studio space. She's avoiding her drug buddies, though. Her apartment's empty for long stretches, which suggests she was staying somewhere else at least part of the time." He drank some water. "Then she rematerializes with a bang at the end of August, beginning of September. Immediately gets her heroin connection going. People see her, she's either high as a kite or weeping or both. She's a mess. Then, in the middle of September, she drops from sight again."

"No one knows where she went?"

"Actually, we do. If the financials hold up, she went back to Idylhaven."

"What?" I asked. "Why did she go back? Is she there now?"

"No, she's not. Last they saw of her was when she checked herself out on September twenty-ninth."

"Where did she go? She didn't just vanish into thin air!"

"We're working on it," Bruxton affirmed. "We talked to people at the gym the dead girl joined. Seems like she was there all the time, unless she was shopping. It looks like she met her friend Kaylee at the gym."

"Have you found Kaylee Quan yet?"

"No."

He didn't seem particularly bothered by that, and his nonchalance bothered me. "This is all you've got?" I asked.

"It's a lot."

"You haven't found out anything about where my sister is *now*. Your big lead is from September. You know it's January, right?"

Bruxton shifted uncomfortably in his seat. "We haven't found any leads on your sister, so we're following up on other angles."

"What other angles? You're making it sound like Claudia disappeared months ago."

"It sounds like she went underground months ago. Dropped her old friends, found some new ones. Who knows what she was involved in? Quite a rap sheet she's got."

"If you're trying to accuse Claudia of something, you're dead wrong," I snapped. "She wouldn't hurt anyone."

"You sure about that?" Bruxton barked back. "Maybe she changed after you stopped speaking to her."

Whatever patience I'd had evaporated at that moment. He'd hit me where it hurt, and he knew it. "I think it's time you left," I said. I stood and Bruxton followed my lead, but he didn't move toward the door. We stared at each other for a moment before I broke the silence. "Maybe if you were as good at doing real police work as you are at digging into my family history, you'd get somewhere."

"What's that supposed to mean?"

"You knew when you met me that my mother had killed herself. That's going back more than a decade, but one neighbor mentioned it and you went looking under every rock. Some serious detective work there." I'd been angry when Bruxton had brought up my mother's death in the interrogation room, but I'd been so determined to make the police see that my sister wasn't dead that I'd tamped down my feelings. Now they were boiling over and I couldn't seem to stop myself. "If you cared as much about finding Claudia as you do about listening to neighbors gossip and rooting through my family's dirty laundry, you'd find her."

Bruxton stopped chewing his gum. "I'm sorry. I should've been straight with you."

"About what?"

"If we're going to figure out what the hell is going on, we've got to be honest with each other. Can we sit down?"

He popped more gum into his mouth. "I should've talked to you about this before. It's been awkward. I need to clear the air with you."

"About what?"

"I'm a cop. It's my job to find out what the hell's going on." He was chewing frantically, making his sharp-jawed face more animated than usual. "Sarah Lyons told us your mother died on New Year's Eve, but she didn't know all the details. I did. I was there."

"What are you talking about?"

"Eleven years ago. You'd gone back to the city on New Year's Eve, then you got the call to come back home. You had to get on another bus and come back up to Ithaca in the middle of the night. A cop met you at the bus station. She took you to the hospital to identify your mother's body, then brought you into the station. That was where I saw you. You were so . . . dignified. It was hard to believe you were just eighteen. You were worried about your sister, kept asking for her."

I was afraid to say anything. It was like talking to someone who'd read your diary, only far, far worse. "What were you doing in Ithaca?"

"I was on the force there," said Bruxton. "I worked narcotics then."

I wondered how much else he'd seen. The police had found Claudia on Sunday morning, drunk and high on pills a friend had scooped out of her parents' medicine cabinet. *Mom's dead?* she'd said to me when they'd brought her into the police station. In the next breath, she'd added, *Now you have to take me to live with you in New York.* The excitement in her voice had crackled like electricity. It was the first time that my sister had truly frightened me. *What did you do?* I'd whispered back. *Nothing,* she'd answered, giving me a dirty

look. Everything the police found was consistent with a suicide. My sister hadn't beaten our mother or forced pills down
her throat. But my mother had never attempted suicide without an audience. She didn't want to die, she wanted to be res-
cued. *Were you there?* I'd demanded of my sister. *Of course
not,* she'd said, and I'd known she was lying.

"You bastard," I said, feeling my chest constrict. I wanted
to curse him out, but I couldn't get any more words past my
lips.

Bruxton reached over the table and touched my wrist.
"I'm sorry, Lily. I screwed up. I thought you were in denial,
lying to yourself and to us. I was wrong."

I recoiled from his touch and focused on breathing, worried
I'd lose control and start weeping or screaming at any second.
I'd felt naked in front of Martin, but this was worse. Martin
knew only what I'd told him; Bruxton had actually been there,
watching me at the lowest point in my life. I was ashamed beyond words.

"I want you to trust me," said Bruxton.

"Why?"

"Because I want to help you. I want to get to the bottom of
this. Believe it or not, I want to find your sister as badly as
you do."

"That's only because you want to pin that woman's death
on Claudia!"

We stared at each other while the words hung in the air. It
was nothing but the truth, but I'd never planned to say such a
thing aloud, least of all to a cop.

"Lily, your sister is tied up in this. That doesn't mean she
did anything to the woman. But that woman was drugged
before she died. Even if the heart attack was an accident, the
drugging wasn't. And it's just too big a coincidence that this

woman's death was made to look like your mother's suicide." Bruxton leaned forward. "The way I look at it, there are two main possibilities. This girl died by mistake, and someone tried to cover it up."

"What's the other one?"

"This woman was killed for a reason, and whoever did it wanted the world to believe it was Claudia."

The second possibility made me shudder. But it didn't hurt me like what came out of Bruxton's mouth next. "I should get going. By the way, Norah and I decided to pull the LUDs for the apartment for all of last year. Turns out your sister and your old friend Martin Sklar spent a lot of time on the phone together."

"Excuse me?"

"Actually, most of the conversations were last March. But they were both making the calls. Sometimes they talked an hour or more." He stood up. "Who knows? Maybe they both missed you."

18

"Mmm, greens." Jesse swooned as he came into the kitchen and kissed me on the cheek. "Honey, I am most definitely home."

He'd called me just as Bruxton was leaving, asking if he could pick anything up for me. The studio he shared with a couple of other photographers was barely a ten-minute walk from his apartment. Knowing he'd be home soon had kept me from jumping into a cab and heading uptown to confront Martin. Instead, I was pan-searing tuna steaks when Jesse came in. When I heard the door I threw spinach and mustard leaves into a pan with the kale and some onion. I'd often pictured Jesse and me settling into sexless companionable bliss in our eighties, and over dinner I remembered why. He wanted to know everything about my meetings with Melissa Ardito, Sarah Lyons, and Rachel Heidegger. I told him all of the chilling things Bruxton had said. In the end, I admitted that I'd had drinks with Martin at the flamenco bar, even though I knew what his reaction would be.

"He's a low-down, no-count lowlife," Jesse ranted. "What poor excuse for a man would make you meet him in a bar in exchange for information about your sister?"

"That's not how it happened," I insisted. "You're deliberately misinterpreting what I said."

"Oh, yeah? I'm not misinterpretin' the part about his kid bein' nuts. Apple doesn't fall far from the tree."

"That's not fair. Ridley's not nuts, he's just . . ." I struggled to come up with a word. Damaged, I thought, but that seemed too judgmental to voice. But Jesse wasn't really interested in the boy.

"You told me yourself what a lousy parent Martin is. Spoils the kid rotten, won't discipline him for anything, wants to talk everything out."

"Martin was shipped off to boarding school when he was seven. He's trying to avoid all the mistakes his father made with him. Martin's misguided. He's not a bad parent."

"Really? If he's not, then what is?" Jesse sat back in his chair and crossed his arms.

"A bad parent doesn't care that there's no food in the house for the kids, so long as she has her gin." I looked down at my plate and pushed some food around, regretting the words. There was an awkward pause, then Jesse reached out and patted my hand.

"You're right, Lil. He's the kind of guy who wants to be his kid's buddy. Heart's in the right place, I guess, but misguided."

I nodded. "By the way, Martin offered to hire a private investigator to find Claudia."

"Wonders never cease." Jesse chewed thoughtfully for a moment. "That's the first decent idea I've heard out of Sklar's mouth. Ever."

I put my fork and knife down. "Here's what I can't get my mind around. Martin and Claudia were obviously in touch. Why is he lying about that? Yet he's admitting she asked him for money." I shook my head. "Why not just admit that they talked to each other sometimes? Otherwise, why would Claudia have asked him for money in the first place? Why didn't she ask me, or Tariq?"

"You don't have thousands of dollars to hand out, and maybe Tariq turned her down. You mention Tariq to the cops yet?"

"He was on the list of Claudia's friends that I gave them. I didn't tell them about his crazy girlfriend." We'd debated that already. Jesse was certain that I should, but I knew Tariq wouldn't appreciate it if I did. There was no guarantee he'd tell me what was going on with Claudia, but I was positive he'd hold back any information he had if he thought I was a rat. I moved my food around the edge of the plate, then prodded it toward the center again.

"What's wrong, Lil?"

"There was something Rachel told me. She said Claudia's boyfriend had jilted her when his old girlfriend came back to town. That was Labor Day weekend."

"You think somethin' *romantic* was goin' on between your sister and . . . Martin?"

I nodded, too upset to look at him.

"Oh, Lil." Jesse got up and came over to stroke my hair. "I'm sure nothin' like that happened."

"Claudia had a boyfriend, but she wouldn't tell Rachel his name," I said. "She said she didn't want me to find out. She and Martin were definitely in touch. And I came back to New York that weekend. What if—"

"Honey, there's just no way."

"Claudia came on to him a couple of times when she was living with me. She tried to sit in his lap once."

"And how did that go? He ratted her out, and didn't he refuse to stay over if she was there?" Jesse pointed out. "Look, I despise Martin Sklar. I think he's a low-down, dirty creep who can't be trusted. But I've been in the same room with him and your sis. He looks down on her like she's trash." He touched my chin and lifted my face so that I couldn't avoid his eyes. "I'd never defend him. But honestly, I can't see him hooking up with her. Going from you to your sister would be too big a trade-down for him."

"That's harsh," I said, but his words made me feel a little better. Martin liked shiny, polished trophies with smooth skin. Claudia's tattoos and track marks would have been off-putting for him. Still, if the relationship was a secret from the rest of the world, maybe Martin was indulging his dark side.

"Sorry, Lil, but your taste in men stinks. It's like your fatal flaw. You're smart and witty and kind and you look like Ava Gardner, but your love life is the pits. Just like Ava's. Look at the men she married. Mickey Rooney? Then that control freak Artie Shaw. Then Sinatra." He shook his head. "You ever think that the reason you like Ava Gardner so much is because you relate to her life?"

"What do you mean?"

"Well, her daddy died when she was thirteen, same age you lost yours, Lil. She had a lot of relationships with older men . . . Like maybe she was looking for a daddy."

"Is that what you think I'm looking for?" I asked, trying to keep my voice steady. Claudia had said the same thing to me before. "Do you think I want Martin to be my father?"

"Your problem is that you think you deserve creeps," Jesse backpedaled. He'd intuited that a nerve had been struck. "You deserve better."

"Are you done with the pep talk? Your dinner's getting cold."

Jesse ruffled my hair. "And you can cook! I forgot that part." He sat down again. "Does it make you feel any better to be a gay Southern boy's dream girl?"

"A little bit."

"You know one of the worst things about you livin' so far away? We never do spontaneous stuff anymore. Everythin' has to be all planned out when one of us visits."

"What did we do that was so spontaneous?"

"You used to throw together these parties at the last minute," he said. "You'd call at four and say, *Why not come on over for supper tonight?* When I got there at eight, you'd have a bunch of folks around. I liked that."

"I still throw parties." That was one of my luxuries; I loved having my own place and being able to invite people over at a moment's notice. "You know that I hate to be alone."

"So why haven't you come home yet?"

"Spain has been great for work. I've been traveling all over the place."

"Okay," said Jesse. I had him there; he'd go to hell in a handbasket if he thought he could get a return ticket. "But if you came home now, you could write other books. Don't you miss your friends here?"

"Of course I do." I was often lonely in Spain, but I didn't want to admit it. I worked from home and I was alone there most of the time, unless I jetted off to Paris or Prague for work . . . where I was also alone.

"You haven't called anyone since you got in, have you?"

I shook my head and took another hit of shiraz. "I meant to call people after I got here. I thought I'd be inviting them to a memorial service for my sister. Then—with everything that's happened—I don't know what to say to anyone. I feel like I'm in limbo."

"You are. It's hard to feel settled with all that's goin' on. But you should be seein' people. Otherwise all you're gonna think about is Claudia and your ex."

I went to bed after eleven with a deeply unsettled mind.

Where was Claudia? What was that other woman doing in her apartment, and why had she died? And Martin . . . I couldn't figure him out at all. After staring at the ceiling for a long while, it hit me that I wasn't going to learn anything new as I lay there. The alarm clock said it was after midnight, but New York is the city that never sleeps, I reasoned as I threw the comforter aside, pulled on jeans and a sweater, and kicked aside my boots in favor of flats. I'd always felt safe walking around the Village and even my ratty corner of the Lower East Side when I'd lived in New York, no matter what time of day. I left a note for Jesse, just in case he woke up and noticed I was gone, then put on my coat.

Outside, the ground was dry, but the temperature was dropping and the wind was picking up speed. It was normally a twenty-minute walk between Jesse's place and my old building, but the weather made me pick up my pace. The Lower East Side was louder at night than I remembered. I'd always thought of Essex as the dividing line between the haves, to the west, and the have-nots to the east. But since Schiller's Liquor Bar had parked itself at the corner of Rivington and Norfolk, the have-nots seemed to be losing ground. Still, the hipsters were nowhere to be found east of Attorney Street. There were groups of teens and young men, refugees from the projects, milling around like they were waiting for the action to start. No one accosted me, but when I got to Claudia's building I felt relief, as if I really were coming home. The sensation lasted only a moment, because there was a huge man parked on the stoop. He was hunched forward with long legs spread apart. He was dressed in black, his head obscured by a hood. The only details I could make out in the street lights were the stark white high-top trainers on his feet and the red glow of the cigarette in his mouth. I stopped dead, wondering if he'd try to rob me or push his way into the building if I opened the door. His hooded head turned in my direction and he startled me by tossing the cigarette into the gutter and bolting. He lumbered toward Pitt Street and disappeared around the corner. I looked over my shoulder to see what had startled him, but there was nothing threatening that I could discern. Hurrying into the building, I unlocked the door and closed it behind me, but no one tried to follow me in. Paranoia had struck again.

Heading up the stairs, I heard a sitcom laugh track on the third floor and some Gregorian chanting on the fourth, but otherwise the building was quiet. The elderly tenants were likely asleep and the younger ones were probably out. On the fifth floor, the police tape dangled at the side of Claudia's door. When I put my key in the top lock, it wouldn't turn. I moved it in the other direction and locked the door. Great going, NYPD, I thought. At least they'd managed to secure the bottom lock. I let myself in and turned on the light, stunned by the sight around me. The tidy apartment had morphed into a disaster zone. Books had been pulled out of the shelves and dumped on the floor. Paper was scattered everywhere, as if a tornado had torn through the room. The sofa cushions had been pulled out, their casings unzipped.

I hadn't planned to tell the police that I'd come over here again, but I wanted to scream at whoever had pulled apart my sister's place. Couldn't the Crime Scene Unit have put anything back? I picked up the books and haphazardly reshelved them, setting the Poe volumes together and fitting the others wherever I could. The painted porcelain bunny rabbit that had been my father's last gift to Claudia lay on the floor, cracked and missing an ear. For some reason, that bothered me more than the rest of the destruction. I wrapped him up

in my scarf and settled him into my leather bag. A small piece
of blue stationery lay on the floor, catching my eye.

> *My dearest C,*
>
> *Words cannot express how proud I am of you, or of
> all you have accomplished in such a short span of time.
> You are as mighty as the phoenix rising from the ashes,
> a woman of astounding beauty, intelligence, and wit. It
> delights my heart to see you blossom, and I hope that I
> shall always be with you, every step of your journey.
> You are forever in my heart, as I am in yours.*
>
> *A*

First *M*, now *A*? What book had it fallen out of? I scanned
the shelves. There was poetry by Rilke, Byron, Shelley, but
wait . . . I put my hand on a hardcover titled *Rising from
the Ashes*. I stared at the cover, a dreamy image of a woman
and soaring bird that looked like a cheap rip-off of a Pre-
Raphaelite painting by Dante Gabriel Rossetti. The name of
its author was Dr. Alexander Gorevale. I flipped open the
first few pages, but there was no inscription. Was I imagining
a connection? The phrase "rising from the ashes" was commonplace, so the fact that it was used in the book title and the
note could have been a coincidence.

There was a small black-and-white photograph of Gorevale on the dust jacket. He was gray-haired and lean-faced,
perhaps in his mid-thirties, serious in a tweed jacket. The
book was twenty years old, so he had to be in his fifties now.
The brief author biography told me that after earning his de-
gree in psychology at Cambridge University, Dr. Gorevale
opened his practice in London, later moving to Dublin, and
then Boston. In addition to teaching at Radcliffe, Dr. Gorev-

ale saw patients in both Boston and New York. I put the note inside the book and dropped them into my bag.

A large accordion file lay empty atop a pile of papers. I knelt to examine what was underneath. It took me a few moments to realize that I was looking at my own work. Articles I'd written over the past eight years for various magazines and newspapers were there, some of them glossy and colorful, others printed in black-and-white from a Web site. I pawed at the pages, wondering when and how my sister had developed an interest in my work. When she spoke about it—a rare event—it was to tell me not to waste my time with fluff. *Deep down, you're pretty superficial,* she would tease. *You should put your talent to better use.* There were photographs too, one of me standing next to a moai, a stone monolith from Easter Island, and another of Martin and me from a charity gala he'd sponsored. Someone—my sister, no doubt—had drawn horns on Martin's head and a Vandyke goatee on his chin. "Very mature, Claudia," I said out loud.

While I tucked them back into the file, I realized there were other articles, not mine, mixed in. ARSON DESTROYS HISTORIC CHURCH, read one headline. It was about the Church of St. Aristarchus, the one Bruxton insisted that Martin had burned down. That was why I knew the name; Claudia had mentioned it to me. She'd called me last March and asked, *Do you remember that old church I used to sleep in?*

Which one? I'd asked.

St. Aristarchus, off Canal. Someone set fire to it.

What happened?

A kid decided to torch the place, she'd said. *He thought nobody would miss it. Crazy, right?*

I found four stories about the fire, and put all of them into my bag. Why would Claudia collect articles about that? I tried not to think about the implications while I went through the desk and sorted out papers. There were five past-due notices from a dentist in Lenox, Massachusetts, dated from May, June, July, August, and September; I dropped them into my bag, too. The recent credit card statements from multiple banks told the tale of a shopping spree gone wild. There were charges of thousands of dollars from designer boutiques, charges in the hundreds from spas and online retailers like Amazon. One of the smallest charges surprised me the most, a bill from the iTunes store for more than three hundred dollars. How did anyone download that many songs in one session? The fake Claudia, with her food issues and retail bingeing, had as big a problem with addiction as my sister.

Inside the bedroom, I turned on the light. This room was as much of a disaster as the living room. The suitcase that had been lying on the bed on my first visit was overturned on the floor, its guts scattered. The mattress and boxspring had parted ways and the comforter dangled forlornly to one side. Cosmetics were strewn over the dressing table; jars lay open, oozing and congealing. It was a disturbing sight, but it reminded me of the chaos Claudia carried with her wherever she went.

The black Prada dress was still lying over the back of the chair, a wraith waiting for another chance at life. I held it up to my shoulders, contemplating what it would look like on. It was a sleeveless knee-length sheath that had a long keyhole cutout that would hint at cleavage without being gaudy. I wondered who had picked the dress, and where it had been worn. The tie at the top of the keyhole was black leather, punctuated by silver rivulets, which gave it a gothic touch that made me guess it was my sister's, unlike the pastels and prints I'd seen on my last visit. Melissa had said that Claudia had shown up at the art gallery in a beautiful dress and shoes. I contemplated my reflection for a moment before pulling off my sweater and jeans and shimmying into it. It fit perfectly, and I stared at myself in the mirror. I knew that my sister had long been jealous, wanting to claim anything I had as her own. But for a moment, I was envious of her. She'd slipped into the ether, leaving me lost and frantic with worry about what she was doing with Martin.

I reached for the closet door, filled with childish curiosity, but as I turned the knob my phone rang. I rooted through my bag for my cell, then flipped it open without checking the call display.

"Lil?" Jesse's voice was urgent. "Where did you go runnin' off to?"

"I'm at Claudia's place," I said. "Why aren't you sleeping? What's wrong?"

"You're not gonna believe this. Guess who just turned up at my door?"

Before I could answer, I saw in the mirror that the closet door was swinging open, propelled by a pale hand. As I started to turn, the door hit the side of my head, and I fell to the floor.

19

I heard running feet and the front door open. By the time I stood up footfalls were faintly echoing from the stairwell. The taste of blood seeped into my mouth and I ran my tongue over my teeth. They were all in place, but I'd bitten into my lower lip. I didn't understand what had just happened, but I knew I had to get help. As I stumbled back to the living room, my head throbbed with each step. The front door of the apartment lay open, but the hallway was empty under the faintly greenish glow of the ceiling lights. There was no point in knocking on the door across the hall; the Decarnos would never help me. I took a lungful of air, and tripped down the hallway, touching the wall for support. I banged on 5C and 5D. Someone had to answer.

A moment later, I heard soft footsteps on the floor inside 5C. "Who is it?" called Sarah Lyons. I could feel her eye on me behind the peephole, and suddenly the locks turned. She was wearing a long, silvery silk robe, her startled face shiny and greasy under a heavy cream. "Lily! What on earth?" She touched my face with one manicured hand. I realized I was barefoot and still in Claudia's dress. "That's a nasty cut on your lip. It's all swollen up."

She led me into her apartment, putting one arm around my shoulders and the other supporting my arm. A few steps and I was on her sofa. Sarah disappeared and came back with an ice tray and a clear plastic bag. She popped a few cubes into

THE DAMAGE DONE   161

the bag, then handed it to me to hold against my mouth. Then she vanished again and rematerialized with a dish towel to keep my hand from freezing against the ice.

"Thank you," I said after a minute. "I'm okay, just shaken up."

"What happened?"

"I was going through some things at my sister's apartment." My voice was muffled by the towel. "There was someone there, hiding in the closet. They hit me with the door."

"Did you see who it was?"

"No, just their hand on the door." Almost unconsciously, I glanced at Sarah's perfect French manicure and my eyes snagged on a beautiful, antique-looking diamond ring sparkling on the fourth finger of her left hand. Even in my badly shaken state, my magpie instincts were strong. I glanced at my own nails, chipped vermilion. The hand on the closet door was delicate and pale, the nails unpolished, ragged and dirty.

"Could it have been your sister?" Sarah asked. "Could Claudia have come back to her apartment?"

Her question made my breath catch. Would Claudia have hidden in the closet, attacked me, and run away? "I—I don't know," I said, but I was thinking, *Yes.* Yes, definitely. My mother used to punish Claudia and me by locking us in a closet. It made me frantic, but Claudia took to the shadows. When she'd lived with me I'd occasionally found her sitting cross-legged in the bedroom closet with the light off. *It lets me be alone with my thoughts,* she would say. Suddenly I remembered Jesse's call. He'd said someone had turned up. Could that have been Claudia? If it was, who had been in her apartment?

"Do you want me to call the police, or would you rather do it?" asked Sarah.

"I need to call my friend first." I looked around for a phone but didn't see one. Sarah's apartment was almost devoid of furniture. I was sitting on a clear Lucite chair that had a twin on the other side of a black wrought-iron table. The minimalist chic could have been a stage setting for a very modern play. I was uncomfortable there, as if I were an out-of-place prop.

Sarah passed me a cell phone. "I don't have a land line," she explained.

When I dialed Jesse's number, I only got voice mail. I called his cell phone and got a recorded voice, too. Where had he gone? It hit me suddenly that maybe someone attacked him, too. Maybe the same person who had attacked me . . . No, that was paranoid. I sounded like my mother, and that was always a bad sign.

"Can I get you something to drink?" Sarah's voice interrupted my thoughts. "Some brandy might be in order. Don't laugh. That was my mother's cure-all for everything."

There was nothing shocking about what she'd said, but her words crackled through me like electricity. Brandy had been my mother's cure-all, too, and it was administered when Claudia or I had a cold, a cough, or couldn't sleep. My mother was, after all, an alcoholic. Before I could answer Sarah, a phone started softly trilling in the background.

Sarah heard it, too. "That's from your sister's apartment," she said. "I can hear it when there's no other noise. No one else has that old-fashioned ring."

"Who the hell would be calling there in the middle of the night?" I didn't like the first thought that occurred to me—what if Claudia had been waiting in her apartment, knowing someone was going to call her? "I have to get over there." I went to the door, still holding the ice.

"Wait." Sarah rushed out of the room and came back with two threatening-looking kitchen knives, one still encased in plastic. "I've never even used this one." She tugged the cover off and handed me the new knife. It had a six-inch blade that gleamed in the light.

"Good thinking," I said, impressed. If I was wrong about it being Claudia who'd hit me, I'd be glad of a weapon. Sarah took the ice and towel from me and we went to the door. I opened it and Sarah followed me out and locked it behind her. The apartment doors in the building had two heavy-duty locks each, but they didn't latch unless you pulled them with force. That was lucky now, because I was able to turn the doorknob and walk back into Claudia's apartment. I'd left the lights on. As I reached for the phone, it stopped ringing. "Damn it! Do you remember what you're supposed to dial when you want the last number that called you?" I asked Sarah, but she shook her head.

"We should make sure no one else is in here," she said. We moved together, room by room, knives in hand. The apartment was small but stacked with hiding spots. There were four closets, including the small linen closet in the bathroom, and we checked under the bed and behind the furniture and everywhere something larger than a cat could be. The apartment was empty.

"It's a mess in here," said Sarah. "Do you think she did that, or was it the police?"

"I wish I knew." I went back into the bedroom, pulled the dress over my head, and put on my own clothes. My cell phone was still on the floor and I picked it up. The screen had a crack in it, but it was still working. I called Jesse and got his voice mail again. What had happened to him? I wondered if I should call his building and have the doorman check on him, then remembered there was no doorman on duty between midnight and seven. Should I call the police? Suddenly I was afraid for him.

I returned to the living room, restless and angry now that my fear had ebbed away. Sarah was standing with her back to me. "Thanks so much, Sarah," I said. She didn't move or speak. "Sarah?" As I moved beside her I saw that she was clutching a piece of paper with both hands, staring at it with an agonized intensity. "Sarah?" I touched her arm and she flinched.

Her eyes cut to mine and back at the page. "I started to pick things up and . . ."

"What is it?" I reached for the page but she wouldn't let go until I tugged it gently out of her grasp. It was a consent form from a doctor's office for a dilation and curettage, dated September 2. The last time I'd set eyes on my sister had been September 4, just two days later. *Reason for procedure: incomplete spontaneous abortion*, it said. I blinked and read it over again.

I could hear Claudia's voice in my head. *You think I just gave in to temptation, don't you, Lily?* That was what she'd said to me that night, when I'd confronted her. I'd assumed that she had been lying to me for months about getting off heroin. What if she'd been telling me the truth? *I've been abandoned and I've lost every fucking thing I care about. But you don't care, do you, Lily? You're just horrified and ashamed. You didn't even ask me what happened. You don't even care why I'm like this.* Guilt and shame coursed through my own veins. I'd never given a thought to the possibility that Claudia had gotten herself clean and had suffered a sudden relapse. She'd had a miscarriage and I hadn't been there to help her.

"Pregnant. She was pregnant," Sarah said, and I wasn't

sure if she was talking to herself or to me. Her hands were shaking. Before I could say anything, I heard a key in the door. Someone turned the cylinder of the first lock, then the second. Sarah froze in place but I moved forward, knife in hand, pointed in front of me at arm's length.

"Put your hands up where I can see them," I said.

There was a pause. "Lil? Is that you? It's me." The door pushed open and I saw my friend, his brown hair sticking out at all angles as if he'd hurtled out of bed in the middle of a nightmare.

"Jesse! What's going on? You didn't answer your phone!" My words came out in a jumble.

"Damn, I left my cell behind when I rushed out," he said. "You gave me the fright of my life when you screamed and the line went dead. I called you back and it just went to voice mail. I gave myself a fright thinkin' the worst." He shook his head. "That's some knife you got there."

I hugged him and realized he wasn't alone. A lurking, hulking shadow in the hallway behind him stepped forward. The dim hallway lights made his chestnut skin a couple of shades darker, and his obsidian eyes more intense. He always reminded me a little of Cary Grant, but darker and more formidable even in a well-cut suit. "Tariq?"

"She walks in beauty, like the night. Hello, Lily." He inclined his head at me. It was a nod of recognition, and a reminder that we kept an adversarial distance from each other. "I am glad that you are safe. Perhaps you would consider putting that knife down."

I looked at my hand and realized I'd put up the blade. As I lowered it, I felt embarrassment. "What are you doing here? I thought you were in Pakistan."

"Where do I begin? Suffice to say I received a telephone call in Pakistan, informing me that you had visited my flat, and that Claudia is missing." Tariq paused. "My source may have mentioned that you overturned a table in the parlor and made something of a mess."

I stared at him in disbelief. "Did your source tell you that your crazy friend Tati attacked me?"

"I'm just thankin' the good Lord you're safe, Lil," Jesse interrupted. "I was goin' crazy with worry. Never run off in the middle—" Jesse broke off as he noticed, for the first time, that another person was in the room with us. "Hey there, ma'am. Are you doin' all right?"

"This is Sarah," I said. "She's a neighbor. She took care of me tonight after someone attacked me here." I looked around and was surprised to see that Sarah's eyes were wet and glassy. She looked shell-shocked.

"You were attacked?" said Jesse. "What in hell did you get into over here?"

I was too surprised to answer him. "Are you okay, Sarah?"

She nodded slightly and recovered her composure. "I should go. It's been quite a night."

"Thanks so much for everything you did," I said. "I'm so sorry to bother you in the middle of the night. You were amazing."

She brushed against me lightly as she headed out the door, and Jesse stepped to one side and Tariq moved to let her pass. "You need to go to the hospital, Lily," she said as she re- treated down the hallway. "A doctor needs to take a look at that bump. The fact you're up and walking doesn't mean you don't have a cerebral contusion." Then she unlocked her apartment door and slipped inside. I felt guilty. I hadn't liked

Sarah when I'd first met her, or at the police station, but her willingness to help me when I'd been hurt touched me.

"Odd bird," said Tariq, sotto voce.

"What are you doing here?" I demanded.

"I returned from Pakistan," said Tariq. "Did I not yet mention that fact?"

"Why are you *here* in the middle of the night?"

Jesse butted in. "He came by my place, bangin' on the door and shoutin'. Don't think I'll ever hear the end of it from my neighbor across the hall. She said she'd call the cops, and she's mean enough to do it."

"You took ten minutes to answer the bloody door," said Tariq. *Bloody,* that was as bad as his language ever got. He still sounded like the Eton schoolboy he'd once been. "I should simply have dealt with the lock myself."

"Sure, if you wanted your fool head blown to smithereens." Jesse turned to me. "He wanted to see you, and I told him there was no way on the Lord's green earth that I was wakin' you up to get interrogated."

"Fortunately, Lily left that note on the table," said Tariq. "Otherwise, I would still be twiddling my thumbs back at your flat."

"Then I had to hog-tie him so he didn't go rarin' off and surprise you here. That's why I called you, Lil. But the line went dead and you didn't answer when I called again, so I came over here with him." He tucked my hair back behind my ears. "I'm sorry, honey, I shoulda just let him come over here straightaway."

Across the hall, the door opened. "We are calling the police," shrieked Mrs. Decarno. "You shouldn't be allowed to carry on with men in this hallway. It is a disgrace! You are nothing but a tramp, Claudia Moore." She had shrunk since I'd last seen her, or maybe it was just that her skinny neck couldn't support the weight of her big head and mouth anymore. The lines on her face were deeper than wrinkles, more like scars.

"Wrong sister. I'm Lily," I called back.

"Not *that* old bat again," Tariq groaned. Mrs. Decarno's eyes narrowed to slits.

"Come on, now," said Jesse softly. "She's an ole lady. Leave her be."

Mrs. Decarno propelled herself into the hallway on her skinny, blue-veined legs, which were on display between the hem of her furry robe and fluffy slippers. Mr. Decarno's fat globe of a head poked out the doorway, but his body stayed inside. The missus always had been the vicious one. "I should have known *you* were back, Lily," she snapped. "That explains all the men buzzing around here like flies. Your sister is a low-life drug addict, but she's not a prostitute like you."

"Just a minute here . . ." said Jesse.

"What do you mean, 'all the men'?" I asked.

"Him for one," Mrs. Decarno said, jabbing a bony finger at Tariq's chest. "I saw you over here, three days after Christmas, carrying on like a maniac. You kicked her door."

"I hope that you enjoyed the show, madam," Tariq commented.

Mrs. Decarno glared at Jesse. "Haven't seen this one around in a long time, but there've been others. Plenty of others."

"What others? When?" I demanded.

"There were two of them over on New Year's Eve," hissed Mrs. Decarno. "Obviously close friends of hers, if you know what I mean."

"I have no idea."

"Two men and one woman! Disgusting," Mrs. Decarno spat out.

Jesse started to speak, but I interrupted him. "Did you see the men? What did they look like?"

"How should I know? I saw their backs, not their faces." Mrs. Decarno shrugged. "Makes me sick. What's the world coming to?"

I remembered what Bruxton had told me earlier, about how the power had briefly gone off at the building on New Year's Eve around eight P.M., and how the security camera had been broken. Had the two men come up to my sister's apartment after that, and had my sister's impostor let them in? The police knew very little, it seemed, but they'd been certain that there was no forced entry at Claudia's apartment.

"Did you tell the police about them?" I asked. "This could be incredibly important."

"Important to you, maybe." Mrs. Decarno looked me over and wrinkled her pruny face. "But you're a tramp."

"Look, I just need to know—" I started to say, claiming enough composure to pretend I was above the fray, when Jesse opened his mouth.

"It's high time you shut your yap and listen up." His voice wasn't loud, but it was fierce. "You've got some kind of dirty mind whirlin' around in there. You pack up the show and go on home now. Tomorrow you're havin' another talk with the cops."

"You think you're going to tell me what to do in my own building?"

"You know what I think?" said Jesse. "You're sick with jealousy over other gals. You couldn't be nice and kind and beautiful, so you hate anyone who is. But I'll bet anything your husband doesn't feel the same way."

Mrs. Decarno's mouth formed an outraged O. I retreated into Claudia's apartment, stuffed the form about her miscarriage into my purse, and threw my coat over my arm. When I returned to the door, Mrs. Decarno stood tall in her doorway giving Jesse the evil eye. "Let's go," I said. I locked the door behind me. Jesse led the way, and I followed him down the stairs, with Tariq bringing up the rear.

"Funny thing, growing up in Oklahoma," Jesse murmured. "You learn that what's on people's lips is what's going on in their own heads." I remembered him telling me this before. I knew it had a lot to do with his own sexuality, and how people responded when they discovered he was gay.

Near the foyer, he spoke again. "You've still got to tell us what happened back there, Lil." He stopped mid-step. "Are you feeling okay?"

"Fine, just a little dizzy."

But that wasn't entirely true. My head seemed to be spinning again, and the only reason I didn't collapse on the stairs was that Tariq reached out and grabbed me.

20

"Do you truly think that it could have been Claudia inside the flat?" asked Tariq. I'm not sure what it said about my sister or our relationship that neither Tariq nor Jesse were startled by the idea that she had slammed me with a door. We were sitting in the back of a tricked-out Range Rover that probably had its own zip code. Inside, it looked like the Earl of Chesterfield had sent over his decorator. The seats were burgundy velvet and there was an Oriental rug on the floor. There was a polished bar between us, made of beveled wood with gilded edges. All the SUV was lacking was a chandelier.

"It could have been," I said, picturing the hand. When I concentrated, I was sure the fingers were small and delicate enough to be Claudia's. But the nails were so grubby, as if they'd been digging through Dumpsters. Even when she'd been living on the street and subsisting on church meals, she'd had a certain amount of pride in her appearance. She covered up her track marks, and she kept her hands and face clean. "I'm not sure."

"We've gotta take you to the hospital, Lil," said Jesse.

"We cannot risk a hospital. It is essential that we keep this quiet," said Tariq.

"Well, ain't that great. Tariq just parachuted in with some rules and regulations for us, Lil." Jesse leaned forward. "I'm gonna tell you this once. You got no say in anythin' Lily decides. Got it?"

I put my hand on Jesse's arm. "I'm not going to the hospital."

"Lil, I don't wanna be the one to say you're addled, but bein' smacked in the noggin can't be doin' your brain any favors. C'mon now."

"I can't go. I'll tell the police what that witch Mrs. Decarno said, but I don't want them to know that anyone attacked me at Claudia's. If there's a chance it was my sister . . . Look, if I go to the hospital, they'll be suspicious that something happened."

"For cryin' out loud, Lil, somethin' *did* happen!"

"I know a physician, an excellent one," said Tariq. "He will be discreet."

Jesse dug in his heels. "Lily needs some of those brain scans you can only get at a hospital."

"My physician has top-scale equipment, and he will be able to make those scans. It will be precisely like visiting a hospital, only without the four-hour wait."

Tariq made a call. When we arrived at a nondescript brownstone in the east Sixties, I realized that his physician, Dr. Khan, was the man I'd seen enter his apartment building after I'd tangled with Tati. Dr. Khan was in his mid-forties with a pudgy, chipmunk face and the energy of a puppy, even when we arrived at two in the morning. He questioned me about my vision, if I'd thrown up, or had any clear discharge from my ears or mouth. He examined the bump on the side of my head, then gave me a vision test and stared at my eyes. His own were the color of bitter chocolate. "You have some scratches on your neck. Were you attacked by an animal?"

"You could say that," I answered, wondering if I needed a rabies shot. "But some people might consider her a person."

Dr. Khan raised an eyebrow. "It will be necessary to make some scans. We must rule out any internal bleeding."

This basement office was clearly part of a suite of medical labs. It was unusually well equipped; I had an MRI right there. Dr. Khan seemed inordinately pleased. "Very good news. No fracture and no hematomas. You are a lucky young woman."

When we piled back into Tariq's SUV, I put my head back on the warm velvet cover of the neck rest. A blink of an eye later, we were in front of Jesse's building.

"Wake up, Sleeping Beauty," said Tariq.

I looked at him, leaning over me, his face close to mine, and I kicked him. "What the—" He gasped.

"Sorry. Force of habit." I sat up straight. "What time is it?"

"Almost four A.M., Lil." Jesse was smiling. "You were out like a light." He helped me out of the SUV and held me steady while my legs wobbled. Upstairs, Jesse and I collapsed onto a couch together, and Tariq sat opposite from us, languid as a panther. He didn't seem tired, but jet lag might have been working in his favor at this point. It would have been time for lunch in Pakistan now.

"I have questions for you." My voice sounded slurred to my own ears. "Do you know where Claudia is?"

"Lily, I did not return from Lahore, leaving the house of my mother, because I know where Claudia is."

"How come you have to sound like such a know-it-all?" Jesse interjected. "Couldn't you just say no like a normal human? That too much to ask?"

Tariq stared at him with his opaque, dark eyes and straightened his tie. I noticed his hands, thick as slabs of beef with long, meaty fingers. I remembered Claudia's commentary about his unusually impressive physical attributes and gave my head a shake. "Do you have any clue at all where she is?"

"No," said Tariq. "Do you?"

"I have no idea. When was the last time you saw Claudia?"

"I am not entirely certain," Tariq said slowly.

"You saw her, or you didn't. Which was it, Tariq?"

"I have seen her and not seen her, if you will allow me to explain." Tariq's tone was calm, but there was an undercurrent of annoyance. He didn't like to be challenged, or questioned. "Claudia and I have not been in contact very frequently this year. I have been out of the country for a good share of the time. Unfortunately my absences coincided with yours, Lily. When you suddenly decided to stay in Spain, Claudia was bereft."

I bit my lip to keep myself from answering Tariq's accusation. I needed to hear what he knew.

"However, I believe in retrospect that perhaps the fact that you and I were both absent may have forced Claudia to reconsider her appetite for self-destruction," Tariq continued. "In April, she made the decision, entirely voluntary and entirely her own, that she would go into a rehabilitation center."

"I know. She told me." I remembered being annoyed that she'd disappeared for weeks without a word, but then feeling elated when I found out what she'd been up to. *I'm so proud of you,* I'd told her. Even though she'd gotten my hopes up before, I clung to the idea she'd one day manage to kick her habit. *Oh, shut up, Honey Bear,* she'd responded. *If I'm going to be somebody's role model, I can't be such a screwup.* It had struck an odd chord at the time, but we'd had so much to catch up on I hadn't thought much of it then. "Did you give her the money to go?" I asked Tariq.

"Yes. I had been pressing her for some time on this issue. I was glad she acquiesced. The next time we saw each other, it was already July. She was, well, wonderful really. We had dinner on the Fourth of July weekend and she was . . ." His eyes stared into the distance without focus, as if he were drinking in the sight of her in front of him, and his clipped voice softened. "She was vital and spirited and happy. Well and happy."

"And after that?" I asked.

"We saw each other next at the end of August. Claudia was unsettled, but she would not explain why. She insisted that she was fine, but I know her too well."

He seemed lost in thought for a moment, and I remembered that Rachel Heidegger had said similar things. In fact, she'd even seen Claudia around the same times Tariq had. Had Claudia been out of the city the rest of the summer? The police had said that the apartment was empty for weeks at a time. Tariq let out a frustrated breath. "I did not wish to press her on what was wrong, because she was still doing well. She was not using heroin. She would not even have a single glass of wine, and she told me she had quit smoking. I thought . . ." Tariq stood and began to pace, wound up and edgy. "I should have known something was wrong. She telephoned me a few days later. She sounded desperate and I went to her flat. She was falling apart. She was back where she had started, bent on self-destruction. I tried to comfort her."

"Oh, you're such a good friend." Sarcasm dripped from my mouth like venom.

"I know what you are implying, Lily, but it is not what happened. Claudia was broken in mind and spirit and I held her until she calmed down, at least a bit. I told her that she had to go into some sort of treatment facility or she would kill herself. She told me that she wished she were dead."

"She said that?"

Tariq nodded grimly. "I arranged for her to go back to the

rehabilitation center she had visited in the spring. Idylhaven, I believe that is the name. Claudia had read somewhere that they could cure impossible cases. I do not have much faith in that sort of thing, but I could not think what else to do."

"I guess that was a way to ease your conscience," I said. "Since you're the one who got her hooked on drugs in the first place."

Tariq stopped pacing and stared at me. This was at the core of my contempt for him. Before Tariq, Claudia was a problem child who dabbled with drugs. Tariq had introduced her to a wider array of illicit substances, and his deep pockets meant that Claudia could indulge as much as she wanted. By the time they broke up, Claudia was a hard-core addict.

"I have done things that now make me ashamed," he replied hotly. "But you cannot blame me for Claudia. She has been drugging herself since she was twelve, starting with the pills in your own mother's medicine cabinet. You know that."

He was right, but I didn't want to admit it. "Claudia resisted rehab for years."

"That was a long time ago, when circumstances were markedly different," Tariq answered. "Have you ever read Rilke, Lily? *If my devils leave me, my angels will, too.*"

"You get what he's sayin'?" asked Jesse, rising to his feet. " 'Cause I'm gettin' a Coke. You want a bite to eat?" His eyes cut over to Tariq, including him in the invitation. Jesse was a natural-born host, even when he wanted to strangle his guest.

Tariq ignored the offer. "When did you last speak with Claudia?"

"The beginning of September. Labor Day. I came back to New York and I saw her then."

"I did not mean the last time you saw her in person. I am

aware that you reside in Spain." Tariq was exasperated. "When did you last *speak* with her?"

"September."

He stared at me. "You have not spoken to your own sister in four months?"

I hated that Tariq had put me on the defensive, but I was guilty of being a bad sister. After our last, horrible fight, I'd taken sordid pleasure in pretending Claudia didn't exist. "I e-mailed her. I called her in December, several times. I sent her a present at Christmas." That was scraping the bottom of the answer barrel.

"Really, Lily, was that the best you could manage?" Tariq's contemptuous eyes bored into mine. "Your only living relative, your own flesh and blood. You were in quite the rush to disown her, were you not?"

I was ashamed and fought to hide it. "What did you mean when you said you weren't sure when you last saw Claudia?"

"Anything that I did, I did out of concern for your sister." Now he was on the defensive. "What did you do, Tariq?"

Tariq looked at his hands and sighed. "Claudia has her own life, I respect that. When we had dinner together in July, it was clear to me that she had fallen in love. She was bursting with energy and hope and optimism. It has been a rather long time since I had seen her like that." He stared off into the distance again. From the wistfulness in his voice, I imagined Claudia shimmering in front of his eyes, a mirage brought to life by the memory of their own love affair.

"Did you meet him?" I asked bluntly. Tariq had met Martin several times; if Claudia had become involved with my ex, Tariq would know.

"No," Tariq admitted. Jesse came back into the living room

with a couple of bottles of water and his soda. Tariq took a bottle and twisted off the cap. "However, I had one of my associates investigate the situation. I discovered that Claudia's lover was a pseudopsychologist of some small renown. He made Claudia believe he would cure her of her demons when all he wanted to do was lure her into his bed." Tariq's jealousy uncoiled, cobralike.

"Does the name Alexander Gorevale ring a bell?"

Tariq stared at me. "She told you his name?"

"I found one of Dr. Gorevale's books in her apartment."

"Claudia would not tell me who the man was, so I became suspicious," he said. "This Gorevale fellow had quite the history. He fancied himself a rake, though I have trouble regarding a man who had intimate relations with his own patients anything but criminal."

The loathing in his bearing made me shiver. "Fancied?" I asked. "Past tense?"

"Past tense," Tariq affirmed.

"He's dead?"

"Yes." Tariq was eerily calm, as if daring me to inquire further.

"Did you have anything to do with Dr. Gorevale's demise?" I asked, remembering what Claudia had told me about Tariq. *Pakistan is different—someone hurts your family, you have to hit them back twice as hard. Someone attacks your cousin, you have to kill him and maybe his brother, too.* I'd never seen Tariq be violent, but underneath his sharp suit and polished manners and elegant language, I knew he was dangerous.

"The question is an insult."

Jesse muttered, "Anything hurts like that, hurts in proportion to the truth."

Tariq ignored him. "In September, when the illusion of love shattered, Claudia took it hard. I still cannot imagine why. That musician she dated and that artist she lived with were both better men. At least they had talent, unlike a washed-up old charlatan who forced himself on vulnerable women."

"Did you know that my sister had a miscarriage?"

"She what?" Jesse yelped, hitting the table with his foot and making it rattle.

Tariq stared at me. "This is, what, a theory of yours, Lily?"

"No." I dug into my bag and pulled out the folded page from the hospital. Tariq took it from me, read it over, and swallowed hard. "That is why she took it so badly," he said, softly. "I could not for the life of me work out why she would be wrecked over an old fool like that." He bowed his head so that I could no longer make out his expression. "I teased her about not drinking anything at dinner in August, but I believed it was just part of her new health regimen. She never said . . . she never mentioned . . ." His voice trailed off and he stood up and went to the window, his back to me.

"When did you hear from her next?"

Tariq took so long to answer, I wondered what had caught his attention outside. "I received a call from Claudia on September the twenty-fourth," he said finally.

"You rehearsing for the cops?" asked Jesse. " 'Cause it's sorta funny you pulled September twenty-fourth off the top of your head."

Tariq's glare over his shoulder was withering. "That happens to be my birthday." He turned back to the window. "Claudia told me that she was feeling much better, but she said she would not be able to see me for a while. She said that she had realized that she fell into old patterns easily. There was some tedious axiom she repeated, something about old friends, old habits. One of those mantras they employ to brainwash people in need."

"You're sure it was Claudia who called you?" I asked.

"Beyond the shadow of a doubt. I respected her wishes and kept my distance. I was in Pakistan most of the time, in any case. At the end of October I came back to New York and rang her. A woman answered and took a message, but Claudia did not return my call. I understood that she needed to do things her way, but I thought she could at least have a brief word with me. When I came back to New York again in December, I went by Claudia's flat. That was on the twenty-first. A woman answered the door. She told me that Claudia could not see me, that Claudia did not want any contact with her old life."

"What did the woman look like?"

"Dark hair, hazel eyes, fit. Too much makeup. About Claudia's height, and a size four." Tariq probably knew the woman's bra size, too, though he relished the part of the gentleman too thoroughly to say such a thing. "She bore a passing resemblance to Claudia, the way that a lesser painter might copy a Gainsborough. None of the brilliance of the original, none of its charm, just a dull, flat imitation."

"She looked kind of like Claudia, though?" I thought of the woman I'd seen in the morgue. Her rosebud mouth was like Claudia's, only less plush. Her freckled skin didn't have my sister's porcelain perfection, but makeup could have evened up the differences. Claudia lived hard, but something in her bone structure or bearing or both made her stand out in any crowd. The woman I'd seen laid out on the slab was unremarkable, even though she must have been attractive in life.

"A transitory glimpse, shall we say," Tariq answered. "She claimed to be Claudia's sobriety companion."

"What the hell's a sobriety companion?" Jesse interjected. "Didn't that seem strange to you?"

"I believe that some Hollywood celebrity had one, and now it is all the rage," said Tariq. "It is a bodyguard one hires to guard against one's own worst impulses. That was one of the reasons Claudia couldn't see me anymore—her nanny would not allow it. That was why I didn't find it strange. Not at the time."

"But later . . ." I prompted.

"I let it go then, but I did wonder about it," said Tariq. "I left something with the supposed sobriety companion. It was something Claudia wanted passionately. Or at least, she had wanted it, back when I saw her at dinner in August."

"What was it?"

"She had pawned something that she wanted to find again. However, the point is that she did not call me about it. I went back to her flat on Christmas Eve, and this nanny character claimed that she had passed the package along. That was when I began to have the building watched. Two of my people reported seeing Claudia, but I am quite certain it was just the imitation of which they caught a glimpse, not my Claudia."

Hearing Tariq use the possessive made my stomach churn. "It took you how long to figure out that Claudia wasn't in the apartment?" I asked, incredulous.

"I have been to Pakistan four times in the past six months. That is in addition to other travel for my business interests. I have been distracted, I admit that."

"You went over there and acted like a crazy person on December twenty-eighth," I said.

"Was that how it was reported? No one answered the door, and I became agitated. The old bat across the hall screamed that she would call the police, so I left. I flew to Pakistan the next day."

"Why did you get all worked up in the first place?"

"I received a message that Claudia did not want me to contact her again. At the time, I was livid." Tariq looked at his hands. "Later, I realized that the *message* was probably Tati's own creation."

"The same Tati who attacked me yesterday?"

"The same. I owe you a sincere apology for that, Lily. Padma told me all of the shameful details. To treat any guest in that way is inexcusable. To treat the sister of my . . . of my dearest friend in that manner is unforgivable." Tariq bowed his head, formally and respectfully.

"Tell Tati I'm up for a rematch anytime."

"You would have to travel to France if you wished that," said Tariq.

"France?"

"I sent her packing as soon as I arrived home."

"Because she attacked me?"

"There were several reasons. That was the most recent," Tariq said, folding his arms. "She meant nothing to me."

"So you kept her around because she had a physical resemblance to Claudia?"

Tariq looked out the window again before he answered. "If all that you can have is the shadow of the original, you tell yourself that is better than nothing at all."

21

Looking at my bruised face and scratched neck, I wondered where the real Lily had gone. Had I vanished when my sister disappeared? I wasn't sure what I was doing anymore, except getting myself into fights and trouble, both of which had always been Claudia's department. I felt a little more like myself when I started searching for information about Alexander Gorevale online. Claudia's one-eared china rabbit sat on the night table, keeping me company. The *New York Times* had printed an obituary.

Dr. Alexander W. Gorevale, a psychiatrist who disputed traditional notions of social roles and relationships and who contested popular methods of addiction therapy, died on September 28 at his home in Nyack, New York. He was 53.

The cause was myocardial infarction, which was caused by an adverse reaction to sildenafil citrate, according to local authorities. There were also traces of several mood-stabilizing drugs in his system.

Dr. Gorevale's theories briefly became popular with the publication of his first book, *Rising From the Ashes.* He wrote that entrenched family and societal roles inhibit the growth of an individual, preventing them from achieving their true potential by forcing them to corrupt their own natures with the expectations of others. Dr. Gorevale's provocative theories were overshadowed by his personal life. He was accused of sexual misconduct, and while the charge was dismissed, his reputation suffered when it was revealed that he had had a consensual sexual relationship with a patient. The ensuing scandal forced Dr. Gorevale to leave Gorevale House, the residential treatment facility he founded in Massachusetts. Dr. Gorevale's later books *The Triumph of the Individual* and *False Morality, False Promises* never equaled the popularity of his first. Dr. Gorevale was arrested in 2005 after a patient almost died while in a detoxification program under his supervision; he was later released after proving that his therapy was commonplace in Europe, but Dr. Gorevale had to pay a heavy fine to the State of Massachusetts and an undisclosed amount to the family of his patient. Dr. Gorevale's medical license was suspended for two years.

Alexander Gorevale was born in England. After a private-school education and Cambridge University, he opened his practice in London, later moving to Edinburgh, Dublin, Boston, Portland, Philadelphia, Baltimore, and New York. Dr. Gorevale, who described marriage as "government-sanctioned slavery," never married, nor did he have children. His will awarded his estate to Harvard University, with the stipulation that the school would name a prize for him. Harvard has not yet indicated whether it will accept the bequest.

I read it a couple of times, letting the facts sink in. So, Dr. Gorevale had been getting too close to some of his female patients. Perhaps that explained why he'd moved around more often than a pawn on a parkside chessboard. Typing *sildenafil citrate* into a search engine, I discovered it was a generic name for Viagra. Talk about those who lived by the sword dying by the sword. I reread the obituary. The list of places where he'd run his practice was longer than the jacket of the book had revealed. I took out the handwritten note again. *I hope that I shall always be with you, every step of your journey. You are forever in my heart, as I am in yours.* The phony bastard. How many patients had he pitched that line to?

My cell phone rang and a number appeared on the cracked screen. It was Martin, and I let him go to voice mail. I told myself that I wasn't ready to deal with him before noon, but that wasn't it. I could believe that Claudia had fallen for her therapist; the things I'd heard from Tariq, Rachel Heidegger, and Melissa Ardito all supported this. But Gorevale had died in September, and Claudia and Martin had been in touch after that. I didn't know what had happened between them, but the possibilities unsettled me.

E-mails from old friends in the newspaper business were trickling in, but they weren't anything I wanted to read. Jesse had told me that a local television news station had run a story about Claudia and the dead body found in her apartment. One particularly inept journalist wrote, "It's rare to get a suspect as attractive as your sister." I closed the laptop without responding.

There was no way I could wait any longer to wake Jesse. I had to talk with the only sane person I trusted completely. I made coffee for him, hoping that the combination of the aroma and the sunlight streaming in the window would get him up off the sofa, where he'd passed out after Tariq had gone. By the time I brought Jesse a cup, he was sitting with his head in his hands.

"Oh, what a beautiful mornin'," I teased. He grunted, which was about as much of a response as anyone ever got when he was in that state. "Do you want anything to eat?"

Grunt. I went back to the kitchen, chopped up some spinach and onion, tossed them into a skillet with eggs and feta and scrambled it together. "I'm too lazy to make an omelet," I explained, sliding a plate and a fork in front him. When I came back to the living room with my own plate and more juice, Jesse's breakfast had vanished.

I retrieved my laptop from the bedroom. "I know this probably isn't how you want to start your day, but have I got an obituary for you."

That got one eye open. "The shrink? What's his name?"

"Alexander Gorevale," I said, and slid the computer in front of him. It took Jesse a very long time to read the piece. I held my breath, tapping my foot against the sofa. "What do you think?"

"The ole coot OD'd on somethin'? Suspicious."

"He OD'd on Viagra."

"Holy moly." Jesse's eyes went round. "It's amazin' the creep never got himself a bullet between the eyes."

"Maybe this isn't poetic justice, but it's close."

"If he was dosin' up on Viagra, there musta been some girl around. Somethin' fishy about it." Jesse took a long swallow of coffee. "There's somethin' downright wrong about every angle in this thing. Your sister. Your ex. That girl who drowned in your sister's apartment."

"She didn't drown, remember?" I reminded him of what Bruxton had told me the night before.

"Doesn't change a thing," Jesse argued. "Makes it weirder. Like someone wanted it to look like Claudia was dead. You think Tariq killed that ole coot your sister hooked up with?"

"No."

"But you flat-out asked him if he did it," Jesse pointed out.

"It was just that Tariq sounded so happy about Gorevale

being dead." I hadn't told Jesse what Claudia had hinted at, how he might have killed someone in Pakistan. "Claudia and Tariq haven't been a couple in a long time. She dated other men. She lived with another guy and Tariq didn't shoot him or anything." If Gorevale had died violently, I would have suspected Tariq's hand in it, but there was no way he'd poisoned the shrink with Viagra.

"Okay, forget that theory." Jesse gulped more coffee. "Hold up, I've got another. Tariq's frantic about finding Claudia. What d'you think he'd do to that girl in the apartment if she refused to tell him where Claudia was?"

"He'd threaten her."

"Imagine Tariq and one of his goons showing up at your door? Maybe that's why she had a heart attack. Maybe she did die unexpectedly. Fine. But whoever sank her in the bathtub knew about your mama. That's a pretty short list of folks, but Tariq's on it."

I didn't want to lie to the cops. Not any more than I had, anyway. When I called Detective Renfrew on Wednesday morning, I said that I'd dropped by Claudia's last night and found the place a shambles, but I didn't mention the intruder. Then I told her about my sister's miscarriage and Mrs. Decarno's news. "Two men were at Claudia's apartment on New Year's Eve. Mrs. Decarno is such a witch, I wasn't sure if she mentioned it to you, but she saw them."

"Why doesn't it surprise me that she spends all day watching your sister's place through her peephole?" said Renfrew. "And no, she didn't tell us about that. We'll have to reinterview her." There was a pause. "When did she happen to mention this?"

"Last night. By the way, did you find Kaylee Quan yet?"

"We did, and we've been told we can only ask questions through her lawyer," Renfrew said. Bruxton would have probed harder for how I'd gotten the information. Renfrew seemed just as perceptive, but more willing to let small sins slide than her partner was. "Looks like they're circling the wagons for some reason."

"Can she do that? I mean, get away with not answering questions?"

"We cops don't like people to know this, but people don't actually have to talk to us," Renfrew said in a conspiratorial tone. "We can force the issue, but they have the right to have a lawyer do all their talking. We can't drag Kaylee Quan downtown, unless we arrest her."

"That's terrible."

"Sucks for us. By the way, we need you to come down to the station today. Want me to send a car?"

"That's okay, thanks. What's happened?"

"I think we've found something that belongs to your sister," Renfrew said. "We need you to identify it."

22

I dressed carefully to see the police again, choosing a blue vintage belted sweater and a gray pencil skirt. My new motto—when in distress, distract—was wearing thin. There was a bruise on my temple that crept out from my hairline, and I was a little too relieved to discover it could be mostly hidden under makeup. Apparently I didn't care what happened to me, as long as no one else knew. I put on the silver bangle from my father and pulled up my boots and trudged back to the Lower East Side with a heavy heart. It was a cold day with a biting wind and I kept having to stop and turn my face back from it, or else it actually made my eyes well up with tears. By the time I got to the police station on Pitt Street, I was sure I was a mascara-streaked mess. I'd planned to stop in the foyer and fix myself up before I went upstairs, but Bruxton was there, dragging on a cigarette in front of the door.

"Look what the cat dragged in," he drawled. The sunlight accented his harsh edges but showed them to his advantage. We hadn't parted on the best of terms the night before, but I appreciated him coming clean with me, even if I still resented him.

"Your charm never wears thin," I said. The corner of his mouth twitched and he offered me a cigarette. I hesitated for a moment before accepting. With everything that was going on, having the occasional one couldn't be that bad.

Bruxton gave me a hard once-over after he gave me a light. "How'd you get that bruise?"

"Bruise?" I wiped under my eyes. "It's probably mascara. The wind is making me tear up."

"No, this." He touched my temple so tenderly I stepped back in surprise.

"I was sleepwalking and I tripped," I improvised. "Does it look bad?"

"Not terrible. You sleepwalk a lot?"

"Only when I'm under stress." He gave me a strange look but dropped the subject. It was a lie I had a lot of experience telling, after all. The marks and bruises I got from my mother had to be explained when I went to school. Sleepwalking? One teacher was so skeptical that she called child services, but after talking to a credulous counselor who assured me that it was not unusual at all to have developed sleep problems after my father died, I realized I had an ironclad excuse. Only those closest to me knew I rarely managed to get into a deep sleep.

"You want coffee?" Bruxton asked. We walked to the cart on the corner. "My partner told me old lady Decarno's news." His tone was casual. "How'd you happen to hear it?"

"I saw her yesterday. I just assumed you knew, but it hit me this morning that she might not have mentioned it. She's kind of evil." I sipped my coffee. I'd forgotten how well coffee and cigarettes went together.

"Did that thought hit you the same time you got that bruise?"

"Very funny. Did you talk to her yet?"

"No, but we will." Bruxton took a long drag. "You know, there are a couple ways we can play this."

"What do you mean?"

Bruxton exhaled plumes of smoke and gave me a dark look. "I spend all day listening to perps and witnesses bullshitting me. Then I've got to deal with the DA's office, which is worse again with its stupid fucking politics. Now I've got you feeding me this line of crap. If you're going to lie to my face, put some thought into it first, okay?"

"Sorry," I said in a small voice.

"Look, I get it. You want to protect your little sister. You've been doing that your whole life. There are things you won't tell me because you never tell anyone the full story. You'd rather keep it locked up. But don't tell me a bald-faced lie and think I'll be fine with that."

"Okay."

"Okay," he responded. We stood silently looking at each other.

"Renfrew said you'd found something of Claudia's?"

Bruxton nodded. "Let's go upstairs." He took a last drag on his cigarette. We tossed the butts on the sidewalk and walked back to the door. "You want to tell me how you really got that bruise?"

"No," I said.

He held the door for me and we went upstairs without another word.

Renfrew had been understating matters when she'd said they had *something* of Claudia's. Arrayed on a table in the interrogation room was a series of objects in clear plastic bags. There was the pink iPod, a pair of diamond stud earrings, silver trinkets with an identifiable Tiffany & Co hallmark, and what I took for a two-carat princess-cut diamond ring. There was also a prescription for something called "lorazepam," with Claudia's name on the label. "I don't think any of this belongs to Claudia, except the pills," I said, picking up the bag that contained them. The vial was dated last June. The prescribing physician was Alexander Gorevale. For a moment I felt like hunting him down and strangling him, and then I remembered he was already dead. No wonder Claudia had told her friend Rachel that she didn't want me to find out about him.

"But these things were all sitting in her apartment just the other day, right?" asked Renfrew.

I nodded. "Where did you find them?"

"A creep with a long rap sheet took them to the wrong fence. I know you're familiar with the name Malcolm Sabado. He was on the list of your sister's associates you gave us, and you said you'd seen him on the street."

"He had all this?" I stared at the table. My face was burning. Demented as it sounded, I'd been hoping that it had been my sister who'd hit me with the closet door. That would have indicated she was close by, which would have meant something to me, however tenuous our connection had become. Instead, I'd inadvertently covered up for a drug dealer, little Mal Sabado, several inches shorter than Claudia or me, with bones as delicate as a girl's. What an idiot I was.

Renfrew was quietly sympathetic as I spilled the story to her. She took copious notes. "CSU is printing the apartment again," she said. "I'll make sure they do the closet door."

She left the room for a few minutes and I put my head into my hands. My temple was throbbing under the bruise. I could picture Mal's face when I'd seen him. *Maybe she moved?* he'd asked me with that creepy little grin of his. I'd confirmed that she hadn't. I may as well have escorted him to her apartment and let him root around. You could never trust a junkie, I knew that; the craving for a fix was never far from their minds, and that need superseded all others. I rested my fingers on the silver bangle on my wrist. Claudia knew how much it meant to me, but that hadn't mattered to her.

"You want some more coffee?" Renfrew asked when she came back. I shook my head. "I keep meaning to mention that I love that bracelet. You're always wearing it."

"It was a gift from my father." It was dawning on me that the woman missed nothing. She had seen the bracelet when she first went to the apartment, when it was sitting on the scarred top of the dresser in the bedroom, and then it had appeared on my wrist. I unclasped it and handed it to her. "There's an inscription."

" 'For Lily, With Love Always, Dad,' " she read aloud. "It's a beauty. Nice to have a memento like that from your dad." She handed it back to me, then reached behind her neck, unclasping a necklace and handing it to me. It was a gold heart the size of a quarter and just as flat. I turned it over. The engraving read "Straight Shooter." "My dad gave it to me when I joined the NYPD. He was a cop, too."

"It's lovely." I returned it to her. "He must be so proud of you."

Renfrew grimaced as she reclasped the chain. She was wearing a teal blue pantsuit today with a dove gray blouse, and the heart pendant disappeared beneath the neckline. "He died a long time ago." She shook her head sadly. "But yeah, he was proud. He wanted my brother to be a cop, too, but Ben went to law school instead. Pop never forgave him for that. It was up to me to keep up the family tradition."

"Once a daddy's girl, always a daddy's girl." I smiled at her.

"Like the song goes, my heart belongs to Daddy. Not that I don't love my mom, too. Without her watching my boys when they're not in school, I'd be toast."

I felt a pang of envy. I'd never been able to count on my

mother. My phone rang just then, and I fished for it under the papers I'd taken from Claudia's apartment the night before. ARSON DESTROYS HISTORIC CHURCH. It was Martin, yet again.

"My ex," I said, obliquely explaining why I wasn't answering the call. I immediately regretted introducing the topic. Talking about Martin and his reasons for being in touch with Claudia was painful enough with Jesse. I liked Renfrew, but I wasn't going to unload the saga on her. I'd had too many confidences betrayed by female friends to let down my guard easily again. "Can I ask you about a rehab center called 'Idylhaven'?" I said quickly. "Detective Bruxton mentioned it last night, and I heard from a friend of Claudia's that she'd been there twice last year."

"This friend have a name?" We were back on familiar footing. I told Renfrew what Tariq had relayed to me. What the police had found roughly matched his story: Claudia had gone to Idylhaven in April and again in September. Both times she had checked herself out. Since she hadn't been ordered to the center by a court, she was free to come and go as she pleased.

"Here's one thing that struck us funny," said Renfrew. "Claudia checked herself out on September twenty-ninth. Then she rents a car on September thirtieth and drives it to Newark, New Jersey, where she drops it off at the airport."

"Wait a minute. Where did she stay on the night of the twenty-ninth if she wasn't at Idylhaven?"

"The same question occurred to us. We've called every hotel and motel and bed-and-breakfast they've got up there—and there are plenty—but we haven't found anything."

"Did she take a flight on the thirtieth?" My sister hated planes, but maybe she'd gotten over that.

"Nope. And she doesn't have a passport—we checked—so she hasn't left the country, unless she's gone to Puerto Rico or Guam. Your sister seems to have developed the ability to vanish at will."

I bit my lip. Claudia was street-smart, but she was never a planner. She went on impulse, crashing from one misadventure to the next. There was no way she was doing this alone. While I disliked Tariq, I believed that he was as worried about my sister as I was. Since he wasn't helping her, that left one major suspect: Martin.

23

Before I left the police station, Renfrew made me promise not to go into Claudia's apartment until the Crime Scene Unit was finished. "And no more trips alone at night," she warned. I got the message. After making a brief detour to the Essex Street Market, always one of my favorite spots in the neighborhood, I returned to my old building. Mr. Pete was on the stoop, a bottle of window cleaner in one hand and a gray cloth in the other. The building was run-down, no doubt about that, but Mr. Pete insisted on keeping it as shiny and clean as possible.

"Miss Lily!" he said, grinning at me. "So good you back. Pretty flowers!"

I'd picked up a colorful bouquet at Essex Farm, and a box of truffles from Roni-Sue. That was the least I could do for Sarah. I had to thank her for helping me the night before.

"Detective Norah find sister yet?" Mr. Pete asked.

"Not yet."

He nodded. "Police slow. They here all the time. Questions, questions. Upstairs now."

"I know. Detective Norah told me they're in the apartment."

"Yes, yes," said Mr. Pete. Something caught his eye and he waved. I looked around and saw a nondescript, dark-haired man on the other side of the street. He glanced over his shoulder at us and walked away. Mr. Pete squinted after him. "Distant vision not so good. Maybe he not detective."

"I guess you've had a lot of cops come through here now."

"No, not cop. Gregory Robinson, private investigator. Like Magnum PI."

"Wait, private investigator?"

Mr. Pete nodded. "Miss Loretta call me to complain. Yesterday, man knock on door, won't go away. I go up. I make him show ID."

It took me a moment to remember that Miss Loretta was Mrs. Decarno. "Did you find out anything else about him?"

Mr. Pete rattled off an address in midtown. I wrote it down, amazed at how good his memory still was. I wondered who Robinson was working for, and what he was doing sniffing around the building.

"Video camera fixed," Mr. Pete announced. "This morning. No good for building not to have."

I thanked Mr. Pete and walked up the stairs. When I got to Claudia's door I paused, listening to the heavy footsteps inside. It seemed like a harmless thing to do, but I realized I was mimicking Mrs. Decarno, whom I thought of as a spider. I smoothed my skirt and walked on.

Sarah answered her door wearing a black angora sweater and winter-white wool trousers with black suede pumps. At her throat was a necklace of gleaming pearls that I took for the real thing. I thought of myself as someone who loved clothes, but I realized I was at the foot of a true master. "You look like you're going out," I said quickly. "I just wanted to say thank you for last night."

"They're lovely." Sarah took the bouquet from my extended hand. "That is so thoughtful of you, Lily. You didn't have to do a thing." She smiled at me. Last night's adventure wasn't showing on her. "Won't you come in?"

"Thank you." I stepped inside and shrugged off my coat, which Sarah hung in the closet. Her apartment faced Rivington, but it didn't get much more light than my sister's. All of these old tenements dwelled permanently in the shade.

"Can I get you a drink?" Sarah asked.

"I don't want to be any more trouble."

"You're not." She smiled at me sweetly. "Make yourself at home. I'll be right back." She disappeared with the bouquet.

I set the bag from Roni-Sue on the glass-topped table and looked around the room. Mrs. Felesky had filled it with colorful memorabilia from her days as a showgirl, with every flat surface covered by framed photographs. Sarah's apartment was stylish black-and-white Spartan. There was little furniture, and nothing on the walls except for a pair of mirrors in etched Venetian glass. I remembered sitting in a clear Lucite chair the night before; now that I was no longer dazed, I realized Sarah had a pair of Louis Ghost chairs, the famous Philippe Starck design that replicated the silhouette of a Louis XVI design. Everything in the room was opulent but understated, much like Sarah herself. I'd wondered why someone who could afford an Hermès Birkin bag lived in such a down-at-the-heel building, but I understood as I looked around. Sarah had impeccable taste but limited funds, and she knew how to spend money for maximum effect. It hit me, just before she came back in, that there were no bookshelves and no books.

"I hope that you'll enjoy this, Lily," she said, handing me a faceted crystal tumbler filled with clear liquid.

I took a drink. "Coconut water? I love it." I'd first tasted coconut water when I'd visited Trinidad. In New York, most people thought that I was asking for coconut milk, which was entirely different. "I haven't had this since I moved to Spain."

"I discovered it while on holiday in Trinidad," Sarah said. "Believe it or not, Fresh Direct delivers it now."

"Trinidad? That's where I discovered it, too." My bracelet clinked against the glass as I took another drink. As I glanced at the silver bangle, with its distinctive Celtic scrollwork, I wondered if Sarah recognized it from Claudia's apartment. I was sure she thought I'd simply taken it, and I felt a sudden urge to explain, as I had to Renfrew, that it was mine all along.

"Would you like to sit down?" Sarah asked, gesturing to one of the Louis Ghost chairs. "Oh, you brought chocolates, too? Thank you, Lily."

"I was just admiring your apartment," I said as I settled into a chair.

"Most of what I own is sitting in boxes in California. I came out here on a whim and I haven't decided how long I'm staying. But it's important to surround yourself with beauty, wherever you are, don't you think? I'm so glad you stopped by." She smiled at me again. "I wanted to apologize for something last night. I became so upset when I found that paper . . . that your sister had . . . that she'd had . . ."

She couldn't seem to say the word. "A miscarriage?"

"Yes." Sarah looked relieved that I'd let the word into the air. "I saw that page and it just brought me back . . . I never tell people this but . . . I've had three miscarriages. I was never able to carry a child to term."

I gasped. My mother had had three miscarriages, and I'd always believed those tragedies were puzzle pieces that explained her instability and her drinking. My sister had suffered a miscarriage that sent her into a downward spiral. I felt an instant rush of sympathy for Sarah. "I'm so sorry. That's awful."

Sarah took a sip of juice. "I often wonder how different my life would be if I'd had a child."

I didn't know what to say. When I was young I used to dream about having a big family, enough children to fill a house and block out memories of the past. But I'd become more realistic since then. What sort of genes would I be passing along to my children? Would they have paranoid delusions, like my mother? Would they be prone to addiction, like Claudia? Still, when Martin and I had had a pregnancy scare a couple of years ago, he'd been so affectionate and tender that he'd almost revived my fantasy about family life. When a doctor informed me that I wasn't pregnant after all, I was relieved but Martin had been forlorn. He had genuinely wanted to have a child with me.

"I might not have ended up divorced," Sarah said. "I know, it's silly to think that way. What's past is past. But sometimes I wonder. Do you ever feel like that?"

"I've been wondering lately if I made a mistake in breaking off my engagement," I admitted. Knowing that Sarah had experienced the same trauma my mother had—worse, really, since she'd never had a child—made me feel oddly close to her. "I felt like I couldn't trust my fiancé, but since then it isn't like I've met anyone else I could trust, either." My disastrous attempts at dating in the past year had made Martin seem, if not like a knight in shining armor, then at least one who hadn't been too badly tarnished. His occasional trips to Spain reminded me of what I missed about him, and made it easy to overlook the dents and scratches he'd accumulated over the years.

"That sounds like my former husband. He had an affair. Actually, he'd had many silly little affairs over the years, but I never minded that. We had this ideal of an open relationship. We were free to see other people if we wished, but we belonged to each other." Sarah stared out the window, but her mind wasn't on the things in front of her eyes. "Only this one affair was different. It was as if he'd discovered his grand *amour*, the old fool." There was a catch in her voice. The subject clearly stirred up a lot of emotions.

"Did you know the woman he had the affair with?"

"No. It was someone he knew from work."

"Did he end up marrying her?" I couldn't resist asking.

"No. I believe she ended up dumping him."

"My fiancé had an affair with a woman he worked with," I blurted out. "At least, I think he did. He lied about business trips with her. I don't know. He's always denied it, and the woman is married to someone else now."

Sarah looked my face over carefully, then took a tiny sip from her glass. "Was it all a misunderstanding? You might still work things out."

"I don't think that's possible. I think . . ." For a second I hesitated, then plunged in. "I'm wondering if he might have had some kind of . . . relationship . . . with my sister." I'd wanted to talk about this so badly, but I had no one else to say the words to. Jesse hated Martin, so he couldn't be sympathetic, and I didn't have anyone else to confide in. I'd always felt unfairly judged when people found out about my screwed-up family. Since college, I'd kept the past to myself, only offering that my parents had died in an accident when I was young. The only person I'd opened up to was Martin.

Sarah's eyes were wide with shock. "But . . . Lily . . . would she do that?"

"Before Claudia disappeared, she called him and asked for money. He admits that much. He says they talked on the phone a couple of times, but that she never picked up the check."

"You think they had more contact than that?"

I nodded.

"Would your sister really do that to you, Lily? It's . . . well, it's awful if it's true."

"Claudia was always coming on to him. She tried to sit in his lap . . . she came out of the shower and dropped her towel . . ."

Sarah's eyes stared at me with genuine horror. "She did that?"

"Claudia acted like it was some big joke, but she flung herself over him." Talking about it made the memory more vivid, and it made me angrier.

"That rotten bitch," Sarah hissed. She put her hand over her mouth. "I'm so sorry, Lily, I shouldn't have said that. Ever since my husband . . . well, let's just say, I find it difficult to be sympathetic to, shall we say, the other woman."

"I know what you mean." I took a long swallow of coconut water and tried to compose myself.

"How did your fiancé react to what your sister did?" Sarah asked.

"He was uncomfortable. He wasn't interested in her, at least not then, anyway."

"Is there a chance she's hiding out at his home, or that he knows where she is now?"

"I don't think so. He seems anxious to find her. He even suggested that we . . ." Hire a private detective. Duh. It hit me suddenly who Gregory Robinson's employer might be. If Mr. Pete was right about his address, Robinson's office was a couple of blocks east of Martin's.

"Lily?"

"He wanted to hire a private detective. I just realized, he may already have gone ahead and done that." Actually, if the detective was nosing around the building yesterday, that meant Martin had hired him before we talked at the flamenco bar.

"But that would be a positive thing, Lily, wouldn't it? You have to find Claudia. I mean, the real Claudia. It's the strangest thing, I feel like I know her even though we've never met."

"I know. Everything about this situation is strange."

"There's something that's been bothering me," Sarah continued. "The woman who called herself Claudia knew all sorts of things that turned out to be true. I knew about you, that you were a journalist and living in Spain. I knew that your mother died . . . well, in a very tragic way." She put her manicured hand over mine and squeezed for a second. "This girl knew all sorts of things about your sister. How did she know? What was the connection between them?"

"I don't know," I admitted. "No one seems to."

"But they *had* to have known each other," said Sarah. "There has to be something that the police are missing. If you can find that connection, you'll find your sister."

24

Once I started looking for the man following me, he wasn't hard to spot. I caught sight of him in the reflection of a shop window, then again, after zigzagging a few blocks and pulling out my lipstick case on the street. He stared at me in the reflection over my right shoulder, then feigned interest in the cars on the street when I turned around. His appearance was unremarkable. He wasn't particularly tall and he had an average build. He was white, his coat was black, and he was wearing jeans.

I walked alternately north and east. Stopping at the Strand Book Store at Broadway and Twelfth Street, I fingered the well-used paperbacks that sat on shelves outside, even in winter. The man stood across the street from me, waited a bit, then went around the corner. When I moved around the block he reappeared. How did I shake off a professional stalker? If I pointed him out to a cop, what evidence did I have? The man was always at least half a block away from me, and I was sure that he'd be able to feign surprise and pretend that I was the crazy one. Assuming that he was working alone, I needed to find a building with multiple exits. That wasn't as easy as it sounded. Several stores had entrances on both the north-south avenue and the east-west street, but all you had to do was stand at the corner and you could watch both.

My anger and frustration were mounting. Why was I running away from him? I made a 180-degree turn and headed

straight for my shadow. I was close enough to catch his startled frown before he darted across the street mid-block. After
a taxi passed, I followed him. He glanced over his shoulder
and I almost smiled; this wasn't what he'd bargained for.
Finally, he decided to make his stand in front of a store
window, staring into it fervently as if hoping I'd pass by, so
I could be the target again.

"Hey, Gregory!" I called loudly as I came up to him.
"How'd you get out of jail?" A couple of passers-by turned
their heads to look at us.

"You've mistaken me for—" he started to say, but I was
just getting started.

"I can't believe they'd let a child molester out of jail," I
yelled. "How many kids have you attacked since you got out,
Gregory? Are you still going after little girls, or are you going after little boys, too?"

People were stopping in their tracks and craning their necks
to watch the show now. Gregory put up his hands. "Look, I'm
not—"

"You are a disgusting excuse for a human being! I can't
believe any court would let a child molester like you go free."

There was an angry murmur rippling through the crowd.
A young woman pulled her little boy back. "You keep away
from people like that, you hear me? That is a bad man."

"You're crazy, just like your little sister," snapped Gregory. "You should get your head examined."

I could feel the blood draining from my face. His poor
choice of words didn't even register until a stocky man with
a clean-shaven head stepped forward. "What did you do to
her little sister?"

Gregory turned away but found his exit blocked. When he
turned back the bald man punched him square in the jaw.

Gregory went down like a flyweight against a heavyweight champ. Then a woman stepped forward and kicked him in the ribs. She was wearing Uggs, which probably cushioned the blow, but still, it had to hurt. I stood there, staring at the angry mob, now more guilty than elated.

"Look, cops!" I called. People's heads looked around and the crowd dispersed. The man who'd punched Gregory ran down Broadway. I ducked into the subway, thinking that had worked a little too well. But as angry as I was at the private investigator, that was nothing compared to how I felt about Martin.

I'm sorry, but he's in a meeting and he can't be disturbed," the secretary said, her voice sharp enough to cut glass.

"He's going to be disturbed if I don't get to talk to him right now." The office was quiet and my voice seemed vulgar and loud. The room, from its black-and-white carpet and the steel-blue walls, to its lacquered black desk and gray sofas, whispered a kind of subdued, masculine glamour. I knew I was out of place, but I didn't care.

"You can't simply show up and think he'll be able to rearrange his schedule—"

"Just let him know I'm here."

"You'll simply have to wait."

"Fine," I answered, but instead of sitting down, I went for the door behind her and rushed down the corridor. I hadn't been in the building in some time, but the layout hadn't changed. My boots clacked on the gray marble floor, and I could hear the secretary's heels before she said anything.

"You can't!" she called. "I'm calling security!"

No one tried to grab me. This was a hive of private offices, and many of the doors were shut. You could have yelled *"Fire"* and this crowd wouldn't have come running, unless there was money to be made. I was faster than the secretary, or maybe she just didn't want to catch up with the crazy lady. Either way, I got to the corner office, opened the door, and stepped inside.

Martin regarded me with a mix of bewilderment and bemusement. "Well, this is a surprise." Into the speakerphone, he said, "I'm sorry, gentlemen, but I'm being called away. You'll have to wrap this up without me." I heard a German-accented voice and another accent I didn't recognize thanking him, then Martin cut the connection.

"I'm so sorry, Mr. Sklar," said the secretary as she rushed in, panting. "I tried . . . to stop her . . . but she wouldn't—"

"Lily is a dear friend. If she didn't live in Spain you'd be used to seeing her in this office, and you'd know she's an unstoppable force."

With a bumbling apology, the secretary went out the door, head low, pulling it closed with the softest click behind her.

Martin stood up. He was wearing a double-breasted gray suit with a dark blue shirt, French cuffs cinched by ladybug cuff links. His playful side was in full view, and there was no hint of the weariness and frustration of the night before. "May I take your coat?" He made a point of looking me over. "You look absolutely beautiful. Are you bored senseless hearing that?" He kissed me, aiming for my mouth but getting my cheek. For once, my body didn't betray me to him.

"You need to work harder on your lines. Try for something original."

"Will you sit down while I rack my poor brain for inspiration?"

"Don't go to the trouble. I'm here to get the answer to one question. Why did you hire a private investigator to look for Claudia?"

Martin looked surprised. "I thought you'd be pleased, Lily. I told you last night I would do anything I could to help. I meant it."

"When I saw you last night, you'd already hired an investigator. Gregory Robinson. He went to my sister's building yesterday. Or are you going to claim you didn't hire him?"

"I hired him," said Martin. "I don't see what the problem is. I wanted to do something to help you, and I thought this would. I've used Gregory's firm many times in the past. They're good at what they do. I trust him."

"Is following me part of his job description?"

"Of course not. Why would it be?"

"He was shadowing me today," I said. "He followed me to Claudia's building. Mr. Pete recognized him. Then he chased after me when I left."

"That's completely inexcusable. I would never have imagined Gregory's firm doing such a ridiculous thing. They normally do good work for me, but this . . ." Martin's annoyance seemed genuine. He was all about the big picture, not the details, and I realized that even though he'd hired Robinson, he probably hadn't discussed tactics. "I'll call them immediately. I promise you it won't happen again."

"The point is, why did you suggest hiring a private investigator last night when you'd already gone ahead and done it? And why didn't you tell me?"

"Lily, sweetheart, I want you to sit down. Are you all right?" He looked at me more closely. "Did someone hit you? You have a bruise on your forehead. I think I should call a doctor."

"Stop pretending to humor me!" I said, raising my voice. I went to the window and stared down. From fifty stories up, midtown Manhattan looked like an ant colony. People scurried around in predictable patterns, a dance similar to what Martin and I were doing now. As much as I wanted him to hold me and tell me that everything would be all right, I knew I couldn't believe him. I had to stand my ground. "Why did you hire the private detective, Martin?" I asked, turning around.

"I wanted to help. What else can I say?"

"You can tell me the truth about why you're so interested in finding Claudia."

Martin's brow furrowed. "She's your sister."

"I'm supposed to believe that . . . that you're doing this because . . . of *me*?"

"Of course. Why else would I?"

"I think you've got your own agenda. You want to find her for your own reasons."

Martin's mouth tightened. When he spoke, there was anger simmering in his voice, but it was at a low boil, controlled. "Think about it. What *agenda* could I possibly have?"

"I don't know. But I'm going to find out."

"You're upset, sweetheart. I know that. This is too much for you to deal with on your own, and you know what I think of the police. Tell me how you got that bruise."

"You're changing the topic." I stared at him, my whole body quivering. "You are hiding something, and I'm going to find out what it is. You're looking for Claudia for some reason of your own."

"Your sister is nothing but a scheming lowlife!" Under his tan, Martin's face reddened. "Why would I care about finding her?"

"Because you're having an affair with her!"

We were both still for a moment, the words hanging in the air between us.

"You think I'm having . . . an affair . . . with her?"

"Yes," I said, in a small voice. "Are you?"

Martin stared at me for a moment, as his expression relaxed, shock easing into relief. "Lily. Lily, you dummy. How could you even think . . ." He laughed and shook his head in obvious amusement. If he was acting, he was giving the performance of a lifetime. "Me, with *her*? Are you serious?" He closed the distance between us and put his hands on my shoulders. "Has hell frozen over?"

"Claudia was always coming on to you. That time she sat in your lap . . . and the time she—"

"Lily." Martin stroked my face. "Anything she ever did, I told you about it. I feel sorry for her, because she's your sister, but I wouldn't stand in the same room with her otherwise."

"You've called her. The police showed me the phone records from the apartment. You were calling her almost every day last March."

"Is this a joke?" asked Martin. "Last March, when I went to London, Prague, and Istanbul, then attended the Maastricht Art Fair, and *then* spent a week in Madrid trying to convince you to come home? I wasn't in New York for more than four days last March."

He was right. I'd been so upset I wasn't thinking straight. The police had to be mistaken, even if I didn't understand how. "Then why are you so determined to find Claudia?" I was trying not to sniffle, and failing.

"I would do anything to lure you back. Don't you have any idea how I feel about you?"

I was in danger of getting caught up in a tidal wave of old emotions, and it terrified me. "I think you lied to me about her phone call."

Martin froze for a second. "Lied?"

"There was more said than you told me."

"Lily." He pulled me so close that I could feel the warmth of his breath on my face. "I didn't tell you everything she said, but only because I didn't see the point."

"What did Claudia say?"

Martin sighed. "She said she'd always been attracted to me and . . ."

"What?"

"She said she could do things in bed that you wouldn't even be able to imagine doing."

Claudia, that little rodent. When I found her, I was going to wring her rotten little neck. "What else?" I asked.

"Please don't make me repeat it all. It would make me blush." He pulled me closer. "Tell me you miss me. You're in my mind all day and night." He kissed me, gently at first, then hard and demanding. I put my arms around his neck and he backed me against the desk, pulling up my pencil skirt so that I could wrap my legs around his waist. When someone knocked on the door, we ignored it, and they eventually went away.

25

"You have to come with me tonight," Martin murmured when it started to get dark outside. "There's a business dinner in Boston. I can't believe I have to go, but I do." He was nuzzling my forehead and holding me close. One thing I'd always found endearing about Martin was that he never wanted to roll over and sleep after sex; he longed to talk and kiss and stay entangled, as if he'd forgotten where he ended and I began.

"You can't be serious." My eyes were shut and I felt too drowsy and sated to move. We were in bed at the Artemesion, Martin's midtown hotel, four blocks from his office. We'd rushed there after our shameless romp in his office and taken a suite. It wasn't normally the kind of place that rented by the hour.

"I know it's terrible timing, sweetheart, but I have to go. I'm building a hotel there. It's a quick trip, just dinner tonight and a breakfast meeting. We'll be home by noon tomorrow, I promise. We'll pick up a dress and shoes for you at Bergdorf's on the way to the airport. Please, Lily?"

"Martin, I'm trying to find my sister. I can't just run away with you." Of course, that was basically what I'd done that afternoon. I opened my eyes and started to sit up.

He lifted himself on one elbow. "I'm being an insensitive oaf again, aren't I?" He touched my face, kissed me, then reached for a champagne flute on the bedside table. "It's just, why worry about her? She has her life and you have yours." He drained the glass. "Sad as I was when you went off to Spain instead of marrying me, I was glad you cut her loose. She's a vampire who'll drain the life out of you."

"She's my sister. She's the only family I have." I reached for my own glass.

"If you married me, you'd have a family," Martin said. "You would have me and Ridley, and the children we would have together." He kissed me again. "Think about it."

"I will."

"I need to take a quick shower. You're not going to leave yet, are you?"

"You think I'm going to run out while you're in the shower?" I couldn't help but smile. "There's an idea."

"Don't you dare," he said, kissing me gently. "You've run away from me too many times already. One day I'll tie you down, and you'll never leave again." He got out of bed and went into the bathroom, not bothering to close the door.

I sat, sipping champagne, listening to water beating against the tile of the shower; there was no city noise up here. The suite was opulently bland, bedecked in safe beiges and sandy tones. The only interesting thing about it were the framed black-and-white photographs of towering Greek and Roman ruins. Not one was of the remains of the real Artemesion, the temple to Artemis that was one of the Seven Wonders of the ancient world; I'd seen it myself on Turkey's Aegean coast, and I knew there was nothing left of it but a lone, fractured column with goats and geese grazing in the surrounding grass. Why would a visitor to New York want to see photos from another continent on the wall, anyway? I obviously understood nothing about the hotel business, even though I'd written about it for years.

Martin's cell phone buzzed. He'd left it on the nightstand, apologizing that if his lawyer called about Ridley, he would have to answer. I looked at the screen and saw *Robinson Investigations* in bold letters. That wasn't about his son. I felt an echo of my fury when I'd realized that I was being followed. After the buzzing died, I scrolled through Martin's call log. My own name and number came up repeatedly, as did Robinson Investigations and Gene Kressler, his lawyer. *Bloom* came up, and I remembered that it was the florist's that Martin liked; I was disappointed that I hadn't seen the flowers before Jesse disposed of them. There were names I didn't know, but their numbers gave away their locations in London and Istanbul and Tel Aviv and Hong Kong; hotel business, I guessed. And then there was a name I recognized. It came up so quickly that I went past it and had to scroll back, just as I heard Martin turning off the water. Kaylee Quan. Why would Martin call her? I forced myself to put the phone down, but I wasn't fast enough. "Did someone call?" Martin asked from the doorway.

"It wasn't your lawyer," I said. "Something called 'Robinson Investigations.'"

"Thanks." He disappeared briefly, but I knew he wouldn't leave me alone with his phone again. As he came back into the bedroom, a towel wrapped around his waist, I slipped out of bed and started to dress. "Great view," he said.

Pulling on my skirt, I turned toward the window. It had a privacy screen so that we could see the city lights, but the city couldn't catch a glimpse of us. I was glad the room was dark so he couldn't see my eyes. "It's beautiful."

"I mean you, Lily. The city's a distant second." He reached for me but I stepped away, pretending to focus on belting my sweater. The rejection didn't faze him. He came up behind me as I stood in front of a mirror and wrapped his arms around me. "I don't want you to leave," he whispered. "I'm afraid if you do, you'll never come back."

I could see our reflections in the mirror, dark silhouettes obscured by the bright city. It was strange that neither of us wanted to turn on the lights in the room. It was as if we were each determined to keep the other in the dark.

When I arrived at Jesse's, there was a note for me, in his loopy handwriting, that read *Studio—back by 7.* It was a relief that he wasn't there. Jesse was the sharpest person I knew and he'd figure out, sooner or later, that something was very wrong.

I was tempted to call Kaylee Quan; I'd memorized her number and typed it into my phone as soon as I left Martin and got into the hotel's elevator. What was he doing, calling her? Quan was stonewalling the police, and I knew she'd hang up on me once she heard who I was. As I paced around Jesse's, I wished I had a cigarette. I took a shower and reapplied my makeup, trying to cover that stubborn bruise and thinking all the while about what to do. Quan was someone I needed to see in person. I put her number into a reverse-lookup directory and came up empty. All the detectives had said was that she worked out at the same health club as Claudia's impostor. Wait, that was it. The credit card bills listed Sinotique Health Club & Spa, next to an exorbitant charge. I typed the club's name into Google, pressed return, and pulled a black dress over my head; Sinotique's address was on the screen before I'd zipped up the back. The club was all of seven blocks from Jesse's building. I looked at the clock. It was just after six-thirty, prime workout time for New York gym rats. I pulled on my boots and coat and headed out the door. Too impatient to wait for the elevator, I took the stairs down and escaped into the cold night air.

Would you be able to page her?" I asked the receptionist. "I hate to bother you, but Kaylee forgot to sign this before she left the office, and we could lose our biggest client."

The receptionist chewed her gum and looked worried. "I'm really not supposed to page members unless it's, like, life and death, you know?"

"I understand. It's just that Kaylee will probably kill me, and everybody else in the office, if this doesn't get signed."

We went back and forth like that for a minute. I'd just convinced her to page Kaylee, when a tall, willowy Asian woman in a severe black suit swept by. "Oh, there she is," the receptionist said, relief in her voice. "Mrs. Quan!"

The woman glanced in her direction and chose to ignore her. Her cell phone was up to her ear, but she wasn't speaking into it.

"Thanks so much," I said. My boots clattered on tile as I ran after the woman. "Kaylee!" I called once we were outside.

She turned to stare at me. "Do I know you?" Her irritation was palpable.

"I'm Lily." I put my hand forward. "It's nice to finally meet you. You were a friend of my sister's."

"Your sister's?"

"Claudia Moore."

Kaylee took two steps back. "Stay away from me or I'll have you arrested. Leave me alone. I mean it." She turned and stormed away. I stared after her, wondering what my next move could possibly be.

26

Jesse made his best attempt at cheering me up that night. He pulled together a group of our old friends and dragged me to dinner with them at Rosa Mexicano, a raucous restaurant west of Union Square. It was the sort of place you had to shout to be heard, but no one seemed to mind. I downed three pomegranate margaritas and tried to forget what I knew. It didn't help that Sinotique was two blocks away, a reminder of my abject failure to find out anything about my sister's whereabouts.

After we hugged our friends good-bye, Jesse and I were left alone for the first time all evening. "You want to stroll on back to the ole homestead? It's cold out but I need to walk off some tortilla chips."

"Sure."

"What's up? I couldn't ask much at supper, Lil, but you owe me. What happened today?" He knew all about Mal Sabado stealing valuables from Claudia's—I'd told people about that at dinner—but nothing about where I'd spent my afternoon. I wasn't ready to tell him about Martin and face his furious reaction. Instead, I told him about my visit with Sarah.

"She's bang on about there bein' a connection between your sister and that impostor. That woman knew all about your folks, right? So your sis had to have spilled her guts to her."

It bothered me that the police still didn't know who the

woman was. She didn't fit the description of any missing person in their databases, and so far the facial recognition software had failed to match her photo. "There *has* to be something in that apartment. Whoever that woman was, she must have had her own ID when she got there." I looked at my watch; it was just after eleven. "Do you want to come with me? Renfrew made me promise not to go over on my own at night."

"Woohoo. I'd love to escort you, ma'am." Jesse turned to the street. "Taxi!" A yellow cab stopped, as if on cue.

"I thought you wanted exercise. It's not that cold," I complained as we got in.

"Sure, for somebody who used to live in Buffalo. It's freezin' out. I'll get to the gym tomorrow." Jesse pulled the door shut behind him. He gave the cabbie my old address and explained the best way to get there; the Lower East Side was more awkward than most Manhattan neighborhoods for cars to navigate. Jesse chatted with the cabbie for most of the ride. I'd never met anyone like my friend. He could get the notoriously nasty cashiers at Duane Reade to smile at him. By the time we arrived at the building, we'd heard all about the man's family in Bangalore. "Pleasure meetin' you," said Jesse, and they shook hands.

"You're unbelievable," I told Jesse as we got out of the cab. "I think he was going to ask you to his family reunion."

"I never yet met a man I didn't like." Jesse grinned. "Well, 'cept one."

We turned to the building and I stopped in my tracks. There was a huge man looming in the tiny foyer between the outer and inner doors of the building. He was taller than Jesse, at least six foot four, with hulking shoulders and a stocky build. He was dressed all in black, with a hood over his head and a cigarette in his mouth. He looked like the same man I'd seen the night before, on the stoop. Now he was shifting from foot to foot, staring at us.

"You stand back, Tiger Lily." Jesse put his right hand in his jacket pocket and I wondered if it was a ruse or if he had something to use as a weapon. Before I could ask, the lurker opened the outer door and stepped out.

"Hi," he said.

Did he know me? I didn't recognize him at all. Most of my sister's friends were emaciated addicts; this guy looked like a linebacker. "Hi," I answered.

"How you doin'?" asked Jesse.

"Okay." The man's voice was a low rumble. "I guess you're wondering why I'm here."

"Pretty much," said Jesse.

The man pulled back his hood. That was when I recognized him, and the shock made my mouth fall open. "Ridley?" He was almost a foot taller and at least sixty pounds heavier than when I'd last seen him a year ago. No wonder the police had taken him for an adult; he looked like a brooding thug, not a boy about to turn sixteen. He had Martin's dark hair and handsome features, but as he came closer I saw his face was marked with acne. "You shouldn't be smoking!" I chided him.

"You smoke," he mumbled.

"I quit when I moved to Spain." Well, mostly, at least. "You're too young." I couldn't say it would stunt his growth. "What are you doing here, anyway?"

"Waiting for Claudia."

"Waiting?" I asked. "Is she meeting you here?" He shook his head. "Why are you waiting, then?"

"She has to come out of rehab sometime." Ridley dragged on his cigarette and dropped the butt on the ground, crushing it under his giant white sneaker.

"How do you know she's in rehab?" I asked.

"She told me." Ridley stared at the sidewalk while he spoke. He was always like this when he spoke, mumbling a few words and refusing eye contact.

"When did she tell you, Ridley?"

"September." His eyes flickered up to my face and down again.

"Have you talked to her since then?" Ridley shook his head. "Did you see Claudia in September?" He shook his head again. I was fighting not to show my exasperation. "Ridley, how did she tell you she was going to rehab?"

"Phone."

"She called you?"

"I called her." He glanced at me again. "We talk sometimes. She likes me."

That would explain the calls that Martin had denied. I knew that Ridley had called Claudia a few times after they met. When Martin and I hosted a dinner or party, they seemed to spend it in a tête-à-tête. Martin had joked about his son's crush on my sister. No wonder Claudia mentioned Ridley to me from time to time. She probably knew more about him than Martin did.

"Do you have any idea where she is, Ridley?" I spoke slowly, as if to an overgrown child. "She's gone missing and no one can find her. I'm worried about her."

Ridley nodded. "My dad's a liar."

"What do you mean?"

"I showed him an article online that says she's missing.

He said she's not. He's lying." It was the longest string of words he'd put together.

"Does he know where Claudia is?"

Instead of answering that, Ridley looked into my eyes. "Did Claudia tell you about the fire?"

"The fire?" I repeated, suddenly realizing what he meant. "At the church? St. Ari—"

"St. Aristarchus." Ridley stepped off the stoop and onto the sidewalk in front of me. I had to put my head back to see his face. It was like looking up at a brick wall. Jesse, who'd kept silent all this time, put his hand on Ridley's arm. Ridley shoved him away without even a glance, sending Jesse sprawling on the sidewalk. "Are you mad about the fire?" he asked.

"I'm glad no one was hurt," I said.

Ridley's expression shifted. "That's what Claudia said." He put his arms around me in a hug that pushed the air out of my lungs. When he let go, I almost lost my footing. "Bye, Lily." He turned and lumbered away from us along Rivington. The groups of teens and young men on the street gave him a wide berth as he passed.

"That kid's a chip off the old block," said Jesse. My friend was beside me again, staring at Ridley's wake. "Like monster like son."

Claudia's apartment surrendered nothing new that night. The Crime Scene Unit had tried to put things back into some semblance of order, but the place was still a depressing wreck. Sometimes I thought about what it would be like to come back to live in New York, but I knew I'd never want to stay in this building again.

The encounter with Ridley forced me to tell Jesse about

the fire at the Church of St. Aristarchus, and the articles that Claudia had printed. "You mean Sklar burned down a house of God to put up some crappy hotel?" Jesse was a devout Southern Baptist. His voice betrayed an absolute certainty that Martin would roast in hell for eternity.

"He wasn't in New York when it happened. There could be some explanation, maybe."

"Sure, he hired some dope to do it for him. Lil, this guy is poison. How many times do I have to tell you before it sinks in?"

But I wasn't thinking about that. I was hearing Martin's voice from our evening at the flamenco bar. *Has someone black-mailed you?* I'd asked him. His answer had chilled me even then. *A few have tried. They don't get away with it,* he'd said.

"Lil, what's wrong? You're white as a ghost."

"Nothing," I tried to say, but the word died on my lips. Was it possible that Ridley had told Claudia about the fire, and that she, in turn, had tried to blackmail Martin? My sister had stooped to many things, but I'd never known her to go as low as that. But if she had, what would Martin's response be? I fumbled in my bag for my cell phone.

"Lil? Who are you calling?"

Tariq picked up his phone before I could answer Jesse. "I need your help," I blurted out. "You said something last night about having an investigator working for you. I need him to look into something. Please."

There was a pause. "My resources are at your disposal, Lily."

"Can you have him find out whatever he can about a woman named Kaylee Quan? And everything about . . ." I had to take a couple of breaths; my heart seemed to rattle in my chest. "Everything about her connection to Martin Sklar."

27

The Oracle on Lispenard looked even gaudier than Martin's other hotels. It wasn't just ugly, it was a behemoth that was out of scale with its surroundings. Martin's company, Pantheon Worldwide, was known for the grand scale of their buildings rather than the tastefulness or innovation of their design. If that was its claim to fame, I wasn't sure whether the Oracle represented a new high, or a whopping low. I knew that looking at the Oracle left me with an empty, hopeless feeling about what Martin was willing to do for a profit.

I debated whether to go inside, and decided I had nothing to lose. The foyer was a cavernous space that peaked at the top. I turned in a circle, trying to take it all in. "Amazing, isn't it?" said a voice beside me. There was a short smooth-faced man in a navy suit and striped tie next to me. He wore a little gold pin that identified him as a concierge.

"Didn't there used to be a church on this site?" I asked.

The man nodded solemnly. "Yes. That's part of the reason the lobby was designed this way."

"Oh? Designed . . . what way?" The room was a giant barn that had been fashioned out of glass.

"Like a cathedral," the man assured me. He misread my startled expression for admiration. "Pretty cool, right? That's also why the windows are arched. Like stained-glass windows."

I was lost for words. The man smiled and told me if I needed anything, to just ask. I took one last look around, and headed back out to the street. Jesse was right; Martin really was going to hell.

It was Thursday morning and I was trying to keep myself from going crazy. I'd started the day early, hitting the shelters that I knew Claudia had used before. I figured if I arrived before they turned their homeless guests out onto the streets, I could catch my sister by surprise. But she wasn't anywhere I looked. No one seemed to be following me as I made my rounds; maybe Martin really had called Gregory Robinson off.

I went up and down Canal Street looking for Claudia. This was her prime area for scoring a fix, and while Mal Sabado was in jail, she'd have other dealers lined up. As I'd walked toward West Broadway, I'd caught sight of the Oracle. It was a block south of Canal and I was desperate to be distracted while I waited for the detectives or Tariq to come up with a lead.

By noon I'd given up on a chance sighting of Claudia, and I returned to Jesse's to regroup. I had to be missing something. There was a clue I'd overlooked, maybe a dozen of them. But where did I begin? Leafing idly through Alexander Gorevale's hardcover book, *Rising From the Ashes,* I couldn't believe Claudia had fallen for him, or for his nonsensical theories. Gorevale's sophisticated turns of phrase ran along the lines of "Family ties are a load of lies," and he regarded the poet Philip Larkin as an authority on relationships. Larkin's "This Be the Verse" was even quoted in the preface: *They fuck you up, your mum and dad.* Gorevale seemed to view the family as an unhealthy entity that crushed the individual. Had that appealed to Claudia, given how dysfunctional our own family was? Even before my father died, my family had had issues. My mother drank, though nowhere near as much as she later did, and my parents fought, often long and loud. That wasn't anything I wanted to remember, and I slammed the book shut.

Next I pulled out the dentist's bills. Poor Curtis Herrold, DDS, of Lenox, Massachusetts. He was the man who'd fixed my sister's broken tooth, filled cavities, and provided extensive dental care, and he had been shafted to the tune of thousands of dollars. Another black mark against Claudia; they were piling up quickly now. I sighed and dialed his number. "Good afternoon, Curtis Herrold," bellowed a man with a jolly voice.

"My name is Lily Moore. We haven't met, but I'm calling about my sister, Claudia Moore."

There was a pause on the other end. "Claudia?"

"I found some notices that she owed you money and I—"

"Oh, no. I mean, I'm very sorry."

"Sorry?" My ears perked up. "Sorry about what?"

There was a long pause. "She said she was sick," Herrold said. "I'd been sending her bills and . . . um. I was sorry to hear that."

"Oh. When was that?" I asked, confused.

"Um. Some months ago, I guess. I . . ." He'd sounded like he was going to elaborate but the answer had escaped his brain.

"She's missing," I said. "The police are trying to contact her. Do you know where she might be?"

"Me? How would I know anything like that?"

"Maybe you had another address for Claudia? I wondered if you were sending the most recent invoices to another address."

There was a pause. "Um, I just gave up."

"Claudia never paid you for the work you did on her teeth?" I felt my face flame in shame. "How much does she still owe you? Did she pay any of it?"

Herrold coughed. "I'm sorry. It's all right. I've already written it off. I don't expect you to pay."

"But I want to."

"No, it's nothing, really. I couldn't possibly. I see that a lot with the girls they send over from Idylhaven. Some of them have a lot of problems. Especially those meth addicts. They're the worst. Nasty drug, meth. They've got teeth falling out of their heads. Such a shame. Your sister's problems were minor by comparison. I couldn't possibly expect you to pay now. I'm so sorry, but I have a patient waiting. Thank you for calling. Good-bye." I stared at the cracked screen of my cell phone. He'd hung up on me.

"That was weird," I said to Claudia's one-eared bunny, who'd taken up residence on the nightstand. I should have been glad to let go of the obligation, but it grated on me. I had a fear of dentists, but Herrold seemed unusually strange. Was he hiding something? For a moment I imagined that he was the lothario my sister had fallen for, not Alexander Gorevale at all. Maybe Claudia was holed up with the very man who had fixed her teeth. I shook my head and realized I had watched too many movies. Somewhere along the way my brain had dissolved. Or could I blame Martin for that?

While my brain was churning out questions, my cell phone rang. This number was one I knew. "Hello, Detective," I answered.

"I hate caller ID," said Bruxton. "I like phones like that old one at your apartment. Can I run a couple things by you? Who does your sister know in Chicago?"

"No one that I know of. Claudia never leaves New York, or she didn't used to."

"Your sister spent most of May, June, July, and August in Nyack, New York. She was shacked up with Alexander Gorevale. He had a house up there. He croaked in September. My partner told me you'd already talked about him."

"True. I can't say he'll be missed."

"Come on, how can you not love a guy who OD's on Viagra?" Bruxton said. "Anyhow, it occurred to us that your sister might have decided to stay in the area, given she spent months here. That's where we are now. Place reminds me of a fucking Edward Hopper painting."

That made me laugh out loud. "What does this have to do with Chicago?"

"Oh. That nosy broad, Sarah Lyons. She called Norah wanting to know why the phone kept ringing in your sister's apartment. Said the noise was driving her crazy. We checked the LUDs and over the past several days, someone in Chicago has been calling four, five times a day. Yesterday it was eight times." He coughed. "Sorry. The calls are from a couple different pay phones, makes it look like the same caller. Any ideas?"

My mind was blank. "I have no idea. I'll ask Tariq. There's a chance he might know."

"Thanks. By the way, if you see that snotty broad, will you tell her to go to hell for me?" Bruxton said.

"Can I ask why?"

"The great lady of the manor—excuse me, the great life management consultant, whatever that is—read Norah the riot act. Said we weren't doing enough to find your sister. She's so wrapped up in this, you'd think it was her sister that's missing."

After we hung up, I went back to shuffling papers. I set the arson articles aside; I had a reasonable idea of Claudia's interest in that subject. Instead, I focused on the credit card bills. There were so many charges to go through that I felt a little dizzy. The dead woman had used the credit cards for everything, even tiny purchases at drugstores. But most of the expenses weren't tiny. She'd been on a serious binge. Could she have been an addict, like my sister? The police had checked out neighborhood support groups, but they hadn't found anyone who'd seen either Claudia or her impostor. The addiction connection was looking like a blind alley, but I couldn't shake the feeling that it was relevant. The woman who'd died had been anorexic, bulimic, and a diet-pill addict. Claudia's circles of junkie friends had wasted away, literally and metaphorically. Heroin wasn't the impostor's problem, but as she'd whittled down her weight, she seemed to have lost control of other appetites. Aside from the diet pills, there had been no drugs in the apartment, except for Claudia's prescriptions and an unmarked vial that had contained Ambien. Unless Kaylee Quan had swiped drugs from the apartment while she was there . . .

I noticed a couple of car-rental charges on the bills as my phone started to ring. Sarah had mentioned that the woman often went away for the weekend; where had she gone? I picked up the call and noticed with relief that it was Tariq. "Did you find anything about Kaylee Quan?" I asked breathlessly.

"Yes, of course." Tariq's tone was smug. "I wanted to ask if I could interest you in a trip to suburbia."

"What are you talking about?"

"I am going to see this Quan woman now. She is working from home today. Do you wish to come with me?"

"Yes, but . . ." This wasn't at all what I'd had in mind.

"I am outside of your friend Jesse's building. You have five minutes before I leave."

"Don't you dare go anywhere without me." I stepped into a pair of shoes and grabbed my bag and coat, and ran out of the apartment, once again, like a madwoman.

28

"You are full of surprises, Lily," Tariq said. "I would never have imagined Little Miss Prim and Proper going behind the back of the authorities. Claudia would be proud. You are far more interesting than she has led me to believe." He'd been mocking me since I'd gotten into the SUV and I was ready to clock him. His driver sat up front, guided by an Urdu-speaking GPS that was leading us to Long Island; Tariq sat next to me in the back. Up close he smelled slightly of musk and vanilla.

"Stop being so snarky and tell me what you've found."

"You are as impatient as your sister. Perhaps a family trait." I was thinking about throttling him with his tie when he went on. "Kaylee Quan is the second wife of a man who lives in Hong Kong. It seems that he runs his business there, and she handles operations here."

"What kind of business?" I asked.

"Software. It appears to be how they met. They are both from Hong Kong, but she lives here and he lives there. On occasion, she goes back to Hong Kong, or he comes to New York."

"So what is the connection with Martin?"

"There does not appear to be one," Tariq answered. "My investigator could not come up with any history between them. Martin Sklar called Kaylee Quan on January third, when they spoke for two minutes. There was another, equally brief, call the next day. She has never called him. That is the extent of their relationship."

"Obviously there's a connection. Your investigator missed something."

"If he had more time, perhaps he would have uncovered some information from a decade ago. There is nothing recent except this. He is thorough."

"Martin has been to Hong Kong several times," I pointed out. "Maybe his connection is with her husband."

"Whatever it is, we will find out this afternoon."

There was something in his voice that felt ominous. "There are rules. I have questions for this woman, and I get to ask them first."

"Rules? All right," Tariq answered.

"No, not 'all right.' I want your word that you'll keep your mouth closed while I talk to her."

"You have it. Is there anything else?"

"Claudia told me that you could be . . ." I fished for a diplomatic word. "Harsh with people. I don't want you to be harsh." He stared blankly, his dark eyes almost innocent. "No violence," I added pointedly.

"Not unless it is absolutely essential." Tariq regarded me with just a hint of a smirk as I started to protest. "You would not have called me if you had wanted a Boy Scout, Lily. You called me because you need to know what is happening with Claudia. I need to know, too."

"This woman might not be able to tell us anything about Claudia. She was close to the woman who was living in Claudia's apartment. I want to get the connection between Claudia and the woman who died."

"We will obtain it, I promise you that," said Tariq.

. . .

Kaylee Quan's house was off Greenlawn Road on Long Island, where every house seemed to be set back a hundred feet from view, tucked behind a tall hedge and thick-trunked trees. The driver parked the SUV beside the house. "You will wait here, Lily, until I send for you."

"What are you going to do?" I asked, alarmed.

"Calm down. Take deep breaths." He said something in Urdu to the driver and opened his door. "Remember to keep your gloves on," he told me as he got out.

I watched them disappear around the corner. Now that we were at the house, I was panicked. What had I been thinking, trusting Tariq with anything I learned? He was a dangerous person. Even without Claudia's hints of violence and intrigue, I knew that Tariq wasn't on the straight and narrow. He was too arrogant, too macho, to follow anyone else's rules. I already regretted my rashness, but I saw no way out now.

The driver came back. "House, please," he said. I got out of the car and followed him. He turned before we went inside. "Glove, please."

"I'll keep them on," I said. He looked blank. I held up my gloved hands and nodded. He smiled and nodded back. Great, even Tariq's driver was worried about us leaving prints. What could that possibly mean?

I found out inside. The tall Asian woman I'd seen the night before was facedown on the pearly gray carpet of her living room. Her hands were tied behind her back, and she was blindfolded. "Must I restrain your ankles, too?" Tariq was asking as I walked in.

"No!" Kaylee said. "Please don't hurt me."

I rushed up to Tariq and grabbed his arm. "What the hell are you doing?"

Tariq grabbed my shoulder and almost lifted me off my feet. "Calm yourself," he said in a whisper-soft voice. "Breathe deeply. Focus. Good girl." He let go after a few breaths. I'd never hated anyone so much in my life as I did Tariq at that moment.

"What do you want?" said Kaylee in a high, plaintive voice that was nothing like her haughty tone in front of her health club. "I don't keep cash in the house, but there's jewelry. It's in the bedroom."

"Thank you, Mrs. Quan." Tariq sounded as if she'd just offered him tea. "That will not be necessary." He crouched next to her. The merciless, icy calm in his voice made me shiver. "This is how we will proceed. I will ask a question. You will answer. I do not make threats." His voice got even quieter. "And I do not like to be disappointed."

"Please don't hurt me!"

"Would you like to begin?" Tariq asked me, but I shook my head. "Very well. Mrs. Quan, you had the misfortune to come upon a dead body this week. Whose was it?"

"C-Claudia Moore."

"Wrong answer," said Tariq.

"That was what she called herself, I swear. I found out later that it wasn't really her name, but that was what she called herself."

"Did you ever meet another woman who went by that name?"

"No. Never."

"Perhaps a woman with dark hair and pale skin, a great beauty. She would be approximately the same height as the woman who called herself Claudia Moore. Her eyes are as green as emeralds."

"No," said Kaylee.

"She might have been introduced under another name." Tariq's voice was calm but his hands were balled into fists.

"Claudia never introduced me to her friends. We met at our health club."

"Think harder," Tariq insisted.

"I want you to tell me what your friend told you about herself," I said. My voice surprised me; it sounded unconcerned, almost faraway, as if I were asking about a movie she'd seen. "What did she say about her family?"

"She was from Massachusetts. Sometimes she went to see her family there."

"What family?" I asked.

"Her parents, I think. Or maybe just her dad." Kaylee sniffled a little. "She didn't talk much about stuff like that."

"What did she talk about?"

"Her weight. She told me she'd lost fifty pounds. She said she didn't have any pictures of herself because she used to be a fat chick. She loved to shop."

"Was that what you did together, work out and go shopping?" I asked.

"Yes."

"What else?"

Kaylee swallowed hard. "Nothing else."

"That is a lie," said Tariq. "What did I say about that?"

Kaylee stifled a sob. "I had an affair with her. Please don't tell my family. They would disown me." She took a couple of gasping breaths. "I only went to her place a few times, I swear."

"Why did you go right over after you flew back from Hong Kong?" I asked.

"I'd been stuck with my family for nine days," said Kaylee. "I just wanted to see her. I missed her."

"You wrote that card we found in her apartment." I

remembered the words. *I'm going to miss you like the devil over the holidays. Only nine days until I see you again.* "What did the *M* on the card stand for?"

"Mingmei. My Chinese name." Kaylee seemed to be crying softly now.

"Why did you refuse to talk to the police again?" I asked.

"That man scared me."

"What man?"

"I don't know his name. He called me and said he knew I'd stolen something from the apartment. He said if I didn't give it back he would kill me. I told him I didn't know what he was talking about. He said I had a day to give it back." She was crying in earnest now. "He told me someone would come to my house to pick it up. I swore to him I didn't steal anything. I didn't! I went to Claudia's apartment, or whatever her name was, and the door wasn't latched. I went in and found her in the bath. I screamed and screamed and a neighbor heard me. She came in and we called the police. I swear to you, I didn't steal anything."

"Then what happened?"

She snuffled again and I felt like giving her a tissue. "I kept the house dark and hid in the basement. I really thought he'd kill me. Then he called back and told me I was off the hook, that somebody else had taken it. But he said if he ever found out I talked to the police, he'd slit my throat while I slept at night."

29

Tariq and I didn't speak for most of the drive back to the city. Just before the driver took us into the Midtown Tunnel, Tariq spoke. "Are you so appalled that you cannot even look at me anymore?"

I watched his reflection in the window. "Why did you kill that woman in Claudia's apartment on New Year's Eve?"

In the glass I saw his full mouth tighten into an angry line. "Now you think that I murdered her?"

"I've just seen you in action. I know how far you'll go to find Claudia. You'd kill anyone who got in your way. It may have been an accident"—I remembered what Bruxton had said about the woman's weakened heart—"but it was you."

"How could I do that, Lily? I was out of the country."

"Maybe you had one of your thugs do the dirty work. To make it look like she killed herself." I turned to look him in the eye.

"That is really what you think?" He watched me, the reflection of the tunnel lights shimmering in his eyes like ghosts. It was uncomfortably intimate to sit next to him, the knowledge of what we'd both just done hanging in the air between us. "I suppose I cannot blame you, but I promise you, I do my own dirty work."

"You've killed people," I blurted out before I could censor myself. "Claudia told me."

"Did she?" His voice was quiet but flat, without any trace of emotion. "Did she tell you the reason why?"

"No."

"Anyone in this world could kill, in the right set of circumstances. The question is, what circumstances?" I didn't answer, and Tariq went on. "For profit? For passion? For revenge? To protect those whom you love? Tell me, Lily, are all of those reasons equivalent to you?"

"You've left out the only reason to kill another person. Self-defense."

"Yes, there is that."

We drove along in a painfully heavy silence. Tariq didn't seem to care that I suspected him of killing several people. At least, not enough to defend himself.

"The police are treating this as a story that unfolded on New Year's Eve." Tariq's voice was quiet, but it jolted me. "The truth is, it started months before. Alec Gorevale wormed his way into Claudia's life in the spring. They were together for months, and then . . ."

Tariq paused. In the silence, I heard my sister's voice. *I've been abandoned and I've lost every fucking thing I care about.* Had Gorevale left her when he'd found out she was pregnant? I remembered suddenly what Rachel Heidegger had told me. Claudia had called Rachel in August with big news— her pregnancy, I guessed. But when Rachel had seen my sister, she'd been despondent. *She said her boyfriend, the genius, had pretty much thrown her over for his old girlfriend. Apparently Claudia had been staying at his place a lot of the time, but he forced her to go back to her own apartment because his girlfriend was coming back for a visit.* When Rachel had said the words to me, I'd been preoccupied with fears about my sister's relationship with my former fiancé. Now,

knowing that she had been living with Dr. Gorevale in Nyack, the facts took on new importance. Who else had Gorevale been sleeping with? In September, had he finally decided
he wanted to be with Claudia, and tried to woo her back?
Evil old Mrs. Decarno had seen an English man old enough
to be Claudia's father at the apartment. Could that have been
Dr. Gorevale?

Tariq's voice broke into my thoughts. "Whatever happened between them, my Claudia suffered a miscarriage and
afterward attempted to drug herself into insensibility. In the
middle of September, she returned to that rehabilitation
center in Massachusetts. Then that charlatan Dr. Gorevale
died on September twenty-eighth and Claudia checked herself
out of the facility and vanished. Another woman surfaced in
her place, and then that woman died. Do you not see it?"

"No, I don't."

"There are two twisted threads. The police do not understand that they must pull them apart."

"You haven't had any more luck finding Claudia than they
have," I pointed out.

"I made the same mistake that the police did. I have been
looking in the wrong place. The point of intersection between Claudia and her impostor was never New York City.
I now believe that it was Idylhaven."

"Based on what?"

"One reason I have little regard for rehabilitation programs is that I feel contempt for the philosophy behind
them. They encourage people to spill out their guts, as it
were, and feed them platitudes. Think about the woman who
impersonated Claudia, and what she knew of her. It was all
knowledge that could have been gleaned in some ridiculous
group-counseling session."

I'd had a similar thought early on, but the last thing I wanted to do now was agree with Tariq. "Have you found any proof? Anything we could show to the police?"

"I do not trust the police. They do not care about finding Claudia. If they did find her, they would blame the death of her doppelgänger on her."

"Just tell me this." I tried to keep my tone neutral. "Claudia asked Martin for money to go back into rehab. What happened between the two of you that she didn't ask you?"

"Claudia asked Martin Sklar for money?" He shook his head. "Who told you this fable?"

"Martin admitted it. You haven't answered my question. Why wouldn't Claudia ask you for money if she needed it?"

Tariq brushed some invisible lint from his suit jacket, then adjusted one of the French cuffs of his shirt. "She has said that she finds me controlling," he said quietly. "Also overprotective, territorial, and jealous." He rubbed his eyes absently with one hand. "I do not disagree with her assessment. My defense is that I know what is good for her better than she does."

"She can't be told what to do. Never could, even when she was little. She was always a rebel."

"She goes out of her way to horrify people. This gothic love of hers for self-destruction and ruin," Tariq commiserated. Something like a smile moved furtively across his face, but it was gone in an instant. "I can tell you that she detested Martin Sklar. I have a difficult time believing Claudia asked the time of day, or anything else, of him."

"What do you mean, she *detested* him? She propositioned him."

"Of course," said Tariq. "To open your eyes as to what a poor excuse for a man he happens to be. Claudia has always found your fiancé particularly loathsome. She said that he was a charming, shallow ne'er-do-well like your father, and that he'd drive you to drink and an early grave like your mother."

"Don't you *dare* talk about my father." Every nerve in my body flared. What had Claudia told Tariq about him? Was there no secret she could keep? The times she'd broached the subject with me I'd shut her down. *Where do you think Dad went the nights he didn't come home?* Claudia had asked me once, years ago. *It's none of your business or mine,* I'd told her. *Don't ever mention it again.*

"Claudia told me that your father's flaws are not something you wish to discuss. But I will not hold back on the subject of Martin Sklar's. The man has no conscience. Claudia has told me how he is ruining the life of his own son with his manipulations and lies. Did you know that he paid the mother of his son a tremendous sum of money so that she would agree never to see their son again?"

"She got it backward. Martin's ex wanted to be bought off. She didn't care about Ridley."

"That is not what Ridley told Claudia," Tariq answered firmly. "He said that his father has kept him away from his mother and her family."

I didn't answer him. When the SUV stopped in front of Jesse's building, I opened the door to make a quick getaway. Tariq grabbed my wrist and pulled the door shut.

"Let go," I said.

"Will you promise to listen to me if I do?"

I tried to pull free but his grip was solid. "Let go of me *right now.*"

"Or you will do what?" He put his face close to mine. "Claudia made me promise not to tell you something that Ridley confided in her, but I am tempted to do it. She said you would go running to Martin Sklar with it if you knew. She has told me that you are as much a fool for him as you were for your father."

Something in my brain snapped and I slapped Tariq's face with my free hand. We stared at each other for a wordless moment before he released me. "I apologize, Lily," he said as I slid off the seat and out the door. "I did not mean to—" The slamming of the door behind me blocked out anything else he said. I rushed into Jesse's building and into the stairwell, not wanting to give Tariq the chance to come after me as I waited for the elevator.

Upstairs, Jesse bounded to the door when he heard my key rattling in the lock. "Hey, I just came in. Did something happen? You look kinda peaked."

I grabbed him in a hug. I couldn't let go for a long time. For the first time that day, I was with someone safe and sane and human.

I told Jesse what had happened at Kaylee Quan's house, all of it. How Tariq had restrained her, how I'd joined in the interrogation, how Tariq had told her at the end to lie there for half an hour after we left, and that if she called the police she would die and so would her parents in Hong Kong. He'd recited her parents' address and she had cried and pleaded with him not to hurt them. Admitting aloud what I'd done made me feel sick and ashamed, and I had to admit it had brought me no closer to finding Claudia. My sister remained as elusive as a puff of smoke. Was she doing this deliberately to punish me? What had Ridley told her?

"Nobody knows Claudia better than you," Jesse said, after I'd pulled myself together. "What does your gut say?"

I pulled the blanket around me more tightly and stared at

the television. We were watching *The Barefoot Contessa* for the thousandth time, and we'd left the sound off. By now, we knew Ava Gardner's and Humphrey Bogart's lines so well we didn't have to hear them. "My sister hates me."

"C'mon, Lil. Be serious."

I blinked at him, because I was serious. But something caught in my chest and I teared up. Jesse passed me a bundle of tissues. After I moment, I said, "I want to believe that she hates me and that she's doing this to get even with me. Because if that's not true, something's happened to her." I thought of Ridley, sitting in front of her building at night like a lumpen sentinel. "No one has seen her for months."

We stared at the television for a while. "Who'd want to harm Claudia?" asked Jesse. "What about Tariq? In the movies, it's always the husband, or the lover. Like this one."

I watched Ava Gardner on the screen. She was coming out of the water in a bathing suit, waving at the man she loved, blissfully unaware of his secret and how far he would go to protect his own honor. "Tariq is a psychopath. But I think everything he says about Claudia is the truth. I don't trust anything else that comes out of his mouth." I wondered what secret of Martin's he'd been ready to confide. Thinking of it now made my stomach turn. Knowing that Martin had threatened Kaylee Quan made me sick; in his own way, he was as bad as Tariq.

We talked about going to Massachusetts to check out Idylhaven; Jesse was all for it, but I wanted to keep my distance from Tariq's theories and plans. Then we stared at the television for a long time without saying anything. Jesse had made us vodka cocktails, but with a too-light hand. I waited for the second one to hit my brain and make me unwind, but it didn't happen. Jesse told me that I wasn't responsible for Tariq. *You couldn't have known what he'd do,* my friend said over and over. But that wasn't true. Part of me had been aware all along of what would happen. I knew what kind of man he was. Still, I'd wanted answers, so I'd chosen a sadistic thug to help me. I drank another cocktail and tried to forget what I knew. When that didn't work I turned to vodka neat and put my head on Jesse's shoulder.

Bruxton had promised to come over to Jesse's when he got back from Nyack. When the phone rang, Jesse jumped for it. "Hello? Sorry, who's this? Oh. Hold on a sec." He handed me the receiver.

"Hello, is this Lily Moore? This is Padma."

Padma? I vaguely remembered Tariq's pretty young house slave. "Yes?"

"I am very sorry to bother you. Tariq told me I must call you if . . ." Her soft voice broke into what sounded like a sob.

"Are you okay? Did Tariq hurt you?"

"He is in surgery. That is all they will tell me," Padma sobbed.

"Surgery? What happened?"

"He was shot, two times, in the chest."

"What?"

"Tariq has told me not to say things on the phone. Can you come here? Please?" she begged. "I would send the driver for you but he is already dead."

30

Security had been beefed up at Tariq's apartment. In the foyer, a guard stood by the elevator and phoned upstairs to say that I was coming up. When the elevator doors opened, there were two men, wary and hulking, flanking the door. Inside, Padma came running toward me, throwing her arms around me like a long-lost relative.

"Lily," she said. "Thank you for coming. I am so glad you are here. Tariq told me that if anything happened to him, you are the only person I can trust."

When she let go and stepped back, I saw that her eyes were puffy and red from crying. She was wearing a dark blue salwar kameez and she was barefoot, as she had been when I'd first met her. That was the night Tariq's girlfriend had mistaken me for my sister and had tried to strangle me. Suddenly filled with foreboding, I looked around the room. The parlor was elegant and refined, as if nothing untoward had ever happened here.

"May I offer you some tea?" asked Padma. I followed her over to the sofa, and watched her pour a cup for me out of a silver samovar with shaking hands. It hit me suddenly that she was taking her boss's shooting very hard. Too hard. What was she up to? Jesse had wanted to come with me, of course, but I'd persuaded him to stay at the apartment in case Bruxton came by. I took the cup and saucer that Padma handed to me, but I didn't take a sip. What if there was something in the tea?

Padma curled her legs under her on the sofa. "I cannot believe this is happening," she said mournfully. "The police inspector would not tell me anything. I have been praying for Tariq. There is nothing else I can do." She spread her hands in a gesture of helplessness.

"They must have told you something. You know Tariq was shot. What happened?"

"The inspector called tonight, wanting to speak with Tariq's next of kin. That was how they phrased it, as if he were dead already. I told them that I was all the family he has in this country."

"That was smart. The police wouldn't tell you anything if you'd told them you were an employee."

"An employee?" Padma looked stunned. Her spine straightened, just a little. "Tariq is my cousin."

"Your cousin?" I set the teacup down, worried I'd cause more damage to the room if any more shocks were delivered.

"You didn't know?"

I felt the red blush of humiliation flush my skin. "When I met you, I thought you worked here because you were cleaning up after the mess Tati and I made."

"Ah, I understand. Of course, you thought I was a maid." Padma patted my arm. "I am gratified to do whatever I can to help my cousin. He has done more for me than anyone else in the world."

I wondered what she meant, but I let it pass. "So, you told the police you're family. And they said . . . ?"

"The inspector told me that Tariq was at a hospital, that a surgeon was operating on him to remove two bullets. One had pierced his lung, and collapsed it." Padma became teary again for a minute, then she looked at the clock. "They said they would call again when he was through the surgery. That was more than an hour ago." She looked stricken.

"How did he get shot?" I asked. "Who did it?"

"He would not tell me that, not exactly. He asked me a strange question, though. He said, how did Tariq know a man named Martin Sklar?"

If I'd still been holding the cup, it would have slid out of my hands. I'd had a vodka-induced headache before I'd arrived at Tariq's, but now my heart was pounding in time with my temples. "Is Martin hurt?"

"I do not know. The inspector said my cousin had accosted Martin Sklar before being shot. I did not know Tariq's connection to this man. I had never heard his name before."

Tariq had accosted Martin? "Do you have a computer?"

"In the library."

She led me down the hall. Tariq had a state-of-the-art desktop with a massive screen, but my nervous fingers fumbled on the ergonomic keyboard. "What else did the police say?"

"Ali is dead." The way Padma said his name was like a sigh.

"Ali?"

"Tariq's driver."

Of course. The baby-faced young man who had reminded me to keep my gloves on in Kaylee Quan's house was now dead. "Did Tariq call you before this happened?" My eyes were glued to the screen. The *New York Times* had nothing. I surfed over to New York 1's Web site, where there was a tiny breaking-news item.

"I had not heard from Tariq since he went out to meet you today," said Padma.

The words on the screen made both of us fall silent. MID-TOWN SHOOTING LEAVES 1 DEAD, the headline read.

Two Pakistani nationals suspected in a kidnapping plot have been shot in midtown. Real estate magnate Martin Sklar was their intended target, but was unharmed in the shooting. The would-be kidnappers may have a terrorism connection, says a source. One of the attackers has made four trips to Pakistan in the past six months.

"What the hell is going on?" I thought of Tariq's comments about Martin in the car that afternoon. Was he angry—or jealous—that Claudia had reached out to Martin for help? I reached for my phone and snapped it open, pulling Martin's cell number out of memory. My call went straight to voice mail, where a robotic voice informed me the mailbox was full before it hung up on me. Same thing at his apartment. I felt like throwing the phone into a wall and screaming, but Padma was there. When I looked at her I was stunned to see her small hands balled into fists.

"He goes to visit his mother in Pakistan, and they call him a terrorist," she said. "His mother, who is slowly dying of cancer in Lahore." She choked on the last word, bringing her fists down so hard on the table that the computer bobbled from side to side. She sank to her knees, crying.

"Calm down. Try to breathe." My own anger and confusion faded next to Padma's blast of fury. In my words, I heard the echo of Tariq's voice that afternoon, and I felt ashamed. "This is just the first crazy thing they've written. The reporters don't know anything, so they're making it up. That's what they do." I knelt on the floor and rubbed her back. Padma took a couple of deep breaths and lifted her head slightly, resting it on my lap. Her hair was black and lustrous and wavy, like Claudia's, and as I stroked it I remembered how I had calmed my sister down like this so many times after our father died. Our mother was lost in her own grief, too fragile to ameliorate ours. Sometimes we would stay like that for an hour, and Claudia would make me recite "The Raven" by Edgar Allan Poe, a poem I'd memorized for a Halloween talent show at school. *Leave my loneliness unbroken,* I thought now, remembering fragments of verse and wondering why Claudia and I had taken comfort in something so dark and foreboding. I looked at Padma and felt a fierce urge to protect her. "I know it's hard right now, but it's going to get better."

"The police inspector has not called again," Padma sobbed. "That means Tariq is in surgery still."

"Tariq is tough. I think he could pull through just about anything." I didn't have to like him to mean that sincerely. Cockroaches were survivors, too.

"He was almost killed because of me."

"What do you mean?"

Padma turned her face up to look into my eyes. "Claudia did not tell you?" I shook my head. "Tariq is the only man of my family who will speak to me, let alone shelter me."

"Why?" Padma's face still had the round contours that hinted of baby fat. She was still a teenager. But as she rolled up one sleeve I saw deep, pink trenches dug into her flesh.

"Acid burns," Padma said softly. "There are such marks all over my body. Everywhere but my face."

I stared at them, horrified. Claudia's arms were pitted with old track marks that had become infected and hollowed out into rough-edged craters. But those missing bits of flesh were like pinpricks next to the gouges out of Padma's skin. "How . . . ?"

"My family became involved in a dispute. The men of the

other family wished to teach my father and brothers a lesson, and so they attacked me. Of course, my family cannot accept such shame."

"Such *shame*? You're the victim."

"In Pakistan, it is different. My sisters cannot marry if I have been dishonored. Unless I am dead." I gasped; when I tried to speak, I couldn't find any words. "Your sister reacted the same way," Padma said. "You and she are so similar." She wrapped her fingers around my hand and held it against her cheek. "I would have been killed if Tariq had not intervened. He . . . dealt with the men who attacked me. Then he brought me here."

It took me a moment to put the story together in my mind. Claudia had hinted that Tariq had killed someone in Pakistan, and now I understood why. "His life is in danger every time he goes back," Padma said, breaking into my thoughts. "The men who attacked me are from a family allied with terrorists. They put a bomb in his car in the summer. It went off before he got in, but he was badly harmed. He would not wish me to speak of it." She lifted her head and sat up. "You are a good person, Lily."

"How can you say that? You hardly know me."

"Your sister did some bad things to you, and you still took care of her," Padma answered. "To my family, I am like one who is dead. They wish I were a ghost. Not because of anything I did, but because of what happened to me. At the time I accepted it. But . . . it makes Tariq angry, and now it makes me a bit angry, too." She regarded me guiltily. "Do you think that wrong?"

"Of course not." After everything that had happened to her, Padma worried that she was a bad person.

We got up off the floor. "I'm going to call a couple of people.

Maybe I can find out what's happening with Tariq," I said. The cops wouldn't talk to me, but Renfrew or Bruxton would be able to wrangle information out of them.

"Can I bring you some tea? You did not have anything to drink before," said Padma. "Perhaps something to eat, too. It may get very late." There was a sweetness about her that made my throat constrict. Most of the nurturing I'd had in my life had come from Jesse. It felt unfamiliar, and a little uncomfortable, to have this girl who had suffered so much fussing over me.

She left the library and I dialed Martin's number's again. Nothing. Wasn't it his responsibility to call me to let me know what had happened? What had Tariq said to him—and how had Tariq and his driver ended up as the ones getting hurt?

31

"I hate hospitals, everything about them," Renfrew said. "The way they look. All those beeps and bells going off. But mostly it's the way they smell. Did I mention that?"

"A few times now," I answered. We were sitting together in a Bellevue waiting room with stained walls and moldering chairs. We'd bought coffee down the hall but had somehow never gotten around to drinking it; our paper cups, now cold, sat on a Formica table. Bruxton was outside, smoking. Jesse was wandering up and down the hallway. Padma was in another room, listening to a doctor explain her cousin's condition. Tariq was still in surgery.

"So we're clear on that. Okay," said Renfrew. We lapsed back into silence. She and Bruxton had already filled me in on their trip to Nyack. My sister had indeed been living there with Alexander Gorevale from May to August, but no one had seen her since. Gorevale's neighbors were used to the good doctor hosting a series of female companions at his rambling old house. They'd known my sister as Cassandra, and she was notable for the fact that she spent so long at Gorevale's house. The last woman who'd spent so long with him was Alexandra, who hadn't been seen in five years. Then there was Serena, who appeared regularly, every couple of months. *Are these real women or soap opera characters?* I'd asked them. *No wonder he needed all that Viagra,* Bruxton had quipped. Gorevale was suspicious and secretive, keeping his neighbors at a distance with a pleasant smile and conversing only about the weather.

"For the record, I hate hospitals, too," I added belatedly.

"If you ever feel like time is whirling by too fast, you can always come to a hospital, where time just stops." Renfrew looked at her watch. "It's not budging. You ever spend much time in hospitals?"

"That time Claudia overdosed. A bunch of times with my mother. What about you?"

"My pop was shot," Renfrew said. "Six months before retirement. Trying to stop a robbery at a bodega. Off duty, to boot."

"I'm so sorry."

"Worst part was that they hooked him up to machines in the hospital, so his heart kept beating and he kept breathing even though he was brain-dead. I'm sure they did it because they wanted to be able to transplant from him, you know? But we couldn't decide what to do. My mom thought it would be like murdering him, turning the machines off. Part of me felt like that, too, even though I knew he was dead."

I felt my throat constrict as I looked at her. Renfrew was staring at the far wall as if she'd been hypnotized. "You don't have to talk about it," I said in a small voice. "Not if it makes you uncomfortable."

"It's not the talking that's hard, it's remembering. Took us six months, my mom and my brother and me, to agree on what to do. We told them to turn off the machines. It was the hardest day of my life."

I didn't know what to say, but the keenness of her pain felt as sharp as my own. "When my father died, my mother wouldn't let Claudia and me come to the hospital," I said. "She told us that he'd been hurt, and she had to go to him. That was

Christmas Eve. Claudia and I waited up for news, but she didn't call. We fell asleep at some point, but in the morning she still wasn't back." I could remember it as clearly as if it had just happened. Claudia, at eleven, wasn't quite a full-fledged rebel yet, and she went along with my idea that we couldn't open our presents until our parents came home. My father had already shown me the bracelet, and I felt a secret thrill, knowing it was there under the tree. I think I convinced myself, and maybe my sister, that everything would be all right somehow if we waited.

"Your father was in an accident?" Renfrew asked.

"No. He was stabbed outside a bar." It had taken me years to piece together what must have happened. He was out for a drink with some of his friends. Another man had come along and asked my father to come outside with him. The man had stabbed my father and left him bleeding on the street. My father was taken to the hospital but he'd lost too much blood too quickly.

"I'm so sorry, Lily. Did they ever find who did it?"

"Yes. He went to jail for a very long time." It hadn't made any sense to me when it happened. The man who was arrested—who apparently had confessed when the police picked him up—was the husband of one of my mother's friends. My mother's friend didn't call or come by, and my mother wouldn't discuss it. It was only when the friend showed up at the funeral, and my mother threw her out of the church, that the first inkling of what had happened hit me. I'd never told anyone, not even Jesse, and when my sister had asked me questions I'd batted her away like a fly.

Padma came back with the doctor, and Jesse, somehow sensing that there was news, sidled into the waiting room.

"Tariq is out of surgery." Padma smiled shyly. "But he is not—how did you put it?—out of the trees yet?"

"Not out of the woods yet," the doctor gently corrected her. Padma asked her to explain Tariq's condition to us. He was in bad shape, and something called a flutter valve had been left in his chest while his injured lung was reinflated, but the doctor was sure he would recover. Tariq would be in intensive care for the next few days and under constant surveillance in case his lung collapsed completely. The surgeon added that Tariq was incredibly lucky, because the second bullet had hit a rib and altered course within his body, missing his liver by a hairsbreadth. Padma would be allowed to see him the next day, if she wished, but only for ten minutes. "He's on some strong meds right now, so he might not recognize you," the surgeon added. "You really should go home now and rest."

"Would you like to c'mon over and stay at my place?" Jesse asked Padma. "There's plenty of room, and you're more than welcome."

"Thank you very much. That is so kind. But it would not be appropriate for me to visit the home of a man who is not a relative," said Padma, averting her eyes. I'd never seen a woman so shy around men. "I hate to impose, but I was going to ask Lily to stay with me tonight. If she does not mind." Her dark brown eyes were pleading.

"Of course," I said.

Renfrew offered to drive us uptown. We made a quick stop to pick up a few of my things at Jesse's, then headed for the Upper East Side. If I'd hoped for a call from Martin, I was disappointed, there was nothing on Jesse's machine, just as there was no call from Martin on my cell.

Padma and I stayed up, talking and drinking tea, until the early hours of the morning. When I finally went to bed, it was in what Padma called "Claudia's room." The walls were painted Chinese red, and every piece of furniture had some sort of human or animal characteristic. The dark wood of the headboard was carved with grotesque, leering faces, the night table had feet with taloned claws, and the dresser had what looked like a curious fox face on each drawer. There were all of Claudia's favorite books—Mann's *Death in Venice*, Lewis's *The Monk*, Goethe's *Young Werther*, Hamsun's *Hunger*, Byron's poetry, and a complete collection of Poe—braced by a pair of watchful gargoyles. Opposite the bed were two framed pen-and-ink drawings, one of writhing humans transforming into snakes, the other of a woman sinking into a pool of black water as hands grasped her from below. I knew without being told that they were my sister's creations; there was one in my Barcelona apartment of a woman melting under the force of a radiant sun. When I'd hung her work in the apartment on Rivington, she'd torn it down. My sister had destroyed most of her own drawings in various fits of temper over the years; the only pieces that survived were the ones she'd given away.

I'd never seen a space that Claudia had decorated before. My sister had spent her adult life shuffling from shelters to squats, taking refuge with friends and lovers, or with me. Now everything in the room reminded me of her, as if the force of her personality had been channeled into inanimate objects. In the closet was a black silk wraith of a robe adorned with red dragons. I scanned the silver hairbrush for a strand of her hair, but it was spotless. In the bedside table drawer was a serpentine ashtray and an open package of cigarettes from Nat Sherman. I lit one up, winced at the stale taste, but smoked it anyway.

When I crawled under the comforter I couldn't sleep. I lay there for a long time, staring at the ceiling and thinking about the fact that Tariq and his driver had been unarmed when they'd been shot. Martin hadn't been hurt at all. I closed my eyes and wondered if Martin had always been the way he was, and I had overlooked it, or if he had changed recently. My sister was right about me: I was a fool for him. *"His eyes have all the seeming of a demon's that is dreaming,"* I thought, remembering another line from Poe. What I had been able to cobble together was this: Claudia knew that Martin had arranged to burn down the Church of St. Aristarchus, probably because Ridley had told her. Claudia had contacted Martin recently—perhaps because she needed money—and had told him what she knew. Maybe she blackmailed him, or just hinted in that oblique way of hers. This all made sense, to a point. And that point was that no one had seen my sister for three months. Only Martin had claimed to speak with her. The only sighting of Claudia was by Sarah Lyons, who'd never actually met my sister and who could easily have been mistaken. Had Claudia told Tariq what she knew about Martin? No doubt, given that she confided almost everything in her friend. Had Martin guessed this and tried to kill Tariq as a result?

Somehow I dozed off around six in the morning. When I woke up, it was after eight, and there was a little bit of wintry sunlight slipping by the heavy silk curtains on the window. I went into the shower and found one trace of Claudia that I'd overlooked the night before. When I opened an unremarkable bottle of gel in the shower, my senses were suddenly hit by the smell of my sister's perfume. Tabac Blond was an almost impossible-to-get fragrance, and as far as I knew the French company that formulated it didn't offer a bath gel version. I lathered up with it, feeling oddly liberated. I'd bought the expensive perfume for my sister but never for myself, feeling that its musky, leathery undertones didn't pair well with vintage silk and lace. But, for some reason, it fit my mood that morning.

Padma was waiting for me in the kitchen, warming up bread in the oven. It was from Tariq's restaurant and it was delicious. She'd already called the hospital a couple of times to check on her cousin. He was asleep and in critical condition, but there was no sign of his lung recollapsing, which seemed to be the greatest risk now. She was going to visit him in the afternoon, when the doctors expected him to wake up. "I wish you could see him, too," Padma said. "I know it would mean a great deal to him."

I doubted that, but I didn't want to argue with her.

"Will you go to Idylhaven now, since Tariq cannot?" she asked me. We'd talked about Idylhaven the night before. Tariq's cousin was as convinced as he was that Claudia's impostor had latched on to my sister there. Deep down I agreed with them, but I was afraid to get my hopes up.

"Yes. Jesse and I already talked about it." I didn't add that my friend had been the one originally gung ho about the Idylhaven angle. "We'll probably drive there today."

"In that case, I will give you everything that Tariq's investigator found."

"Investigator?"

"I do not know his name, but he sent an envelope for Tariq yesterday. My cousin did not find the information immediately useful, but he was hurrying out to meet you. He said he would examine it more closely in the evening. It should still be on his desk." Padma retrieved a heavy manila envelope that was open at one end. On the front was handwritten *For the personal and confidential attention of Mr. Tariq Lawrence.* I pulled out a sheaf of pages, double-sided color photocopies. There were maybe a hundred sheets altogether, and I sifted through a few on the top. They were all young women, some of them quite pretty, but with exhausted eyes and vacant expressions. Their photos looked like mug shots. The text on the pages offered only their names and signatures; instead of personal information, there was legalese, which appeared to swear the women to silence about Idylhaven's policies, practices, and patients.

"Tariq wanted to know every woman who had a connection to Idylhaven in the past year. All of their patients are women, and almost all of their staff, too," Padma explained. "Tariq believed he would recognize the face of her impostor if he saw it again."

I stared at the pages. They didn't seem to be assembled in any order. Sad, desperate women peered up at me. It wasn't exactly like looking for a needle in a haystack, but it felt about as promising.

"Here's what's gonna happen," Jesse was saying on the phone. "You're gonna exit Tariq's place and head on over to Second Avenue."

"Why?" I asked. "The subway is on Lex. I was going to come back and pack for—"

"Don't say it!" Jesse cut me off before I could say *Idylhaven.*

"Is everything okay?"

"You'll see. Just don't blow a gasket." Now he was being as cryptic as a spy in a thriller.

"Why would I?"

"Plenty of reasons, Tiger Lily. See you soon."

I hung up and packed my bag. I'd had a sneaking suspicion that I was losing my mind over the past few days. Jesse's odd behavior made me realize I wasn't the only one. I hugged Padma and promised to call her. Then I went out, past the guards, and to the street.

The temperature had risen, but the trade-off was gray sky and drizzle. I walked to Second, expecting to see the bright baby blue of Ginger, Jesse's beloved Camaro. Instead, a burgundy sedan pulled up beside me and the passenger window slid down. I stared at Detective Renfrew, startled to find her. " 'Good morning, heartache, what's new'?" she said, quoting a song of Billie Holiday's. "Hop in."

"How did you know I would be here?" I asked as I got into her car.

She gave me a sardonic smile and ignored the question. "Hold on." She flicked a switch on the dashboard. On went the light and siren, and we peeled down Second Avenue, cutting through the crosstown traffic at intersections. A few blocks down, she turned it off but kept driving. "Always have an ace in the hole," she said.

"Are you going to tell me what's going on?"

She turned onto Fifty-ninth Street, heading for the Queensboro Bridge. "Word came down from on high early this morning. That woman from your sister's place? Her death's being ruled accidental. Your sister's disappearance is going to the bottom of the Missing Persons caseload."

"But Claudia's still missing, and that woman didn't die accidentally."

"Thought you'd say something like that," Renfrew answered. "Predictable." She shook her head. "Missing Persons just had two huge cases fall into their lap, both involving kids. Nothing else matters till they find them, so don't get worked up about that part. The death? You can make a case for accidental, based on the lack of forced entry to the apartment and the fact the woman didn't have any wounds, defensive or otherwise. Remember, she died because her heart gave out. Nobody choked her or shot her or beat on her."

"But it's obvious that something very wrong was going on. You know that."

"Sure, you, me, and the deep blue sea." She sighed. "But the things that are wrong don't line up with the case. For example, how come Martin Sklar was almost kidnapped last night, and yet there's not a scratch on him, but one of his kidnappers is dead and the other has a machine helping him breathe right now?" Renfrew nodded to herself. "It's funny too, since Mr. Sklar said his bodyguard shot both men. The bullets came from different guns, so that's some fine shooting his bodyguard does. Wild West style, pistol in each hand, I guess. That, or maybe there was more than one bodyguard. Mr. Sklar doesn't seem the type to do his own shooting, know what I mean?"

"Martin keeps his hands clean," I said, staring at the East River as we crossed over to Queens. That was why he hired people like Gregory Robinson.

Renfrew hummed to herself for a moment, a song it took me a couple of bars to recognize. It was "Mack the Knife." She stopped abruptly. "So there's never, ever a trace of red," she said, voice dripping with sarcasm.

"Do you think Martin ambushed Tariq?"

"No one much cares what I think right now," Renfrew answered. "No one cares that there was a call almost four minutes long that Mr. Lawrence made to Mr. Sklar yesterday afternoon. Mr. Sklar doesn't recall it, you see. Maybe some flunky took the phone. He's not sure. What Mr. Sklar is sure of is that Mr. Lawrence had made threats on behalf of the Muslim Brotherhood or 'some terrorist organization or other.' That's a quote. Mr. Sklar's bodyguard swears it's the gospel truth. 'Course, he would also swear that when Mr. Sklar speaks, a choir of angels sings out."

"Are you asking me what I think happened?"

"I'm not asking anything. I'm off the case."

"You can't be," I said. "Claudia is missing. Martin is . . . I don't know what, but he's got a hand in all of this. You can't leave the case."

"I don't get a vote on this, you know."

"What about Bruxton? Is he off the case, too?"

"Brux got suspended," she answered.

"What? How?"

"Mr. Sklar generously offered to come into the station to answer some questions early this morning, and he brought his army of lawyers with him. Brux and I weren't allowed to sit in, so I can't tell you what was said, but Brux decided he was going to get some answers when Mr. Sklar was leaving. And somehow—no one knows how—Mr. Sklar bumped into a wall."

"Martin bumped . . . into a wall?"

"Brux is a big guy. Overpowering personality and all. Probably made Mr. Sklar a little nervous."

"Is Bruxton all right?"

"Pretty hard for Mr. Sklar's bodyguard to shoot him at the station." Renfrew gave me a sidelong glance and smiled. "He'll be flattered you care." She cut her eyes back to the road. Now that we were in Queens, I was lost, and the visibility in the rain was low.

"Did Martin say anything about the fire at that church?"

"Stop right there." Renfrew put her right hand up. "My hearing's cutting in and out this morning, you know that? Otherwise, I could be compelled to tell the brass certain things, or get suspended when I failed to talk." She put her hand back on the steering wheel. "You know what's bad about police work these days? With computers, they can tell exactly who runs a name through the system without authorization. If your cell phone is on, they know exactly where you are. No privacy." She squinted at the road and made a right-hand turn into a parking lot, drove into a spot, and put the brake on. "I hate to say it, but you're on your own, kiddo."

"You're dumping me in a parking lot?" I stared out the window at the big red bull's-eye on the concrete building. "What are you doing—shopping at Target?"

"There's an idea. They're supposed to have a new Ella compilation I want." She drummed her fingers on the steering wheel. "But I should probably get back."

I didn't try to hide my incredulity. Why had she driven me miles away from Tariq's building, to Queens, of all places? She'd been obviously upset when she mentioned being taken off the case, but everything else seemed out of character. "Thanks for the ride," I said, slowly inching out of the car, hoping she'd reel me back in and admit what was really going on.

"Remember, if anyone has occasion to ask—anyone—you never saw me," she said.

I closed the door and she drove off, peeling out of the parking lot. I watched her taillights before she turned, feeling strangely bereft. If anyone had been following me, she'd done me the favor of getting me out of their clutches. But nothing else made sense.

A black sports car pulled up beside me. "You need a lift, miss?"

"Jesse? What are you doing . . ." I dropped the question and got into the car. "Where's Ginger?"

"Norah reckoned it would be a bad idea to take her to the Berkshires. Too easy to trace. Next stop, Idylhaven. Unless you wanna hit Target first."

"Why would I do that?"

"Well, I wasn't able to pack clothes. All I could smuggle out was in my camera bag." Jesse gestured at the back seat. "But I remembered your chocolates."

32

It took three hours to make it to Lenox, Massachusetts, thanks to Jesse's pedal-to-the-metal school of driving. On the way, he explained how he had roped Renfrew—or Norah, as he was calling her now—into getting me out of the city. "She tried callin' your cell to tell you the case was bein' shut down," Jesse said. "It was off, so she called me to get Tariq's home number. We got to talkin' about Idylhaven, and how that's the next place she and Bruxton woulda gone to investigate your sis's disappearance, 'cept now they can't 'cause they're off the case. I told her we were plannin' to go there, and she thought that was smart. Then I told her all about that no-count guy who followed you, what's-his-name Robinson, and she got all worried." And so a plan was hatched. I was grateful for what they had done for me, even if I felt bad about making Jesse as paranoid as I was. Since I'd told Martin about the man who'd followed me, I hadn't seen anyone tailing me, but I couldn't be certain of anything anymore.

We were halfway there when Jesse said, "You know, it just hit me that with all the places we've been together, we never got to the Berkshires before."

"That's not so strange. Plenty of New Yorkers never go to the Berkshires." I'd been there only once, researching a spa story for a magazine. That seemed like another lifetime now. I was sifting through the stack of pages in the folder. I'd already gone through the entire folder and hadn't seen anyone who could pass for Claudia. One photo had made my heart skip a beat, until I realized I was looking at my own sister's face; she had had to sign the same privacy-enforcing document as everyone else. Now I was holding the pages up at odd angles to see if they reminded me of the woman in the morgue. So far, no one had.

Jesse gave me a smile, but the wattage was dim. "I used to spend a lot of time up in this neck of the woods." It hit me, as he said the words, that western Massachusetts was where Jesse's ex was from, and where his family still lived. "Lil, you look like you just swallowed a catfish." Jesse grinned for real.

I closed the folder. "I'm sorry. I'm a totally insensitive jerk. I feel awful."

"Honey, he's the insensitive jerk," said Jesse. "You're the girl who gets away with bein' preoccupied, given that her sister's on the lam."

"I should remember something like that."

Jesse shrugged. "I used to like it up there. I haven't been since what's-his-name two-timed me with Bit Part." Ted's affair had been with an actor of some minor notoriety. "Goin' with you will get the bad taste out of my mouth."

Mouth. The word sank into my brain, jolting my memory. I grabbed the batch of pages I'd already dismissed as useless. Where was she? The woman who . . . there she was. I pulled out the sheet with her photograph. The woman had a face pale as a full moon and equally round; it was impossible to discern any cheekbones. There was none of the angular boniness so common among addicts. Her reddish-blond hair was artfully highlighted and styled, her makeup applied with an expert hand. But the oddly small rosebud mouth belonged to the woman I'd seen in the morgue.

"Trina Greene," I said. "Jesse, this is her."

He glanced at her photo and frowned before turning his eyes away. "Um, Lil? That's a blond."

"Right. Bruxton told me the dead woman's natural hair color was strawberry blond, and that she'd dyed it black." I was growing more excited as I spoke.

"Fair enough. But, as we say in Oklahoma, that there's a big-boned gal."

"You didn't see the woman in the morgue. It's her." What had Kaylee Quan said? *She told me she'd lost fifty pounds. She said she didn't have any pictures of herself because she used to be a fat chick.* I was looking at the fat chick, another Idylhaven inmate. Tariq had been right after all.

We got to Lenox in time for a late lunch at a diner. We were the only people in the restaurant, and the waitress who served us was a chatterbox. Unfortunately, she didn't recognize my photograph of Claudia, and she'd never heard of Trina Greene. "It's like something right out of *Law & Order,*" she announced.

It was cold outside as we walked around the town square. "You should see this place in warm weather," said Jesse. "Tanglewood—that's what they call the bandshell—has the Boston orchestra visiting all summer. You can go to Edith Wharton's mansion. What's it called? Damn, that'll probably wake me up at night . . ."

The Berkshires were a bustling hive in the summer months, and the fall attracted a share of tourists following the changing colors of the leaves on a trail that came down through Vermont's Green Mountains. But in the winter, we were highly conspicuous as the lone tourists in the area. Well, not the only ones, but the others would be sequestered at one of the area's two prime spas, Canyon Ranch or the Cranwell. We were probably the only tourists not swathed in seaweed at the moment.

"What do you want to hit first?" asked Jesse.

"I want to round up everyone in town and ask them if they've seen Claudia, or if they know Trina Greene."

"Hmm." Jesse still wasn't sold on the idea that I'd found the right woman. "How 'bout after that?"

"I don't know. Maybe we should go to Idylhaven and make sure Claudia isn't there under a fake name."

"They know what she looks like, Lil. She's been there twice before."

We'd been on a mad tear to get to the Berkshires, and now that we'd arrived, we were stymied. "I guess we could go to the car rental place and check if it was really Claudia who rented the car to drive back to New York."

That wasn't as smart an idea as it sounded. The rental shop was miles away from the town of Lenox. It had perfectly fine records, but all it really showed me was that they had a photocopy of Claudia's license and a form with a squiggle for a signature. "It could be Claudia's, I guess," I said, squinting at it.

"Great detective work," said Jesse, his elbows on the Formica countertop and his head resting in his hands. "You're a real Miss Marple, you."

"Do you remember anything about the woman who rented the car?" I asked the ruddy-cheeked man behind the counter.

"That was three months ago, miss." He shrugged, his long white hair flopping into his eyes.

"Could it have been this woman?" I held up the photograph of Trina Greene.

"That's funny," the man said after examining it for a minute. "It doesn't look like her—her hair was black, not blond—but I remember thinking, boy, that girl gained some weight after she got her license photo. It looked good on her. Not fat, you know, just nice and curvy. Hey, we all put on weight over the years." He patted his own beer belly.

"How did she pay?"

"Cash," he said, pointing to a notation in the file. "The rental fee plus the special deposit for paying in cash."

"Do you know a woman named Trina Greene?"

"Haven't heard the name," he said. "You know if she was local?"

That was the problem. I knew so little, I wasn't even sure what questions to ask.

Back in the car, Jesse turned off the radio. "How come you never told me you were coverin' Claudia's rent check every month?"

I glanced at him warily. His eyes were on the road and he had one hand on the wheel. "I wanted to make sure she had a place to live. She couldn't live with me. When I tried it, it just about killed me. But I could give her a place to live so that she wouldn't be homeless."

"You couldn't stay, but you felt guilty about goin' away," he said in a mild voice that had no judgment in it.

"I felt like I was suffocating, being in the same city as her. It was like she drew all of the oxygen out of the room, the building, the city."

"But you only moved after you broke up with Martin Sklar."

"There was a lot going on around that time."

Jesse seemed to be taking a deep breath and getting ready to say something when my cell phone rang. The number was blocked but I answered it anyway

"Lily, it's Sarah Lyons," said a familiar voice. "Are you all right? I just saw in the paper that that Pakistani man, the crazy one who was at your sister's apartment with you, was shot last night."

"The police told me about it, but I haven't seen him. He was shot twice in the chest, and he's still in critical condition."

"It says here that he was shot by Martin Sklar's bodyguard." Sarah's voice sounded odd. "That wasn't . . . that wasn't the same Martin you told me about before, was it? Not your former fiancé?"

"Actually, it is." I hadn't intended to tell her Martin's name, but I'd been rattled when I saw her and must have blurted it out. "Any reason you were wondering, Sarah?" With everything that had happened since, I regretted telling Sarah as much as I had.

"I'm sorry, Lily. I don't mean to pry. Is there any news yet about Claudia?"

"Nothing, except that the police aren't looking for her anymore."

"What?" she practically shouted. There was a pause. "Oh, Lily, I'm so sorry. What will you do?"

"I'm still looking." I stared at the snow-covered trees as if Claudia might pop out between them like a startled deer.

"Please let me know if there's anything I can do to help," said Sarah. "Anything at all. Day or night, I'm here for you."

Jesse and I needed thirty minutes to locate Idylhaven. Leafy and obscure, the gates sat a mile down an unmarked road between Pittsfield and Dalton. We must have driven past it a dozen times before we recognized it. There was no signage, and it was broad enough for one vehicle but not for two to pass. The naked trees should have made it easy to see, but layers of ice and snow blocked our view, and the little road wove around the trees, so it was impossible to see where it led. "They sure don't wanna be found," said Jesse, steering the car with surprising tenderness. It was a bumpy ride, suggesting an unpaved road beneath the fresh snow. As we cleared the forest I saw a grand fountain in front of the house, frozen in winter. The mansion itself was a three-story neoclassical wonder with towering columns and broad balconies.

"Here goes nothin'," Jesse said as we climbed the steps.

Zelda Tapply, how do you do," the tiny old lady said, holding out one withered hand as if waiting for her ring to be kissed. It *was* quite a ring, a star sapphire that would have made the pope proud. I touched her papery fingertips briefly. She had white hair and a complexion so translucent that I could see tangled blue veins behind it. "Of course, I would do anything to help." Zelda shook her shriveled head slowly, as if it would fall off with a quick motion. "I've been beside myself with worry about Claudia since the police called."

"Anything you can tell us would be helpful," I said. "Do you have a file on Claudia's stay here?"

"I'm afraid we aren't able to share our patient files. It conflicts with patient confidentiality." Zelda smiled at the man who carried in the tea tray. He was dark-haired, pasty-skinned, and pudgy-faced, reminding me of Bela Lugosi in *Dracula*. Only this vampire had a gun holstered on his hip. Guard and houseboy, all in one.

"We're looking for anything that could help us find Claudia," I said. "Since she was at Idylhaven right before she disappeared, this is obviously the place to start."

Zelda smiled indulgently, as if dealing with a particularly stupid child. "I do understand your concerns, Lily," she said, while Bela Lugosi poured tea. "I have already discussed this matter with the police. Our patient files are confidential." She spread out her pale gnarled hands in a gesture of regret. "Of course, I would be happy to tell you anything that isn't confidential." Her servant half bowed as he left the room.

"What exactly would that be?" asked Jesse.

"Won't you have some tea?" Zelda poured milk into her cup. "I can tell you that Claudia signed herself out of our treatment center on September twenty-ninth. That was at three P.M. I had to look that up for the police."

"Signed herself out—does that mean her treatment program was complete?"

"Not necessarily. Every patient is different."

"So when Claudia left, she was in the middle of detoxing?" I asked.

Zelda steepled her fingers together. "While I can't provide specific details, I can say that our ideal scenario for a patient with your sister's issues would be to stay here for six weeks to two months. A residential program, with counseling, medical support, and continuing support is necessary to combat her particular addiction."

"Look, I know my sister was a heroin addict. You can say the name of the drug."

"Very well. Since you know the drug, you should also know that the average heroin user attempts detoxification between ten and twenty-five times," said Zelda, sipping her tea. "It's a very long and complicated process, and unfortunately relapses are very common."

"Do you think Claudia relapsed after she left here?" I asked.

Zelda shook her head. "I wouldn't be able to say."

"C'mon, you must have *some* opinion," Jesse prompted.

"I'm sorry, but that's really not my bailiwick. My focus is on administration. A counselor would have a better perspective."

"Then can we talk to a counselor?" I asked.

"I'm afraid not. Again, that would violate patient confidentiality."

I felt an irrepressible urge to put my hands around the sagging skin of Zelda's wrinkled neck and squeeze. There was something in her prim demeanor that made me feel that she was enjoying the process of yanking my strings. Given her eroded, frail body, maybe psychological torment was her only source of fun.

"Now look here," Jesse said, but I interrupted him.

"You have a holistic wellness program here, don't you?"

"Oh, yes," said Zelda. "We believe in addressing mental and physical wellness, and in integrating the two."

"Which is why you provide yoga."

"That's correct," said Zelda. "It has been beneficial to so many of the girls who have come to stay with us."

"Who certifies your yoga instructors?"

Zelda blinked. "Certifies? Ah . . ." There was a pause. "I believe . . ." There was another pause. Zelda opened the file drawer of her desk and rifled through it. She pulled out a manila folder and opened it up. "Here it is. Gillian was certified by Spirit Tree."

Gillian Kendall, I read, upside down. Her address was on a street called Kemble. Kendall on Kemble? That was a ready-made mnemonic trick. "And Claudia participated in the yoga program?"

"Oh, yes." Zelda nodded and closed the file. "We encourage all of our girls to do so."

"Claudia told me Trina Greene got her into yoga," I said. I knew Zelda wouldn't tell me anything about another Idylhaven patient, so I tried to work Trina's name in naturally.

Zelda's mouth moved as if she had tasted something very bitter. "Trina," Zelda said, her pale blue eyes narrowing at me. Her dislike of the woman was obvious. From personal experience, I knew that addicts were difficult to deal with, but hadn't Zelda signed on for that job? She straightened her spine. "I'm afraid you've caught me on a very busy day. I'm sorry I can't spend more time with you. You do have my hope that Claudia will return safely and soon."

It drove me crazy, to be so close to information about my sister and yet come up empty. What if I pulled the fire alarm? I thought, my eyes scanning the wall for a red lever. I could clear the building and search for Claudia's file. I glanced over the bookcase and stopped dead.

"Alec Gorevale," I said, spotting his book.

"What? Oh, yes, Alec." Zelda glanced over her shoulder at the books. "A great mind."

"Did you know him?"

"Of course," said Zelda.

"Did he have anything to do with Idylhaven?"

I knew what the reply would be before it came out of Zelda's mouth. "I'm sorry, but that is confidential."

33

"I can't believe we got roughed up by a little ole lady," said Jesse. Two hours later, he was still obsessing about how Zelda had routed us. "She's the size of Yoda. We should have distracted her and grabbed her files."

"It's too late for that," I pointed out.

"You sure this is gonna work?"

"No," I answered honestly. "But it's all we've got."

We'd gotten our first break of the day when we located Gillian Kendall, the yoga instructor at Idylhaven. All I'd had to do was call directory assistance with her name and street; it was my second lucky break of the day. Gillian was sweetly sympathetic when I told her about Claudia, but she hadn't heard that Claudia was missing, and she'd barely known my sister. Worse, she had never even met Trina Greene. But Gillian had been incredibly helpful in one way, giving me the name of an Idylhaven patient who'd been at the facility for most of the past year. "Mavis has got OCD and she self-medicates with ketamine, but when she's inside Idylhaven, she's fine," Gillian had promised me. Idylhaven residents didn't have phones in their rooms, so I was going to have to meet this girl face-to-face to find out what she knew about Claudia and Trina.

"Just drop me off here," I told Jesse at the turn off the highway. He tried to protest, but I cut him off. "You can't argue. If Zelda hears the car and looks out the window, I'm toast."

Jesse rolled his eyes. "Have it your way. I'll be twiddlin' my thumbs right here."

The driveway was longer than I remembered from the drive in, and it was covered in snow with glare ice underneath. My high-heeled boots were perfect for peacocking around New York, but they were no match for a Massachusetts winter. I slowly made progress toward the manor house, hugging every other tree I passed. When I caught sight of the fountain, I could have cried with relief, but the tears would have frozen in my eyes. I slunk toward the side of the house, using the servants' entrance that Gillian had told me about, letting myself in with the key tucked into the edge of a terra-cotta pot beside the door. There'd been a trace of bitterness in her voice when she'd told me that Zelda wouldn't let staff members use the front door. It didn't seem that the lady of the manor inspired affection—or loyalty—in anyone.

The advantage of the servants' entrance was that it had its own staircase. I walked up, shedding the ice that clung to my boots on the way. The house was quiet, as Gillian had said it would be in the late afternoon. I got to the second floor, which was dark and gloomy, in stark contrast with the airy, flower-filled atrium I'd seen on my first visit. Each resident's name was on her door, and I found the one I was looking for. I knocked softly.

"Yes?" called a high-pitched voice.

I turned the knob and opened the door. The room was high-ceilinged and painted in stark white. In summer, this might have seemed airy but in winter it felt barren and frigid. "Excuse me, are you Mavis Evans?"

The girl sitting cross-legged on the bed nodded at me. She was sprite-sized, with curly red hair and fair skin. She was wearing a T-shirt and sweatpants, but one leg was rolled up and she had a pair of tweezers in her left hand and a magnifying glass in her right, both suspended in midair as she stared at me. I wondered if this was what Gillian had meant about obsessive-compulsive disorder.

"I'm Claudia Moore's sister," I introduced myself, closing the door quietly behind me.

"You're Lily!" Mavis grinned, as if meeting a celebrity. "I've heard all about you. Wow, you look a lot like Claudia. You're a journalist, right?"

"Right," I said, relieved that someone knew my sister. "I hope you don't mind me barging in on you. I'm worried about Claudia. She seems to have vanished after she left Idylhaven in September."

"September was a crazy, crazy time." Mavis set the magnifying glass on the comforter but kept her tweezers in hand, at the ready. "It was chaos around here."

"What do you mean?"

"Dr. G—I mean, Dr. Gorevale—died around the end of September." Mavis spoke in a rapid-fire way that was hard to follow. "Some of the girls were upset. I mean, really upset. They'd been at Idylhaven before, back when he—Dr. G, I mean—ran the place. Repeat offenders. I don't know why, since he sounded like a creep. But I was sad about Brenda."

"Who's Brenda?" I asked, confused.

"Brenda Collins. She was the cleaning lady at Idylhaven. Sweet, sweet person, kind of mousy but she'd do favors for us. She died a day after we found out about Dr. G."

The name was vaguely familiar; I must have seen it in the file. The pages hadn't distinguished between patients and staff. "How did she die? Was there some connection with Gorevale?"

"Not that I know of," said Mavis. "Brenda's house burned down, and she died in the fire."

I didn't know Brenda, but I shuddered. "That's terrible. You're sure she had nothing to do with Gorevale?"

Mavis shrugged. "Dr. G was at home in Nyack. They told us he had a heart attack." She plucked an invisible hair from her leg. "Bad things happen in threes, I remember someone saying that. Have you ever heard that? I think we were hoping for Zelda to kick off, but of course she didn't. The angels aren't exactly rushing to gather her into heaven."

"I saw why," I admitted. "She wouldn't tell me anything about my sister."

"Zelda's a freak, a serious freak, about privacy. She's always worried that something would damage Idylhaven's reputation. I mean, with Dr. G around, that must have been tough."

"What do you mean?"

"It was kind of a running joke. What does G stand for? Groping, grasping, G-spot." Mavis made a face as if she'd just tasted a rotten lemon. "I guess that's in bad taste now that he's dead. But I heard he had relationships with some of the girls who came through here. That's a gross, gross thing for a doctor to do."

"He seemed to have a relationship with Claudia."

"Did he ever." Mavis's eyes went wide.

"You knew about it?"

"Idylhaven's a pit of vipers when it comes to gossip," said Mavis. "I heard that Claudia had found out he was screwing another girl—or girls—and she'd relapsed. I don't know, that part sounded a little fishy to me." She shrugged slightly. "Claudia and I weren't BFFs, but we were in group together and I knew her pretty well. She's the kind of girl who'd strangle a guy if he pissed her off."

She relapsed because she had a miscarriage, I thought, but I kept that to myself.

"When Claudia came back to Idylhaven in September, she was having a really tough, tough time. Like her withdrawal kept getting worse. Suddenly Dr. G appeared on the scene to help her. It was supposed to be this huge secret, but everybody knew. I mean, there are no secrets here."

"Was he able to help Claudia?"

"He did. It was weird. One of the girls said Claudia wanted to kick H for him. Who knows? But then Dr. G proposed to her. It was a huge, huge big deal because he'd spent his whole life preaching against marriage, and suddenly he wanted to get married. He gave Claudia this stunning diamond ring. She said it was his grandmother's engagement ring. I don't know if that part was true, but it was this beautiful, antique monster ring."

I almost choked. "Claudia got engaged?"

"Yeah. She was so happy. I didn't think anybody could be that happy, let alone goth girl. She was wearing the ring on a chain around her neck, since it was too big for her finger, but she kept showing the ring to everyone. She was like a little kid. I mean, in a good way. She said she couldn't wait to tell you, but she was going to get herself clean first."

"Did you see Gorevale?"

"A couple of times, just coming and going. I knew he wasn't allowed on Idylhaven's grounds. I think there was actually a restraining order or something."

"Did you know Trina Greene?" I asked.

"Yeah." Mavis's mouth twitched as if she'd had another taste of that bad lemon. She was actually silent for a couple of heartbeats. "She was my counselor for a while. Group and private sessions."

"She was a *counselor*?" My voice was loud, even to my own ears. "She wasn't a patient? She worked here?"

"For a couple of years. Miss Popularity. Everybody's best friend. Though, trust me, Trina has some serious issues of her own, especially with food," said Mavis. "Though, actually, I heard she lost a ton, a serious ton, of weight when she was out of work over the summer. It was crazy that she thought Zelda would take her back."

"Take her back?" I was having trouble following the thread of conversation, partly because of Mavis's rapid-fire delivery, but also because there was so much I hadn't heard before. I'd assumed Trina Greene was a patient. What else had I gotten wrong?

Mavis sighed. "If you met Trina, you'd have loved her. Loved! At first, anyway. She would seem so warm, like she cared about you so much. Of course, that was all bullshit. But she was really, really great at getting people to open up to her, though."

Of course she was, I thought. That was how she knew so much about Claudia. That was why she was able to regurgitate parts of Claudia's family history. "Why did she leave Idylhaven?"

"Trina was always looking for her next bigger, better deal," Mavis said. "She talked this girl from a rich family into hiring her as a sobriety companion. So Trina quit and went with her to California. Then, like three weeks later, this girl gets coked up and had a massive, massive car wreck. I heard Trina came back around here, but Zelda wouldn't give her her job back."

"Why would she come back here, then?" I asked. "Is her family around here?"

"No, I don't know where she's from. But she was dating a guy in town and she moved in with him. I guess she was re-grouping till she figured out her next move."

"Who's the boyfriend?"

"His name was Curt. Trina said he was creepy but he had a lot of money." Mavis made a snorting noise. "That was how Trina got you to open up to her. She'd tell you stuff about herself, bad stuff, like she was your girlfriend, and you'd reciprocate. Sneaky-smart, you know? She remembered everything, and she'd use it against you long after you forgot what you told her."

I wondered what Trina had done to Mavis, but knew it was none of my business. "Did Alec Gorevale know Trina Greene?"

"No way. He was gone a couple of years before she showed up. Trina was hired by Zelda."

And I'd run out of questions Mavis could answer. "Thanks for talking with me."

"No problem. How's your brother doing, by the way?"

"My brother? We don't have a brother." For a moment, I had a sense of déjà vu. This was how it had gone with Mr. Pete, when he'd tried to tell me about the *cousin* in Claudia's apartment. "Did Claudia tell you we did?"

"Sure. He's in trouble all the time, but he's a sweet kid. What's his name, starts with an *R* . . . Ridley."

"Oh, our, ah, stepbrother. Right. He's fine." I knew that Claudia liked Ridley, and he'd been drawn to her, but it had never occurred to me that they'd become that close. "Thanks again, Mavis. I appreciate it."

"It's nice to meet you. You're not nearly as scary as Claudia said."

"Scary?"

Mavis nodded. "She's in awe of you."

"No, I think she pretty much hates me."

"She does hate you a bit, but only because she wants to be you." Mavis picked up her tweezers. "Good luck."

I closed the door quietly and turned to the stairs with a lump in my throat. Hearing Claudia's twisted feelings about me from a stranger made my internal compass go haywire. I'd never been the scary one; that was Claudia with her tough look and wild life.

At the bottom of the servants' stairs I peered down the corridor that led to the grand foyer. Jesse and I had passed an office on our way into the building, and I was sure I knew which door it was. The problem was that it was just off the main foyer. How long would my luck hold? I decided to test it and made for the door. Of course it was locked. The knob rattled under my hand but wouldn't budge. I cursed under my breath and kicked it.

"Who are you?" asked a voice behind me.

"What?" I spun around. There was a skeletal woman in her late twenties with long blonde hair and a bubblegum-pink velour tracksuit with JUICY sprawling across her chest. "Oh, hi. I didn't hear you there," I hedged.

"You visiting someone?"

"Claudia Moore."

The blonde's expression was impassive. "Never heard of her. But I only got here a couple weeks ago. My family dumped me here so I wouldn't embarrass them on their holiday trip to Klosters." She was chewing a thick wad of gum, which tangled up her vowels. *Embawwass.* "You want into the office?" She pulled out a key and opened the door. "Membership has its privileges," she said, though it came out *pwivleges.* "I need to use the phone. Help yourself."

"Everyone get a key like that?" I asked her, and she laughed. "Ask Gori."

I almost asked if she meant Bela Lugosi the houseboy, but I held my tongue. The idea of cozying up to Gori to get phone privileges made me sad, and I hoped that Claudia had never done anything like that. The office was tidy but, like Zelda, it was not aging well. There was an ancient monitor housed in beige plastic sitting atop a particleboard desk, with a moldering computer tower on the floor next to it and a printer on a side table. The beige plastic phone looked like a vintage 1985 model, with pulsing red lights and a curly cord. Idylhaven wasn't wasting patients' money on office supplies, evidently. The blonde made her call, whispering frantically while I zeroed in on the gray metal file cabinet. The computer would be a natural place to store files, but given the state of the hardware, I was guessing it wasn't often put to use. The filing cabinet contained manila folders naming patients and their admission dates in black ink. The files only went back four years, making me wonder where the rest were. Had Idylhaven only existed for four years? That would be a question for Zelda. The files were organized by admission date and I scanned through them for my sister's. I went through the past September's files and didn't see it, backtracked through August's and then fast-forwarded through October, November, and December. There was nothing for Claudia Moore.

"Are you going to be much longer?" asked the blonde. "I need to lock the door."

"Give me a minute," I said.

"If Zelda catches me in here, I'll be locked in my room."

"Hold on." I'd just found a slim folder with Trina Greene's name on it. Her résumé and Social Security number were inside. There was an address in Boston. Was it possible that Claudia was there, pretending to be Trina?

"I've got to go," hissed the blonde.

"Okay, just go."

It wasn't until I heard the key turning in the lock that I understood what the blonde meant. I dropped Trina's file and went to the door. The knob wouldn't budge. She'd locked me inside the office. I swore under my breath and barely resisted the urge to kick the door. I was having trouble breathing all of a sudden. *Stop being stupid,* I told myself. *You've got a cell phone and a land line. You've probably even got e-mail here. You can get out.* But part of my brain kept hearing the click of the key in the lock. It made me remember my mother, and that gave me chills. After my father died, the crazy ideas that had always swirled around her brain took on the force of a tornado. She would lock Claudia and me in a closet for hours at a time, muttering under her breath about keeping the bad people away from us. My sister and I would keep each other calm while she ranted. We reacted in different ways. Claudia gravitated to dark rooms and small spaces; I became claustrophobic.

It felt as if the air were being sucked out of the office. I darted to the window and pulled it up. An alarm immediately sounded, and I shut the window quickly. The alarm didn't stop. I pulled open the window again and stared at the ground. It was only a drop of four feet or so, and everything was covered in snow. I pushed myself up to sit on the windowsill, swung my legs around, and jumped. The snow made my initial landing a soft one, but as I crashed through it something hit my legs and clawed at my face. I fought back, realizing belatedly that I was caught in a bush. I extracted myself from it as it scratched at my face and hands, staggering in the snow.

"Put your hands up in the air," ordered a voice I didn't recognize. I turned and saw Zelda's houseboy with a gun in his hand.

34

At the police station, all I could think was that Claudia would laugh her head off if she could see me now. First tumbling out a window and held at gunpoint, then cuffed and tossed into the back of a police car, and finally praying to be bailed out at the police station. I'd made my one phone call already. "You got yourself *arrested*?" Jesse had said, sounding shocked and oddly delighted. "Holy hell, Lil. When you're bad, you're *bad*."

I hadn't done anything really wrong, I told myself. I was looking for my sister, and that meant I had to do some things that were unusual, things that were out of character for me. It wasn't like I'd committed a crime. Still, I couldn't get Claudia's face out of my mind. I'd bailed her out of jail once after she'd hit a guy in the face with a bottle in a bar fight. I'd been furious at being dragged into her troubles yet again. I'd lectured her until I ran out of breath, but she'd just smiled. *You've been arrested again and you don't even take that seriously,* I'd said in frustration.

Maybe you should try it sometime, Lily, she'd said slyly. It was as if she'd had a vision of the future and was sure that one day I'd be the one waiting around in handcuffs.

"Sorry, miss, but we've got to take you to Pittsfield," said a young officer with a crew cut. "Sheriff wants to talk to you."

All I'd done was poke around some files at Idylhaven. It

didn't seem fair. We trudged out to the police car. The cop was decent enough to unlock the cuffs and let me sit in the front seat. I was holding on to that last shred of dignity.

At the Pittsfield station, the officer escorted me to the sheriff's door. I could hear laughter behind it. The officer smiled at me and I knocked uncertainly.

"Come in," called a gruff voice. The officer opened the door and we were immediately hit by a cloud of smoke. I coughed and squinted.

"Guess we should open the window," said Bruxton. Fanning in front of my eyes, I saw him slouching in a chair in front of the desk. He looked better in jeans and a shirt than he did in a wrinkled suit. His sandy hair was neatly combed and he looked like he'd shaved today.

"Sure thing," said the bulky man behind the desk. He was gray-haired and had a walrus moustache and brought to mind Teddy Roosevelt, minus the monocle. A smoldering cigar sat in an ashtray on his desk.

"Tiger Lily!" Jesse got up and hugged me.

"What the hell is going on?" I asked, staring at Bruxton over Jesse's shoulder.

"Got a little time on my hands, as my partner probably told you," said Bruxton, exhaling smoke. "I hear some people come up to these parts to relax, so I thought I would, too. This is my old pal Terry Noyes." I stared at him, feeling elated and grateful and yet completely inept at expressing it. He gave me that crooked little smile, where only one side of his mouth moved.

"Brux told me your sister is missing, Lily," said Noyes. "I'm sorry to hear that." He pulled out a chair for me. "We've been talking about that rehab center. *Idylhaven.*" The way he pronounced the name made his contempt clear.

"I told them all about how Zelda stonewalled us," Jesse volunteered.

"No surprise there," said Noyes. "Zelda's got a lot to worry about. That dump has come close to being shut down a couple of times."

"She had me arrested for trespassing," I pointed out.

"Don't worry about that. The arrest will be voided," said Noyes. "Zelda's terrified of bad publicity. She just wants to scare you off."

"Why?"

"Because the Doctor Feelgood who was behind the place—what was his name, Brux?"

"Alec Gorevale."

"Right, snooty Brit. Stare right past you on the street without so much as a hello," said Noyes. "Anyways, he had some detoxing strategies that were a little unorthodox."

"And illegal," Bruxton added. "Gorevale sedated patients for days while they went through the worst of their withdrawal. It's been done for years in Europe. It can work, but people have died from it."

"One of Doctor Feelgood's patient's almost died, which is how it came to our attention," said Noyes. "That was four years ago. The doc had to pay a big fine, and he almost had his license suspended."

"But he got to keep practicing medicine?" I asked.

"Uh-huh. Till about a year later, when one of the girls over at Idylhaven said he groped her."

"A girl I met there told me he was an octopus."

"Long story short is that Zelda, his business partner, bought him out after that," said Bruxton. "The good doctor moved on to greener pastures. Or, in his case, Nyack, New York."

"He never got charged?" asked Jesse.

"We would've thrown the book at him," said Noyes, "but the girl recanted. She was threatened, I'm sure of that, but I couldn't prove Gorevale did anything."

"Threatened?"

"She was going to press charges, then she dropped everything." Noyes sighed. "I tried to talk to her, but the girl was freaked out. 'That woman is going to kill me. She'll do anything to protect him.' She said that a couple times."

"That woman?" I prompted.

"She wouldn't say who it was. I sort of suspected Zelda Tapply, but it's not her style. Gorevale always seemed to have lots of groupies floating around. Anyway, the girl ran away."

"Do you have her name?" I asked. "I need to talk to her."

Noyes shook his head. "She died of an overdose after that. Boston PD could give you the details. But it wasn't a suspicious death."

"Sounds like there are a few reasons folks would want Gorevale dead," Jesse said.

"Can you tell me anything about a woman named Trina Greene?" I asked. "She was a counselor at Idylhaven, and she was the woman who died in my sister's apartment in New York."

Noyes smiled. "Jesse already gave us that name and we had Bob, the deputy, check her out. She's got no record, not even a parking ticket."

"I'm wondering if my sister could be living in Boston. I found Trina's old address in a file." I'd memorized it before Bela Lugosi had come at me with the gun. Both Noyes and Bruxton wrote it down as I recited it. I nudged Bruxton. "I thought the case was closed?"

"We still need to do a next-of-kin notification," Bruxton pointed out.

So many trails, all leading to nowhere. "Do you know anything about the cleaning lady, Brenda Collins?"

"Died in a house fire," said Noyes. "Grim. Bad ending to a sad life."

"What do you mean?" I asked.

"Brenda's husband used her like a punching bag. Then she'd turn around and lie to cover his sorry ass." Noyes shook his head. "Drive anybody to drink, watching the likes of that."

"You know how it's going to end up, sooner or later," Bruxton threw in.

"Exactly. Her husband killed her, then burned down the house thinking he'd get rid of the evidence." Noyes rubbed his eyes. "It was too bad, since Brenda had been telling people she was going to leave the bastard for good just before that. Probably why he killed her. Bastard like that can't stand losing control of his victim."

"Do you have a photo of her?" I asked.

Noyes called for the young recruit. "Can you find the Collins file, Bob?" A moment later, the recruit trotted in, discreetly closing the door as he left.

"You don't want to see a lot of this," said Noyes, rifling through it. "There was nothing but a charred stump of Brenda left after the fire. Had to identify her through dental records." He pulled a couple of Polaroids out. "That's her."

I looked at the snapshots. The woman staring back looked like she'd been cornered. She had limp brown hair that hung to her shoulders, pockmarked skin, and a weak chin. Her most prominent feature was a black eye that was three shades of purple. Her other eye seemed to dart lazily in another direction, embarrassed by its twin.

Jesse glanced over my shoulder. "Terrible," he said softly. "Where's the husband now?"

"Doing twenty-five to life at Cedar Junction," Noyes answered. "Rat bastard that he is, he's trying to appeal the conviction. Everybody knows he's guilty as sin."

"He killed his wife, then started the fire to cover it up?" I asked.

"That's what it looked like. Couple of witnesses said he told them he was going to do it if the bitch left him. Not that I put much stock in their word."

"Why not?" I asked.

"They're buddies with Corey Kerry. The name wouldn't mean anything to you, but he's a major dealer in these parts," said Noyes. "He's also Brenda's brother. We figured he put his buddies up to it, to make sure the husband didn't go free. Not that you could really blame Corey, since his sister was murdered."

"Hold up—drugs?" asked Jesse.

"Right." Noyes nodded.

"You're not gettin' me," said Jesse. "The cleaning lady . . . from the rehab center . . . her brother's a drug dealer?"

"I get it," said Noyes. "I know Brenda went through random drug testing at Idylhaven—all their employees get it— and she never failed one. Brenda was never in trouble. She was one of those women who goes around quivering, you know, like she's waiting for somebody to hit her. Her husband's a piece of shit, pardon my French. He put her in the hospital a few times. Then Brenda would go sleep on a friend's couch for a week, but she'd always go home in the end."

"Do you know who the friend was?" I asked Noyes.

THE DAMAGE DONE   289

"Sure. Trina Greene."

We were all silent, as if we'd been given a glimpse of a giant jigsaw puzzle, but that the pieces amounted to less than we'd originally thought.

Bruxton's voice cut into my thoughts. "What was the husband's alibi for the fire?"

"He was out drinking with some buddies." Noyes puffed on his cigar. "He later amended that to out getting high with some buddies."

"What a winner," Bruxton commented.

"This was an open-and-shut case," said Noyes. "Only funny thing was the dog." All eyes turned to him and he shrugged. "Brenda had this little white dog her husband used to kick around, mean bastard that he was. But he left the dog out in the yard, tied to a tree, when he set the fire. I always thought that was the damnedest thing." Noyes tucked his hands behind his head and stared into the distance. "All her friends said he was so mean to the dog. I always wondered why he didn't kill it when he killed her."

35

Back at the motel, I threw myself down on the bed and stared at the ceiling. "You know, Lil, they don't clean bedspreads that often," said Jesse, swinging his carry-on bag onto his bed and unzipping it.

"Ugh," I responded, aware that I should have known better. Shuddering, I got up to pull down the bedspread, then threw myself dramatically onto the pillows. "What are the odds that two people from Idylhaven die on the same weekend? Alec Gorevale on a Saturday night, and then the cleaning lady on Sunday."

"It sounds like the cleanin' lady was bound to get killed by her husband sooner or later," said Jesse as he hung up a fresh shirt, pulling at a slight crease. "That's what you call an established MO."

"Excuse me? Since when did you start talking like a cop?"

"That Detective Bruxton is kinda cute," said Jesse, hanging up a pair of jeans. "Don't tell me you haven't noticed."

"The last thing I need right now is you meddling in my love life. I'm here to find my sister. Bruxton's here because he feels bad that the case was closed. That's all."

"You keep tellin' yourself that, Tiger Lily. He's sweet on you."

I went into the bathroom to change into fresh clothes. When I came out, the sight of a handgun sitting next to a toiletry bag stopped me in my tracks. "Tell me you didn't bring a real gun."

"C'mon, Lil. Things have been crazy. I mean, Tariq got shot. Tariq! By your lousy ex, no less." Jesse shook his head. "Things are screwy around here, and until they're set right, I'm packin' heat."

"So you're going to play vigilante?"

"I'm not fixin' to shoot anybody. But when the other guy's bringin' a gun to the fight, you don't pack a peashooter."

I knew that Jesse owned a gun, but I'd never seen it before. It was surprisingly innocent looking, like a misallocated movie prop with its silver barrel and black handle. "I don't understand how you could even want to touch a gun, after what . . . happened . . . with your parents," I told him.

There was a long pause. Jesse avoided looking at me. I wondered what he remembered when he thought about his parents. Their murder-suicide must have cast a pall over every family memory he ever had, the way that my father's death haunted every Christmas and my mother's suicide lurked in the air over New Year's.

"It's the damnedest thing," said Jesse. "You're like a terrier, holdin' on to the bad stuff for dear life. Like you're afraid to exist without it."

"That's not true."

"Lotta bad things have happened to you over the years, Lil. But you hold on to each one like it's some kind of treasure. Like you want to remember it."

"How could I forget? Why would I want to?"

"You obsess. Like with that bracelet. Since you got it back you're clingin' to it for life."

"My father gave it to me," I said.

"My daddy gave me my first gun," said Jesse. "When I was twelve. We used to go huntin' together." He picked up the handgun, looking at it from different angles. "It's at home in Oklahoma. Kind of hard to hide a rifle. My daddy never laid eyes on this one."

"But doesn't every gun remind you of your parents? Doesn't it make you think about how your father could have done what he did?"

"I've spent a lot of time thinkin' on Exodus," Jesse said.

I stared at him blankly. I knew that Adam and Eve were in Genesis, and that the Apocalypse was in Revelations, but everything in between eluded me. I was a very lapsed Catholic who'd been known to pray in times of crisis, but my trips to church were almost exclusively for sightseeing purposes.

"The sins of the father shall be visited upon the sons, or upon the children, if you don't want to be sexist about it," Jesse said, sighing.

"I've heard that before and I think it's horrible. Why should a child suffer for what their parent did?"

"It's not prescriptive, Lil. It's a fact, and maybe a warnin'. Whatever a parent does is going to stay with their child forever." Jesse set the gun down. "That's not the way it's usually interpreted, but that's how I think of it. I asked myself for years how could my daddy do what he did? Didn't even leave a damn note. And just after Christmas." He shook his head. "But then I remember how sick my mother was. She had a tumor on her spine. She couldn't walk anymore. Couldn't lift her head, she was in so much pain. I think she wanted to have that one last Christmas together, and then she wanted to die." He stared at the floor. "Don't know if they ever discussed it, the two of them, but I believe my daddy did what he thought my mama wanted. Then, 'course, he couldn't live without her."

I rubbed his back just below the nape of his neck. "I'm sorry."

"When I think of them, I try to remember what it was like before my mama got sick."

He was quiet a moment. I kissed the top of his head. "Thank you for coming with me," I said. "For taking care of me. For everything. I'd be lost without you."

"I know." We were interrupted by a knock on the door.

"Showtime," said Bruxton. "You ready?"

"As much as I'll ever be," I answered.

We are not in the habit of breaching our patients' confidentiality." Zelda Tapply's thin, angry mouth trembled at the corners. She had transformed into a quivering blue-veined mass of righteousness when we went back to Idylhaven with Bruxton. "May I see your subpoena?"

"I was hoping not to have to go that route," Bruxton said.

"Well, I am afraid you will have to. Though, of course, you don't have grounds for one. Even if you found a court officer willing to sign one, our lawyer would file an injunction." Zelda's lips pulled back in an imitation of a smile. A smug one. "And you should know that I will be filing a complaint with your superiors for bringing *that woman* into this place. She has already been arrested once today." Zelda's rheumy glare made it clear she hoped it wouldn't be the last.

"Here's the thing," said Bruxton. "You can let me see the file now, and this will go away quietly. Or I can put in calls to some reporters I know." He leaned forward, putting his hands on the desk. "That's the thing about being one of New York's finest. City's crawling with reporters. When you've got a place like Idylhaven—a place that almost killed a patient with experimental detox, where a doctor can fuck his patients with impunity—you've got one hot story."

"Dr. Gorevale is no longer affiliated with Idylhaven," said Zelda firmly. "Besides, he's dead."

"This place used to be called Gorevale House," Bruxton snapped. "He founded the fucking institution."

Jesse and I looked at each other. We'd missed that little detail.

"There is no need for foul language," Zelda answered. "Dr. Gorevale has had nothing to do with the facility for the past several years."

"But you still referred patients to him, didn't you?" Bruxton stood straight. "A drug scandal and a sex scandal? The tabloids will have a field day. This place is going to be shut down, and you'll be ticking off your last years in jail."

I remembered exactly why I'd thought of Bruxton as a pit bull the first day we met. He'd scared me then. The only thing that had changed was that he was now tearing into other people on my behalf.

Zelda opened a drawer and handed a thin manila folder to Bruxton. He leafed through it.

"This all there is?" he asked. Zelda nodded primly. "Where's the file from Claudia Moore's first stay here?"

Zelda's lips quivered. "I just have one file."

"I'm going to ask this real slow, so you can follow," said Bruxton. "Was there more than one file on Claudia?"

"Yes," said Zelda, in a small voice.

"How many?"

"Two."

"What happened to the first one?"

"It was sent to Dr. Gorevale when Claudia decided to pursue a private course of treatment with him. Dr. Gorevale was banned from this facility, but we still referred some of the particularly difficult opiate-addiction cases to him." Zelda's blue eyes were watery. "You have to understand, these are incredibly difficult cases. Most of them can't get through the physical withdrawal, and they stand no chance of getting well if they don't. It's a desperate situation, and it calls for solutions that aren't open to us legally."

Bruxton ignored her explanation. "Did Gorevale ever send that file back?" Zelda shook her head. "So all that information is gone?"

Zelda nodded. "You're not going to bring the police into this, are you? I need your assurance—"

"I need to know what's missing from the file," said Bruxton.

"The contents would be similar to what you see there. Notes from her psychologist, from her counselor, from the doctors."

"Her counselor?" I asked. "Trina Greene would have made notes about my sister?"

"Well—yes."

"What about what isn't reported?" asked Bruxton. "What was Claudia's state of mind when she left this place?"

"She was distraught when she left."

"Distraught?"

"We all found out that morning that Dr. Gorevale had died," said Zelda. "It was a terrible, terrible shock. Claudia was, I believe, very close to him."

"Close . . . to him." Bruxton dragged out the words suggestively.

"Claudia had a very difficult time when she came here in

the spring," said Zelda. "There are some people that the replacement therapies don't work for, and I'm afraid your sister was one of them. Alec was her last resort for treatment."

"She had him knock her unconscious for days while she went through withdrawal?" I asked.

"That method has worked for many people," Zelda answered quickly, sitting up straighter. "It's used in conjunction with naltrexone, as it is in Europe. It is not some sort of unproven fringe therapy."

"But it is an illegal one," said Bruxton. "What are the side effects?"

"You have to understand, there are upsides and downsides to every course of treatment," said Zelda. "Methadone, the most common, is itself an addictive drug. You must lower the dosage over the course of several months, but even the slightest change in dosage can cause physical agony. With rapid detoxification, you avoid basically all of the physical withdrawal symptoms. But..."

"But..." I prompted.

"The psychological addiction to heroin is very powerful. Unfortunately the therapy does not address that."

"So what happens?"

"Well, if a patient is closely monitored by their doctor, and has a supportive environment, and counseling, they have the conditions necessary to combat serious addiction."

"And what if the patient was having an affair with her doctor?" I asked.

"Then her recovery would be... fragile," Zelda said.

"So Claudia Moore left here, distraught, on September twenty-ninth," said Bruxton. "Where was she going?"

"I don't know," said Zelda. "Our patients aren't prisoners,

and we cannot hold them here against their will, you know. This center is devoted entirely to voluntary rehabilitation."

"Because if cases were sent to you by the state, the state would have oversight on your operation." Bruxton sneered.

"How did Claudia leave? Did she call a taxi?" I asked.

"She went with Brenda," Zelda said.

"Brenda Collins, the cleaning lady?"

"Yes. Many of the girls here form—I mean, formed—close friendships with Brenda," Zelda said. "She does errands for them, or takes them out if they, ah, need something."

"Brenda's brother was the local drug dealer," Bruxton snapped. "You think that had anything to do with Brenda's popularity among the addicts?"

36

We drove back with Bruxton, picking up a couple of pizzas on the way to the motel. He checked in and came over to our room. "Make yourself at home, Detective," said Jesse. "Figure anything out yet?"

"I don't like loose ends," said Bruxton. "There are too many here. Claudia Moore is missing. Trina Greene is dead. Brenda Collins is dead. Dr. Gorevale, patient molester, is dead. Nothing adds up."

"Tariq Lawrence was shot," I added. "His driver was killed."

"You're making me feel like a wuss for just getting suspended," said Bruxton. "There's been a lot of blood spilled over something we can't figure out. Trina Greene's death was suspicious. Brenda Collins's was clearly murder. Gorevale's is just freaky. Martin Sklar tried to murder Tariq, but what kind of connection could there be between him and, say, Trina Greene?"

"You don't think Martin killed her, do you?" Even though I'd lost faith in my ex, I didn't believe he was running around killing people. Even if he had threatened Kaylee Quan.

"New Year's Eve at your sister's building, someone knocked out the power and took out the security camera," said Bruxton. "That's the work of a pro, not an amateur. Thanks to your nosy neighbor Mrs. Decarno, we know two men went to your sister's apartment that night. Trina Greene was killed on purpose. Every instinct tells me she was."

We were silent for a moment. "I should call Padma to find out how Tariq is doing," I said.

"Why don't we take this party to my room?" said Bruxton. He and Jesse shuffled out with the pizzas and drinks. I called Padma and talked to her for a few minutes. She had seen Tariq that afternoon, just for a few minutes, and she was elated. "The doctor said she had never seen such a strong will as my cousin's," she said proudly. "He is doing much better than they predicted."

After we hung up, I dialed Martin's number, even though I knew I'd get nothing. While the *full mailbox* message came on, I got a call, saw on the cracked screen that it was Sarah again, and let it slide into voice mail. When I went to pick up her message, I was stunned to hear Martin's voice. "Lily, sweetheart, it's me. I just want to tell you not to worry, no matter what you hear. Everything will be fine, I promise you that. Trust me. I love you."

I almost dropped the phone. I listened to Martin's voice again, then examined the call log. No, I hadn't missed his call; he must have called the message center directly. Why hadn't he wanted to speak to me? I listened to it one more time, then sent it into the ether. Sarah's message was next. She wanted to let me know that a woman had come into her building and had knocked endlessly on my sister's door. "I thought it might be the woman I saw in November," she said, her voice bubbling with excitement. "I called the police but the woman ran away." I saved the message, feeling an odd combination of gratitude that she cared, and curiosity as to why she'd decided to get so involved. There was something

about her that niggled at my memory, but I was too preoccupied to think about what it was. I went to Bruxton's room
and gave them an update.

"I'm so confused by everything," I admitted. "I feel like
I'm going in circles."

"Welcome to police work," said Bruxton. "You'd make a
good detective, if you weren't so impatient."

It was well after midnight when Jesse and I went back to
our room. I brushed my hair and fanned it out over my shoulders. "Why doncha put on some more lipstick and eyeliner
while you're at it?" asked Jesse.

"What do you mean?"

"Miss Innocent. I take it you noticed there's a nice hunk of
man meat down the hall."

"You're not seriously suggesting that Bruxton and I . . ."

"Let me put it like this," said Jesse. "He's been lookin' at
you like you're the answer to every riddle he ever came
across."

"He's not my type."

"No, your type burns down buildings and makes money
off other folks' sufferin'. You hang around and feel guilty
about it."

"Guilty?"

"From the time I met you, when you were a bundle of
guilt about leaving your mother and sister. Then guilt about
Claudia. Guilt kept you with Martin, since you could hang
around with someone with some pretty sick kinks and say it
was okay 'cause you were helpin' him."

"Stop!" I said. "Are you giving up photography to be a
shrink?"

"Ava wasn't the self-analytical type, either, Lil. Maybe
that's why you like her so much. She just kind of crashed

through life, pulling up stakes on a whim, moving to Spain, takin' up with bullfighters 'cause she felt like it." He chuckled to himself. "Y'know, maybe she's a good role model for you. Why don't you just go have some fun with a guy for once instead of tying yourself up in knots?"

"I can't." I looked at the floor.

"Can't, Tiger Lily? 'Course you can." He came closer and must have caught the look on my face. "No. No. Don't tell me you . . . you didn't! Not with . . . Sklar?"

I nodded grimly.

"I can't believe it. No, 'course I can believe it." Jesse sat on the bed and his shoulders drooped as if he'd given up on me. "You get away from him for a while, then you go right back to him. You and Claudia are exactly alike."

"What's that supposed to mean?"

"You're addicts. Your sister's problem—I know she had more than one, but bear with me—her addiction is heroin. Yours is pain. You both get hurt, and you run away for a while, but you always end up goin' back for another helpin'."

"You can't compare love with an illegal drug," I protested.

"Sure you can. Just a different delivery method." He shook his head, as if clearing the cobwebs. "Let me tell you somethin', Lil. You can see Claudia's problems, bright as day. But she can see yours, too."

"What, have you been getting calls from her like Martin did?"

"Not recently. But when you and Martin got engaged, she phoned me."

"You never told me that."

"She wanted to save you from yourself," said Jesse. "She said Martin played these head games that made you doubt yourself all the time. She said it was like watchin' your mother and father again. Martin always comes off so reasonable, but there's somethin' not right about that fella."

I felt myself getting heated again. First Tariq and now Jesse. How many people had Claudia blabbed to about our parents? "Claudia said that? What did you tell her?"

"You know I've always hated him," Jesse answered defensively. "I'm not gonna lie. I despised him even before I had reason to. I was jealous when he swept in and swept you off your feet. You were mine first and suddenly I couldn't compete."

"Do you know how dumb this sounds? If you were straight, no one would ever have been able to pry me away from you." I smiled, in spite of my annoyance. "Martin's jealous of you, too. It's as if, deep down, he knows that I'll always love you more."

Jesse grinned back at me, but his smile faded when he spoke again. "The thing is, I was right about him. He can't be trusted. It wasn't just the other women. Don't give me that look, Lil. I said *women,* plural, not just that lady architect you kept worrying about. It was more than that. The only thing Martin Sklar ever loved is himself."

"That's not true. He loves his son." I felt sad even as I said the words. Yes, I was positive Martin loved his boy, no matter how much trouble Ridley caused him. I'd wanted him to love me in that same unconditional, reckless way.

"Fine, can't argue with you there. But if I was a parent, I figure I'd be gettin' my kid help instead of sweepin' his problems under the rug," said Jesse. "But that's not what this is about. I caught Martin Sklar cheatin' on you with another girl. He'd taken her up to the Berkshires for a weekend, and I was here with Ted. He had his arms around her and I thought he'd swallow his tongue when he caught sight of me, but he was smooth as twelve-year-old scotch. 'Course, he knew you wouldn't leave even when I told you."

I stood there, thunderstruck. I remembered the weekend; Martin had told me he had a corporate retreat to go to. When I'd mentioned that Jesse had spotted him with a woman, Martin said that she was one of the corporate trainers and that she was surprisingly attractive for a lesbian.

"I know it sounds bad, Lil, but that's why I decided to help Claudia."

It took me a minute to unknot my tongue. "Help Claudia?"

"That time Claudia sat in Martin's lap? That was maybe a little . . . staged. We figured that the only way you'd leave that bastard was if you caught him cheatin' on you with your sister."

Suddenly I remembered Tariq's words on the drive home from Long Island. *Claudia has always found your fiancé particularly loathsome. She said that he was a charming, shallow ne'er-do-well like your father, and that he'd drive you to drink and an early grave like your mother.*

"How could you?" I asked Jesse. "How could you do that to me?"

"I love you, Lil. I can't stand the thought of anyone hurting you. You wouldn't listen when I tried to tell you how awful Sklar is. Claudia and I talked and decided this was the only thing you'd pay attention to."

I felt as if a bucket of cold water had been poured over my head.

"Lil, this happened ages ago. I'm sorry, I really am. I know you're angry right now, but I'm hoping you'll understand I was just trying to—"

"To help. Sure, I get it." I was chilled but my head felt incredibly clear, as if adrenaline were coursing through my body but not raising my pulse. "I don't want to talk to you right now." He started to interrupt, and I put my hand up. "I can't. I don't want to listen to anything else right now." I walked out the door and pulled it shut behind me, cursing myself three seconds later for not grabbing my coat. I hated motels. Instead of returning for the coat I knocked on Bruxton's door. He opened it, naked from the waist up. His body was corded with muscle, which didn't surprise me, but he was tattooed from his wrists on up his arms, over his shoulders and down his torso.

"Hi," I said. "Do you have a cigarette?"

He handed me the pack, then lit me up.

"You want to come in?" he asked.

"I think I'll just stay out here, thanks."

Bruxton was already pulling on his shirt. "I don't bite, you know."

"Wish I'd known that when I met you."

The corners of his mouth twitched. "Bark's bad enough." He joined me on the walkway and handed me his jacket. "If you're going to stand outside, try not to catch hypothermia." There were four cars in the dark parking lot, and the snow picked up the brightness of the moon almost as well as a street lamp. "You don't see stars like this in the city," Bruxton said.

"Not in Spain, either." We stared up for a while, smoking wordlessly, before I broke the silence. "What's your name, anyway? All anyone ever calls you is Bruxton or Brux."

"Hemingway," said Bruxton. I gave him a quizzical look and he cracked up. "You're an easy mark. Want to buy a bridge in Brooklyn?"

"Cut it out. You've told me you're an alcoholic, and that you're divorced, and that your wife cheated on you. Don't you think you can tell me your name?"

He took a long drag. "When I was getting sober, I read this book, *Lighting Up,* by some broad who said you should live the least secretive life you can. I like that. But there's personal and there's *personal.* You want to tell me more tales of your sleepwalking adventures?"

"You really hold a grudge, don't you?"

"Damn straight."

"Will you be straight with me for a minute? Do you think we're going to find my sister?"

Bruxton made a sound that could have been a sigh and threw his butt into the snow. "Why are you asking me that now, Lily?" He fired up a fresh cigarette.

Ever since I'd found out that Claudia had checked herself out of rehab when Gorevale had died, I'd been pushing away a memory of her face. Not her wicked eyes or troublemaking mouth, but the face I'd seen lying on the floor of my apartment when she'd overdosed. Her skin was clammy and her lips were almost blue. She was barely breathing anymore and there was still a spike in her arm. She'd never told me whether it was an accident. We'd never really talked about it at all. After she came out of the hospital she moved in with me and that was that.

"Claudia came to my apartment a couple of years ago. I was out, but she had a key. She deliberately overdosed. I never understood why. I mean, why there?"

"Maybe she wanted you to save her."

"She couldn't have known I'd come home when I did," I argued.

"Why'd you go back?"

"Claudia called me and she asked . . . she said, *Remember that poem you used to recite for me?*" I could still hear her voice, calm and composed, even though it felt like she was drifting further away with each syllable. I took a last, long drag on my cigarette and ground the butt out.

"What poem?"

" 'The Raven.' That was what she meant." It was hard to explain to another person. No one else would have gotten it. It was like our little in-joke, only it was sad instead of funny.

"Right," Bruxton said. "You told me you both like Poe. All I know from 'The Raven' is *Nevermore.* I wasn't such a hell of a student."

" 'Distinctly I remember it was in the bleak December, and each separate dying ember wrought its ghost upon the floor,' " I recited. It was from the second stanza of the poem, but Bruxton didn't know the difference, or didn't care. He smiled, and in the cold moonlight his angular face was wolfishly handsome. For a split second, I wished he would pull me close and kiss me. I wanted to obliterate thought and memory and drink him in. It was weakness to want to cling to him, and I was disgusted with that part of myself, but that didn't make the craving go away. It was a relief when he turned his face to look up at the sky again.

"You ever hear the line, 'Every junkie's like a setting sun'?" he asked. I shook my head. "Neil Young. Vintage, but not enough for your tastes, I guess."

"What made you think of it?"

He looked up at the stars again, as if debating whether to answer my question. "You know why I left the narcotics division in Ithaca? I was an addict. Alcohol—I already told you about that. Cocaine, pills. I was machine bent on self-destruction. I'd been that way pretty much my whole life, and it was catching up with me."

"Why? I mean, why were you like that?"

"You want another cigarette?" he asked, holding out the

pack. I shook my head. "See, that's the difference between you and me. You know when to stop."

I could think of a few instances that would prove him wrong. "What stopped you?"

"My kid got hit by a car." He caught my alarmed expression. "He's ten now, Lily, and he's fine. But he was in the hospital and no one could find me. I was off getting drunk, getting high." His eyes were hot with shame. "I fucked up my life without a thought. My son healed up okay, but by the time I got myself straight my marriage was over. I blamed my wife—she was the one who had the affair with my best friend—but I was the one who got us into a place where that could happen."

"At least you got yourself together." Something bitter had crept into my voice. Bruxton might have screwed up, but he'd worked to make things right, and that was more than my mother had ever done. It wasn't her fault that we'd lost our father, but she had slipped out of our lives, too, swallowed up by the bottle. Maybe that wasn't her fault, either. But I'd tried to fill the void she left in Claudia's life and I had failed miserably. I'd never forgive my mother for forcing me into a role I had no idea how to play. There were so many things I regretted about my relationship with Claudia, moments I wished I could snatch back, times when I'd been selfish instead of helping her. Whatever she'd become was as much my fault as her own. Maybe more.

"It took me a while," Bruxton said. "Addicts aren't in their right minds. I don't mean that as an excuse. Just a warning. For when we find your sister."

37

On Saturday morning I veered away from Lenox's main street, walking along beautiful boulevards of redbrick Federalist-style houses. Jesse had parked in the center of town. I'd told him I had a couple of places I wanted to see, and he didn't ask what. It was unlike him, but we were both raw from our fight the night before. Jesse was being oddly courteous. "Take care, now," he'd said when I walked away. For some reason, I felt bereft without his meddling. I turned around and saw that he was behind me, but some distance away, and I didn't look back after that.

When I found a small sign that read CURTIS HERROLD, D.D.S. my heart thudded heavily in my chest. The dentist had been odd on the phone, but it wasn't just that. Lying awake in my motel bed, I'd remembered a fragment of my conversation with Mavis. I'd asked her about Trina's boyfriend, and she'd said, *His name was Curt. Trina said he was creepy but he had a lot of money.* Could it be the dentist? I'd wanted to race out of bed and tell Bruxton. Instead, I'd eventually fallen asleep and missed him; Bruxton had gone out early with his friend Noyes to talk to Brenda Collins's drug-dealing brother.

Herrold's house was a three-story structure with a large, gabled verandah and a mansard roof; it appeared to be both home and office. At the door I rang the bell and heard it echoing through the house. One thing that wouldn't stop niggling at me was the fact that Herrold had stopped sending past-due payment notices to Claudia after September. What did he know that the rest of us didn't?

The man who answered the door was in his early fifties, with a large round head that had a few tendrils of ashy hair scraped over the top. He was an inch or two taller than me, with a belly that made his shirt gape as it sloshed over his belt. A small white dog nipped at his slippers. "Get back there, kiddo," he said in a jolly voice.

"Cute dog." I knelt so that I could pet her.

"Thank you. She's always into everything." His smile lifted his jowls slightly and revealed perfect teeth. When I stood, his grin vanished. "Do . . . do I know you?"

I introduced myself. "We never met in person, but we spoke on the phone. You said Claudia owed you money."

"Oh, I . . . I just wrote that off. I never . . . I never thought you'd come all this way . . . I mean, it was just a couple of cavities I filled. It was no big deal."

"That's nice of you. I'd like to ask you a few questions, if you don't mind."

"I'm just going out. I'm sorry. Don't worry about the money. It's all settled." He was retreating, trying to close the door.

I stepped inside and smiled at him, pretending I hadn't noticed his hands were shaking. "It's really important, and it will just take a minute. So, how do you know my sister?"

"She was my patient."

"And you . . . filled her cavities?" I prompted.

"Yes." The dog whined at his feet.

"Did you get to know her at all?"

"Just a little. She was a nice girl," he said. In the back of my mind, a bell went off. *Was?*

"Trina Greene has been living in my sister's apartment for the past few months. How do you know Trina?"

"Trina?" There was something in the way he said it, a wistfulness that underscored the name, that connected the dots in my brain. The man in front of me was, with the exception of his teeth, exactly how I'd envision a troll, which must have made him a perfect mark for Trina's charms. "Trina's still in New York?" he asked hopefully.

"Trina's been impersonating my sister since October. What I want to know is, where's my sister?"

"Why . . . don't you . . . ask Trina?" There were little droplets of perspiration on Herrold's temple.

"I'm asking you."

"Why would I . . . why would I do anything to her?" The little white dog cocked her head from side to side and put her two front paws on his foot.

"I didn't say you did." I was more anxious by the second. "Is that Brenda Collins's dog, by any chance?"

"Br—Brenda?" His lips quivered.

"The woman who died in the fire."

"What do you . . . want?"

"I want to know what happened. What did you do?"

"Nothing . . . I . . . nothing. Go away!" He turned and lumbered toward the back of the house. He stopped at a doorway, gave a little shudder, and went inside. The little dog yelped and went in after him. I ran down the hallway, unwilling to let him dodge me now, and charged through the doorway he'd entered, stopping dead in the center of the room. Herrold was standing behind a desk, holding a gun and pointing it at me.

"What the hell are you doing?" I was more angry than scared. "Is that a real gun?"

Herrold ignored my question. "You said Trina's at your sister's apartment?" Sweat was trickling down his face now and the gun was shaking in his hand.

"Yes."

"Don't move or I'll shoot." He spun an old Rolodex on his desk with his left hand. I took a step back and he cocked the gun. "I told you not to move!"

I froze in place. The Rolodex was flanked by framed pictures, all with their backs to me. Did he have children? Maybe I could appeal to his sense of decency . . . And then I saw what was on his wall. There was an enormous photograph of a blond, plump Trina sitting on Herrold's lap, one freckled arm slithering around his neck. Across from it was another picture, this one just a portrait of Trina. She was squeezed into a black, corsetlike dress that her breasts popped over the top of while she dangled a red stiletto pump off one foot. She was more attractive than I'd realized, but she looked hard and cheap. Claudia was tough, but also dreamy and romantic.

"The police are outside, Curtis. They're waiting for you. They know what you did and you're not getting out of here."

"Shut up," he said. "This is all your sister's fault."

It took him three tries to dial the phone, because he kept glaring at me. He put it on speakerphone and I heard it ring, and then a woman's voice, as breathy as a Marilyn Monroe impersonator's. "You know the deal, don't you? So leave a message."

"Trina?" Herrold said, after the beep. "Trina, dammit, where are you? Why aren't you answering your phone? Trina, baby, I've been waiting for you to call me. Where have you gone now?"

"She's never going to call you back. She's dead."

Herrold dropped the receiver. "What . . . what did you say?"

"Trina Greene is dead. She died in Claudia's apartment."

"No!" Herrold cried. "No, no, no, no. My poor baby." His

sweaty hand was shaking so much I was terrified the gun would go off.

"She died on New Year's Eve," I said coldly. "If you didn't hear from her before then, it's because she didn't want to talk to you."

"Trina wouldn't do that. We're getting married. I gave her a diamond from Tiffany's."

"Let me guess: a two-carat princess-cut solitaire?" Herrold nodded dumbly. "Trina stuck that in the back of a drawer. She was showing off a much bigger, much nicer diamond ring to everyone in New York."

"She loves me," Herrold whispered in a warbling voice. "Something's wrong with her cell phone, that's all."

"Did you hear what I just said? Trina has been impersonating Claudia for months. Now she's dead. Where is my sister?"

"I don't have to talk to you."

"Maybe not, but you'll talk to the police."

"The police? They know?"

"What did you think, I just wandered in here alone?" I wondered if I could sprint down the hallway and out of the house without him getting off a shot. My luck wasn't that good. "I came in here to get the truth, before they arrest you."

"Arrest . . . me?" There were tears in his eyes. "I didn't do anything to Claudia, I swear. I just . . . I just did what Trina asked me to do."

"And what did Trina want?"

"She said I had to . . . to switch the records."

"Switch the . . ." I couldn't catch my breath. "The dental records."

Herrold blinked back tears and nodded quickly. "I didn't kill anyone, I swear."

"Kill . . . anyone?"

"It wasn't Trina, either. Brenda called her and told her Claudia had overdosed at her house. It was an accident, but Brenda was terrified she'd be sent to prison. Brenda's brother would've gone to jail, too."

"So it was Brenda's fault."

"Yes, exactly." He nodded so hard I heard his neck creak. "They didn't know what to do. They finally got a hold of Brenda's brother and he came up with a plan to . . . hide what happened. Brenda had to get away from her husband anyway . . . Corey said it was like killing two birds with one stone." His eyes were darting wildly as the words tumbled out of his mouth. "And Trina just wanted to help Brenda, Brenda was her good friend, so she had her come in here and I X-rayed Brenda's teeth. Then Trina . . . she made me switch the X-rays with your sister's."

I was reeling. The body the police had found at Brenda Collins's house, the body that was burned beyond recognition, was Claudia's. My sister was dead.

Herrold couldn't seem to stop talking. "Corey said somebody had to rent a car using your sister's license, and it couldn't be Brenda so it had to be Trina. So Trina dyed her hair black and put on makeup like your sister wore. She had to get Brenda out of town. That's the only reason she went to New York. She stayed for a while to help Brenda find a place . . . and then, I don't know, she just ended up staying longer . . . like she never planned to come back."

Herrold lowered the gun and held it by his side with a twitching arm. "What are they going to do to me?" he pleaded. "I didn't hurt anyone, I swear. Trina promised she'd marry me. I only did it to help her. Your sister's death, it was an accident. Nobody should go to jail for an accident."

"You're going to go to prison and rot there for the rest of your miserable life."

Herrold's purple tongue flicked over his lips. "I bet you're lying about the police. I didn't see anyone outside." His blubbery face took on a sly look. "I bet you're lying about Trina, too."

"Maybe I'm making up the fact that there was plenty of acid damage on her teeth because she was a bulimic. They found that during the autopsy," I shot back. "But why should you care? Trina was just using you. When she moved to New York she hooked up with someone rich who took really good care of her, in case you're wondering why she hadn't called you in all this time. You know Trina likes the finer things in life."

He sank into the chair behind the desk. It groaned under him in protest. As he looked up at me, his lips trembled like a big baby's. He felt sorry for himself, the bastard. For Trina, too, even though she had abandoned him. He didn't give a damn about Claudia. His fat, round head dropped to his chest and he started to sob. "Trina . . . Trina . . ." he burbled.

I stared at him, every inch of me filled with hatred. I wanted to grab the gun and shoot him, but that wouldn't be enough punishment. "Death is too good for you. You deserve to suffer."

Someone pounded on the front door. Herrold lifted his head, his face filled with terror. In the only swift, unclumsy motion I saw him make, he raised the gun, put it against his temple, and fired.

38

Jesse answered the door when the police came. I heard their boots beating down the hallway, then one shouting, "The body's in here!" A minute later I felt hands on my shoulders as someone lifted me to my feet from the cold tile of the kitchen floor. I was still clutching my cell phone and someone took it from me. "My sister's dead," I said, breaking down completely. I sank back to the floor and the police let me stay there for a while. In the background, I could hear the frantic yipping of the little dog over their voices, until someone took it out of the house.

Horrible as watching Herrold shoot himself was, it was nothing compared to finding out what had happened to Claudia. He deserved to die, I told myself. He'd switched Claudia's records. Trina Greene and Brenda Collins had killed her. Maybe they hadn't started out with a plan to murder her, but if Herrold was right and Claudia had accidentally overdosed, the two women had lost no time taking advantage of the situation. However it had happened, my sister was gone.

I'd been devastated a week ago, when Renfrew called and told me that my sister was dead. But, I realized now, that was nothing. Deep in my heart I'd always been afraid that Claudia would die young. She had soared through the world with the force of a comet, a bright heavenly body bound to burn out fast. I thought I'd accepted that as her bargain with the world. I was wrong.

"Lily," said a gravelly voice next to my ear. When I opened my eyes, Bruxton was kneeling on the floor.

"He switched the records," I blurted out. "Brenda Collins didn't die. Claudia did."

There was a flicker of understanding in his eyes. He touched my hair, murmured something, and held me against him so that all I heard was his heartbeat. Then he gently lifted me to my feet, keeping his arms around me. "Don't say one word till we get you a lawyer," he whispered.

"Jesse banged on the door. Herrold thought it was the police. He shot himself." I recited the facts, though none of it really made sense to me. Claudia was gone and nothing would bring her back now.

"Lily, stop talking."

"I didn't shoot him."

"Please shut up, Lily." He stroked my hair and said more than my brain could take in.

Later, at the police station, what Bruxton said made sense. Though the ballistics expert and investigators agreed Herrold's death was a probable suicide, the fact that I was in the house when it happened made me a suspect. My lawyer turned up, bow-tied and folksily cheery, but when it came time to get down to business, the man was a hammer. As I stared into space and saw Claudia's face hovering there, he dealt with the police. Thirty minutes later I was out the door of the station, with Jesse hugging me and a warning from the cops that I needed to apprise them of my whereabouts, should they need me for further questioning. My lawyer shook my hand and told me everything would be all right. Then he hugged Jesse and told him how much he missed him.

"That's Ted's dad," Jesse explained as the lawyer walked

away. "Ted might be a piece of trash, but his family are some of the finest folks I ever met."

Bruxton joined us. "I have to stay here a while." He lit a cigarette, handed it to me, then fired up another for himself. "You two should head back to the city."

"No. I want to stay. I want to see her body."

"You don't want to do that, Lily," Bruxton said firmly. "It's been three months. Seeing her won't help."

"I don't want to leave her," I begged.

"I know. We've got to sort out this mess, though. When we do, we'll bring Claudia's body back to New York, okay?" Bruxton sounded like he was negotiating with a morbid four-year-old. He tried to put his arm around me and I pulled away.

"It makes sense, Lil," said Jesse. "Let's get you home now. It'll be okay."

"How can it be okay? My sister is dead."

"I'm sorry, Lil." Jesse gave Bruxton a helpless look.

"We'll get photos of Brenda Collins and canvass your sister's neighborhood with them," Bruxton promised. "We're going to find her, Lily. I promise."

He said it as if that would make a difference now.

Jesse and I were mostly quiet on the drive home. I was locked inside myself, drowning in grief. My sister's face would float in front of my eyes and I would start to choke, trying to draw breath but feeling my lungs burning. The car was freezing because I was smoking again, and being trapped in a car with cigarette fumes was too much, even for Jesse. He reached over and squeezed my hand from time to time.

"If it's any consolation, I know how you feel," he said at one point.

"How?"

" 'The righteous shall rejoice when he sees the vengeance,' " Jesse recited, his voice steady and his eyes on the road. " 'He shall wash his feet in the blood of the wicked.' " He glanced at me. "That's Psalms."

I nodded. Psalms had gotten it right. "I want Trina Greene to suffer. I want Herrold to suffer. Now I need to find Brenda Collins to make her suffer, too. She's the only one I can do anything about now."

"The first two are roastin' in hell, and the third one might be there, too." Jesse reached for my hand. "Leave it to the Lord. Right now we need to take care of you."

I knew I was lucky to have such a loyal friend, but all I wanted was for a bottomless pit to engulf me. Jesse's cell phone rang as we got closer to New York, and he answered it. "Hey. You heard what happened?" Jesse was silent for a long time. "I don't fuckin' believe it," he said finally; I'd only heard Jesse curse like that a handful of times in all the years we'd known each other, and even in my anguished state, I knew something was wrong. "Thanks a lot, Norah." Norah? Detective Renfrew, of course. "I'll talk to her, see what she wants to do."

I waited anxiously, dragging hard on a cigarette, while he got off the phone. "What now? What is it?"

He glanced at me, worry etched into his face. "I'm not sure how much more you can take just now, Lil."

"Whatever it is, just tell me. Please."

"They found the cleanin' lady, Brenda Collins. She's been in Chicago the past six weeks, got on a bus and ended up back in New York yesterday. Norah said she was hangin' around your sister's apartment. They have her at the station now."

I stared at him and remembered Sarah's message. She had

told me about the woman she'd seen yesterday; she'd even called the police. I knew I was indebted to her, but I didn't feel gratitude toward anyone right now. All that I'd felt since I'd learned that Claudia was dead was cold, hard anger. Trina Greene was gone, and Curtis Herrold had just removed himself from the picture. That left Brenda Collins as the focal point of my rage. "Can they give that bitch the death penalty?" We were quiet for a while after that.

That night, Jesse ordered in four kinds of takeout, hoping that I'd eat something—anything—but all I needed was vodka. Jesse bit his lip as the night got darker and I got drunker. Norah Renfrew came by, taking my hand and telling me how sorry she was. She said much more than that, but I couldn't take in the details. Mostly I stared at the television, oblivious to what was playing, and drank. Bruxton came by after midnight, and the only thing I heard him say clearly was to Jesse. "Are you going to let her do this to herself?" Jesse's answer was whispered, indistinct. For a fleeting moment I was afraid what he would tell Bruxton about me, about my family, but then I remembered that Claudia was gone and I didn't have a family anymore.

At some point, I passed out. I woke up, drank some more, and passed out again. Later, I saw the first streaks of pale light coming in through the living room windows. Jesse had taken off my shoes and tucked a blanket around me. Bruxton wasn't there, but Jesse snored beside me on the couch, one arm around me and his face pressed against my hair. He woke up enough to say, "Back to sleep, Lil," when I started to get up. Sinking back down into the pillows, I remembered that I'd lost Claudia all over again.

Drifting in and out of consciousness, I knew I really was

alone now. Claudia was dead. I felt untethered, as if I might do anything, now that there was nothing left I cared to do. It was morning when I got up, shed my blanket, and showered. By the time I was done dressing and painting my face, Jesse was in the kitchen, frying eggs. Vodka bottles dominated the recycling bag, their contents presumably poured down the sink.

"You're eatin' something, Lil, I don't want to hear—"

"Okay," I acquiesced, and sat at the table.

"Okay? Okay," said Jesse, sounding confused. "How you feelin'?"

"Horrible. You should have gone to bed last night. You didn't have to stay next to me on the couch."

"'Course I did. Want some OJ? I'll pop some toast in a sec."

We ate breakfast, not talking very much. It was peaceful, just sitting with Jesse, being under his care.

"Would you do something for me?"

"You name it, Lil."

"Would you get me some chocolates from MarieBelle? I don't know why, but suddenly I've got such a craving for them." I sat with my chin resting in my palm, absently staring into space.

"Want me to get them now?"

I looked at my watch. "You can shower and be there when they open."

"What are you going to do?" His eyes were sad and his face was drawn.

"You look worried."

"I just don't think you should drink any more right now," he said softly.

"I won't."

"You promise? No drinking today."

He was like a terrier. "I promise."

"Good to have some rules," he said, standing and kissing the top of my head before he left the kitchen. I waited until I heard him turn on the shower to get up. His carry-on bag was still in the hallway, not yet unpacked. I opened it and took out the gun, made sure the safety was on, and dropped it into my purse. Then I put on my coat and left the apartment, closing the door behind me with the quietest click I could manage.

39

I stared up at the apartment building from the street, thinking about how many times I'd been there over the years. The Dakota was a landmark, notorious as the setting of John Lennon's murder, but a work of beauty. It was light enough now that the gas lamps had been turned off. Often I'd thought of the irony of Martin building shiny eyesores but choosing to live in historic splendor. Inside the opulent lobby, I asked the doorman to tell Mr. Sklar that Lily Moore was visiting. "Go on up, miss," the doorman told me as he put the phone down.

I took the elevator to the eighth floor. The hallway had been redone since I'd last visited. The Dakota was crazy about upkeep, Martin had told me that. They were always touching up, not only repairing flaws but filling in before any could be spotted. Martin opened the door before I got to it.

"Sweetheart, I'm so sorry." He kissed me, aiming for my lips but I turned my face down and he had to settle for my forehead. "I just heard an hour ago. My poor darling. Come here." He reached for my arm and led me into the apartment, closing the door behind me with a quiet click, not bothering with the locks. He held my face in his hands, caressing my hair and cooing at me that everything would be all right now. I recoiled and turned my face away. "I know you're upset, sweetheart. Come sit down." He put his arm around me and led me to the sofa in the living room. He held me against him and murmured something in my hair. For a heartbeat I let myself relax against his chest. If only it could have been that way between us.

"She died on September twenty-ninth," I said, pulling away from him. "There was a house fire near the rehab center she went to. My sister's dental records were switched with another woman's, so no one realized she was dead." A tear ran down my cheek and I brushed it away.

"You don't have to talk about it. I heard enough details on the news. My poor Lily."

"It sounds like she died of an overdose, but the police told me it would take a long time to confirm that. They have a lot to figure out."

"I'm sure they do, sweetheart. There's nothing you can do to help her now. Leave it to them. My only concern right now is you." He stroked my hair and rubbed my neck. "I'm taking you away for a few days. Your choice: Maui or Barbados. I'd like Maui but it's a much longer flight."

I stood up and walked to the window. Martin's apartment overlooked Central Park, and even now the view amazed me. Wherever Martin was—his office, his hotel, his home—he was always looking down on the world. Maybe that was why he felt he could play God. "Why did you lie to me about Claudia?" I turned to look at him. "Why did you tell me she called you in December? She was *dead* long before December."

Martin's brow furrowed. "I thought it was Claudia. I would've sworn it was her." He gestured helplessly. "I didn't really remember what Claudia's voice sounded like. I thought it was her."

"What did she actually say to you, Martin?"

"I don't remember exactly. I was so distracted, and tired. I'd just come back from a trip." There was wariness behind his gaze. He was waiting for my reaction, gauging every step of his high-wire act by my quiet fury.

"You told me she asked you for money. I believe that part. But the woman who called wasn't going to rehab. She was blackmailing you."

"It doesn't matter what she said. None of that matters now." There was no trace of regret in his expression. "All that matters is you and me. What does the rest of this count for, anyway?"

"What matters is you lied to me!"

"Lily, sweetheart, I know you're upset—you have every right to be—but Ridley's sleeping. Please don't yell. Talk to me."

"All right. Let's talk," I said, fighting to control my anger. "This is what I've figured out so far. You burned down the Church of St. Aristarchus. No, sorry, you paid somebody else to do it, since you were out of the country and anyway you'd never get your hands dirty. Claudia found out that you did it." I didn't add that Ridley had told her everything; the boy didn't need more trouble. "Because my sister was incapable of keeping a secret, she told people. She mentioned the fire to me, and she told Tariq everything. She told her counselor at the rehab facility she went to in April. That was the woman who blackmailed you."

Martin leaned back on the sofa and gave me an appraising look. "You know, as beautiful as you are, the most amazing part of you is your brain. Let's say you've more or less hit the mark. I'm truly sorry I told you that Claudia called me. I thought it was her. It seemed like the kind of cheap stunt she would pull." He shifted uncomfortably. "I'm sorry to speak ill of the dead. I know she was your sister, and you loved her. But I'm not going to be a hypocrite and pretend I'll miss her."

"Why stop now, Martin? You lied to me about everything. And you tried to murder my sister."

"I had nothing to do with your sister's death. How could you think—"

"I know you didn't give her the overdose. But when you thought my sister was blackmailing you, you sent your henchman Gregory Robinson to kill her." I set my purse on a chair and rested my forearms on the back of it. "After all, once you start giving money to these people, who knows where it will end?"

Martin got to his feet. "I understand you're just not yourself right now, Lily. But really—"

"You had the keys to the apartment. You knew all of the details of my mother's suicide. It was perfect, pretending that my sister decided to kill herself on the same date, in the same way. What a stroke of genius."

I reached into my purse and pulled out the gun, smoothly releasing the safety, and pointed it at him.

"What the hell are you doing?"

"Shh, Ridley is sleeping," I reminded him. "Does this help your memory at all?"

"You've lost your mind. You need help."

"That's not a smart thing to say to the person with a gun."

"What do you want from me?" His face was taut with anger.

"The truth. I want you to tell me what happened at the apartment on New Year's Eve. I want you to admit you thought you were murdering my sister."

"I did nothing of the sort," Martin insisted.

"You're a liar!" Ridley shouted. He stormed out of the shadows in a fury, barefoot and wearing only pajama pants. There were tattoos on his oversized shoulders and biceps, and strange, raised scars on his torso that were too intricate to be accidental. "Everything you say is a lie. You killed that woman. I know you did."

"No, I didn't," Martin said through clenched teeth. He and Ridley were standing toe to toe, the boy looming over his father.

"You sent Gregory over there. I heard you plan it." Ridley's voice was deep and clear; there was no mumbling now.

"Gregory didn't kill her." Martin wasn't giving an inch.

"Liar."

"Gregory told me that when he and his man got there, the woman was dead," Martin insisted. "They took her computer and her cell phone and they left."

"Liar."

"Gregory said her body was already in the bathtub. He told me he didn't do it." Martin spoke slowly, his eyes locked with his son's. They'd forgotten I was in the room.

"Ridley, I want you to tell me what happened," I said. "The whole story, from the beginning."

Ridley turned to look at me, bumping against his father and knocking him back in the process. "You've got a gun. That's cool."

"It belongs to a friend." The gun was heavy in my hand, and I felt ridiculous suddenly for pointing it at Martin. I lowered my arm. "Will you tell me what happened?"

Ridley nodded and looked at the floor. "It was my fault. I shouldn't have—"

"Shut up, Ridley," Martin interrupted. "Leave it alone."

"I don't want to be a liar like you." Ridley looked at me; his eyes were so much like his father's, but there was sadness behind them, not anger. "I told Claudia everything. She was my friend. She was mad at me about the fire, though." His eyes went back to the carpet.

"Why would she be mad at you?"

"Because I started the fire," Ridley said. "At the church. I'd wired a remote detonator and I wanted to try it. And my dad kept talking about this old church that nobody used anymore. He said it was in the way, like it would be great if it burned down. I thought it would be cool to do it." He glanced at me briefly. "Claudia saw me on Canal Street that night. Later she kind of put it together, and she asked me if I had anything to do with burning down the church. I told her the truth. She was so upset. She said homeless people sometimes stayed in the church, that I'd taken away their home." He rubbed his face with one giant paw. "She said she'd never speak to me, ever, if I did anything like that again. Then she made me give her the remote detonator."

"Claudia had the *detonator*?" I looked at Martin. "Was that what you thought Kaylee Quan had taken from the apartment?"

Martin nodded sullenly.

"I don't get it. Why didn't Gregory and his friend look for it when they went to the apartment on New Year's Eve?"

"That's because my idiot son forgot to tell me he'd handed it over to Claudia," Martin snapped. "He only told me that part after New Year's. When that woman called to blackmail me, she said she knew that Ridley had started the fire at the church. I didn't want to believe it was true. I'd thought the fire was just a happy accident for me. But when I asked Ridley about it, he said, 'Did Lily tell you?' I asked how Lily would know about it, and he said Claudia must have told her."

"I thought maybe you ratted me out to my dad," Ridley

said. "Like that time I wanted to try heroin. Claudia always says secrets are like poison, they kill you sooner or later. I knew she'd tell you sometime."

"So that's how you found out that Claudia knew," I said, staring at Martin. "And that's why you called me in Spain. To see if I knew, too."

"I needed to find out whether you were somehow involved, even accidentally," said Martin. "If you'd known the truth I would have paid Claudia—that woman, whatever her name was—off. But you didn't know anything about it, so I sent Gregory to have a talk with her instead."

"A talk? That's why Gregory took out the surveillance camera? Because he was going to have a talk?" My voice rose in incredulity.

"I did not discuss his methods with him," Martin answered.

"He went there to murder her, because you told him to."

"I never once uttered the word *murder,* or *kill,* or anything like that," Martin maintained. "I didn't order him to do anything except deal with the problem."

"That's exactly what you said: *Deal with the problem,*" Ridley shouted. "That was like telling Gregory to kill her. You know it, but you're a liar. I heard you on the phone with Gregory. You said, 'How's this for a happy coincidence? Her mother killed herself on New Year's Eve. Like mother, like daughter.' Go on, deny it. I know you."

"Ridley, all of this would have been so much easier to deal with if you had just told me the whole story in the first place, instead of coughing up a little piece here and there." Martin turned to me. "I was sincere about wanting to find your sister, Lily."

"Of course you were. Once you found out that the dead woman wasn't Claudia, you must've figured she was just my sister's business partner. You figured Claudia would turn up again to blackmail you." I laughed, but the sound was more like something had caught in my throat and started to choke me. "That's why you kept turning up, why you kept calling me. Why you hired a private detective to follow me. You were trying to figure out if I knew where my sister was."

"Or if she suddenly got in touch with you. I couldn't rule that out." His expression softened. "But that wasn't the only reason, Lily. I love you."

"Shut up," Ridley and I said at the same time. The boy glanced at me, then lowered his eyes again. I put the safety back on the gun, and set it gently back into the zippered compartment of my bag. "Martin, were you always a disgusting excuse for a human being, or is this a more recent development?"

"Don't say that, Lily," he answered. "You're being heartless and unfair."

"Don't tell me I'm hurting your feelings." I tried to keep my voice steady. "By the way, why did you decide to shoot Tariq? Was it just because he knew about the fire?"

"He called me in a fury, saying he knew all about it, and that he knew I was lying to you." Martin's voice was weary. It must have taken up all of his energy, spinning a convenient lie for every occasion. "He thought that I might have kidnapped or harmed Claudia. I told him that I was frantic about finding her, too, and suggested that he come over to talk. A couple of Gregory's men waited for him. It wasn't like I had much choice at that point. Everything was damage control."

We stared at each other for what felt like a long time. It was as if our mutually agreed-upon illusions had finally dissipated. *Anyone in this world could kill, in the right set of circumstances,* Tariq had told me. *To protect those whom you love.* I wanted to hate Martin, but I felt empty and exhausted, and he suddenly seemed pathetic to me. It wasn't hard to understand that a father might kill to protect his child. But this particular father was at the root of his son's problems. He would wonder for the rest of his life what had gone wrong with Ridley, but it would never occur to him to look in the mirror.

The silence was broken by Ridley. "Did you find Claudia yet?" His eyes were on me, sadness tempered by just a little flame of hope. That was extinguished as he read my expression. I closed my eyes and put my hands over my mouth, struggling not to break down here, in Martin's living room, of all places.

"She's dead, Ridley," Martin said. "I'm sorry. She died of a drug overdose."

"Claudia?" Ridley choked on my sister's name. I watched his face crumple. His huge shoulders and chest started heaving and there was no sound in the room except his ragged breathing. Martin started to put his arm around him, but his son recoiled. He ran from the room, his footsteps echoing down the hallway. Then there was the slamming of a door, and silence. I wiped tears from my cheeks while rummaging for a tissue in my bag with the other. Martin handed me a wad of Kleenex and I mopped up my face.

"I'm sorry, Lily, about all of this. I wish I'd told you everything from the start. It wouldn't have helped your sister but . . ." He took my hand.

I stared at him, dumbfounded. Surely, after all that had passed between us, he wasn't stupid or arrogant enough to think . . .

"I love you," he said. "I can count on one hand the number of people I give a damn about in this world. There's Ridley, and my mother, and you. When I met you, I thought I'd dreamed you into existence. You're everything to me."

As delicately as I could, I extricated my hand from his grasp. "You need to understand that it's over between us. I don't want to see you again. Don't call me. Not ever. Is that clear?"

"Don't leave me again," whispered Martin. "We need to work this out."

I laughed. Not the throttled sound I'd made earlier; this was astonishment at the absurdity of the situation and the incongruity of his words. "Please leave me alone. Forever."

His mouth was set in a grim, determined line. "We're not done."

"Oh, we definitely are."

"You might think you're finished with me, Lily, but I'm not done with you. I never will be." He leaned in so close that I felt his lips brush my ear, as if we were lovers again. "You can't leave me, not for long. I need you and you need me. " He bit my earlobe, not hard, just teasing. "You know how relentless I can be. And you love it."

He was almost panting. I felt desire too, but only to pull the safety off the pistol and shoot him. Instead, I reached into my bag and grabbed the gun by the barrel, hitting Martin's face with the handle. I heard something crack and he cried out, and I ran down the hallway back to the elevator.

40

After I left the Dakota I walked aimlessly for blocks. It was another cold January day, but the sun was shining brightly as if in defiance of my mood. What had I hoped to accomplish by confronting Martin? Even though I hated him for being ready to murder Claudia to save his son, the woman he had killed wasn't my sister. Trina Greene was at least partially responsible for Claudia's death. No one else had profited from it as much as she had. Heroin had stolen Claudia from life, but it had an assist from the two women who watched her die without calling for help. As I walked and shivered, I wondered if perhaps I owed Martin a debt for killing Trina. Martin's obsessive and frantic determination to protect himself and his son had avenged my sister, however inadvertently.

When I went into a bodega to buy cigarettes, I realized that my father's bracelet was no longer on my wrist. Where had I lost it? I'd been wearing it when I'd left Jesse's. Had it fallen off my arm when I'd struck Martin? There was no safety chain on it, just one single, fragile clasp. I felt the need to storm back into the Dakota and hunt it down. That was crazy, I knew, but I was panicked at losing the bracelet again. I couldn't find my cell phone, either. I suddenly remembered an officer prying it out of my hands at the dentist's house. I'd never thought to ask for it back. How stupid, in retrospect. Outside I lit up and called Jesse from a pay phone.

"I just wanted to tell you I'm all right. I needed to talk to

someone," I said to his voice mail. "I'll be back soon, I promise." I felt guilty as I hung up the phone. I went into the subway, fully intent on going back to Jesse's. But it was the
weekend and trains were rerouted for track maintenance work.
I ended up getting off the subway at Canal Street, where I
was irresistibly drawn east, until I found myself on familiar
streets in my old neighborhood. I crossed Delancey and got
to Rivington, then went into my sister's building and climbed
the stairs to the fifth floor, finding the police tape dangling
from the door of Claudia's apartment. I wondered if I was
about to be attacked again, if Martin had sent his henchmen
and they were already waiting for me inside. But when I unlocked the door and turned on the light, no one jumped out. I
peeked into the closet, then the kitchen, bathroom, and bedroom, but no one was waiting there. Inside the closet, I found
only expensive clothing and shoes. Under the bed there were
lurking dust bunnies. I was alone.

I sat on the bed. I really was alone. Truly alone. My family
bonds had felt like restraints, but now they were gone and I
felt anything but free. I wondered what Claudia's last moments were like. When a person overdosed, did she drift in
bliss until her heart gave out? Or was it agony, as I always
suspected my mother's death had been. I tried to picture it,
but my mind kept retreating to the unfinished parts of this
puzzle. When had Trina Greene decided to start impersonating my sister? From what her boyfriend had said, it sounded
like Trina was just supposed to rent the car and drive to New
York, to make it look like my sister had left the Berkshires.
When had she realized she could take it further? Had she
seen it would be easy, since Claudia had no family but a sister
living a continent away, and only one close friend who would
miss her if she were gone?

There was a knock on the door and I went to answer it. Through the peephole I saw that it was Sarah, and I sighed, not wanting to have a conversation with her now but knowing that I had to. When I opened the door, Sarah grabbed me in a fierce hug. "I'm so sorry, Lily. Jesse told me everything. I'm so sorry."

"Jesse told you?" I asked, letting go and standing back.

"He came by, maybe an hour ago, thinking you would be here. I told him I'd check on the apartment and let him know if you came around. He told me what had happened to Claudia and I couldn't believe it. How . . . unfair. How absolutely, horribly unfair." Sarah seemed to be on the verge of tears. She was elegant as always, wearing a silver lace blouse and black trousers, but she no longer looked like an Amazonian version of Grace Kelly, but like a deflated, exhausted middle-aged woman who'd had too much cosmetic surgery.

"I just can't believe it," I said.

"Do you want to talk at my place?" Sarah asked. "I have some of those lovely Portuguese pastries you like from the bakery downstairs."

I wondered what she meant. When had we discussed pastry? "I don't have any appetite, but thanks anyway. I think I'll just go through some of Claudia's things."

Company was the last thing I wanted, but I knew I was being an ingrate. Still, I'd remembered what it was about Sarah that had been bothering me, and I didn't want to deal with it now. I called Jesse from Claudia's landline, leaving another message. "Sarah told me that you were looking for me at Claudia's. That's where I am now. I'll be back soon, I promise."

I went into the bedroom. My purse was still sitting on the bed. As I looked around the room, I knew I would have to deal with all of this stuff at some point. It made me want to get on the next plane to Spain. I opened the closet and rifled through the clothing. It would be easy enough to give away the items that Trina Greene had acquired, but some of my sister's things were mixed in there, too. Living with Alexander Gorevale had given her a certain confidence and polish. As much as I hated to think of her being preyed upon by him, I wished that I'd seen her in that state. I'd been looking forward to seeing her on my Labor Day trip, but I'd waited too long to visit. I'd left everything until it was too late.

There was another knock on the door. It was Sarah again, this time holding a silver tray and two beautiful white china teacups. Her Hermès Birkin bag hung from the crook of one elbow.

"Make yourself at home." My tone was grudging. Sarah had been pushy from the moment we first met, and I'd finally figured out why.

"I thought you might like some tea, Lily." She set the tray on a chair and handed me a cup and saucer, then took one herself. "I was thinking that perhaps I could help you plan the funeral."

"That's all right."

"No, really, I want to help." She gave me a bright smile that revealed her perfect, pearly teeth. When I didn't return it, she lowered her head and sipped at her tea. "I know that this must be such an agonizing time for you. Do you like the tea?"

I'd been ignoring the cup. The smell was pleasant, like cardamom and cinnamon, but when I took a drink all I tasted was alcohol. "What's in this?"

"Brandy. Mother's cure-all for everything, remember?"

I looked down at the delicate cup. There was something revolting about it to me, suddenly.

"I should have asked you before putting it in," Sarah said.

"Don't worry about it." I set the cup aside.

"Your friend Jesse said that Claudia died of a heroin overdose. It must be so hard for you, knowing that you couldn't save her."

"Yes," I whispered.

"Everyone wanted to save Claudia. Isn't that funny? Like some poor little bird that fell out of a nest. Have you thought about music for the funeral?"

My answer popped out of my mouth before I could censor myself. "You know, there's only one thing I've decided about the funeral so far. I want to make sure my sister is buried with her engagement ring."

Sarah's eyes widened. "Engagement ring?"

My sister had always been regarded as the impulsive one, hopscotching from one crisis to the next. I'd been the quiet girl that adults liked because I got good grades, watched old movies, and tamped my restlessness down in front of prying eyes. But now that restraint was vanishing. "You know, the really beautiful, big, antique diamond ring that the woman who died here was wearing? That was actually my sister's engagement ring. I guess her impostor took it before she burned Claudia's body. I mean, what good is a ring to a corpse, right? That must have been what you thought."

"What *I* thought?" Sarah set her cup down.

"Remember the woman who discovered the body in the bathtub? She told me that a neighbor had heard her scream and had come into the apartment. That was you, wasn't it? And before the police showed up, you had the chance to take the ring." Her face was turning red now. "The bad thing is, you can't wear it outside, because it's so distinctive. But you had it on your hand that night I knocked on your door after midnight."

"The night that I . . . that I *helped* you after you'd been attacked."

"You did help me, Sarah. But you also stole that ring."

She stared at me for a moment, then reached for her hand-bag. "I shouldn't be surprised," she said suddenly, her voice cold and flat.

"Surprised?"

"That you are just like your sister, a grasping little rube who thought she could get away with stealing what rightfully belonged to others." She pulled her hand out of her purse. There was something black and bright yellow in it. Her arm jerked out and touched my chest. There was a sizzling sound and pain surged through my body as if I were on fire. A gar-bled sound emerged from my mouth and I fell to the ground, shivering and gasping.

"One would prefer to see one's enemy suffer, don't you agree, Lily?" Sarah stood above me, regarding me like an in-sect. "It might sound like a strange term to call Claudia my *enemy*. After all, we had so much in common. At one time I was very much like her, a patient of Alec Gorevale's. The good doctor transformed my life, as he did so many others. Really, he was quite amazing." She gave me one of her frigid smiles.

"Gorevale?" The realization hit me with the force of a slap. Something one of Claudia's friends had said, about how Claudia had had to leave Gorevale's house, because his girl-friend was coming back for a visit. Sarah had been living in California, caring for her mother. She had been Gorevale's absent girlfriend.

"The problem with falling in love with your doctor is that he always has other patients. Alec was always getting entan-gled with patients and I was always having to free him from the net, so to speak."

"Claudia," I mumbled. All I had to do to reach the phone was get my hand up to the top of the desk, but when I tried Sarah took it and unplugged it.

"Alec became enamored with her, but I could live with that. Alec had all sorts of girls, and he thought nothing of them, so why would I care? But he became obsessed with Claudia. Like an old fool." Sarah's voice was steady. "Alec, who had always preached against marriage and family, all of a sudden wanted to have one with your sister. I had wanted him to marry me years ago, but he didn't even want to live together, and I'd respected that. I trailed around after him from place to place. Then, when my mother became very ill, I moved to California to be with her. Alec and I carried on our relationship long-distance. It seemed like a good arrangement. His little trollops were never around when I came to visit. What a fool I was. He even gave Claudia his grandmother's engagement ring. I'd dreamed for years that one day he would give it to me."

While she was talking, I started crawling to the front door. She was so wrapped up in what she was saying, she didn't seem to notice.

"When I got pregnant, years and years ago, I thought Alec would marry me then. Oh, he preached against family ties, but I thought a baby would change everything. Do you know what he did? He told me he would never, ever see me again if I had the child. He forced me to have an abortion."

I was moving slowly, but getting closer to the door. Suddenly, Sarah grabbed my hair and jerked my head upward. My eyes teared up at the pain.

"Not that way, Lily." She pulled me toward the hallway. "Did you know that Alec refused to come west for my mother's funeral? Mother died in September, and he left me to deal with it alone. He couldn't leave Claudia, he said. Then he actually thought he could get rid of me. He offered me a financial settlement, 'as if we'd been married,' he said. As if! What was I if not his wife?" Her voice was sharp and clipped. She was angry, but more than that she was aggrieved at losing what was rightfully hers. "He was so stupid, he actually believed me when I agreed. I offered to make a special farewell dinner, and he complimented me for being so mature. *Mature*, he said. He was throwing me over for a child."

"You poisoned him," I whispered.

"I did. Viagra is such a marvelous drug, hard to detect when you break the pills down to powder." Her eyes were glassy. "I went back to California, but I was miserable. I knew I'd never be happy unless I got rid of the little bitch who stole Alec from me. Your little sister ruined my life."

"That's why you moved here."

"Yes, exactly. I had my revenge planned just perfectly. I was going to have some fun playing with Claudia's drug-addled brain, you know. I was going to be the good mommy she never had before I killed her. Instead, I found this snobby bitch who was obsessed with exercise and shopping. Everything Alec had written down in his files about her was wrong. If she hadn't been wearing his grandmother's diamond I would have sworn she was the wrong woman." Sarah shook her head. "I made a terrible mistake on New Year's Day. I thought I was being so clever, mentioning her mother's suicide to the police so there would be no investigation. But when it turned out it wasn't Claudia Moore who died, it just made everything more suspicious."

"What happened on New Year's Eve?" I asked.

"It all went to hell. That woman who lived in this apartment went into cardiac arrest with one shot from the Taser.

I hadn't expected that. It was such a disappointment, after all my planning. It should have been satisfying, ridding the world of that bitch, but she died before I could even tell her who I was. I put her in the bath anyway, but it wasn't the same."

She dragged me to the threshold of the bathroom. "Why?" I panted. "Why did you pretend you saw Claudia on New Year's Eve?"

"How else was I going to be involved in the investigation?" Sarah answered. "I thought she was alive, and I was desperate for you to find her. When you found her, that meant I did, too. Someone had to pay for what happened." She let go of me and stepped over my body. "You know, it's nice to finally have some closure," she said. "Do you like bubble baths? I think something with a nice scent would be appropriate." Then she turned and smiled that frozen smile again. I didn't see her hand, but I heard the sizzle of the Taser a nanosecond before my body involuntarily flipped and convulsed. Now, I was lying on my back, nauseous, caught in a twister. The room was spinning around me so swiftly that I wasn't sure whether I was floating or on the ground. I panted for air, my heart rattling against my rib cage. There was the sound of running water, then Sarah's cool voice again, but I couldn't make out what she was saying. She appeared suddenly, her face inches from mine, then vanished from my field of vision. I could hear her voice in the distance, but her words were indistinguishable from the running water.

For a moment I swooned, then came to when cold water slapped down on my face. Sarah was pouring it out of a plastic bottle she must have taken from the fridge. "I want you to be awake for this," she said. She disappeared again and the sound of the water filling the tub stopped dead. I pushed my feet down on the floor, moving my quivering body back a few inches to the doorway of the bedroom. That was as far as I could go.

"Really, where do you think you're going?" Sarah came back, holding the Taser, and caught sight of my purse on the bed. "You don't think I'm going to let you call anyone on your cell phone, do you?"

All I could think about was Jesse's gun. If I could just get to it . . .

Sarah stood, watching me, with her arms crossed and her head cocked to the side. "You look so pathetic lying there. It's just not the same, doing this to you instead of Claudia. Not at all what I'd hoped for." She shook her head, sadly. "Did you know your sister told Alec that she thought you were heading down the same road to oblivion as your mother? She told him all about your terrible taste in unfaithful men. Talk about the pot calling the kettle black."

My fury gave me just enough adrenaline to reach the bag. I pulled it down and put my hand in, touched the cold metal of the gun immediately. All I had to do was take the safety off, but I fumbled with buzzing fingers that were still shuddering from the electric current.

"Now what have you got there?" Sarah asked idly, stepping over me. She pulled the bag away, but the gun was still in my hand. She screamed and I pulled the trigger.

There was a soft click and nothing.

Before I could try again, Sarah grabbed the gun with both hands. My own were too weak to hold on to it. She stared at the weapon for a moment, her finger on the trigger and her expression frozen in horror, as if just realizing how close she'd come to being shot. I grabbed the Taser she'd dropped and pressed it against her leg. The gun went off and Sarah fell on top of me and everything went dark.

EPILOGUE

Claudia's funeral was a small affair, officiated by Rachel Heidegger at the Woodlawn Cemetery chapel in the Bronx. The old borough had gotten my sister back, after all. At the chapel, I leaned on Jesse's arm when I had to stand. Sarah's attack hadn't left any permanent marks on me, but in the two weeks since it had happened I'd felt so brittle that I thought I might shatter at any second. Bruxton was on my other side, casting concerned looks my way and working a mound of nicotine gum over with his jaw.

After the service, Claudia's friends talked in small groups. I recognized a few of them, and they came over to pay their respects. Renfrew—or Norah, as I thought of her now—came over afterward. "What you said about Claudia was beautiful," she commented, hugging me. "Too marvelous for words."

A reporter came up to me and shoved a digital recorder under my chin. "Lily Moore, can you tell us about your relationship with Martin Sklar?" he asked.

Cameras had been banned inside the chapel, but voice recorders were easy to slip in. I'd been stupid for thinking that the media interest would die down with the delay in the funeral. Couldn't there have been some scandal at the governor's office to knock my sister's story off the front page?

"At the funeral? Are you fucking kidding me?" snapped Bruxton. He'd finally told me his first name a week earlier and, after I'd laughed, I realized I'd never be able to think of him by any name but his last. *If it's any consolation, there was a very popular leading man in the 1930s with the same name,* I'd told him, and he'd glared at me. *Is that why you're such a tough guy, because you have such a . . . a . . . nontough-guy name?* I'd asked. *You're too damn smart for your own good,* he'd growled. I thought of that now as I watched him wrench the recorder out of the man's hand, throw it down and crush it under his heel.

"Police brutality. I'll report you," the man said.

"Have fun," said Bruxton. "Want to get better acquainted with police brutality?"

The man backed away slowly.

"I need some air. Let's go outside," I announced.

"There's gonna be more of those cockroaches out there," Jesse cautioned.

I sighed. I'd thought I was a part of the media. Jesse had, too, since he was a photographer. But the circus that had swirled since my sister's death had been reported bore no resemblance to what I thought of as journalism. I'd sometimes wondered how I'd grown so lazy, swanning from city to city and resort to resort, penning frothy articles instead of the investigative pieces I used to dream about. But travel writing was a class act next to the tabloids. "There won't be any cameras, though," I answered. "Let's go."

I'd seen a sign at the cemetery's entrance when I'd first visited, a week ago. At the time, the photography ban made no sense. What if a person wanted to keep an image of a loved one's grave? It turned out that Woodlawn allowed that. Their ban was targeted at those who profited from filming other people's grief. I was grateful for that now. When we stepped outside, reporters swarmed.

"There she is!"

"Lily, can you tell us if you'll attend Brenda Collins's trial?" That was a trick question, I thought, since the former cleaning lady had made a full confession to the police. She'd run out of money in Chicago, and with Trina Greene gone, she'd lost the strength to keep running. *I thought it would be great to chuck it all in and start a new life,* she'd told the police, *but it was so hard, lying to everyone I met, keeping my story straight, worrying all the time about being found out.* The District Attorney's office was still working on the details, but a plea agreement had been struck. Brenda had been able to fill in the missing pieces of the puzzle. She told the police that Claudia had accidentally overdosed at her house, and that she had panicked and called her friend Trina. After Trina had driven them both to New York, they stayed in a crumbling hotel west of Times Square. Trina had been curious about Claudia's apartment; she'd visited, then stayed a night, then two, and decided to stay a while. Brenda holed up in the hotel for a couple of weeks, then went on to Michigan, where she had a cousin. Her cousin's husband had gotten tired of her staying there, so Brenda returned to New York and found Trina living high on the hog, as she put it. *Trina's always wanted to be a big-city girl,* Brenda had said, *she hated it in the sticks.* Trina hadn't hatched a plan to take over Claudia's life, it had been a simple matter of getting away with a few things and wanting to see what she could do next. *She knew Claudia's sister paid the rent, and she thought it would be exciting to live in the city for a while. I mean, the sister lived in Spain—it wasn't like she was going to show up at the door, you know?*

Trina told Brenda she couldn't stay in New York. Since rooming with the Michigan cousin hadn't worked out, Trina shipped a fearful Brenda off to Chicago, telling her she'd be able to get a job in the big city. Brenda hadn't, but she'd stayed in touch with Trina and had been able to explain how her friend had come to blackmail Martin. *Claudia was feeling a lot of guilt about a kid she knew, Ridley. She said he was like her little brother, but the kid was pulling crazy stunts, screaming for attention from his dad, who completely neglected him. Ridley set fire to a church, and when his dad found out, he bought the site to build on it.* However, Trina hadn't known Ridley's last name until *New York* magazine published an article about the Oracle and Martin Sklar and the controversy surrounding the church fire. Trina had realized that Ridley's father was very, very rich, and she'd hatched her blackmail plan.

"Lily, are you afraid that Sarah Lyons is going to come after you when she gets out of the hospital?"

That was a good question. Sarah would have undoubtedly recovered quickly from the electric shock I'd given her with her own Taser in Claudia's apartment, if she hadn't just grabbed Jesse's gun. The shock had made her convulse, inadvertently pull the trigger, and shoot off part of her left hand. She wouldn't be wearing Alec Gorevale's diamond on her ring finger anymore. She'd failed the court-ordered psychiatric exam and was in a padded cell somewhere. Sarah was mad, but not the kind of crazy the court believed. I was certain she'd duped the evaluator into believing she was nuts. In Sarah's apartment, the police had found Dr. Gorevale's extensive, obsessive notes about Claudia. It was suddenly clear why Sarah had known details like my mother's three miscarriages. Ironically, Sarah had been able to do with me what she'd planned to do with my sister, using old confidences to gain my trust. It was all there in Dr. Gorevale's tiny, precise handwriting. I'd told the police everything that had happened in my sister's building, but I'd pretended that the gun was Sarah's. I'd already dragged Jesse far enough into the mud with me, and I reasoned that since Sarah had to keep up the pretense of being crazy, she wouldn't be able to argue the point. So far, it had worked.

"I can't believe the nerve of these folks," Jesse said. "Sick, that's what they are."

"Lily, are you still sleeping with Martin Sklar?" asked another vulture. Every reporter's beady little eyes zeroed in on me.

"That's it," Bruxton said. He stepped forward and the first vulture fell down, clutching his stomach. "You should watch out, it's slippery around here." The reporters stared at Bruxton, but no one had seen exactly what had happened. "Back off," he snarled at the rest of them.

"Thanks," I whispered, as he came back to my side. "Just don't lose your badge again."

"That's it, I'm taking you into protective custody," Bruxton whispered back. He'd made it clear over the past couple of weeks that he'd give me his moral support, but that, if the choice were his, he'd like to add a physical element. I'd warned him that I wasn't sure when, or if, that time would come. I was sorely tempted, but trepidatious. Jesse had been right when he'd told me that my taste in men stank; even though my friend had since made it clear he approved of Bruxton, I knew I was an emotional wreck who would be better off getting a pet than getting into another man's bed. My caution wasn't solely because I didn't trust my own judgment. Knowing that Bruxton was an addict, albeit a reformed one, made us closer, but it put up a wall between us. I wasn't sure if an addict could stay reformed forever.

When I felt a hand on my back, I turned and realized Padma

was there. She was wearing a plain black salwar kameez and no jewelry. I knew that it was because Islam forbade decorative attire during mourning. We'd spent a lot of time together in the past few days, as she'd helped me plan the funeral. "Everything you said was beautiful," she said, throwing her slender arms around me and kissing me on the cheek. "Claudia appreciates all of it, I know."

Tariq was behind his cousin. He was wearing a severe black suit and walking stiffly, but looking startlingly well for a man who'd survived two bullets and a collapsed lung. He'd been stoically silent when I'd visited him in the hospital to tell him about Claudia. He'd asked me to come back in an hour, and when I did, his eyes were bloodshot, and everything that could have been broken around him—including the window of his room—was shattered. But he'd been warm, even consoling, with me that afternoon; I hadn't seen him since then. Now he leaned forward, hesitated for a moment, and kissed my forehead. "Somewhere in heaven, Claudia is laughing about all of this fuss, you know." His voice was a rough whisper because of his lung.

"That would be exactly her style," I admitted.

Tariq nodded politely at Jesse and Norah and Bruxton. "Would you mind if I have a word with Lily, alone?"

Bruxton and Renfrew stepped back. Jesse moved in closer. "No quick moves, Tariq. I'm sure by now you know what Tiger Lily's capable of." He smiled at me and moved away.

Tariq smiled. "He is rather cheeky, is he not? Claudia always called him 'Puck,' after *A Midsummer Night's Dream*."

I watched Jesse, talking animatedly to Padma and the cops. He was gesturing wildly, and I saw Bruxton's mouth twitch. "She always had some funny ideas about things."

"I suppose so," Tariq whispered, his tone gentle. "You may already realize this, but that black car parked over there belongs to Martin Sklar."

"I know." Martin had sent flowers for me to Jesse's place, and an enormous arrangement for Claudia's memorial to Woodlawn. I hadn't spoken to him since I'd been to his apartment, and I didn't intend to. It wasn't realistic to think we'd never cross paths again, but whatever emotional bond we'd had was severed.

"It does not trouble you? His keeping watch on you, I mean."

My eyes went to the car, but then they went to the tiny rows of mausoleums lining the pathway, and to the tombstones and monuments beyond that. So much life and loss. Martin's being there didn't scare me. It made me think of Frank Sinatra at Ava Gardner's funeral. Brokenhearted at his former wife's death, he had sat in his car while her body was laid in the ground. Unable to be with her in life or death. "He just doesn't believe that it's really over between us," I said.

"I understand how he feels." Tariq's dark eyes were watery, but he kept his composure.

"Will you walk with me?" It wasn't fair to ask that of Tariq, who was moving stiffly and very slowly, but he took my arm and we walked farther from the chapel and the road. January had warmed up in the past few days and the snow had melted into the ground, making it marshlike beneath our feet. I'd hoped we could see my father's grave, but realized Tariq wouldn't make it over or around the rolling hills that separated the chapel from it. That would wait for another day.

"What I cannot stop thinking is that there is nothing we could have done. *Nothing*," Tariq rasped. He was already out of breath and I stopped walking, pretending to take in the view. "It was futile, everything we did."

"I know." I realized that Tariq and I were tormented by Claudia's memory in different ways. Tariq would never recover from his inability to save her. For him, that meant failure as a man and a lover and a friend. My pain was simpler but just as poisonous. Close as we were as children, a chasm of resentment and guilt had grown ever wider between us, never to be healed. A river of anger and frustration would follow me as long as I lived, its currents threatening to pull me in like an undertow.

"I made the mistake of confronting Sklar in a rage," said Tariq. Each word was an obvious effort. "I thought he might have abducted Claudia and I lost all control. In the end, I was of no use to her at all." It was strange to finally realize how deeply he loved my sister. I'd thought they were bonded by drugs and lust, but something deep and powerful had taken root even in that thin soil.

"You were her best friend, Tariq. In your own way, you wanted what was best for her. We just didn't agree on what that was."

"Excuse me," said a low voice behind us.

"Ridley?" Martin's son was wearing a black overcoat with the collar pulled up. I guessed that it was an attempt at hiding, now impossible for him because of his size. He shifted awkwardly from foot to foot, his polished shoes making a soft squish in the muck. "What are you doing here?"

"I'm sorry about Claudia." His broad shoulders hunched and his eyes swept over my feet. "I miss her."

"I know, Ridley. I do, too."

"My dad said we shouldn't go in to the service but . . . we wanted to come." Ridley glanced at me. "You're not mad?"

"Claudia would be happy you're here," I said. "I'm glad you came, too, Ridley."

He nodded, and I believed he understood what I meant. Ridley was Claudia's friend, and he deserved to mourn her with others who'd loved her, even if his father didn't. "You didn't tell the police about what I did. The fire, I mean."

That wasn't entirely true. The NYPD was looking into the arson at St. Aristarchus again, and I'd told Bruxton and Norah that I'd realized that Ridley had confessed to Claudia; their verdict had been that my testimony wouldn't hold up in court. I hadn't mentioned that Tariq knew the story, too, nor that Ridley had given the remote detonator he'd used to Claudia. Perhaps she'd just thrown it out; no one knew what had happened to it. Tariq would eventually take his revenge on Martin, but I wanted to believe he wouldn't involve Ridley.

"You promised Claudia you wouldn't do anything like that again," I said. "I hope you meant it."

He nodded solemnly. "My dad . . . wanted to say . . . sorry. About everything." Ridley's voice was unsteady, as if reciting a half-learned speech. His eyes were as green as his father's, but they couldn't meet mine directly, darting instead to the tombstones around me.

"Oh." I was stunned that Martin had sent Ridley to speak for him. I'd read in a newspaper that Martin Sklar had fallen and knocked out four teeth. Only he and I knew what had really happened. And Ridley, of course.

"Is that all?" Tariq snapped. Even as a whisper, his voice was harsh.

Ridley flinched as if he'd been struck. "My dad wanted . . . here, take this." Ridley thrust a small black velvet drawstring bag at me and fled. I watched him lose his footing, fall into a headstone, and get up again. He vanished from view as he rounded the chapel.

I untied the bag. Inside was the silver bangle from my father. Rolling it around in my hands, I felt lighter, almost giddy, for a moment. *For Lily, With Love Always, Dad.* "I can't believe it."

"How the devil did he get his hands on *that*? He must have stolen it from Claudia's flat." Fury simmered under Tariq's words.

"No, I found it at Claudia's and then I lost it. He's just returning it to me." I snapped it around the wrist of my glove, heartening slightly at the reassuring click. "I couldn't believe she'd had it all this time."

"What do you mean? I only brought it to her in December."

"What?"

"Claudia had sold it some time ago for . . . well, she had sold it, and she went to great lengths to retrieve it. When I had dinner with her in August, she was determined to locate it. She could not even remember to which pawnbroker she had taken it, but her guilt at taking it haunted her. I thought it would impress her if I were able to do it. Of course, I was out of the country a good part of the time, so I had several people working on it."

I stared at him, speechless. Claudia hadn't been hiding it from me all this time. She had sold it for drugs, as I'd originally feared.

"When I visited Claudia's in the middle of December, it was because I had managed to retrieve it," Tariq whispered. "I gave it to the woman who answered the door. When I did not hear from Claudia, I knew that something was terribly wrong. Claudia would have sold her soul to get that back for you."

"I had no idea. I thought . . ." I'd assumed the worst about my sister yet again and I regretted it. The bracelet had always symbolized my father's love. Now memories of Claudia were mixed in, too. How she would have mocked me for being so overly sentimental about a bauble. *Deep down, you're pretty superficial,* as she liked to tease me. "Did she tell you it was from our father?"

"She did. She told me that he always found very special presents for his children." He touched my wrist, openly admiring the bracelet. "Claudia told me he was a wonderful father to both of you. She said she had been very lucky when he was alive."

My eyes were welling with tears, but I smiled. "That's because he always took her side when she was in trouble at school or anywhere else." My father was the same way with me, but those occasions were rare. With Claudia, no matter how good her intentions, something always went sideways.

"I know," said Tariq. "Even when our girl was being good, she was bad."